THIS TIME
THE GRI

A novel in twenty three apparently
unrelated parts

Peter Campbell lives in the chilly north of Scotland with his partner and three demanding cats. This is his fourth published book.

By Peter Campbell

THIS TIME WE GO DOWN TO THE GREEN TOGETHER

PETER CAMPBELL

Dojoba Press
2014

Published by Dojoba Press 2014

First paperback edition

ISBN 978-0-9930314-0-3

For Douglas, as always

For Hilary, long overdue

Acknowledgements

My thanks go to Gillian Pressley, Eliza Moon, Kate Murdoch and C Macdonald for their careful reading of this book, and their invaluable suggestions. Without their input, this book would be considerably poorer, and would feature so many punctuation errors it would be unreadable. Any that remain are mine alone.

ONE

What shall we do with the drunken sailor?

Put him in the fo'castle with the lice and the rats, amidst the wooden bunks with their atmosphere of vomit and dysentery, a blanket thrown over to muffle his beery snoring, his propulsive farts, his incoherent shouts at wrongs imagined or recollected.

Oh, but here comes the captain! Footfall heavy as a giant's, down the galley, vibrations evident even over the sough and roll of the ship, the wind's velocity, a fee-fi-fo-fum would not be unexpected, pipe in his mouth belching out nacreous smoke, opening doors, slamming them shut, shouting, where is he, bring him to me, and he is as solid and unstoppable as a locomotive which, come to think of it, he somewhat resembles, its momentum, its vapours, calling all aboard, all aboard, his joke as men were pressganged, their dull and groggy futures glimpsed through a stupored haze.

Where is he? Oh, not here, definitely not here, captain, the four men standing lined in front of the doorway, blocking his view, feeling the heat of his face close to their own, not daring to flinch or look away, no aversion of eye contact, else that heavy fist would rise and fall, or the hand replaced by a hook, or his steeled feet. There would be bones broken and flesh blooded, and they'd be sent to the hold, the ship's own personal hell. Not that it's necessarily much better up here...and oh, wait, has the drunken sot *shit* himself? Something noxious drifting their way certainly, though it may be, it could almost certainly be, the reaction of their own fear.

The captain passes, a swift glance back to make sure they still stand to attention, and then he's turned the corner, pistoning, seething, roaring, the glass of his eyes holding corralled souls, who knows what destination they're heading to, what final terminus awaits them. Quick now, quick! Before he returns! Lift the drunkard between them, an arm and a leg each, out the doorway, bumping, the corridors too narrow to easily manoeuvre, even for experienced hands, muttering, cursing, but not too loud, because the captain might hear. In fact, is that him turning back? Heading this way, motion increasing until it threatens to become a scream?

Hurry now, down this passage and that, the clatter of their shoes on wood, the drunk hanging face down, threatening to call out again, until one of them clamps his heavy hand over the sailor's mouth, threatens, don't you say a word, says it in such a way there's real fear in those inebriated eyes.

Ahead is the galley. Steam forms so thickly there is a chance they can hide in there, amongst the arcing fat and lancing, boiling liquids, the ovens so heavy and intense the heat can be felt even a full corridor away, the thud and screech and thraw of bodies being dissected, someone's meal soon, even if the odours are less than appetising, certainly this far into the journey where they may well come with a maggot or two, if you're lucky, the green, sour smell of meat salted and lain for weeks, months. Though it's fish for the captain, good for the eyes and the brain, keeps him alert you know, keeps him active, proof in his voice cacophonous behind them, I can hear you, I can see you, yet they are not in his sight, surely not, plunging into the steam, avoiding the one-armed cook who averts his eyes, his retinue of effeminate cabin boys who find sudden interest in the sputtering vats of

4

porridge. It's better that way, to confess ignorance when questioned, for the questions will surely come.

Where to hide him? The cupboards are full, and cramped, the metal tubing will lift flesh if touched, and amongst the practiced weave of the kitchen there is little room to move. They push him into an upended cask, a repository for flour at one time by the look of it, the source of flat tack that sits heavy now in someone's stomach, maybe even their own. Is it tempting fate to put him here, amongst all the foodstuffs? What if the captain wants a little snack? It's much too easy to imagine him gnawing on cracking bones, tongue catching at the tasty marrow, the rip and pull of flesh like that picture they've seen somewhere and couldn't stop looking at, some future fold of time feeding back here, flash of a kitchen with its protective warmth, snow crusting the windows, small hands leafing the pages of a book, and here is the picture, the very one, Saturn devouring his children, the one they sat looking at, that terrible compelling image...

The hiding place is a little obvious maybe, especially as one foot sticks out still, quickly covered with a hessian sack, but there's no opportunity to find anyplace better. And not too soon, for the captain is in sight now, his eyes glowing red, pipe still wedged into his mouth adding to the general fug, screaming where are they, and there's only time to leap into the dumbwaiter, one, two, three, four, to careen down and down, a descent that never seems to stop.

They land in a bruised and panicked heap, limbs so entangled it's difficult to say where one person begins and the other ends, though there is a gradual resumption of identity as they pull apart. Momentary relief is replaced by terror as they realise that - someone certainly has a strong sense of irony out there - they are in the captain's cabin. There is his bed, a deep-based unvarnished box, and a writing desk covered with handwritten notes they dare not read. In the corner of the room a black and white movie plays on the television, featuring a Hollywood actress who looks familiar but who they cannot name. The sound is muted, but she appears about to be abducted, something indicated by the stealthy approach of an intruder, so the background music is no doubt going tum-tum-TUUUUM! Which is oddly appropriate to their situation, though, come to think of it, what is a television doing here anyway? Double-take and it's gone, some manic dream, some collective hallucination they've experienced. In fact, isn't the captain's cabin situated on the deck *above* the galley, and at the opposite end of the ship? Something very strange is going on here...

There's a mad scramble to exit the cabin, but before they can do so there's a roar from above, loud enough to make the deck tremble, followed by screams then a crash as something plummets down the dumbwaiter shaft. The first thought is that the captain, mad enough to do it if anyone is, has leapt down the shaft in pursuit. One of their number pisses himself, a hot spreading flush, and there isn't emotional room left even for embarrassment, but maybe later, if he survives all this. It isn't the captain though, because out comes sliding the body of a cabin boy, violated perhaps, certainly dead, for no-one's neck should be in that position...

Minutes later there's further panic as the dumbwaiter rises and then descends again, but it is only someone above, sending down the sailor. The luck of the drunk, there's not even a bruise, and he comes rolling out of the hatch with an almost-swagger, a dusting of flour over his body which must have come from the barrel. And, oh shit, he's leaving floury footprints over the floorboards, the perfect trail for the captain to follow, as if his preternatural tracking instincts were not enough. What to do? They dust him down with the blanket from the captain's *very bed,* his body's ghost trapped there, and there's a bubbling hysteria between them all, it rises and rises, and only escape will quell it.

A hurried rub over the floor removes the last traces of flour or enough of it so it is not immediately evident. More importantly, the direction of their flight will not be so easy to follow. Except...the door is locked. Panic, clamour, woeful moaning ensues. One sailor remembers the heavy key fob that swings permanently from the captain's belt. The door is solid and apparently immovable. The dumbwaiter is still useable, but who knows what waits above (or below, it is all very confusing). That only leaves the window, which is barred, but it is debatable whether this is to keep others out or the captain in. And OH GOD here he comes, the tread of feet unmistakeable, and there is the turn of the key in the lock. They stand motionless, and breath does not even come, it is held in abeyance until the very air seems to shimmer. If ever there has been the need to cry, to weep hot, self-pitying tears, now is that moment. Lives do not recapitulate, not exactly, but there are flickering moments of love and loss, and thrills and disappointments, all within those few seconds as the door begins to open.

Relief! It is only the maid, pail and mop in hand, come to clean the captain's quarters. She has a hard, questioning look, a look that says she and not the captain holds the power in the ship, and this is what keeps her safe, unquestionably, the only woman in this vessel full of men, for none would dare... They amble out, insouciant, no, nothing going on here, except the grubbed bed and that dead cabin boy lying there, nothing to do with us you know, mind the drunk, he's been taken a little unwell, nothing a spot of fresh air won't rectify.

Once out the door, they run. No decorum now, it's a determined rush, the inebriate hanging between them, no looking back, no telling what might be seen back in that bedroom, unbidden...

Stairs lead them down into a room containing the base of the capstan.

Ropes lie coiled and stinking, and there are heavy links of chain. It is, mercifully, silent and dark. They stop, no room even for breath, and let the sailor fall. They too slump, and take advantage of the still, the absence of noise, only the water slapping on the sides of the ship and voices far away, from decks above, reaching them. No telling how long it will last, though none of them hold any illusion relief will be anything more than momentary. Still, it gives pretence enough of safety to produce a few sly laughs, recent events recounted with shared recognition as the story is retold and retold again. One day it will be handed down, fathers to children to grandchildren and beyond, twisting and changing with each retelling, so it becomes unrecognisable from its source. This emotion too fades, and they slip into silence of a contemplative sort.

Their eyes fall to the sailor, who is lying face down on the floor, face mashed against a length of rope, shirt part undone, trousers half-mast to reveal a bare bottom, pert and certainly not unattractive, wan as a guiding moon in this half light. They look at each other. It's a long journey, and distractions are few. Moreover, it's dark here, no-one would know...

The fear enhances their libido, somehow. In turn, four engorged cocks find their way into those tight, surely virginal cheeks, discharge what seems to be an eternity's worth of longing and terror, not a little hate even, and he doesn't seem to complain too much, they can even pretend there's some enjoyment in there somewhere, those moans of pain are awfully ambiguous sometimes, and at the end, when he lies unmoving, bottom still in the air but slicked now, it seems to them he has changed somehow, because don't those features look more feminine? His body has curves, little pads of fat in all the right places, a young woman's body, surely, certainly, maybe one on the cusp of puberty, breasts budding, face still to lose its softness, to discover the disguise of lipstick and blusher, the mask that will hide never-forgotten sorrows.

There is no time to wonder. The captain's voice comes again, harsher now, as if he has seen, somehow, their transgressions, maybe even engineered them in some fashion they cannot and will not ever understand. The captain knows, and he wants them to know he knows. Yet, even with that fear, they continue to lie, still, breath heavy, contemplating fates avoided, if only temporarily, the cold seepage of the decks below them, cries and glottals rising, and through the gaps in the floorboards a dim light reveals bodies huddled, sex and age indeterminate, finding refuge in their own private hells...better they think than this one anyway, though they will soon discover the depth of that illusion...

When the cry comes once more, they carry the sailor down into that gloom, the pallid light hinting at a sickness, a constant infirmity inhabiting the very ship itself, and into which they are subsumed, with the possibility there will be no way of ever getting out again.

They descend, far, far down, into the ship's belly, into its guts, no sun or air down there, just the lowing of beasts slowly dying, the humans dying even more quickly. It is the place no-one wants to go, not ever, but these are desperate times, and there is the chance, somehow, that they can slip amongst those bodies, amongst the lost, find a territory as yet unexplored.

This is the repository of the almost-dead, dumb faces merging into and looking out of blackness, skin forgotten by sun, transparent almost, eyes that one day will seal from disuse. These are the healthy ones. From further back come the cries and moans of the sick, the sour, inescapable smell of vomit and diarrhoea. Did they ask to come here, these people? Do they remember blue skies and shingled beaches, open hillsides and night time gatherings around fires to chase away the night's cold, the hard, inescapable wind? Do they remember dreams of what their future would hold? Not this future, surely, chained and crowded beyond imagining, in a terrible heat, with lice and disease for company. And although the sailor would be difficult to locate in these crowds, in this darkness, it is beyond imagining they could abandon him here.

He is sober enough now to half-walk, through the people who sit, curious but uncommenting on their arrival. The captain is still far away, but nearing. The darkness brings fear, true, but it also brings safety. They push their way through bodies sweat slicked, that issue a stench both alien and familiar. All are young: no place here for the old. They head for new and terrible lands in which their health will be prized, their strength, their fire, although nothing will be left of that by the end, not at the conclusion of the longer journey they dare not even think of at this point.

The bodies seem endless. Towards the back, light begins to rise. There is a hinterland here, dreams escaped, coalescing to form their own refuge. Men are gathered in small groups, playing card games, smoking, not saying much really, their actions a dull whiling away of hours and days until the time their bodies, apart, arrive at their fierce new world, if they arrive at all, death always being the strongest possibility. Separate, women tend to the children, or talk in low voices, a language alien in the way it rises and falls, vowels inverted, not at all like the sailors' own harsh accents, roughened by the sea's dangers, a life that seemed perilous, until they saw this, at least. Some of the faces look oddly familiar. Crickets sussurate, night birds shriek and flutter, and, further back, calls of beasts have turned to fable. A loam scent now, the damp, heavy smell that comes with the release of rain. Someone even dares to laugh.

It is only an illusion. They walk decks slippery with shit and vomit, and the bodies of the dead, still chained, poxed and infested with lice, and the smell is the most terrible thing somehow, even more than the sights they see. Only the desperate would come here, or the unwilling. Even the drunken sailor is mute, as if they are venturing ever deeper into something more dreadful even than what lies behind, than what roars and follows, certain even in the dark of their direction. Hurry, hurry, push past people too lethargic to complain when they stand on the edges of clothing, on legs on feet on arms, though there is a subdued violence too, a resentment that will rise and conflagrate one day, not now but years later, in other times, in other lands...

It is a relief to descend again. A steel ladder leads down to animal holding pens, their occupants even more certain of their fate than those above. Dull cow eyes stare forward to certain slaughter. Sheep have the vacant expression of the terminally depressed. Chickens contemplate suicide by clambering high then falling, their useless wings flapping by reflex. Better that than the inevitable, rote decapitations they see daily, no attempt even to hide the certainty of their fate. At least those above have some chance, no matter how desperate, how unwished for, to reach their new world.

It's difficult to hide him here, for there are so few animals left. They force him onto his haunches, head down and given the strictest of instructions not to move, and leave him amidst the dung-strewn straw of the cattle. In this light, surely infernal in origin, he almost blends in. The boat rocks uneasily, seas restless, or it may be its instability is more evident down at this level. The four of them go scattering thiswaythat, stomachs a little uneasy, even after all their time on board. They have their own hiding places to find, because there is nowhere else to go, there is only ascent, and that is impossible when they will meet the captain mid-way, perhaps even on the ladder itself. Time to extinguish the Tilly lights, quick, quick, fingers nervous and fumbling, but it is too late, here he comes, down the ladder, belching smoke and fire, sparks drifting dangerously to the straw below. Find a patch of darkness, and wait, still, trembling, hoping he will pass, his roar mute now, it is the most dangerous time when that happens, it always happens in silence. Let him pass, let him pass, let him pass. Do not dare even to breathe. His footsteps, they can hear them approach, closer and closer.

The boat lurches, it rocks, because a storm is coming, yes it is coming, it is coming. It is coming.

TWO

Here she comes, stottering down the brae with her heels too high, her white latex trousers too tight, and her T-shirt three sizes too small, so the fat bulges out from her belly and peeks beneath the t-shirt's hem, looking like the repulsive innards from some butchered animal. She has hair beyond brassy, and looped fake gold earrings, and the slap's trowelled on so thick you could lift it off and there it'd be, a perfect mirrored mask of her features.

"Here, Jeannie, ya heifer," I call.

"Carol, ya heathen," she calls back. Though I doubt she even knows what a heathen is.

Jeannie and me go way back. She lived next door to me when I was wee and she'd stomp around the garden, overweight even then, with her ma looking glaikit from the kitchen doorway, making sure her lassie didn't land head first in those bonny chrysanthemums that grew in the borders. Which she was inclined to do, like. Which she's still inclined to do, come to think of it, although drink's usually involved these days. She's not short of a shilling is Jeannie, but there's not much sense there either, unless you count an encyclopaedic knowledge of Heat magazine and who's doing who amongst our loosely defined band of friends.

You always knew that was the way she'd turn out. She was the unlovely, dumpy one in school and there's not much has changed, except she's maybe learned to disguise it a bit better behind her knock-off designer labels (eBay, because she'll not resist a bargain) and her manner, which gives new meaning to the term brash. Subtlety's not our Jeannie's strong point, I'm telling you.

I mean, look at her here. Chav's not in it. She's lacking the obligatory accessory baby but not much else, though I'm sure that'll come too, the way she puts it about. She's heading towards me smoking a fag and blowing a grey fug around her features, and she's got those thick, clattering bangles around her wrist, gold in someone's imagination but not mine, and nails grown so long they'll meet at some infinite point, painted the sort of violet your granny'd sometimes wear if she was getting dressed up to go somewhere nice.

"Did you hear," she says, breathless, not quite alongside me yet.

She's got this kind of alarmed look on her face, but excited too. She's got some news to tell me, you come to recognise the signs.

"Hear about what?" I say, and it'll be some tale about how thon scrag at the other end of the village is shagging her mum's boyfriend or suchlike, or how Ferdie's been hauled back into jail again for stealing drink out of the Co-op, or Elaine's had another big win on the lottery but she's keeping it quiet so everyone in the village doesn't know, even though her house has been done up twice, and the laddie at the newsagents blabbed it all to everyone anyway, 'cause he'd sold her the winning ticket.

"Gordie's dead."

I can't believe what I'm hearing. Gordie? Not dead, surely? "That's never right. I saw him last night. He was with Craigie and that crowd. Down the street it was, they were pished and carrying on."

"Well, maybe that explains it. They found him this morning and he was face down in the river with his head all smashed in." She sidles closer. "Just under the bridge, it was."

"Aw, that's awful. You're sure it's Gordie? Who was telling you?"

"Everyone's talking about it. You must be the last one to hear. I cannae believe no-one's told you." She drops her voice (or drops it as far as she's able) and whispers, "They're saying it's maybe deliberate. That he jumped."

She has this sort of shocked look on her face, but it's kind of excited too, you know? Like we've felt death come brushing past us, and there's thon chill, alive feeling you get when something terrible's happened, but it's not affected you, or those really close to you.

"Not Gordie. He wouldn't do that on purpose. Christ, no-one loves life more than he does. Did."

I'm trying to imagine it, but it'll not come. What I keep on seeing is a body lying in the water and there are these two coppers looking down on it from the bridge. They're wearing trench coats and they're rushing on down to see who it is. Then they're turning the body over but I can't see the face, though it's a man, you can tell that. I can see the coppers' faces though, and they're the two guys out of Taggart.

Fuck, I watch too much television.

Later, we're all down in the caff. It's one of thon places that have pretensions of sophistication but what you're really paying for is an overpriced cup of coffee and a slice of something so sweet you'll develop type two diabetes overnight. There six of us: Kevin, Marline, Jeannie, Roddie, Digger and myself. There's only one topic of conversation, and it's everybody's topic of conversation today. A wee place like this, you can't expect much else. You can tell from the expression on everyone's face, it's like a skelped arse, because fate has taken down your breeks and given you all a good hard wallop to remind you what life's all about.

"I telt you," says Jeannie, because she's holding court, "it was an accident waiting to happen. Or, no, no an accident, because maybe it wisnae, but there was always something there, you could see in his eyes, they'd thon wild look to them."

I can't mind his eyes. When I'm visualising his face, it's got that gaunt, maybe a bit hollowed quality, but that's what came of driving his life too fast, because he never stopped, and it was all the fags too, and the drink at the weekend. His eyes though, when I'm picturing them, they're black, beyond black, like there's wee bitties of coal pressed into the sockets.

"It's his family I feel sorry for." Marline's got her hands cupped around a mug of coffee for warmth, even though it's not cold in here. "I mean, his mother, she disnae keep well anyhow, and this'll be the last thing she's needing. And the father's no use, is he? He'll be half way down a bottle of rum by now and boaking it up by midnight. We've all seen it."

Aye, they're not the best of families. Hardly a family at all, now Gordie's gone.

"You're quiet, Carol," says Digger, which is rich coming from a man who's not known for his conversational skills. I mean, that's practically a speech by his standards.

"I'm just thinking," I says. "It makes you think, something like this happening."

"Does it no. That could have been any of us." That's Roddie. Roddie knew Gordie best out of all of us. Not best friends, mind, because Gordie was the type that was friends with everybody and nobody. He'd be the one who'd make everyone laugh on a night out, and you'd not want to be away from his company then; but at the same time he'd not come greeting to you at three in the morning with whatever dark things pulled at his soul. No, he'd not come to you or to anybody. Some people do that, use laughter as a shield. I don't know if anyone really knew him well, because of that.

"My ma, when she heard, she told me about this lassie she knew, threw herself into the sea when she was young? One minute the lassie was there, the next she was gone. It makes you wonder, it does. Like I said," Roddie continued, "it could be any of us."

"Aye, but it's no us, is it?" Jeannie doesn't like the conversation wandering too far without her contribution. "We're no that daft. And dinna you look at me thon way, Marline, because there's no one of us who's no thought it already. I mean, Jesus Christ, you dinna throw yourself over the edge of a bridge when you've got your entire life ahead of you."

"That's harsh, Jeannie," says Marline. "You don't know what it was he was going through. Maybe was an accident. All we've heard is rumours."

"I heard there was a note. But I'm no supposed to tell anyone that, so dinna any of you repeat it. It was Bobby that telt me, there was a note left for his mam. I dinna know what it said though."

That's maybe true. Bobby's one of Jeannie's many conquests. Or she's one of his, even if it's not much of a conquest, to be truthful.

"Live while you can, that's my motto." Jeannie gulps down her mug of coffee, then orders another. "Anyhows, I'm going for a fag. Who's joining me?"

The six of us are standing outside the caff doorway, shivering, because it's turned cold, even if it's nominally summer. Kevin's the only one of us who doesn't smoke, but he may as well, the combustion we're generating. He's probably inhaled the best part of twenty Lambert and Butler just by keeping us company. It's quiet, quieter even than normal, as though people are maybe thinking it's disrespectful to been seen enjoying themselves. Or maybe it's that grey, dirty cloud pushing overhead that's doing it. You just know it's going to piss rain in a wee while, and that'll set everyone's mood spiralling down even further. Look at us, for example: we're all standing here silent, not speaking, lost in a collective dwam that's descended on us. Though it's relative, like. Jeannie's dwam is the sort that the roadrunner'd have, or thon mouse, what's his name, Speedy Gonzales. She's flitting from thought to thought, you can see it in the flicker of her eyes, downcast, drilled in to some bittie of her none of us are able to access, though she'll gladly offer all the sordid details later on when (inevitably) we're pished and the whole day's events land on top of us with their already nostalgic tang. See, she's pulling on that fag there, and squinting against the smoke, and you can see the wee thoughts running back and forwards through her brain.

22

You'd almost say she looked deep, if it wasn't for the clothes, like.

Suddenly she looks up and announces, "Fuck this. I don't want to be here. Let's go for a spin in the car."

So there's four of us now, in the car, racing along the side roads, watching the scenery blur into this whip of green and brown. Digger's driving, because it's his car, and he's the sort that'll not let anyone else get their hands on his precious vehicle, even if it's this mud-coloured clapped-out thing you wouldn't think would even get started, much less reach the speeds we're achieving just now.

Jeannie's counting roadkill.

"That's the eighteenth splatted rabbit. I'm telling you, they must be throwing themselves below the wheels of cars when they see them coming. Do you no think, Carol?"

I'm not looking at the road, I always feel sorry for the wee creatures when you see them reduced to this unravelled mixture of guts and fur.

"I'm averting my eyes, Jeannie. I was traumatised when I saw Watership Down on the telly when I was a bairn."

"Och, they're only rabbits. Plenty more where they came from. Nineteen."

This time I do look and at the side of the road, sure enough, there it is, something that's not even recognisable as once having a bunny-shaped form.

"Do you mind that song? Bright Eyes? I had it when I was wee, it was on a tape my mother had. And we'd the film on video." Kevin's the third passenger in the car, Marlene and Roddie having excused themselves, which you can maybe understand, them being closest and all. Or maybe it's just they know what Digger's driving's like, because he's fair bombing along the road, and no doubt adding a few himself to the body count.

Anyhow, Kevin's continuing, "I always had nightmares after seeing that. It was a weird film. All I can remember is blood, and thon ghost rabbit floating everywhere."

"I'd have nightmares too, after hearing that song." Jeannie's got the window wound down now and she's sticking her head out to get a better view of the road, her hair's whipped up and flapping. "Some people just have no taste, I'm telling you."

Aye, that's true. Though Jeannie's not one to talk, because I've passed her house when the bedroom window's wound down and it's blasting out Boyzone.

"Twenty. Twenty one."

Digger decides to drive even faster. The car goes rattling up and down the bumps on the road, which is not the smoothest of surfaces in the first place.

"Jesus, Digger, have you got a death wish for us all, or something?" I'm in the back and holding on to the front car seats to keep myself from battering against Jeannie, who has just bashed her head off the window frame.

"Aye, slow down man. It's no a race to get anywhere." Kevin puts his hand on Digger's shoulder, like he's comforting him, or something.

And he does slow down, does Digger, though he doesn't say anything, because that's not his style. There's nothing in his expression to give anything away,

24

apart from a hard, distant look in his eyes. Mind you, that's the look he always carries.

"What's up?" says Jeannie. "We're hardly moving." She's rubbing her head as she's saying this, and she's not even aware of the fact.

We've stopped at some side road somewhere. To be honest, we've travelled so fast, and so far, I don't even know where we are any longer. Around these parts everything tends to look much of a muchness – dun-coloured, flat, boggy land leading to hills that are mostly bare and uninhabited, unless someone has set up a pine plantation as a tax dodge. We've come a fair bit anyway, because there's a bothy here, set off from the road. We've only stopped because Jeannie's needing a wee. She's behind the bothy somewhere with her knickers pulled down, and no doubt trying not to crouch too near to the ground, because Kevin had shouted, "Mind the sheep ticks!" just before she disappeared out of view. The rest of us are standing at a discreet distance, even though we're all curious to see what's in the bothy, even if we already kind of know it's going to be crushed drinks cans and sheep turds and newspapers from two years back, much like any abandoned building you go into around here, in fact.

"OH-YOU-CLINT!"

That's Jeannie's voice.

Funny, how that's Jeannie's one bit of prudery. She'll not say cunt like any normal, decent person would. It's CLINT instead. There's no knowing where she picked that one up from. Anyhow. She comes roaring around the corner, pulling her breeks up, which is difficult since she normally has to lie flat on her bed and weld them onto her legs, I've seen her do that, and she's looking all red and flustered. None of us are concerned really: we're used to Jeannie's overreactions.

"There wis a deer," says Jeannie, "and it was LOOKING at me when I wis having a pish."

Kevin's laughing. "That'll no hurt you, Jeannie."

"Aye, I know that, you daft bugger, but it gave me a fright and I jumped and stung my fanny on a bunch of nettles."

Oh that's it, we're ending ourselves. It's one of those times you laugh and laugh and it becomes a kind of hysteria that has its own momentum, it goes beyond whatever started the laughter off. Even Digger's affected. He's lurched to the ground, crying, and hurpled in thon sore way because your body's not obeying you, it's doing its own spastic, involuntary thing. He's laughing still, even when our own laughter has stopped, and eventually we have to get him and lift him up off the dirt track he's lying on. When he looks up his face is this grimed mess that clearly marks the path of his tears.

"I dinna like places like this." Jeannie's half-in, half-out the bothie's doorway. "I always think they might be haunted."

You can sort of see her point. Who comes here? Not many people, by the looks of it. Hikers with shorts and hairy thighs, lugging their backpacks over a landscape most of us have the sense to stay away from. Over there, for example: a dark sweep of rain racing over the ground, visible from miles distant, though it'll be on us before we even know it.

I'm already inside, in the shelter. "Come in, Jeannie," I says, "or you'll get soaked right through in a moment."

"Aye. Maybe."

In she comes, wobbling on her too-high heels and her legs kind of wrapped around each other even when she's walking, as if she's desperate for a wee again, or maybe it's her nervousness showing. She's right superstitious, is Jeannie.

"It's awful dark," she says.

"It is when you're blocking the doorway," says Kevin. "Hurry the fuck up, will you? That's the rain just on."

As indeed it is. It comes splooshing down in that hard, overpowering way, so loud that soon you'll not be able to hear what it is people are saying.

"Jesus," says Jeannie. "we'll be floating back."

The rain gets even louder.

She's already forgotten her fear of ghosts, watching the rain instead, which seems solid, like slate, you can't even see through it, and there's this wheechter of a wind come up as well so the rain's coming in the doorway almost horizontally, driving us back to the room's corners where we're standing on things you try not to look at, because you suspect they're dead or – maybe even worse – alive.

"Do you not look at that and it makes you feel awful small?" I say, but there's no reply, and for a wee while I feel kind of insulted, but then I realise it's because no-one can hear me. A stream of water is running across the floor now, branching out, and Jeannie's dancing out of the way, worried it'll stain her shoes, because they cost her two weeks pay, even if they look like they've come out of Primark or some such place. The wind must be calming down a bit, because I can clearly hear her shriek, just before a clap of thunder comes along, one of those deep, heavy rumbles that sounds like this hulking bit of machinery trundling across the sky, and you can feel the ground shaking in response.

"Ah fuck," says Kevin, "it's a thunderstorm. You cannae beat a good thunderstorm."

Jeannie looks shit scared though. She's not as tough as she makes out.

"As long as I'm no out in it," Jeannie says, "then it'll no hurt me."

"That's not much consolation if this place is haunted like you said." I'm just saying that out of badness, because I don't like her to get too cocky, especially as how I'm not too fond of thunderstorms myself.

"I wis just jesting. It's just an old building. Isn't it?" She looks around wide-eyed, like something wicked's about to jump out at her. "I saw a ghost once," she says, "at my nana's funeral. It wisnae my nana I saw, mind, but in the church there was this bonny creepy man sitting in the pews a few seats down from me. I asked my mam who he was, but she couldnae see him at all."

"You was probably pished," is Digger's opinion.

"I was only eight then. Hell, Digger, I didnae start on the drink for a few more years after that, at least. Naw, he was a right creepy clint, I'm telling you, all dressed up in this old suit like they'da worn a hundred years ago. Put me off the church forever, that did. I've no set foot inside one since."

"You'll need to though. For Gordie's funeral." Kevin's edged that bit nearer to Jeannie. I'm sure he fancies her. He's got this elated look the storm's put there, the weather does that sometimes.

"Do they do that? If he jumped? I thought they dinna."

"They wouldnae do that, surely." Yet in the back of my mind something's reminding me what's she's saying was true, at one time. Maybe I'm getting confused about that, mind you. I was never the church-going type. Jeannie now, she will be, not straight away, but later when she's settled and has her kids, if not her man. She's the type that needs that sort of security.

"Whose idea was it to come here anyway?" Jeannie says. "We should have stayed in the caff."

The four of us stare out at the rain, and listen to the thunder, and we fall into a sort of trance standing there, waiting for the storm to pass.

We're in the pub. It's the weekend. What else do you do at the weekend in a place like this? Drift from place to place. Go here and there. Talk to this person and that. Find something to pass the hours which are both endless and too short. Come Monday you'll be back on the drudge, that wee job you have in the supermarket or the office or the newsagents, where you're stacking the shelves or handling that phone call you've been putting off all day, or selling your token newspaper and packet of fags, wondering how much longer it'll be before this place closes and you have to join the others in the Co-op shop or, more likely, down at the dole office. That's what Jeannie does, works in Co-op, three days as week. I'm the lucky one, at uni, though during the holidays I help my uncle out on the estate he runs.

Digger's gone home, or so he says, but he's probably off to shag that lassie out of MacLennan Street he's seeing. Instead we have Heinrich, a German who, for reasons only known to himself, has come here on holiday. Jesus, you think, you have the entire country to come visit and you choose here? So that's Jeannie and Kevin and Heinrich and myself. Heinrich's a jolly chap, with blond hair and strapping Germanic thighs, and in your head you can kind of picture him prancing about in his lederhosen and brandishing his bratwurst sausage. He's as bent as bent can be, I'm sure, but Jeannie doesn't seem to have realised that, because she's coorying in alongside him awful close. Kevin's looking a mite jealous, but I'm sitting between him and her, so there's not much he can do about it.

"So," Heinrich's saying, "you have never left here?"

"I went to Glasgow a few times when I was wee." Jeannie snuggles up even closer. "Ma Auntie lived there at the time. In one of thon big blocks of flats you see when you come into the city? You'd look out the window at night and the whole city was lit up. It was like the Christmas lights was always on. You couldnae get me away from that window. So they telt me anyway. She's dead now, my aunty. The cancer, you know?"

"Ah, that is such a terrible disease. My mother, she too went the same way. That is when I decided that life is too brief a thing to stay in one place. Now all the time I travel. Europe, of course, and Asia. Next year I will be going to the USA."

"All them places? You must be loaded."

"I am only careful with my money." Though it doesn't look it, the way he's been ordering the drinks in. We've only been here an hour and we're near bladdered already. "Also, when I was younger I was in an accident. It was very bad, and there was a lot of compensation paid. I am part metal these days. When I go through the airport security, all the alarms keep ringing."

"Do you have scars?" Jeannie's hand now starting to creep up his shoulder. I said before, subtlety's not her strong point.

"Many, many scars. It is not very attractive, I think."

"Show me one. Just one. I'll no go ugh at it, ah promise."

Heinrich unbuttons his shirt, and underneath there's this criss-cross of weals and knots of flesh that's torn and congealed into a pink, woven layer. It's like he's been melted and it's not set right.

Jeannie touches the skin.

"Ugh!" she exclaims, and lets out this little shriek that's half horror, half delight.

To his credit, he doesn't look too offended, though he buttons up his shirt real quick, like. While he's doing it, I'm sure I see a glimpse of flashing metal.

"Heinrich," I says, "that's not a pierced nipple I saw there was it?"

"Both nipples," he explains proudly. "In fact," and here he leans forward, conspiratorially, "not only my nipples." He straightens back up. "I think our drinks are almost done. We will have more, yes?"

With that he disappears to the bar waving that endless supply of twenty pound notes he seems to have. He's more than a wee bit tipsy like, tripping over Auld Sandy's golden lab that's occupying its usual spot mid floor, while Sandy himself is sleeping, head tipped back and - I was going to say snoring - but it's more like they're hacking down a pine forest with chainsaws.

"He's nice," says Jeannie. "And worth a bob or two as well. He didnae say what the accident was though. Do you think he minded me asking?"

"I - "

"And thon piercings. Do you think he's got one of them ring things in his todger too?"

"Fuck me." Kevin's standing up. "What a hoor you are. Money and cocks, that's all you think of."

"Dinna be like that," I'm saying, "it's just Jeanie's way," but he's off from the table, tipping over empty glasses in the process.

"Christ," says Jeannie, "he's a dour bugger tonight."

"Do you not think there's a reason for that, the way you've been ignoring him all evening?"

She's not listening though, and here's the reason why: up at the bar, Kevin has Heinrich in a headlock, he's ripped his shirt, and he's twisting on those nipple rings of his. Jesus, I'm scrunching up my own boobies at the very thought. Heinrich's not saying a word. Maybe it's some Germanic stoicism coming through, or maybe it just hurts too much to even speak. He's not putting up a fight either, even though Kevin's laying into him and there's blood everywhere, dripping from his nose and all that.

Jesus, Heinrich, you'll mind your time here, right enough.

Tam The Barman sorts it out. There's no-one will argue with him, not when he's six foot four and built like a brick shithouse. And he's a total fucking psychopath. Strange thing is, it's Heinrich he lays into and not Kevin, though Kevin does end up fleeing through the front door, face down onto the pavement.

I'm inclined to step in and say it's not Heinrich's fault, but one look at Tam The Barman's face convinces me otherwise. I don't know - maybe he hates Germans or something. He can be a right cruel cunt at times, anyway.

Eventually the bobbies come along and sort it all out, and the two of them are led away while Tam The Barman goes straight on back to serving his pints and nips and chatting with the regulars like nothing's happened, even though his shirt has a long lash of blood down the front.

"Thanks a fuck, Kevin," I says, although he's not here to hear me. "We'll need to buy our own drinks now."

Jeannie drains her last vodka and lemonade.

"Men," I tell her. "is there not one of them that doesn't think with their cocks? Do you want another? I'll buy."

"Nah," she says, "I'm no wanting to stay here now. Let's go."

So now it's just the two of us, the same as it began.

*

Jeannie wants to go to where Gordie's body was found. I'm not sure why, and it's dark, and it's bonny and cold, and we're half-pished.

"You're not wise in the head," I tell her.

We go anyway.

Our route's a footpath that leads through a field, and then heads down a steep brae to the main road that travels across the bridge, the burn pushing far below it.

Even from a distance we can see the burn is running high and brown and muddy, maybe from the storm that hit us earlier in the day. There's no-one there. I thought maybe there'd be other people around, drawn to the tiny bit of excitement this place has offered in long enough, or maybe the morbidly curious, which I suppose is what we are.

Jeannie's got mud splashed up the side of her trousers, but she doesn't seem to mind, and she's shivering with the cold, because she's not brought a jacket. Maybe that's why she's ploughing on so determinedly, because stopping would mean hypothermia. It's me that has to shout, "Jeannie, hang on, it's not a race we're running," but she doesn't stop, not till she's there, on the bridge, looking down at the water with a strange, giddy expression on her face. For one moment, I get the feeling she's going to jump. That puts the shits up me, I can tell you.

Instead, she waits until I join her and says, "Poor Gordie. You can hardly imagine it, can you? He was no right in the head, wanting to do that."

She's got her arms all wrapped around herself, as protection against the cold. Her teeth are fair jittering too.

"You can't tell what people are going through, Jeannie. With some, it's all a front, their smiling and their laughing, and their hard man acts. It's not easy in a place like this, where everyone knows you. The slightest wee crack and everyone's all over you."

"I know that. I'm no daft. Everyone thinks I am, but I'm not. I mean, I'm no clever like you are, no in that way, but I've got a bittie common sense, people dinna credit you for that."

"You're too hard on yourself," I say, though, actually, she's right, that is how people think of her. A bit large, a bit plain, a bit thick. Even her ma said that. 'She'll never be no poet laureate, that one.' Well actually, what she said was Poet Lariat and what I think she actually meant to say was Nobel Prize winner, Jeannie's ma not being the fastest of critters herself. Unless Jeannie has a secret passion for writing rhyming couplets in her bedroom I've not heard of before. "Do you never think of moving away? There's not much to keep you here, is there?"

"It's what you know, isn't it? I'm no brave like you, Carol. I've got my job, and it's no much, but it gets me by. A few years, maybe I'll be settled down with some guy, and some bairns of my own. Maybe with Kevin."

She must see my startled expression, because she continues, "Aye, maybe he's the one. Och, he's wild just now, but he'll calm down, and, let's face it, I'm not likely to get any better. There's a future there, I can see it."

She's still staring down at the water, and then she hoiks into her pocket and brings out this coin she tosses into the burn. You can't even see the splash, it's too far below, and it'll be carried away in the current or settled down in the silt for some fish to swallow.

"That's for you, Gordie," she says.

Then she says: "Let's go back."

THREE

Overnight, the birds fell from the sky. When we woke, our neighbours were already clearing away the cold, almost weightless carcasses. My grandmother handed me a heavy snow shovel, while she wielded a wide, bristled broom, and together we lifted the detritus of blackbirds and wrens and starlings and gulls and pigeons. Afterwards we burnt their corpses: the sparking, heavily smoking conflagration carried the scent of burning keratin I have subsequently always associated with death.

I missed the morning and evening irruption of birdsong, but my grandmother claimed herself glad to be rid of its sleep-intruding cacophony. In the event, both of us soon adjusted to its absence, forgot in fact it ever really existed. In those days, reality was as malleable as paper, a surprising, delicate origami construction. Each new fold revealed something unexpected and occasionally exciting. I suppose it was all exciting, but familiarity makes one so blasé.

Shortly after, I began to be visited at night by a man who had the head of a bird. I cannot be sure what sort of bird it was - an ibis perhaps, or a curlew. I do know he used his long, curved beak to prise apart my not unwilling buttocks, before plunging in a penis that so trembled with excitement it almost immediately left a hot, enthusiastic deposit of semen.

My grandmother knew nothing of these visits, at least not at first. Yet when she washed the sheets she must have seen the runneled stains, the telltale seepage of brown, but if so she never made comment. Perhaps she refused to acknowledge the evidence, this blatant expression of blossoming sexuality (the stains were not

the bird man's alone), a property she had successfully
quelled since the death of my parents. Since I was now
in my early twenties, she must have considered it a
battle long won.

Let me describe my grandmother to you: a trim,
contained woman, greying hair drawn back in the
severest of buns. Her hands, perfectly manicured, were
nonetheless calloused on the palms, evidence of her
determined nature for, once she had decided something
must be done, then she would launch into its solution
with an almost frightening intensity. Perhaps she took
this from her own mother, who personified the term
Dour Scot, or from her father who, it was rumoured,
had been Japanese. Evidence of this coupling could be
seen in the cupola of her eyes which combined the
naivety of a Japanese anime with an earthy brown that
spoke of the salt of the earth. In deference to this
assumed but never confirmed parentage, she had taken
to wearing a long, smock-like coat that gave her the
distinct air of an oriental, while beneath her clothes
were proper Marks and Sparks best, conservative
woollens. She painted her fingernails purple.

There: I have described my grandmother to you, and
yet I have given almost no real detail. My grandmother
once described me as a creature of the most maddening
ambiguity, but in truth the same description could also
be used to describe her own character.

We lived in one of the village's few grand houses, the
sort with window ledges so thick you could lay an entire
meal out upon them. The windows themselves, single
paned, barely fitted the frames which, warped, let in the
most unholy wind, summer or winter, so it sounded

throughout the house as if someone was in perpetual distress. We were the only people who inhabited this much too grand Victorian folly, having long since isolated ourselves from the outside world. Our only contact came in the form of cursory nods of greeting to our neighbours and a few, inescapable words to the delivery man who supplied our groceries on a weekly basis. Any other visitors we simply ignored. I have a vague recollection of being taken into the village to purchase clothing as a child, but as I grew older these trips stopped, and my clothing simply appeared, like so many things on which we relied.

The bird man, then, represented an intrusion into the uneasy equilibrium in which we found ourselves (uneasy for me, that is: I cannot speak for my grandmother). He was a very tall man. I say man because, his avian head apart, he was most definitely masculine: his preternaturally hard, though somewhat attenuated penis attested to this. A constrictively formal black suit, threadbare at the edges, was his habitual attire. It was the sort of uniform a funeral undertaker would wear. A faint odour of burning clung to him, and I could never be sure whether he smoked or whether the incineration of his avian cousins hovered around him, ghost-like. Undressed, his flesh had the necrotic whiteness of alabaster.

Did he speak to me? Not at first, and later only sounds that emerged as high, fluting phrases and, sometimes, an excited, dangerous skaw-ing. Occasionally, I thought I could detect words, or almost-words, in the noises he emitted, but this may have been pareidolia. When he spoke, his head tilted to one side, and his hard, unblinking eyes remained fixed, while his strange ibis-like beak clattered out consonants so imperfectly it would have been impossible to translate them, even assuming they contained any sort of meaning. The truth was almost certainly this: these were random sounds, splintered, in which I would find my own reflection.

I knew when he would arrive. At first, a regular, determined tapping came at the window: that was his beak. Then the wind rose and the windows (French in style, their lock inadequate) flew open, the diaphanous curtains flapped then billowed, and there he was, dark-uniformed as always, his head visible initially, then his hands, which grasped the window ledge. He seemed to rise without effort, almost floating through the open window and into the room, where he proceeded to bugger me, mechanically, though with great enthusiasm, before leaving again. Sometimes he left a token on my pillow: a blackened rose or a key grown twisted; but most of the time he left only a nacreous deposit of semen which dribbled onto the sheets, smelling quite strongly of fish. I suspect he fed on fish, diving and hunting on the shoreline some miles from our house. I had never seen the sea, but on cold, still nights its sound would carry, as regular as a heartbeat. That sound always frightened me.

The tokens left were stored in a box, secreted beneath my bed. At night, waiting for his arrival, I would pull the box out and examine these enigmatic objects of desire.

Of course, I professed to love him.

Irregular at first, these visits became more frequent, his appearance never less than anticipated, and I could no longer contain my gasps of pleasure as I rode, with increasing confidence, his not entirely adequate, but seemingly tireless, member.

My grandmother must have heard. Even our house, with its endless refraction of rooms, could not have contained my long, ululating cries which neither hand not pillow would smother.

In the mornings my grandmother prepared breakfast. This was her duty because she rose early whereas I did not, being a more nocturnal creature by inclination. Breakfast was a ritual, and the menu never varied. Two eggs, soft-boiled. Three slices of toast, neatly triangulated. A cup of tea, served in gold-rimmed china. Butter too hard or too soft, under cover of an austere white dish. That was my grandmother's contribution: mine was to eat what she prepared, dipping soldiers into the egg's soft yolk, while she watched with a look either critical or approving, I was never sure which. The eggs were reptilian, and had a heavy, slightly musty taste. She herself did not eat. For someone so robust, she nourished herself sparsely, allowing herself a few, spare slivers of pleasure. The gratification for her, I am certain, lay in this very act of abstention. If I had, and she did not, she could claim the power of virtue.

It was on one such morning she announced, "Caley, do you ever miss having friends? Do you feel lonely, here in the house by yourself?"

I was uncertain how to answer, never having had friends, or even acquaintances, beyond the casual. Our isolation was absolute. I smiled at her by way of reply.

"Sometimes I think it would be nice to have a *special* friend, someone you can turn to. Don't you think?"

"Mm." I pretended to busy myself with my breakfast while appearing as non-committal as I was able. I could not avoid, however, the betrayal of my reddening cheeks.

"Though you could say *I'm* your special friend. You could think of it that way, couldn't you? Just you and me."

I nodded, grateful to be released from the line of questioning. I understood though: if she did not know, then, at the very least, she suspected.

I did not attempt to communicate my grandmother's suspicions to my visitor, fearing his visits would stop. Even discovery would be better than that. Besides, I reminded myself, I was an adult. I was a man. I had never thought of myself in this fashion before. At night, waiting for his arrival, I rubbed my fingers over my chin's stubble, marvelling at its severity, its insistence, its masculinity. Was he aware of that when he fixed me with those hard, yellowed eyes, with their look of peculiar determination? Did he see the tracing of hairs on my back when he pressed his cold, clothed body next to mine, and did he register the depth of my cries, the slapped bass of their ardour?

In truth he probably looked at me as he would an insect: an alien, desirable morsel for consumption, conveniently soft-bodied, unhesitatingly compliant, beating in a bewildered fashion around the light of his strangeness. There was no sense of complicity in his fixed, unending stare, nor any expression of enjoyment in the nightly ritual he initiated.

Repetition allowed me to observe details unnoted before. The bed sheets were often left with a thin residue of sand, and a faint lambency patterned the walls at his moment of climax, as if we plunged underwater. Once, I am sure I saw a flitting shadow pull back from the bedroom's large, copper-rimmed keyhole, as though we were being watched, as we coupled in those inevitable, brief moments of passion. It struck me that all of the rooms in the house were lockable; and my grandmother held the keys.

This image of my grandmother as key keeper and, perhaps, as jailer, is one that remains with me. Such an unlikely, cruel captor, with her powdered cheeks and overripe breath, her eyes cleft at the edges, her hands that trembled slightly, even though their grip was surprisingly and alarmingly firm. The way she walked, the start of a limp in evidence, so I could hear her sometimes, in the rooms upstairs, or outside my room, or in some far corner of the house, somewhere I could not quite place. Though at other times I could not tell where she was at all, no matter how closely I listened. I suspect her movements were audible only when she intended them to be. That I failed to exercise such self-control may have been my downfall.

Our house was one governed by ritual and, in retrospect, I realised my crime: I had allowed uncertainty to gain a foothold, and this threatened the carefully preserved stability. Routine was my grandmother's way of creating stasis, for she hated and feared change, as with so many older people who find comfort and perhaps even power in routine.

When things began to fall apart, her obsession with order grew greater. The window was the great delimiter. In daylight, the garden (trees, coltsfoot, cottage plants grown ferocious) would cry with little fluted gasps of despair whenever the wind gusted; but this was as nothing to the evenings when shadowed figures leapt, almost glimpsed, amongst the undergrowth, and the moon waxed, unbidden, and turned the colour of blood orange.

Further afield, events had grown much worse: we heard the news on the short wave radio which crackled and hissed, broadcasting the most alarming stories, even when switched off, or with the volume muted. My grandmother countered such events with the strict application of routine. It was understandable, perhaps. But then she was no different even before the world began to shift and subtly melt, to blur, and so perhaps I am only finding excuses for her behaviour. In truth, her version of reality could scarcely be called less awry than the one she attempted to inhibit. Nevertheless, I was the one to invite disaster. I knew this and, on some level, welcomed it.

How subtle her systems of control: the clothes I wore, for example, were dun and asexual, so when seen from a distance I could be identified as neither male nor female. My features, moon-faced, small featured, must have enhanced the ambiguity, as did my name which could be applied to either gender. Perhaps she was attempting to keep me a child forever, to suppress my emerging sexuality.

These things occur to me now, but they are only made obvious in retrospect. I suppose you could call it hard-won wisdom, a process begun with my visitor's arrival. Wisdom or possibly corruption: on that point I remain unsure.

Certainly I was naïve in the expectation my grandmother would not feel the impulse to confirm or curtail my nightly visits. If any doubts remained, the tiredness I always felt must in itself have been a signal, my eyes hollowed and darkened, and the words I spoke stumbling, confused, as everything attained the heightened, dream-like quality marking the wavering shift between wake and sleep. Even objects I touched, or the light, too bright for my always weary eyes, seemed more illusion than reality.

Even if fatigue had not made it obvious, the sense of excited anticipation I at first carried with me would have. As would the invariably stained sheets, or the heavy, metallic smell of semen occupying my room, even when I opened the windows as far as they would allow, or as I dared, especially when shadows flickered and leapt amongst the trees, and cries that were like the calling of lemur monkeys came ever closer.

One day, fire fell from the sky, drifting, like bright-dyed feathers, spiralling down, until it extinguished on thankfully sodden ground and on the roof of our house.

That was the first night my visitor did not come, and I knew: he was afraid of flame. I fell to sleep late, and slept late into the morning, far beyond my normal hour, so far in fact that, when I pulled the curtains back on waking, the sun was almost in its noon position in the sky.

While I had slept, the walls of my room had been hung with mirrors. One was positioned above the head of my bed, and two on either side. Another, longer, thinner mirror had been placed by the bedroom door, so that on rising I encountered my own bewildered reflection. Above the door was a parabolic reflector, catching and transmitting all the images in the room.

In the hallway were further mirrors still; and they continued throughout the house, each strategically positioned to catch each other's depths. I could stand in the house's far recesses and follow the trail of reflection upon reflection that formed a recursive tunnel, and look upon my own bedroom, its every corner visible.

I had heard no noise; my sleep had been sound. At some point my grandmother (and it could be no other person than my grandmother) had erected this surveillance system. It was winter then, and snow lay in deep drifts on the ground. The mirrors caught the snow's light, so the house, too, was filled with brilliance. I felt naked in its exposure.

Breakfast was served as always. Even though I had risen late, and even though it would be lunchtime soon, there were routines to follow. My grandmother did not remark on my tardy arrival, nor did she mention the mirrors. I did not expect her to. With her, only the unexpected was worth comment, and then only if she, herself, did not expect it: as on the day, for example, the trees in the garden filled with coiled, leering serpents, snaking deadly red between the branches, so they resembled the trees' animated, hubristic fruits. That only lasted a morning, and then the serpents were gone, leaving skeins of discarded skin to hang from the foliage, rattling in the wind. Or the time the sky turned the bitterest shade of indigo for weeks on end, casting the landscape into perpetual, inky darkness. These were events of note, and she spoke of them still, in her blunt, didactic manner. Of the mirrors though, there was no mention.

After breakfast, her sharp, watchful eyes followed me throughout the house, no matter where I tried to find refuge, and, even if I did not look for confirmation, I could feel her gaze, which was always present. If there was consolation, it lay in the fact I could sometimes look into the mirrors and monitor my grandmother, just as she monitored me. Only this provided any sense of reprisal, but even this was unfairly weighted, for the mirrors did not angle into all the rooms of the house she frequented, whereas she could sit in them and watch my movements with ease.

When the evening came - quickly, for now the days turned dark with fingerclick immediacy - I retreated to my room as normal. My grandmother kissed me goodnight, as she always did, and when she held my hand, it seemed there was warning or possessiveness in the way her touch lingered ever so slightly longer than necessary. She had age-leathered hands, to match her face, which had gained the sexless weathering of the old. Momentarily, she stood in the doorway before closing the door, turning to walk down the corridor; but I could see from her inverted, multiplied image that she watched me still. I watched her, watching me. I closed my eyes, as if by doing this she too would avert her gaze. With some embarrassment I undressed, aware of her observation, and I covered my chest and genitals as an adolescent would, before slipping beneath the bedcovers.

Later, the shadow came, and the tap came: three sharp raps on the glass. The window, as always, opened of its own accord. A hard, dangerous blast of the rawest air was enough to send me shivering deeper beneath the bedcovers, though I dared not turn my head, or open my eyes more than the barest crack. What would she do, I wondered, when she saw him? The bird-headed man pulling out of the shadows, his priapism already evident, coming closer.

At precisely this moment all the mirrors in the house cracked. They fissioned inwards into the thinnest of shards, before falling to the floor with a simultaneous smashing, a splintering and crashing that caused me (I must confess) to shriek like a child. From my grandmother there came no sound, or at least none I could hear or, more importantly, observe, for I could no longer see her, just as she could no longer see me.

Had my visitor's arrival caused the mirrors to shatter, or had I in some way externalised my terror? Was it perhaps simply coincidence? Whatever the reason, I was saved. I was pinned and stripped and buggered in his coldly efficient manner, and then he left, with only the track of his passage through shards of glass to show he had ever been there.

The following morning my grandmother cleaned up the debris with a brisk efficiency. I did not offer to help, nor did she ask. The atmosphere in the house was as brittle as the fallen shards, and I was glad when she sent me (oh, how strange the errand, for we never received visitors) out into the garden to scrape snow from the path with a heavy bladed shovel I could barely carry. The day was cold but still, and the sound of the blade scraping on the path hypnotic, and soothing.

I returned indoors to find my bedroom locked. My belongings had been moved to another room, one that, once upon a time, had been a child's nursery: bars still covered the windows. I accepted my banishment submissively, as though the move had been planned and agreed months before. It was a tiny room, which smelt of damp. Of the seven bedrooms in the house, none were less welcoming than this, the smallest, least accessible, the darkest. It was directly opposite my grandmother's.

It strikes me now that perhaps she was trying to protect me, and in doing so reduce me to a state of infantilism. The nursery had not been mine. It was decorated in both claustrophobic pink and insipid blue. Stored in one corner was a box filled with toys from another era, forgotten now, dust shrouded, its one-eyed teddy bears and once ambulant vehicles bearing the marks of either love or abuse; it was difficult to say which. I felt sad and nostalgic and bitter to be in that place. It carried the odour of the forgotten, and I too feared I would be forgotten, so my life would return (how distant and frightening it seemed now) to the period when I was unaware of the touch of another's flesh, or of pleasure, no matter how perfunctory or one-sided it might be.

At least this time I dared to ask my grandmother why she had chosen to move me from the room I had lived in for long as I could remember.

"There are dangers in the garden," she said. "You have bars on the window now. Remember, they're for your own safety."

It seemed to me she trembled a little as she spoke, suppressing emotion perhaps. I had never noticed before, how old she looked, the way her lipstick bled into fissures around her lips, and her hands which shook (I was certain) had the stretched thinness of fabric soon to perish. I thought: you're not so strong, not really. But still I was afraid of her.

I slept that night with no expectations. I say slept, but in fact I lay awake for a long time, before falling into that borderline state which is neither waking nor sleep, and in which small worries become enormities. What little light intruded through the window (I had left the curtains undrawn), and the sound the house made as it cracked and sighed, seemed a deliberate intrusion. Even my own breathing, rapid and uncertain, was a deliberate provocation. I waited for him to come. I did not expect him to come.

He arrived with the smell of old grass cuttings and wet soil, as though he had spent the day curled in some hidden corner of the garden, one of which I was unaware, and into which winter did not fully intrude. He brought the cold of the night too, so the touch of his hands was like that of the dead, and I moaned not with pleasure but at the chill of his grasp. I did not know where he had come from: the bars on the window were intact, and the door remained locked. He simply appeared, stepping out of the room's corners, as though part of the shadows. Which is where, in fact, he returned once he had made his inevitable deposit, his brusque violation in which I was gladly acquiescent. Then there was only the night's shifting light, struck from the snow, the house's restlessness and, somewhere, a sound that may have been someone crying, almost soundlessly.

Did she know? Did she hear? In any case I was not moved again, and remained in that room, which I grew to think of as my own. The visits continued, and this routine defined my world, just as my grandmother's own routines defined hers.

On those rare occasions he did not appear, I wondered what prevented his visit. Did he see someone else apart from me? Did something, somewhere out there in that exterior world I knew so little of, prevent his arrival? I wondered what he did during the day, and what it would be like to see him in daylight. I only observed him in darkness, for those brief, repetitious moments, the brute coupling accompanied by the bird-like sounds he periodically made. Did he not have the head of a bird? I thought of him always, sometimes distantly, sometimes with an intense and overwhelming longing. It was infatuation, and jealousy.

I should have known that final night, the night of his last visit, that something was wrong. My grandmother was nowhere to be seen, which was unusual. Her attention had increased, not lessened, over the weeks and months. Maybe she had abandoned her quest. Maybe she was tired, and had gone to bed early. There were so many possibilities. I did not know. Truthfully, I did not think.

He came as always. I had already undressed, and lay naked, slipped beneath the bedcovers that never offered quite enough warmth. He came with his faint fish odour, less than fresh, and the smell of smoke, accompanied by the gelidity that always signalled his arrival, as though he had somehow opened an entrance to the world outside, the one my grandmother tried so desperately to keep at bay. There was the push, there was the thrust, there was the brief moment of pleasure, mine certainly, although as always he gave no overt sign of his. Certainly not affection, never affection.

As he left, I lay face down, so I did not even see his departure, and fell almost immediately to sleep. If I had remained awake, could I have prevented what happened? I wonder about that often.

It was the sound that disturbed me. The sound and the light. There had been a cry, and then another. A luminance filtered through the window, throwing the bars in relief against the wall opposite. I eventually rose, not wholly awake, and looked out. In the garden, my grandmother stood. She held the heavy snow shovel in her hands, and stood guard over a fire that flared, throwing out black, oily smoke, casting sparks high into the night sky. Shadows moved amongst the trees, almost liquid, accompanied by mewing cries of alarm, but they did not approach, for the light kept them at bay. I suppose I knew even then, even if I did not believe; and I stood watching until the fire died and then was extinguished, at which point my grandmother turned and hurried inside, before the shadows overtook her.

The following morning, I stood attentive while my grandmother buried the body in the garden. There were only carbonised ashes, heavy as clinker, fragile as paper.

She dug the hole herself. It was a shallow hole, but long, and the remains, laid out, almost formed the shape of his body. There was nothing there now, nothing of what once was, and I imagined my life, the life I had foreseen changing in ways more fantastic than the world transforming daily around us, was similarly buried, mounded over with dirt, scuffed flat with a scraping of the shovel, tamped down with the soles of shoes. I do not know why she did not simply scatter the ashes, but perhaps it was one last concession to ritual, the restoration of order. I did not cry. I did not feel anything.

She came that night, when I lay awake; awake but not listening, not expectant, but unable in any case to sleep. The door was unlocked: there was no sudden melting out of the shadows, no window blew wide to allow an entrance as ambiguous and sudden as a dream. No, there was the turn of a key in the lock, and footsteps, uncertain at first, then determined.

She wore a crudely painted bird's-head mask, with a filleted beak whittled from wood. There was a plume of dyed feathers I recognised as having once adorned an extravagant hat. There was a man's suit too large and crumpled, and which smelled of mothballs. Her eyes peered identifiably through the hollowed sockets of the mask. She sported a large, priapic phallus between her legs, one smooth and metallic.

"Caw," she said. "Caw." He had not spoken like that though: nothing about his speech had been so immediately familiar. When she pressed close, she smelled of cold cream and scented powders, rather than his intimidating, alluring fish odour, his tang of sea air, the almost taste of salt that clung to him.

She buggered me that night, with a surprising and vicious enthusiasm. I cannot say it was entirely unpleasurable, even if I shook with fear and surprise. Then, this done, she exited the room again, in a manner as clumsy and unconvincing as her entrance.

This set the pattern for the nights to follow.

In the morning, the birds returned, as though they had never gone. They gathered on the windowsills, and on the eaves of the house, and in the denuded trees, calling out as though it was spring, as though the many months in between had only been a fevered nightmare, and the sun that cut through the window marked an end to the disturbance, to the anticipation, to the fear, to my cherished dreams.

FOUR

Where the braes fell away, the trees were sheltered from the worst of the winds, but still they grew crooked, slanted back to the land. Towards the bottom were rowans, and silver birches, and willows, and other trees she could not name, pushed close amongst the ground-hungry gorse. Pines stood further up, as if they needed the expanse of sky to contain them. From the top, looking down, you thought you could never descend that slope, it was so sheer, but in fact it was easy to do: a mud track showed the way others had gone before, and she was young and strong and entirely unafraid. For her, the descent was easy.

At the bottom of the slope, a burn blocked her path before the ground on the opposite side rose again. Sometimes she could cross this, in the summer months, when the water levels were low, but in spring and winter it was impassable, the rush of brackened water pushing past, its roar.

"Mind you watch what you're doing down there. I don't want to find you floating out to sea someday."

That had been Kirsty, her sister. She had developed a horror of heights and would not even go near the brae's edge; and, besides, she said she was too old for that sort of thing now, traipsing through fields and getting her shoes clarted. Kirsty had started to wear a bra, and lipstick, and had begun to show definite interest in boys. Their father's disapproval was evident, even if he did not say. Claire noted this, and stored it away for future reference: she was that sort of girl.

She would come here alone, in the early morning, or towards evening, when others were not around. The bottom of the brae was one of the few spots in the village where their house could not be seen. Then her company was sheep strayed from their unbounded fields, down the slopes, finding the onward meander of their journey carried its own impetus. They perched on the most perilous spots, with nothing between them and the drop below, and they stared at her, as though she was the intruder here. Sometimes she came across a sheep's carcass, where it had fallen to the bottom, swollen and bursting with flies.

She loved this place.

"Where did you get to?" Kirsty was sitting at the kitchen table eating cornflakes, reading her book, looking up briefly when Claire entered.

"The usual."

"You might as well set up home there. See anyone?"

"Naw, too early. There were deer though, up in the fields."

"Sign of a cold winter that, them coming down so early. Here puss." She bent and placed her cereal bowl on the floor, where a ginger and white tom looked on, expectant. The cat began to lick the remnants of milk and cornflakes from the bowl.

"Nan'd better not catch you doing that."

"She's asleep yet. Dad's got the day off, so we'll not see him, and Howie's in his room reading his comics. It's just you and me." She stood and looked out the kitchen window. "The ground's all frosted still. You must be frozen. Here, let's see your hands."

Claire held up her hands which were cold, and red.

"Och, Claire, you've no sense. Where's your gloves?"

"I forgot to take them."

"Well, mind not to put your hands too close to the Raeburn, or you'll know it. Here, I'll make us a pot of tea, and that'll warm you."

Kirsty reached up to the cupboard and brought out the tea tin. It was a cylindrical biscuit tin, so old the colour had started to flake away. On the front was a scene of a robin perched in the snow. She placed this beside the teapot on the worktop.

Claire filled the kettle, carried it to the Raeburn, then sat back at the table.

"What're you reading?" Claire lifted the book and examined the cover. It showed a woman in khakis, wearing a pith helmet, knee high in long grass. She turned with an alarmed expression, away from a group of crudely drawn African warriors in grass skirts and bone necklaces. Each carried a spear. " 'Carolyn in the Jungle.' "

"It's good. Better than the cover looks. Want to read it when I'm done?"

Claire nodded and, intent, began to flick through the pages.

"Mind not to lose my place."

"I won't."

The kettle started to whistle. Claire reached over and lifted it from the heat, without looking up from the book.

"I think I've lost that one then?"

"Mmmm?"

"You always did like your adventure stories." Kirsty poured water in the teapot, shook it around, then emptied it in the sink. "And climbing trees, and mucking around in the dirt. You're a proper tomboy sometimes."

"Mmmmm."

"Daydreaming too. You're such an odd creature." She scooped tea into the teapot, added water, and left it to brew.

From upstairs, the sound came of their father hefting himself out of bed and clumping down the passageway to the toilet.

They both looked upwards.

"The beast awakes," said Kirstie.

If she followed the burn, it took her through the mire, thick with irises in spring, but firm enough to support her weight in winter, its surface iced over. Beyond that, willows pushed into the water's edge, stark now, their roots so thick they tangled together to form a tunnel that, when the burn receded, was wide enough and dry enough to crawl beneath and hide. Not today though: the water was high, slipping over the edges of the banks. She had to climb onto the bowing trunks and step from branch to branch, tree to tree, until she reached higher ground, where she could walk on land once more.

Here, further up, was where the rowans were. The leeched light turned their bark black, and the twist of their branches meshed against the sky. Past the rowans, the ground cleared and she could walk to a ruined building, its purpose unguessable now, long disused, grassed over, the old road leading to it hidden beneath withered bracken and gorse. This way took her further and further from home. She walked as far as the building, then looked to the way she had come. The rowans resembled old, humped women gathered on the hillside. Then she turned back, because it was growing dark, even though it was only three in the afternoon.

"Do you not get lonely, wandering off on your own?"

Claire shook her head. She was in Kirsty's bedroom, lying on her back, watching branched shadows move on the ceiling, pushed by the rising wind.

"Our nan thinks it's not healthy spending so much time out there like you do." Kirsty stood in front of the open wardrobe in her bra and pants, deciding what to wear. She lifted a blouse out, and a skirt. "What about this one?"

Claire sat up to look at the clothes Kirsty had chosen.

"I tell her she's worrying about nothing. It's not as if you've no friends. This one?" Kirsty lifted out another skirt. "Yes, this one." Answering herself. She held it to her waist and examined herself in the wardrobe mirror. The skirt was checked black and white and red and reached below her knees.

"You know it's mum she's thinking of," she continued. "She's worried you'll turn out like her. But that's nan for you. Anything that's a wee bit different and the world's going to end. If she had her way we'd all be married off to some farmer lad by the time we hit sixteen, and spend our lives knitting and having babies. I tell her, no fear of that, nan. Aye, and as if she's the perfect role model and all." She reached down and tousled Claire's hair into a tangle. "What's up with you tonight? Cat got your tongue?"

"Don't!"

"I knew that would get you going."

"I'm not in the mood to talk. Am I not allowed?"

"Aye, well, we all get that sometimes." She slipped her skirt on, examined herself, then adjusted it. She pulled her blouse on without unbuttoning it. "Oh. Oh yes. Karen-bloody-Carpenter."

She removed the blouse, then the skirt, and found a replacement in a red, polo-necked sweater and bell-bottomed jeans.

"Is David going to be there?" Claire sat up, suddenly interested. "You wouldn't be going to all this trouble if he wasn't."

"He might be." She laughed. "Are you after him too?"

"I think you two ought to get married. Then you can get your own house and I can move in with you."

"What's brought this on, eh? No, I'm going to the cafe, and my mates will be there, and David might, and I say *might* be there as well. And no," – seeing Claire's expression – "you can't come. It's me and my mates, and they're all too old for you."

"My friends are boring."

"You'll just have to make new ones then, won't you?" Kirsty looked at her watch. "Here, is that the time? I said I'd be there in half an hour. I'll need to phone Sam and ask if she'll come and pick me up." She looked out the window. The trees whipped in the wind. "Not that it's a night for walking anyway."

"I like nights like this."

"How did I know you would say that?" She bent and kissed Claire on the head. "I've got to be going."

She hurried out the bedroom. Claire lay there on the bed still, and when her sister was gone, reached to the bedside table, lifted Kirsty's book, and began to read it again.

She hid in the tunnel beneath the willow trees. Something had died there and lay in a grey and matted lump at her feet. The tunnel was formed of roots so thick barely any daylight entered: they tangled together into a fibrous mass before sinking into the ground. The only sound was the stir of the leaves and water from the burn trickling past. It was midsummer and the water level low: she could step across it in places, and it was little more than a few inches deep. A cabbage white fluttered at the tunnel's end, where the grass had grown high, but the breeze caught it and lifted it out of reach. She hummed to herself in a tuneless fashion.

Far off, her father was calling her name, but she paid him no attention. It was safe where she crouched, and there was a buzzing warmth she could easily fall into.

"Claire!" and again: "Claire!"

In her hand she held a necklace of red, opaque beads. Kirsty had given them to her. She counted the beads in their endless circle, until her thumb grew sore, and she had to get up because the heat was making her dizzy, even with the wind rising. She no longer heard her father, only the susurration of grass, the roots around her which cracked and shifted as though she was on a boat, and for a moment she imagined she was marooned on a vessel in high seas with a storm growing; but that was a dangerous thought because she did not want to think of the sea, even though she was never far from it, even though its salt odour penetrated inland, to where she crouched, carrying with it the coarser scent of rotting kelp.

Eventually, she emerged from the tunnel. The brightness was disorienting after having spent so long in the shade, and her legs had grown numb besides; and so she fell down onto the cracked silt and exposed stones of the dried-out bed, scuffing her knees and the palms of her hands. She washed her hands in the trickle of water from the burn, and then drank it too, even though the water was brackish brown and slow-moving. Peated fibres spun through it when she held it cupped, and the wavered reflection of the hills around her, which were nothing but green, in all its myriad forms.

From the position of the sun, it was late-afternoon. The beach would be full today with the sun to bring the families there, and they would head on home with their shoulders and backs burnt raw and swollen, shaking and peeling in the days to come, waking at night, when the heat would flare from their bodies, as if trying to match the colluding temperature of the settled air.

A jet pushed ahead, and left a score of white across the sky. She watched its progress, shielding her eyes from the sun, then rose and began to climb the braes.

At the top, children played. They were dressed in shorts and ran foolhardily barefoot through a field often used by grazing sheep. The boys were bare-chested, but the girls wore T-shirts. Although they were younger than she was, she recognised most of the group and waved from a distance, though she skirted the field's perimeter and did not approach them. The children were kicking a bright-coloured ball between themselves, so light the wind was strong enough to catch it and send it curving above their heads.

Seeing her, one of the boys ran over, though she did not wait for him, and he had to call to her.

"Claire!"

She still did not stop, so he hurried to catch up with her, and was breathless when he arrived.

"Why didn't you stop? I was shouting to you."

She turned to look at him and crooked her head, but did not speak.

"Your dad's looking for you. He's been searching for hours, he said."

She nodded, but did not reply, and walked on.

"You're fucking weird, you are," the boy shouted, but she stared ahead and did not look back. Then, as an afterthought he called: "Sorry about your sister."

She carried on down the field which sloped and led to the road. From there the road continued on to the harbour, so she turned in the opposite direction, towards the bridge. It was a high bridge, with stone walls low enough for her to lean over and look to the vertiginous drop below. The burn was a thread, and she followed its path upstream with her eyes until she located the spot where she had hidden beneath the willow trees. Even if anyone had thought to look there, they would not have seen her: she could have remained there forever and no-one would have found out. Lifting a stone from the road she dropped it over the edge, and watched it fall into water so shallow the rock bounced rather than submerged, and she could hear the faint sound of its impact, even over the wind. She continued up the road, which was hazed, heat rising and wavering from the tarmacadam, taking the long way home.

It was past her tea time when she arrived back at the house. The smell hit her when she entered: one of her grandmother's inglorious stews, and she was glad she had missed it, even though she was hungry.

Her father: "Where on earth have you been? I was looking and looking for you."

"Don't let your father worry like that. Don't you think he's enough on his mind?" Her grandmother had saved some of the stew, which had dried out and lay in an unappetisingly congealed mess on Claire's plate. Smash to accompany it, and tinned peas withered small and hard.

"Och, don't be hard on her. She's not had it easy either, have you, lass?"

Her father sitting opposite her at the kitchen table with a lager and his cigarettes before him. Her grandmother at the head, assuming her role of matriarch.

"You're too easy on her, that's your problem. She needs to learn some consideration for others."

Claire sat and ate in silence, listening but not responding to the conversation around her.

She went to bed early, tired from the heat and wanting to escape the over-attentiveness her return had brought. She fell asleep quickly, and soundly, but was woken at three in the morning by her father, who had been drinking. He came to her and roused her, and he lifted her, and pressed her to him.

"My wee lass," he said, "I was so worried about you."

She could feel the fierce heat of his body, and smell the sweat that had gathered and dried on his clothes. He was shaking.

"My wee lass." He kissed her on the cheek, and she could feel the rasp of his chin, which was unshaven.

"Down there. That's where I used to go."

Claire pointed to the footpath down the brae, less evident than it had once been, parts of it grown over now.

"You'd not want to have a fear of heights would you? I'd not risk it." James peered uncertainly towards the edge, as though the very act of looking would make him fall.

"It's not as bad as it looks. You'll maybe slip at bits, but it's not sheer, and there are trees all the way down, you'd not go far."

"Still."

"And it's another world down at the bottom, you could be far away from here. That's what I used to imagine, I was stranded on a desert island somewhere, and there was no-one around but me. Though one day my dad came looking and found me, and that was the end of that."

"Aye, I think you're part hermit. Even dressed like that and all."

Claire had her hair dyed blue and shaped into spikes. She wore a studded dog's collar around her neck and a leather jacket, and the shortest of skirts, coupled with fishnet stockings. Her feet were elevated on black stilettos, with heels so high that to fall from them threatened a broken ankle. When she walked through the field, they left a patterned indentation in the ground to mark the way she had come.

"You're a knob, you are," she said. Then: "We should go down there."

"Aye, right."

"You're just scared. Look!"

Claire slipped off her shoes and left them in the grass, then started to run down the track in her stockinged feet. She reached quarter of the way down then shouted up. "Are you not coming?"

"Fuck me. If I end up with a broken neck, it's your fault." James followed her, his descent less certain.

At the bottom, a mist had started to gather around the water, so the burn could no longer easily be seen. He reached her, said, "In fact, if I don't end up with a broken neck, it's a fucking miracle."

"Imagine we're explorers. It's a lost world and there's an entire civilisation we'll find down there." She laughed to herself. "Christ, I'd forgotten. Kirsty and her book. I read that one I don't know how many times." Then, without offering an explanation, she carried on down the track.

The mist had risen further by the time they reached the bottom, and all that was visible was the outline of trees.

"It's pushing in off the sea." Claire had stopped by the burn's edge, where they could only hear the sound of the water rushing past. "Soon it'll spread out over the land, and it'll be like the whole world's being erased, bit by bit."

"You're a strange one."

"But that's why you like me, mm?"

He reached for her and held her. The combined heat of their bodies was protection against the mist's chill. "Will we go back? Before we lose sight of the way up."

"Wait a bit longer. It's peaceful here, away from everything."

"Aye, and the village is so hectic in comparison. You'd not last in a city."

"We'll go to the city someday, James. We'll hole up with some punks in a squat somewhere, and you can join your band and I'll become an actress, and -"

"And?"

"I've not thought that far ahead. I'm going to become famous, of course. You'd consider that a sell-out. I might throw you a crumb or two from my passing limousine."

"In your dreams."

"At least I have dreams. That's more than some here have."

"Everyone has dreams, Claire. They're just not all as grand as yours."

"Aye, well, if you're going to be disappointed, you might as well make it a proper disappointment. That's what I say anyway." She pulled away from him and stepped forward into the mist, walking so far ahead he could no longer see her, or hear her.

"Where have you gone to now?"

No reply. He followed, walking into the still landscape he could not see, and found her, eventually, crouched beneath the curl of the willow tree roots, quietly laughing.

FIVE

I heard you died today, Bodie. Dear old Bodie. I haven't seen you in such a long time, and now when I do, you will be lying there in a coffin. Cancer, of course. That seems to be the way so many of us go. It must be the cigarettes, for our every movement was nothing when not silvered through a fug of tobacco smoke. These days, I hear they use herbal cigarettes, which to me seems to be combining all of the dangers and none of the pleasures, but I suppose I am old-fashioned that way. Though it was not as if I ever had much regard for danger in the first place, you always said that. It must have been the femme fatales I played: those roles spent dressed in clothes so tight the husk in my breath was not feigned. Silks and furs and lace. Stockings and garters. Panstick emphasised pallor, and lipstick appeared almost black on the screen. Cigarettes and alcohol. I always became lost in the characters I performed. Well, that was my excuse anyway.

It's different now. I am remembered, I know: letters still arrive, but infrequently. Mostly they are written by old men, toying with their memories - and perhaps other parts of their bodies - or overenthusiastic movie buffs who dream of interviewing me. I never answer. I am famous for it, in fact. Nor have I been photographed, to my knowledge, for over twenty years. Not that anyone would recognise me these days. The curves have surrendered to gravity, and my face, still called iconic, is scored so deeply even the heaviest of makeup cannot disguise it. At least I have not succumbed to the scalpel, or the injections that have turned my contemporaries to impudent chipmunks. Sometimes I catch one of my films on TV, banished these days to the wee hours, or the dead weekend afternoon slots, when no-one is watching. How young I looked then, and how unblemished. You can see why people thought I was a beauty.

I suppose I shall have to go to your funeral, although I seldom venture outdoors now and, unless there is someone to accompany me, certainly never beyond the gates of my mansion. The sky is too blue and the spaces too wide. There is the threatening, noiseless green foliage from which all life has been fumigated, either by traffic pollution, or by my gardener, Dammie, who does not dare allow even a lone mosquito the opportunity to survive. Dammie stands for Damien, by the way. His parents must either have been closet devil worshippers or, at the very least, fans of that dreary film.

The truth is, I feel afraid without the order of my room around me. Twenty years of near-isolation does that to you. If the breeze carries in snatches of conversation, as it sometimes does, I am bewildered by some of the phrases used. The television is my real companion now, and the voices I hear there are cracked and clipped with age, like the film stock itself.

Apart from Dammie, the only person I see with any regularity is my maid. She is Korean, ruthlessly efficient, and barely speaks a word of English. Mi Cha, that's her name. I used to have a manservant – yes, that is a little irony you hear in my phrasing – forty years my junior, but he was facile and annoying and, besides, he ran off with another man, which may explain his conspicuous lack of enthusiasm while he attended to me. These days I am content with the company of my cat, and to watch my neighbours, their poolside perfectly visible from my bedroom window, along with their house - less grand than mine, but more welcoming too - which sits alongside. I do not know if they see me looking, but if they do, they never give any indication.

There is a husband, and wife, and two teenage children, one a brattish girl who looks and behaves like a boy, and the other a boy who looks like a girl, which is highly confusing, even to someone like me who grew up in an industry in which so many people were evidently, though never publicly, queer. They only moved in a few months ago, and I find them terribly fascinating, because even their mundanity is unfamiliar to me.

I suppose I am lonely, even in this age of twenty four hour television and the internet. Sometimes, if I am alone in the house, I find myself talking aloud, and I stand on the staircase (spiralled and iron wrought, a grand folly) and pretend I am acting one of my old film roles, lines still remembered after all these years. And I think: how sad, how sad, I am turning into Norma Desmond.

*

Well, I went to your funeral out of obligation, Bodie, though in some respects I rather wish I had not. I know you won't take offence - you were never that sort of person. It was a decent gathering, you had not been forgotten, but what a sad collection we made: faces I almost knew, their names tantalising, and then the dreadful shock of recognition when I finally realised who they were. They stood in the mordant green of the cemetery, or they sat, more than a few wheelchair-bound now and some, frankly, more than a little la-la, steered along by their nurses whilst they made random noises or shouted out at inappropriate moments. The nurses were the only young people there; the rest were old, faded stars like you and me. A few members of the press stood behind the cemetery gates, along with onlookers as decrepit as the people they had come to see. The sun shone, of course, because it always shines here. These days I find it hurts my eyes, and I wear dark glasses for protection. Dark glasses are such a useful invention: they hide age, they hide tears, they hide identity.

I stood at a distance, with my chauffeur-for-a-day in attendance, holding his arm for support. He wore too much aftershave and frowned when I lit a cigarette in his presence, my little spark of tribute to you. No-one looked at me, not during the service, which was as long and as enervating as all such ceremonies are, but when it was done I could see people approach, and that was when I instructed my driver to leave. It was fear, you see. Fear of death, of old age and, especially, the fear I would be recognised, the tatters of my beauty revealed. Still, at least I made the effort, Bodie, I said my farewell, and all the memories returned of those wonderful, dangerous months together when there was passion, if not love.

Afterwards, in my room, I watched one of your films, the one you won the Oscar for. I drew the curtains, I locked the bedroom door, and for a few hours the modern world did not exist. There was only you and I, and those alarming matte backdrops that defied anyone's belief. How terrible to be a victim of one's memories in this way.

*

Mi Cha brought me a letter today, in her usual wordless manner. She is such a small, pretty woman, but her English is so limited I cannot tell if it is accompanied by any degree of intelligence. The letter was in a plain white business envelope, with my first name written on the front.

"How did you get this?" I asked.

"Lady."

Well, I already knew that from the handwriting. Men have such thick, clumsy hands that any degree of delicacy is impossible. This was written in fine, close-knit script.

"Which woman, Mi Cha?"

She shook her head, which either meant she did not understand me, or she did not know. Perhaps I should study Korean to fill the long hours. Or, more rationally, I should hire a maid who knows how to speak English. But I cannot bring myself to let her go. She knows me as well as anyone these days, she is trustworthy, and she cleans the house with a ferocity bordering on callous.

Inside the envelope was a letter written on scented paper. Either that or it had been written by someone who drenched themselves in perfume.

Hi there

It's Matty, your next door neighbor. I just wanted to say hello. I meant to when we first moved in but never did, I must seem really rude.

I'm a big fan of your movies. My dad used to watch them all the time, I guess that's what got me hooked.

Maybe you'd like come over sometime and we can have coffee and a chat? I'm home most days but the kids are out in the afternoon, and we can get some quiet then.

I'd be real honored, and we can get to know each other better. I'd sure like to hear your stories of the old days, when you were famous.

Looking forward to hearing from you.

Matty

I was a little offended by the phrase 'when you were famous', I will admit, but of course she is correct; to think otherwise is delusional.

Then, when I looked, there she was, visible from the window, lying by the poolside, the spot where she spent much of her time, sunning herself. Obviously a lady of leisure. The sun seemed to have no effect on her, for she was as white as white can be, and thin: not the horrible, anorexic look seemingly fashionable for so many women nowadays, but in a way that hinted at illness. She turned in that lethargic fashion sunbathers possess, and I think maybe she saw me, even if she did not acknowledge my presence. She looked lonely there, the sort of person who might be glad of my company and, to be truthful, I would be glad of hers, even if the note suggested it would not be the most intellectually stimulating of meetings.

Of course, I will not accept her offer, but I cannot pretend I am not a little thrilled. I sometimes think what keeps us going is the attention of our fans, as though we feed on them.

*

I'll tell you who she looks like. Do you remember the wardrobe mistress we had, the one so thin it looked as though her body was ready to collapse in on itself? Thinking about it, her name was Matilda as well. How strange: I haven't thought about her in years. She had a daughter, I forget her name, who sometimes accompanied her on set. Maybe you met her? She was the one with dyed blonde hair, trowelled-on makeup and the most abrasive accent imaginable. Still, she dreamed of becoming a movie star, just as everyone in this town does. Or did: who knows what they dream of these days. Such a sweet girl, and clever too, but utterly talentless. She would lift my script and read lines aloud, and you would only call her performance wooden if you were being charitable. That's assuming you could decipher her strangled phrasing. Naturally, I did not have the heart to tell her, though it might have been better if I had.

After her mother died, I still saw her in the studio sometimes, older and certainly more worldly-wise, if no less insensible to her lack of talent. Once she even managed to find herself a bit part in one of my movies. No speaking, of course, or doing anything that even resembled acting, nobody was that foolish. You just knew she'd only gained this smallest of roles by sleeping with the casting director. We spoke briefly, and she was so excited about her part, saying it was only the beginning, that one day her fame would be as great as mine. Hearing her talk that way broke my heart, truly it did.

Years later, I saw her hanging around a side street, and there was no need to guess what her job had become. Just the tiniest of falls from where she had been, but the tiniest of falls is an abyss in this town. Poor, poor girl. How lucky you and I were, Bodie, how fortunate and determined and (yes, I have to admit the truth) ruthless to gain our moment of fame. You and I know the real reason it is called tinseltown, because if you scratch its thin, glittering veneer, so many stories like hers lie beneath.

*

Last night I was woken by an argument next door. It was three a.m., or so the stare of the clock told me. I am quite familiar with that particular hour, for I seldom sleep through the night now. It is so tiring, being old; nothing follows the pattern it should. At least this time I had an excuse.

Matty and her husband were quarrelling. I think I heard the word "affair" being flung about, but it was difficult to tell through the volume of noise, the shouting and the sound of objects thrown. The son became involved at one point, and then I could no longer tell who was arguing with whom. It halted briefly when a car drove off, at great speed, so I suspect a teenage tantrum there, then it began again a few minutes later, just the two of them now. I looked out but could not see anything, only the deserted pool, which had a hollow, mausoleum look, the artificial light reflecting off the water and the tiles, the sun loungers and umbrellas, and it all seemed so still, in contrast to the continuing din.

I suppose I must have fallen asleep then, sitting there in the chair beside the window, because when I opened my eyes it was to rising sun and mist and everything was quiet once more. One of the sun loungers floated, half-submerged, in the swimming pool, while others lay in disarray, so I imagine I must have missed a particularly dramatic moment. How typical. The daughter was awake, or had not yet gone to bed, because I could see her on the patio, eating her breakfast, but there was no sign of the others.

That was last night's thrilling drama. It has left me tired, even more so than normal. At one time there were no sounds here, no neighbours, and nothing to look out on, apart from the spread of trees down the hillside and the cloudless sky. That was before property developers arrived and buildings sprung up all over, obscuring my view and bringing their dirt and noise. Now I am only one house among many. I really ought to move, but it would be such an upheaval, and I am simply too old and too stuck in my ways. Besides, these days, events such as the one that took place last night are the only source of excitement I experience.

You will remember the dreadful arguments on the film sets. There was always the moment's star who complained about the angle of his or her face in the camera lens, the way it failed to emphasise their cheekbones, or the strut of their chins, the way it showed the breakage of lines on their skin. They forgot, in those moments, how disposable they were. I knew though. There was always someone more handsome, more beautiful, more talented than you, willing to work for less pay, willing to sleep their way through the ranks of bit actors, the set designers, the cameramen, the Bs and the As, the directors, the producers, the financiers. Hadn't I done it myself? We were all so desperate, willing ourselves to the top, unaware or ignoring the adage about rise and fall. Everyone was so terribly needy I imagine we must have had the most awfully deprived childhoods. Don't you think? Because insecurity was always the real source of the arguments, which invariably ended with placatory words, and the inevitable respite of the trailer, where alcohol was consumed, and pills popped so they came back onto the set with a washed-out smile, and something rattling behind their eyes that resembled a brain, but only loosely.

That would go on for one movie, or two, or three, or however long they drew the public in, but the instant their pulling power faltered, that was the time their grievances and tantrums counted against them. If they were lucky they descended to fourth or fifth billing, their lesson learnt, but otherwise their decline seemed to have no limit, and even the B movies, the Z movies were denied to them. Eventually they'd be found dead in a seedy motel room somewhere, their only obituary a sideline in one of the scandal magazines.

I was clever: I avoided that, although at times this house seems like its own sort of death. It is too big for me, too empty, and too full of memories. But I will not move, I am too old, it is too much of an upheaval. Oh dear, I have said that already, haven't I? I fear my mind begins to wander.

*

I think Matty may have left her husband, because I have not seen her since the argument, which is not like her at all. In fact, I have not seen anyone, not since the brief glimpse of the daughter this morning. I know, because I kept an eye on the house from the moment I rose. For some reason I am so very eager to find what last night's quarrel was about. The frisson must arise from the knowledge she is a fan. Perhaps, in fact, the argument had been about me. Perhaps she had persuaded her husband to buy the house just to be in proximity to me.

Yes, I have fabricated such sad delusions.

I looked out into empty rooms, an abandoned swimming pool, the patio area which still had Matty's cardigan slung over the back of one chair. They favoured modern, minimalist furnishings, and this made the house look not only empty but lonely. Jinnie, my cat, who seemed to prefer their house to mine, sat outside their kitchen window, washing herself: that was the only indication of life. Mi Cha made me lunch of soup and a sandwich, and I sat in my bedroom, eating, gazing out, imagining myself lounging outside, in the sun, as at one time I used to, before the terrors overtook me. Isn't that sad? You might think as you get older you have less to lose, but the opposite is true. Everything becomes a source of danger.

In the evening, the husband returned. I had moved to one of the many, long-unused guest rooms, one from which my neighbour's driveway could be partially seen. A short, stocky man, he always dressed in uniform, even at home, but I could not work out what the uniform was for. He carried a case of some sort, and emerged from his car holding a conversation on his cell phone, which he held with some difficulty. I think perhaps he has some sort of disability in one hand. Nothing in his expression indicated anything untoward had taken place, and when he disappeared indoors I went back to my bedroom and sat, rereading Matty's letter, only to realise I could not even remember what she looked like. I kept on thinking of the wardrobe mistress instead.

*

I wonder, has Matty taken the children with her? They did not appear the remainder of that first day, or the day after. The husband left in the morning and came back in the evening, and beyond that there was nothing, no movement, no sound, to indicate anyone lived in their house at all. At some point I misplaced the letter I had received: maybe Mi Cha disposed of it, though that would not be like her. More likely, I had put it down somewhere and could not remember where. I began to slip into the past again, watching those old movies, sitting there, smoking cigarette after cigarette. I never lost that dreadful habit, you see.

*

The daughter reappeared today. She must have left in a hurry, not stopping to take any belongings, because she entered the house using the key the family keep secreted in the garden Jardinière. Either that, or I am fleshing out events for greater dramatic effect, and she had simply forgotten to take her key with her.

What I am certain of is this: she did not expect to find her father home. It was mid-day, when he was normally at work, but this day he was not. Did he expect her arrival? Was he forewarned? Or was it coincidence? Whatever the reason, when she opened the door to find him standing there, waiting for her, her surprise was apparent. As was her delight at seeing him, because the two of them embraced, fiercely.

Of course, I did not see anything after that, because the door was closed and, along with it, my access into their world.

Shortly after, she emerged to haunt the poolside, as though she had never been away.

My suspicion the daughter is a lesbian must be true. She has that mannish look about her, surely cultivated. How else to explain the checked shirt, and the heavy belt and jeans? That and her head shaved almost bald. There was still no sign of the son. Maybe he fled the house, shrieking in his emasculated fashion, and lived now with his mother, wherever she may be. Whatever the cause of the argument, it seemed the daughter at least did not bear her father any resentment. Possibly she decided her allegiances lay with him. Fathers and their daughters, mothers and their sons, that's the way it always goes.

Watching her, an idea came to me: I would go out and ask her where her mother was. Whatever was I thinking, Bodie? Really, truly, I am starting to become unmoored from reality. Whatever made me imagine I could leave the safety of my house, and make the journey to their house, all to talk to a woman I had never spoken to before? Me, who, in the last ten years, has barely managed to walk a few yards from my front door without the assistance of others.

So of course I did not, I evaded that momentary delusion. I visualised it though: descending the steep stairwell and out the front door, down the garden, past the statues and the arbours, the lawn with its revolving sprinklers, continuing towards the roadside which cars drive past with a speed never less than careless. My progress would be slow; these days I walk with a limp and have grown unsteady, and have to hold onto whatever object is nearest me, so I do not fall. How different from the last time you saw me, when we had at least the remnants of our youth to cling to.

Even to think of the journey panicked me, but this is the point: I dared imagine it. Perhaps the fear is waning, as inexplicably as it came. Perhaps and perhaps and perhaps.

In the afternoon the daughter went back indoors, later emerging with several bundles of women's clothing. Were they her own, or her mother's? It was difficult to tell. Nor could I imagine why she was taking them out into the pool area. But no; she rounded the house and so, to keep track of her movements, I hurried to one of the guest rooms, or hurried as best I was able. This room allowed a partial view of the front of the house. To see more clearly, I knelt on the windowsill, waiting for her to appear. It was then I made my mistake: I opened the bedroom window to look out and, as I knelt there, must have grown dizzy, the giddiness that comes with age when you move too quickly. And then I fell. Oh, Bodie, I fell.

*

Mi Cha and Dammie were leaning over me. I wish I could say their expressions showed concern, but in truth I was too confused and sore to notice any such thing. I lay in my bed, where they had carried me. Mi Cha had heard a thump and, on finding I was not in my bedroom, nor in any of the other places I haunted (that is to say, toilet and lounge, nowhere else), she had gone through each room in turn, and eventually discovered me sprawled on the carpet, unconscious. Fortunately I had fallen backwards, and not forwards, as that would have taken me out the window to join you in whatever netherworld dead movie stars inhabit. A blanket covered me, but still I was terribly cold and I shook and I ached. Every little part of me trembled, Bodie. It was shock I imagine, a diagnosis the doctor confirmed on his arrival.

I made up the half-truth that I had risen too quickly, had grown dizzy and had fallen.

"You're a fair age," he said. "Something like that will take its toll on you."

As though I didn't know that myself. I had chafed the skin on my shoulder and the palms of my hands, while bruises spread along my legs and back would eventually bloom in the most glorious of colours. His prescription was rest and painkillers, and his bill will be out of all proportion to that moderate advice.

I cannot say the next few days were unpleasant, drifting in and out of the narcotised sleep the tablets brought. It reminded me rather of the jazz clubs we used to visit, the ones filled with more smoke than air, and where our faces supplied the only white amongst the black. We thought we were being terribly daring, which in a way I suppose we were. Those places always left me a little lightheaded, because you would find a way of obtaining reefers, disappearing to talk to some person you evidently knew, somewhere in the crowd, someone I could not see, and we sat there openly smoking them, feeling ever so brave. Nowadays, of course, you are thankful if your children limit themselves to such innocuous activities.

Lying in the darkness I thought about these things, and other moments in our lives finding those memories had greater clarity than events from only days before. The blinds in the windows were drawn so if anything further happened next door, I could not tell.

I wonder: why have I become so anxious about Matty's whereabouts? I have come to this conclusion: I am a sad and lonely woman who has no friends, who sees no-one, who is remembered by very few, and I am desperate for even the slightest sign of recognition, for the fame once mine. That is mine, in a way, but only in the by-lines of books and magazine articles and, these days, on the internet. I have done that ridiculous thing where you Google yourself and see yourself reflected in images and words, all of them slight, many containing the words 'whatever happened to...?' and 'reclusive', which is code these days for 'no-one really cares'.

I have been thinking too about Matty's children. You will have noticed my comments about them have not been the kindest, but the truth is, I always disliked children. No, dislike is too strong a word. I had a fear of children, and what they did to your body, leaving it so misshapen. That was when you had to graduate to character roles, and corsets so merciless they left you staggering, airless, barely able to say your lines. Some managed it, of course, but many more felt obliged to marry some fat, uninteresting producer, in order to provide their lives with an element of security. I dreaded that, the thought of becoming the trophy wife, trapped indoors all the time, with no-one to talk to, finding ways of filling the empty days with pointless amusements. How ironic that is, for I have become exactly like a trophy wife now, except I am not a wife. And, come to think of it, not much of a trophy either.

You know, of course, that is only partially the truth. You were one of the very few people I told about the abortions, late one night, when we had had too many gins, and talk turned from frivolity to soul baring. It was the sort of discussion that seems so profound at the time, but the following day is recognised as maudlin ravings.

There had been rumours, of course, but those sorts of rumours followed everyone in our business, and some of those rumours were even untrue. I am proud to say I did not weep, though a terrible blackness filled me as I told you about them, four in all. Four, even though I had been careful; but it was as though my body's intention had been to betray me. At least I did not have to attend one of those disreputable backstreet clinics. There were other possibilities open for those who had money, like me. It did not make the feeling afterwards any less sour, or the depression any less deep. Each time it happened I turned to the pills, and the booze, and so of course the stories would go around about how 'tired' I was, how 'unwell'. Well, we all knew *that* code.

You were always such a good listener, Bodie, maybe because you'd a few secrets of your own, hidden away somewhere. Who knows? If you had, they weren't for my ears, not that night, nor any other. As for my secrets, well, they were mild in their way, because we all know the darkness this business attracts, but they were not mild for me, not for me.

The fifth time was a miscarriage. When that happened, I left the business. I have never told anyone that before, not even you. I was tired of opening my legs, and the consequences. I was tired of the artifice. I was tired of the forced glamour, and the obligations, and I had enough money to need never work again.

That's one thing about this business: you will either end up blowing your brains out in a doss house, or you will be very, very wealthy. I was one of the fortunate ones.

*

I am feeling better, that's something, isn't it? And I will tell you why: my life has turned into an adventure, albeit one of a rather disturbing sort.

Last night I woke to the sound of a car in next door's driveway. I say woke, but in truth I was awake anyway, for the painkillers have started to lose their effect, and the deep sleep they brought, so welcoming, has been banished. I could not see anything from my window, so I rose and padded, ever so slowly, for I am still sore, to the same guest room in which I had fallen, the one that provides a clearer view of the driveway. From there I watched the husband, sitting in his car, its engine purring. He was dressed in the same uniform he always wore. That indicates repression, don't you think? How very incisive my insights are of late. He sat in that way, staring into space, not moving, and remained there for nearly quarter of an hour, the windows wound up. For a moment I worried he had fed a hose into the vehicle, and was attempting to asphyxiate himself. But no; he suddenly drove off, away from the house and onto the road beyond. I could not see which direction he headed, but from the flash of headlights, assuming they were his, he was driving away from, not into, the city.

This meant his route took him up the hillside, up and up into scrubland. I imagined him there, on those empty roads, driving to who knows what destination.

The idea he was going to commit suicide was still on my mind, I will confess.

So I waited for his return, and for those hours the house seemed very empty, and a little threatening. Stillness amplified every noise and made it a danger. Unexplained sounds do not normally frighten me, because I have become familiar with the way the house stretches and relaxes in the cooler evening air, but they did last night.

It is time I employed a live-in maid. Mi Cha arrives in the early morning, then leaves after she has made my evening meal, and for the remaining hours I see no-one. I have watched too many of those movies, the type in which the heroine is by herself, in a house too large for any one person, and every shot is full of amplified shadows and sound. Thinking about it, I even starred in a few.

*

At eight in the morning the husband came back. I waited all up all night for him. Isn't that pathetic? I don't know where he had been, or what he had done, but he had changed into jeans and a checked shirt, and these were muddied and covered in dust. As he emerged from his car, his walk had the sort of lurch that comes with extreme fatigue, and he headed straight into his house, leaving the car door wide open. On the back seat, the uniform he normally wore was neatly folded.

Half an hour later he reappeared. He had changed, and must have showered, but you could see he was still tired. In fact, I wondered if he might be a little inebriated and invented a scenario in which he had driven away during the night, and had stopped at a bar somewhere, drinking away his sorrows; and then some sort of fight with the redneck locals followed. If this was a movie, there would be that sort of scene, one from which he would emerge either victorious or broken, both paths markers on his road to redemption. You see, I always root for a happy ending, even if it is evident from the beginning this in not the route the story will take.

But maybe I was mistaken. He removed his uniform from the back of the car, and bundled it into a clear plastic bag. I had not noticed before, but he had also changed his shoes, and now wore sneakers, oddly incongruous on his feet. The shoes he normally wore (black, expensive, highly polished) he also took from the car, and placed them in the bag, alongside his uniform. He carried these into the house, then returned.

From the car boot he removed a spade, crusted with earth. Yes, a spade, and a long, discoloured sheet of plastic. He moved these to the far side of the house, which I could not see. I knew they had a garden incinerator there, because I had seen the rise of smoke from it before. And yes: smoke began to rise now.

I know what you are thinking now, Bodie, because I thought the very same thing.

His last action was to wash down the boot of the car with a bucket of soapy water and a sponge.

What I saw did not seem real. His acts pointed to one thing and one thing only. I found myself trembling; yes, trembling, and moaning too, a sound that threatened to turn to hysteria. How quickly the story had changed from domestic feud to murder. But that is not the worst. The worst is that, as he was finishing his work, he glanced up and saw me watching at the window, my emotions surely transparent. I should have acted rationally, and waved to him, as though nothing was untoward, but I was foolish, and drew back quickly, frightened. With that one movement he must have known what I had seen. He knew that I knew.

When next I dared look out again, he had returned indoors, and I did not see him for the remainder of the day.

*

Thrillers were always my favourite sort of films. The heroine in the deserted house (an old mansion if it was a British setting, an apartment if it was American). Or gas stations in the Midwest, on the way to a city somewhere, or a no-hope town. That seemed real life to me, the danger and duplicity, and the struggle. Did I find myself in that situation now? I kept on thinking about the expression on the husband's face (the husband – what was his name?) and the surprise and threat it implied.

I did not know what to do; and so I did nothing. I imagine it must have been shock, or indecision, or fear. When you knew me, I was not like that. We were so daring, the two of us.

To complicate matters, the son returned that very same evening. Wherever he had been, it was evidently not with his mother. The children suspected nothing, apparently. They sat around the poolside, the boy playing an acoustic guitar, and singing; the girl read a book and ate a sandwich. Their father joined them, and lay on a lounger, sipping a drink. The girl said something, and there was laughter. My cat, treacherous, ran along the poolside, right towards the girl, who fed her a morsel from her sandwich.

Now the children have gone indoors, but the father lies outside still, and has fallen asleep. There is a stir of waterflies over the pool, and it is very tranquil.

So I doubt myself even more, and wonder if there is an innocent explanation for what I have seen. I have replayed the events of the night of the argument, and of last night, and this morning, and I have replayed them over and over. Each time I come to the same conclusion. Still, I doubt myself. Maybe Matty has left for a reason quite unconnected to the argument, perhaps nothing is untoward, perhaps they are estranged. Perhaps she is in the house after all, and is ill.

I just do not know, Bodie. I do not know what to do at all.

*

I turned to the internet. How absurd not to have thought of that before. Even the archaic - amongst which I now surely number - recognise its importance. It took surprisingly little time to find the information I sought, even allowing for the distraction of a page in which old set photographs could be seen, and in which I featured, and you, and people I have not thought about for years. I Googled the house address and got the family's name. I Googled the family's name and got their Facebook page. From the Facebook page I discovered where the father worked, and his company website. How exposed we have become in the electronic age.

His name was Aden Austin, and he was media specialist for a rail haulage company, whatever that may involve. Not like the old days when people had easily understandable job titles. His wife was called Matilyn (so: Matty was not a shortened form of Matilda, as I had imagined), the daughter Calamity, and the son Halcyon. At which point you start to question not your own sanity, but theirs, for choosing to encumber their children with such appalling names. No wonder they had turned out as they did. Aden's Facebook page was locked, and I could not find one for Matty, but his children were less careful. Their posts were as innocuous and witless as you might imagine, and contained nothing to suggest they were anything other than a wealthy, averagely dysfunctional family. But then I suppose it is naïve to suppose otherwise, as though violence only comes to the deserving.

*

I may have left it at that, the product of an old woman's delusion, had it not been for Jinnie, my cat. You wouldn't have met her, but would have seen her great-grandmother, or great-great-grandmother, I forget which. That was back in the days when I had many cats, before Mi Cha took them all to be neutered and now only Jinnie remains. She will be the last, I would imagine. She still has her youth about her, so will probably outlast me. I must make provision for her in my will. Isn't that just the sort of things an eccentric old woman would do? Heaven knows there's no-one else I would leave my money to.

Jinnie often climbs in through my bedroom window. A trail of ivy lies thick on the wall, and she uses this to claw her way to the top, sometimes bringing with her unwelcome presents of disembowelled mice and birds. This time she left something that was not so obvious.

"What's that Jinnie? What do you have there, puss?"

She dropped something by my feet, purring around my legs and leaving her track of white hairs.

I knelt, with difficulty, and picked up a necklace of thin, red beads. They were nothing more than costume jewellery, but not unattractive. At one time I would have considered wearing them myself, when I paid attention to such things. The cord had snapped, and the beads were coated with dirt. When I scraped the crust with my thumbnail though, it flaked in such a way I was certain it was not dirt, but blood. It was the darkest umber, almost black, and when I smelt my fingers they had an unpleasant odour, like meat gone bad.

I dropped the necklace then. I could not help it: it was as though my fantasies had become concrete. I dropped them, the necklace snapped, and the loosened beads scattered on the hard, marble floor. They rolled under my bed, and under my dressing table, and who knows where else. Even Jinnie looked bewildered as to which direction they had gone, frantic in her attempt to chase them all, and locating none.

I did try to find them, on my hands and knees, moving painfully over the cold of the floor, and somehow managed to rescue three: but these were unmarked. Then I could not kneel any longer, the discomfort was too great, and I had to rise.

I am certain it was blood - a woman grows to know its appearance, even if that too is a memory these days - but I cannot prove it.

Did I ever see Matty wearing the beads? If I think of her, I cannot see her face, not clearly, only the pale of her skin, the angularity of her body. She wore shorts, and t-shirts, and in the pool area at least, sneakers. For someone who spends so much of her time watching, I am not very observant.

My first thought was to call the police, but was afraid of being branded a hysterical old woman. I had no proof, only suspicions. When you live on your own as I do, when the past is as palpable as the present, it is so easy to make events fit your own version of reality. For surely I was doing nothing more than re-enacting the plot of Rear Window?

Besides, I am so very tired. I have been tired since the fall, and it is as though that simple accident has stolen half the life from me. Even to rise makes me breathless, and I want to sleep all the time, even if I seldom have that luxury. Old age brings many things, Bodie, few of them pleasant, as you well know.

That did not stop me fantasising, oh no. I asked myself: what would I do if I was the heroine in a movie, what route would I take? It was a path as inescapable as the scene in which the female lead descends into the dark basement, or enters the empty house, having heard a noise, and you, the audience, are screaming *don't go there!* Despite which she always does, in that pretty, dumb-headed manner female characters are apt to have. Naturally, the hero will come along at the end to save her, and the danger will be vanquished.

The problem being, there was no hero to come and save me. I lay on my bed, and imagined myself younger and more capable, the age I was before arthritis stopped my joints from moving so freely, a Nancy Drew character of sorts, complete with the bob cut and blue felt hat.

Confronting the husband was out of the question, even if I carried some sort of recording device to capture his confession. I would end up in the hills somewhere, buried in the hard, sandy soil. Befriending him in order to find out more information was equally impractical, especially when I remembered his expression from the morning he saw me watching. No, better to avoid him altogether. The children? They were an unknown quantity. I considered enlisting the help of Mi Cha and Dammie, but my talk would be dismissed as the ravings of a senile, incoherent woman, perhaps justifiably. I could hire a detective, an option I seriously considered, but that would take time, and I knew from roles I had played that speed in these sorts of cases was vital. Finally, the plan I settled on was this: I would sneak into their house when everybody was away, and I would look for clues.

I can hear your incredulity from here, Bodie, and your laughter. The very thought I would do such a thing, me, who can barely venture outdoors without panicking, who moves at a shuffle, who finds it difficult to even think clearly at times. Yet I lay on my bed and it all seemed so straightforward, so simple, so achievable. What is more, I believe I am actually going to go ahead and do it.

*

The light was very bright, I remember that. Yes, the light, and Mi Cha's reaction when I announced I was going out, her expression part bafflement and part alarm. I dressed as I imagined someone would when going for an early morning stroll, which of course meant wearing fashions twenty years out of date, topped off with a wide brimmed hat as protection against the sun. How expansive the world appeared when I stood in the doorway and looked out. How expansive; and how intimidating the distances. My feet barely carried me, but I had anticipated that, and leaned on a walking stick, one I kept as a souvenir from that awful jungle film we appeared in. It had faces carved along its length, you will remember, all wearing an expression of alarm. Well, that is exactly how I felt.

It was as I had imagined it, the journey. Once an architectural conceit, the wide, spreading steps leading from the house were now an obstacle, and a danger. The garden was still and green, and the heat diabolical. The palms lining the driveway posed a threat by their very inactivity. Rose bushes bloomed, their scent cloying. I walked past them all, looking ahead to the wide, iron gates I had made my goal, and I counted my steps, one two, three, four, five, just like that. I suppose it was a distraction.

Fifteen minutes it took, Bodie, just to walk from my door to the bottom of the driveway, all due to the treachery of my feet, the steep gradient, and the accompanying panic. But I did not admit defeat, No, I did not and I would not. I always had a stubborn streak; pure bloody-mindedness others called it.

It was only when I passed through the gates and reached the sidewalk that I was tempted to turn back. It was the speed of the vehicles driving past and the dust they threw into the air, catching at my lungs so I coughed and coughed. Their passage made me dizzy, and the very ground unsteady, as though I did not walk on a solid surface but instead on something spongy and unreliable. You suspect, no doubt, that I was close to fainting; and now I suspect so too. Looking beyond the road, to the ground sloping to the town beneath, I felt as though it carried me downwards with it.

I did not turn back. Instead I walked, ever so slowly, towards my neighbour's house. One and two and three and four and five. A little at a time; that is what I told myself.

Of course when I got there, the gates were locked. You might have guessed that; and I should have guessed that too. Here the practice is to lock the outside world out, something I am more familiar with than most. I stood there, leaning on my stick, and stared at the gates. They were high and ornate and quite beyond my ability to open or clamber over, as were the walls fronting the garden. I cursed my stupidity then, and I curse it now, because I had not thought beyond the barrier of my own house and what I would do after the seemingly impossible fantasy of leaving it. How would I have entered their house anyway? It would be locked, certainly, and alarmed. I stood there, Bodie, and I wept, yes, literally wept with frustration. Then I turned, and I crept back the way I had come. I returned to my room, and I pulled the curtains, and I did not emerge again for the remainder of the day.

*

After some reflection, I have come to the conclusion my excursion was a triumph of sorts. No, I did not achieve my preposterous mission, but I managed something greater: overcoming the terror that has for so long stifled me when venturing outdoors. I feel a little pride when I think of it, and I do not think my pride unjustified.

You will notice my mood is considerably better than when I last wrote. The reason? Matty has come back. After all my suspicions and paranoia, there she was this morning, embracing her husband in the doorway as he was leaving. I do not know how or when she arrived home as, caught in my own delusions and disappointments, all I have seen of late is my own darkened room. Who knows? Maybe she never left in the first place. I only saw her briefly, but it seemed to me she had put on a great deal of weight, which may not be a bad thing when she looked so sickly before. Perhaps she has been on medication and this has caused the weight gain.

I will admit to contradictory emotions. The first was relief: she was safe, and my worries groundless. At the same time I fretted: how divorced from reality my thought processes had become. I do not joke when I say I think I am becoming senile. What other explanation is there? And you might point to the argument, and the beads, and the night Aden left then returned with his clothes covered in dirt, unloading tools that could have been used to bury a body, before washing down the car. I do not have explanations for these things either, but that is not the point; she is alive, and I was wrong, and I begin to wonder how much of what I have told you is truth, and what is fantasy. Maybe I have started to live out a role in one of my old films, and can no longer tell what is real, and what is not.

Still, I should not complain. The day is bright and the sky the purest blue, for once not obscured by haze; the sort of day in which you feel unaccountably happy. Except I feel, strangely, cheated by what has taken place, which is all very odd. I have made a resolution, that, after giving them a little time, I will go around and introduce myself to Matty. She will be a little embarrassed perhaps, but also thrilled. Perhaps we can become friends. I will fully overcome my fear of the outdoors, and she and the rest of the family can come to my house to visit. It will be as it was before, when I held dinner parties, and I would entertain people with stories of the old days, the stars I knew, the world that is now lost and which they would surely be enthralled by.

*

I know you haven't heard from me for a while. I've been very ill for the last few weeks. Maybe it explains why I was so tired after my tumble: some dreadful virus was working away in the background, sapping my strength.

It happened not long after I last wrote. I had that glimpse of Matty, then fell asleep – so much of my life is spent asleep these days, even though it is a broken sort – and when I woke I could not move. Everything had the dizzy, swirling quality you get when you have a fever, and when I tried to rise from bed to go to the toilet, I fell. I fell and I shit myself. Yes, Bodie, look what I have come to.

Again, it was Mi Cha who found me, but she was unable to help me up by herself, even though these days there is nothing to me, I am as frail as a bird. So she fetched Dammie, and he in turn called for the doctor, who wanted to send me to hospital. I refused, of course. The very thought of those cold, hospital lights is enough to send me to the grave, I tell you.

Anyhow, I have recovered, and am up and about again. I must have been weakened by all the excitement recently, even though it was all in my mind. Yes, I am well, if still very tired. I managed two full meals today, if you count watery soup and steamed fish to be meals. Moreover, I am determined, once my strength returns, that I will go out, and I will enjoy the sunshine, and I will see people once more.

Next door, life has returned to normal. The son sits by the poolside, playing his guitar, making a pitiful attempt at singing, while his parents often remain indoors, presumably to get as far away from the noise he is making as possible. The only person I have not seen is the daughter and, who knows, maybe she is home too, for while I have been bedridden I have not been able to rise to enjoy my vicarious life. It strikes me I have turned my neighbours into a film in a way: the picture framed, the characters introduced, the storyline tantalisingly revealed; and now it only waits its conclusion. Yes, when I am well, I will visit Matty, and we will become friends, and maybe one day we will sit and laugh at the sad fantasies I concocted.

*

You remember my resolution? Well, today I went around to my neighbour's house. I feel stronger now, and strength has given me determination. I will not remain indoors, I will go out at every opportunity, and I will enjoy the sunshine, the fresh air, and I will see people again. Perhaps, in time, I will not even be referred to as a recluse, the adjective that accompanies my name everywhere these days.

To be truthful it took me four attempts, one a day, until today I succeeded. The aftermath of my illness defeated previous efforts: my legs shook, fear overcame me, embarrassment overcame me. This time though, this time I persevered.

Yes, just as before, I ignored the white, white brightness of the sun-reflected courtyard and the intimidating, shivering green with its threat of life hidden somewhere within. I still used my cane, stopping frequently, for even the smallest exertion caused exhaustion. Mi Cha was very anxious about my expedition, but I managed to reassure her, in gesture more than words, for neither of us could understand what the other was saying. Dammie was worried too. He was in the garden, and although he did not say anything, I could see him watching.

How proud of myself I was, walking that distance. I did not panic, and continued ever so slowly to my destination. I hyperventilated a little, I will admit. That could be age though: I will say it is age.

I had chosen my moment carefully. The husband had left for the day, as had the son. Matty was at the front of the house, watering plants in their hanging baskets, as I made my way up the long, long driveway. She stood and watched me approach, not moving, saying nothing. I was tired from my walk and not a little frightened, but I smiled, elated, because I had managed to come so far. I imagined her delight at my appearance, though she gave no indication of this, at least not from a distance. In fact, she looked puzzled. Perhaps she did not recognise me? I have grown so very thin, and frail, even compared to the last time she would have seen me. Her opening words confirmed this.

"Hello, can I help you?"

Her voice was coarser than I had imagined, and the accent unfamiliar.

"I wanted to come and see you. I would have come earlier, but I have been ill. You don't mind, do you?"

Her incomprehension was obvious.

"It's Cecilia. Oh, I know I have changed, and it must be a shock to see me like this, but you said you remembered my films and I thought..."

She looked at me as though I was mad. And perhaps I am mad Bodie, perhaps I am, but looking at her, I was certain it was not the same person. She was fuller in body, and younger looking. In fact, I am sure it was not Matty I saw, but the daughter, dressed in her mother's clothing, and wearing a blonde wig.

Yes, she said nothing, and her expression was both intimidating and bewildered.

"Oh dear, have I come to the wrong house? I am so very old and forgetful." I looked around me, and acted confused, which admittedly was not difficult. "I am sorry my dear, I have made such a terrible mistake..."

I think I covered it quite well, for my acting skills have not entirely deserted me, and if I hurried a little too quickly down the driveway, then that was natural, embarrassment would account for it.

She stood observing me, still not saying anything, so on reaching the entrance I turned left, not right, towards the houses leading further down the hillside, and I shuffled until I was out of sight, then had lean against a wall for support, I shook so.

When I turned back towards my house, she remained in view, but fortunately I saw her before she saw me, and crouched down behind the wall (what must I have looked like!) out of her sight, until eventually she turned and went indoors.

That is not the end of it. I kept an eye out for the husband arriving home and when he did, she met him at the doorway. Even before he went in the house there was some sort of argument, nothing major, but he said something, and she attempted to slap him. He caught her arm, and twisted it and, Bodie, I tell you, her wig fell off. She is not blonde, she is dark-haired, and when you see her, there is no doubt, no doubt at all: she is not the same person. It is the daughter, and she and the father and the son, they are all in it together.

I know how ludicrous this sounds, but you did not see the look on their faces when it happened. He pushed her inside, and she still held the wig that had slipped, and they were both frightened, looking around to see if anyone had seen. Which they had, I had seen, but I had grown cunning, and peeked from behind a corner of the curtain, just a crack, so I was not visible.

There you have it. I believe Matty has been murdered and buried somewhere in the hills. To avert suspicion, or for some other reason, the daughter has taken her place. Yes, said like that it is ridiculous, isn't it? I feel as if I have stepped onto the set of a particularly unbelievable B movie, full of absurd coincidences and fantastic revelations. Now I am tired again, and I want to sleep. So much has happened today, and I do not know what to do, although before I do anything I think I must first get evidence to back up my suspicions.

*

Well, Bodie, this story has a bitter ending. I knew it would, for it is too much like one of those films we starred in, where any happiness is short lived, and the characters must pay for their actions, for their foolishness, and their crimes.

This is what happened: I decided my best course of action was to visit the family, under the pretext I was introducing myself, their neighbour. What did it matter if the daughter had seen me before, and the father? I would act forgetful, and a little wandered which, let's face it, is not much of an act. They would humour me, I would befriend them and, using our friendship, I would look for and obtain evidence, though quite what evidence I might find was something I had not considered. Such little foresight: I will blame age for that too. How flimsy and unrealistic the whole plan seems now.

I waited until the whole family was in. I could see them lazing around the pool, all three addicted to the sun. Then I hunted around to find a gift, but could not find anything suitable. I settled on a book of photographs in which I featured (black and white, soft-focussed, makeup emphasising the bold cheekbones I once possessed), and signed it. *A warm welcome to my neighbors.* It would seem rather bizarre to reveal I knew their names.

Then I walked again, out of my house, and up to their house. It strikes me all I have done is watch, and make excursions, in mind or reality. And fall of course. Oh, how I have fallen now, Bodie.

This time it was easier. The gate was open, the garden deserted. It took as long as ever, but the fear had diminished. I wonder now whether I was wholly lucid, for I do not really remember that part of the journey. No-one noticed my arrival, even though CCTV cameras were mounted above the doorway, nestled high in the eaves.

I rang the doorbell several times. I am certain of that. Yes, I rang the doorbell and knocked too. When there was no answer, I tried the door handle, but it was locked. That was when I took the key they kept hidden in the Jardinière and let myself into their house, with its unfamiliar sights and smells.

It goes against me that I did not call out. It was the strangeness of my surroundings, you see. I cannot remember the last time I was last in another person's home. It looked remarkably like my own, I must say, in size and layout, if not in decor. Then, instead of looking for my neighbours, I began to climb, ever so slowly, up the long stairwell leading to the upper floor. I do not understand why, even now.

In turn that led me along corridors that seemed to echo those in my own house, and which contained a series of rooms, all their doors closed. I opened each one in turn. They were bedrooms, and dreadfully ordinary rooms at that, as if they were not part of the grandeur of the building they inhabited.

The largest bedroom belonged to the husband and wife. I stood in it, and looked at the photographs on the walls, and the bed with its covers of the deepest sea green. To rest, I sat on the bed's edge, and then lay down. I was so tired. Why did I do these things? I do not know, Bodie. I just do not know. How warm it was in there, with the sun shining through the part-open window, and the tall trees swaying outside, their rustle I have always found so comforting. Yes, I fell asleep, on the bed, still clutching the book I brought with me. You would think adrenaline would have kept me awake, but now I think adrenaline was the only thing that kept me going those last few weeks.

What woke me was a woman screaming, not at me, but *at* me, if you see what I mean. Her scream was not of fear, but fury. It was the pretend wife, the not-Matty. She had me by my arm and pulled me from the bed so I fell to the floor. Didn't I say my story is one of falling? Just like those old stars, the ones who never managed to hold on to their fame. Her husband stood there too, as bemused as she was furious. There was such rage in her eyes, I remember that. I am ashamed to say that I wept, and I wet myself.

The police appeared and by that time I was incoherent. It was all so far from what I had imagined, the cool sleuth discovering the awful secret, emerging with proof, and the aftermath of glory. I'm afraid I don't recall a great deal more, but how cunning was it for them to call the authorities, to be so blatant about it? My ravings, naturally, sounded exactly that. A murdered wife, a daughter who had taken the wife's place, and furthermore the whole family were in on it, don't you know. The faux-wife protested bewilderment, said she had never seen me before. The husband explained the daughter was away abroad, in Europe. I recall shouting a great deal, and then apparently lapsed into something resembling catatonia.

There are brief memories of ambulances and nurses and then the hospital. I recall doctors and corridors, and the too-bright light of wards. I slept a great deal, was unconscious most of the time, in fact. So they tell me. Naturally, I don't remember.

As it turns out, I'm in the clear. The reason? I have been diagnosed with terminal cancer and so have changed my role from disturbing intruder to object of pity. My accusations are merely a by-product of my illness: it often happens when it gets into the lungs, I am told. It is something to do with oxygen deprivation, I imagine. I have weeks to live, perhaps not even that. I have a drip, and a monitor that bleeps constantly. The staff are very attentive and some even recognise my name from movies they have seen. Mi Cha visits, as does Dammie. They are such loyal employees.

I am certain it was not hallucination though, or fabrication. If only I could return to my room, I might find the letter and be proven right, or I could find the beads with their coating of dried blood that lie still, I am sure, below the furniture. I did mention it to Mi Cha and Dammie, but Dammie only smiled indulgently, and Mi Cha looked at me with incomprehension. There has been a lot of that, though truthfully my mind has never been clearer. I cannot say the same for my body, which is visibly failing. Now I am composing this last message in my head, Bodie, though it will go nowhere, just like the other letters I wrote to you. Perhaps I will come back to haunt the family, and that will be my final role, the B-movie descent I always managed to avoid, the bit part in one of those awful Abbot and Costello comedies. What will I see then? Will I ever understand what has taken place? Perhaps not. Perhaps not. It seems unimportant now, life itself is my priority, though that is diminishing fast, you can see it on my visitors' faces.

What will my obituary be? Not the television news, certainly. A news byline perhaps, a small notice in one of the newspapers that still bothers with such things. How things have changed, haven't they dear? The world is a strange new place. At least in our day they bothered to supply a definite ending.

SIX

Under the rowan tree the mother laid the baby, and she plucked a handful of berries off the tree, squeezing them to produce a thin runnel of juice that ran like blood over the infant's chest. The father lifted a branch the wind had broken free and touched the green-leafed end to the child's body, all the while humming a song, one passed to him by his father and his father before. The baby cried and screwed up her face, and it began to rain and washed the juice of the berries away while her parents watched. Then they took her home.

Under the oak tree the girl looked to the topmost branches with their dark crows' nests clotted at the top. It was windy and the branches shook, and the leaves sounded like the sea she heard when she lay awake at night, but still she climbed. Her limbs were short and could not wrap the trunk, but she found handholds in the whorls and fractured bark. The climb was dangerous for her body was light, there was scarcely any weight to it, so the wind threatened to pull her free. Yet she did not fall. She looked continually to the uppermost web of branches, the furthest reaching, the most fragile, and willed herself to the top.

At the top of the oak tree she looked across to the surrounding trees, the descending canopy, down to the cluster of rowans where her parents had taken her as a child. Crows swooped and clipped at her, but she paid no heed, nor to their frenetic cawing, and instead reached up into the first of the nests where there were five blue eggs. She placed one of these inside her mouth and the rest inside the furred pouch slung around her waist. Apart from the pouch she was naked. She bit down on the egg and pretended she could fly.

Beside the rowan tree they buried her mother. It was winter and the ground so hard they could only cover her body beneath a mound of stones. The family stood around and mourned, but not for long because the chill was too intense, and her death had not been a surprise anyway. She had always been feeble, and the effort of bearing children had taken the rest of the energy from her. There were no flowers for her grave, so they each placed in turn a spray of pine, hoared with frost. The girl was the last to leave, and she stood until the cold drove her away, because she did not wear much in the way of clothing. There were crow feathers in her hair and madness in her eyes and she talked to herself and sang cryptic, tuneless songs. Her father suspected she was a changeling. When she left, she ran as though something dreadful followed, and she did not stop until she caught up with the others. She would return two weeks later, on her own, and find her mother's body gone. Some animal, winter-starved, had exhumed it, dragging it somewhere off into the still, rimed hills.

Under the ash tree her father took her sister, while she watched, laid flat and panicked in the tall, concealing grass. Disturbed, moths fluttered up from their hiding places, blinded by the sun's severity, and whispered dreadful things to her. Her sister's body was tanned and plump, unlike her own, which had the frailness of a bird's. She had to press her hand to her mouth to stop sounds escaping and, when it was finished, and they had left, she hurried down to where they had lain, as though she would find some evidence of what had taken place. There was nothing though, only crushed grass and dockens, and a few tangled strands of her sister's blonde hair, caught in the bark of the tree.

High up the Scots pine she watched them wade the river, a group of four men, all attempting to stay upright in the deep, running water. Her father was not amongst them. The body was caught against an outcrop of rock, folded back over it, and from a distance it did not look like a body at all. Heavy rains had made the passage dangerous, so the men linked arms in a chain to lessen their chances of being swept away. Her brother stood on the riverbank, still, too young and too small to help. His arms were held straight to his sides, as though he was afraid to move. The man closest to the river's edge shouted to him, and he ran downstream to where a large branch floated in the water, lodged at the side of the bank. Lying on his stomach, he reached down and attempted to pull it from the current, but it was either jammed too firmly or he did not have the strength to lift it. She called to her brother to be careful, but her voice came out muted, the words stolen from her. Instead she screwed her eyes shut, as though the scene would be gone on opening them again: but it was not. The men retreated to the safety of the land, and her brother stood helpless, looking down at the branch he had been unable to move, and the body still clung there, resisting the river's passage, one bare arm flapping free, a silt of hair spun around the upturned face, the partially exposed breasts, the face death had made unrecognisable.

Beside the rowan tree, she lay on the spot that had been her mother's grave. It was raining heavily, and somewhere her father was searching for her, but she did not care. There were deep, dark bruises that ran the length of her near-naked body.

Under the cover of pine trees she hid with the rain hitting hard in the high branches and the dead needles beneath her. It was dark and there were animals moving somewhere in the darkness and she was afraid. She had stolen a haunch of cooked rabbit and some bread, and she held them to her as though they were all she possessed, which they were. She waited for the approach of her father, his footsteps, the way she had lain in fear so many nights in her own home. He would not look for her until the morning, she realised that, but it did not make her feel any less afraid. The sound of the river was clear where she lay, and she imagined her body in the water, carried by its uncaring rush, turning over and over.

Under the cover of wind-blown hawthorn she talked to the starlings. They settled in the branches and chattered angrily, and she answered back, imitating their harsh song, lying in the shade of the trunk bent near-horizontal, its brief blooms making their appearance and covering her with pale pollen. The tree was near to the top of a hill and she did not recognise the landscape before her, the unmarked green of lowlands and hillside, with distant patches of smoke to show someone was alive in this emptiness, this place so far from any she had travelled to before. Here the people she passed even spoke differently, the fall of their voices unfamiliar. A crow settled at a safe distance, watching, pecking for grubs in the grass, and she called to it, and it called back and flew away and then returned. She found herself smiling, even though she had not eaten for days, and her head was light and her body unsteady, and when she walked it was as though she was always on the verge of falling.

By the grove of trees people would leave offerings of food and drink, either in veneration or appeasement. She stood amid the heavy trunks, near-naked, padding over the mudded or leaf-mulched ground, calling to the crows which spun and cawed overhead. There was little to distinguish between her call and the crows', so perfectly did she mimic their sounds. The crows would swoop down and rest on her bare shoulders or sometimes on her head, their sharp claws clutching at her hair, which had grown unkempt and reached halfway down her back. She no longer spoke: or at least not the language of man. Sometimes she would climb up high in the trees, and sit there amidst the crows' nests, and the wind would blow and she would sway, unafraid, clinging to the unsteady branches while the sky passed grey or blue overhead. She would feed the crows pieces of the food people had brought, and they grew excited at her approach, and called to her with anticipatory, demanding cries, the cries chicks give to their parents. People saw these things and hid their eyes, or tried to come close to touch her; but she always ran away cawing, and climbed the thick trunk of the nearest tree, so the crows would rise and circle, filling the air with their sounds, as though they too were afraid.

Amongst the oak and rowan and hawthorn and pines she grew old, and she watched the crows hatch and grow and die. She planted their bones below the soil she stood on and slept on, and imagined they would grow, as the trees did; but they did not.

By the ash tree she lay and the snow settled around her and on her, and it was not cold at all. The snow was not cold, nor was the ground, and she watched the drifting flakes with a distanced sort of pleasure. Crows sat on the lower branches of the taller trees, and flapped around the ground, not wanting to settle, watching her. She lifted her arm and waved dully at something unseen, something risen from her past, and then she let it fall again. When she died, a crow landed on her face and plucked out both her eyes, and ate them.

SEVEN

They were on the beach, the sand wet and pliant beneath Cissie's feet. The sun was out, but the wind was sharp, and she only wore a bathing costume.

"I'm cold," she complained.

Kagan, wordless, took her cardigan off and draped it around her sister's shoulders. The arms reached almost to her knees.

"You're too thin," said Kagan. "When you grow up a bit you'll get a nice layer of fat like me, and then you won't feel the cold so much." She patted the swelling bulk of her stomach, by way of emphasis. "I really ought to lose weight, I really should."

They walked as far as the rocks, which were dark, and slimed with seaweed. There was almost no-one at this end of the beach. The tide was far out and had left behind long, foul-smelling strands of kelp.

"Let's stop here for a bit. I'm getting tired." Kagan smoothed her skirt beneath her, and found a flat slab of rock to sit on. Its surface was covered with the tiniest of barnacles, and seaweed dried to the texture of tatami. She lit a cigarette and turned her head to exhale thin streams of smoke. "Don't tell gran."

Cissie nodded, the admonition by now familiar, and clambered over the rocks, arms outstretched for balance.

"And don't get my cardigan wet!"

"I won't." Cissie tied the arms of the cardigan in a knot behind her waist, to make sure. It was warmer here anyway, sheltered from the wind.

There were pools of water caught in the rocks' recesses, filled with bright coloured fronds of weed. Sometimes she could catch the movement of crabs, small and thin-shelled, or insects – were they insects? – she could not name, threaded and curling. She dipped a finger into the pool, which felt warm, but unpleasantly viscous. There was movement and something slipped into the pool's depths, too quick for her to see.

She stared at her reflection in the water, her pale stretched features. Even the sun had not brought her colour back, and there were still days when she moved in an unruddered, powerless manner.

"We thought we were going to lose her." Her grandmother had said that to one of her friends, with the careless manner of the old who have forgotten their own depth of understanding when they were children.

She touched the water with her fingertips, and her reflection dispersed.

"What are you looking at?" Kagan came up behind her, and crouched down so she too looked in the pool. "Watch your fingers. There might be anemones in there, and they really sting if you touch them." She shook her hand, unconscious of the memory possessing it.

"There's a crab. See?" Cissie pointed at its pallid shell, barely visible now.

"Baby crab. It won't hurt you. What's that?"

There was a translucence below the water, lined against the rock, as though hiding.

"It looks like a fish?"

"It's not a fish. I know what it is." Her sister was trying not to giggle, Cissie could tell.

Kagan searched around and found a discarded ice lolly stick. With this she lifted the object from the rock pool. It hung ruptured and dripping.

"What is it?"

"A rubber johnny."

Cissie had no idea what a rubber johnny was, but she knew it was in some way rude. She could tell from the glee in Kagan's expression, the way she pulled a length of hair across her mouth, as she always did when embarrassed.

She reached to touch it, but her sister pulled it away.

"Don't!" Then, by way of explanation. "It's dirty."

She lay the condom down on the rock. Cissie could see the stone through it, its dark, sharp cavities. They sat for a while, watching, wordless. Finally, Cissie gave in to temptation.

"Is it alive?"

"Don't be silly. It's made of rubber. You don't get anything living made of rubber, do you?"

"So what is it?" Met with her sister's mute smile: "Tell me!"

Kagan leant forward and whispered. "Men use it. It's to stop their girlfriends having babies."

This was incomprehensible to Cissie.

"Do you remember Amanda? When she had her baby? Her boyfriend was using one of these and it burst."

Cissie remembered Amanda, but only vaguely. She was even older than her sister, and she only knew her by sight. Still, she nodded.

"Come on, let's throw it out to sea." Kagan lifted the condom with the stick, walked to the edge of the rocks, then flipped it into the water.

"Off to heaven," Cissie said. She still had the idea it was, or had been, alive somehow.

"Or hell. It's looks so dark and cold out there."
Then: "Don't tell gran."

Cissie nodded.

They walked back the way they had come, along the beach. There were children in the water, paddling, while the adults remained on the sand, sitting on blankets or propped in deck chairs. Their father sat at the far end, near to the abutted sea wall, catching the reflected heat of the sun. The wall ran far beyond the beach, and out to sea. Their grandmother was there too, but she had a blanket draped around her shoulders: she was at the age now, she said, when she felt the cold all the time. She was unpacking food from a cool box.

"You two have a good walk then?" Their father looked up as they approached. In unconscious parody, he had a knotted handkerchief over his head, and had rolled his trouser legs midmast, to match his shirt sleeves. He was on his fourth beer, and his voice was a little too loud.

"We went as far as the rocks, and had a look in the rock pools," said Cissie.

"Find anything interesting?"

"We found –"

Kagan interrupted. "Crabs and insects. You know." She stood her distance, conscious of the odour of tobacco that lingered, but Cissie ran to her father, kicking up sand.

"Don't! You've got it over everything now!" Their grandmother shook grains from the food she had unpacked.

"She's only playing, aren't you, love." Her father lifted Cissie up and whirled her round. He reached to tousle Kagan's hair, but she moved out of reach. "My lovely girls."

"Are you having something to eat? I made some sandwiches. Fish paste or ham."

"I'll have a coke, thanks."

Her grandmother handed Kagan a bottle. "Let me get the opener."

"No need." Kagan prised the bottle top off on the edge of the stone wall.

"Ttch. I wish you wouldn't. You'll end up cracking the glass one of these days, and doing yourself an injury."

"You're always fussing."

She tipped back the bottle, and drank it down in a single, fizzing mouthful.

"Ttch."

"I was thirsty."

Their father sat down onto the ground, Cissie in his lap. "Come and join your dad. It's nice, the four of us together like this."

"A proper family outing." Their grandmother, approving. "Or would be, if your brother had bothered to come along."

"He'll be at Ernie's and'll have forgotten the time, as usual. And no, I'm not sitting. I'll get my dress dirty. I've already got sand in my shoes." Kagan gazed up towards the sea wall. A walkway ran its length, rails on either side. "No, I'm going up there, have a proper look out at the beach. You coming, kiddo?"

Cissie nodded, and ran towards her sister, before looking back at the sandwiches.

"They'll still be there when you come back. On you go now." Their father was in the process of opening another can of beer.

Heavy, granite boulders shored the wall. Although a series of steps led up alongside, they used the boulders to climb to the walkway, Kagan leading and Cissie following. When they reached the top, they looked out over the sea, deep and churning around the wall's far reaches.

"You know," said Kagan, "you could fall into that water and never be seen again."

They sauntered along the wall, which was wide enough for them to walk hand-in-hand.

Then, as an afterthought, she added: "So you be careful."

"Kagan?"

"Mmm?". She was looking back at her father and grandmother, trying to see if they were far enough out of sight for her to sneak another cigarette.

"What about India rubber men?"

"What?"

"India rubber men. They're made of rubber, aren't they?"

"Are you still thinking about that? No silly, they're not made of rubber."

They walked on.

"Kagan?"

"What now?"

"Are you and Dave going to get married?"

"Maybe. Maybe one day. A long way off, though. I'm not going to end up like the other girls my age. They no sooner get married than they have children, and they look like they're ancient all of a sudden. Babies, they take so much out of you. I hate the thought of that."

She sat down suddenly, removed her shoes, and hung her legs, feet bare, over the wall, below the railings. She tapped her shoes on the concrete, heel down, and emptied out a scattering of sand. Lifting her foot, she showed Cissie her red and blistered heel. "I should have worn something more sensible. Silly, wearing heeled shoes on the beach."

"I'll carry them for you, you can go barefoot like me."

"Don't be daft, I think I can manage that." She reached over and ruffled her sister's hair. "You know, you look so much like mum sometimes." Then: "Let's go. I want to sit at the far end. You can see fish sometimes, way down in the water." She tapped her shoes one more time, then slipped them back on. "I've appearances to think of, after all. Can't be seen looking anything less than my best."

There were fewer people visible here, as beach gave way to tide, and the breeze was stronger. Waves slopped lazily against the wall, and sent their salt scent higher.

Cissie looked over the beach. Her grandmother had pulled the blanket further over her shoulders and was looking out to sea. Her father stood and, she could tell, watched them.

Cloud drifted across the sun, and she shivered, the remainder of the day's warmth suddenly stolen. She wondered where the condom was now, drifting out to the ocean's expanses, or inland again, trying to find the haven of the rock pool once more.

Kagan had gone ahead. She had found pebbles thrown up on the sea wall and was tossing them into the water. Cissie ran to catch up with her.

"I'm trying to make them skip, but they're the wrong shape. You try." She handed Cissie a stone, flat and hammered. "See? You throw it like this."

She bent her knees, crooked her arm, and sent the stone flying. It hit the water and disappeared immediately beneath a wave.

Cissie followed her example. Her stone skipped one, two, three times.

"You're showing me up! That's real beginner's luck, that is." Kagan laughed and handed Cissie another stone.

This one skipped twice before it was caught by a wave. Her own attempt again disappeared straight below water.

"Come on," she said suddenly. "let's go to the very end. I'll race you."

They ran along the wall, giggling, feet cracking off shards of shell and drifted pebbles. The water was much deeper here, enough to submerge the rocks shored on either side.

Kagan reached the end of the wall long before Cissie, but then had to sit down to catch her breath. Small boats were tethered to the right, with a metal ladder, rusted, that led down into the water. The beach seemed far off now, its population made minute.

"Are there fish, then?" Cissie lay on her belly and looked down into the sea, but it was too gloomy and dark to see anything. A slick of oil and foam floated on top. Weed clung to the wall, revealed by lapping waves.

They sat there in silence, watching the water's movement.

"It makes me all dizzy, watching that." Cissie sat up. A sudden surge sent spume flying into her face. She giggled.

"Well, you be careful, and come back from the edge a bit." Kagan stood. "It just makes me all dreamy. Like watching snow falling. You forget things for a bit."

Grey cloud pushed in across the sky, and the sun was hidden. Far off, on the beach, they could see people rising, starting to leave, and the wind had increased.

"We'd better go back. Gran will be wondering where we've got to, and it's looking like it might rain."

They stood. It had turned cold now, not cool, and Cissie shivered.

"We shouldn't have come so far." Kagan turned back to look out to the sea, which had turned choppy, and grey. "It's been a lovely day though, don't you think?"

Cissie nodded, prancing a little to keep warm.

"I'll race you back. See who gets there first. See if you beat me this time. It'll warm us up too. Though mind you don't trip." As she said this, Kagan climbed onto the railing, and waved to the people on the beach, as though they watched her. "Ready? One...two...three...!"

And then she rose, and stood on the uppermost rail, and dropped deliberately, defiantly, into the deep, cold, engulfing water.

*

Cissie stood at the far end of the sea wall. It was as it had been before, but her body was different now. Her reflection, caught in puddles layered across the concrete, showed her taller, and older. It was, in fact, Kagan's body. She had blonde hair, not black, and it hung loose, not plaited into pigtails.

A strong wind whipped the sea into high, surging waves. The sun was very bright, it shone with an intense, unnatural luminescence, so she could see down into the very depths of the ocean, its rocky cavities and weeded beds. Kagan had been right: you could see fish here, whipped into shoals, still or cutting through the stirring seaweed fronds.

She looked back, and the beach was full, but her father and grandmother were no longer there, replaced by a blackness where they had been sitting. It was like a photograph on which ink had been spilt.

When she looked towards the sea again, Kagan was sitting on the metal barrier that separated sea wall from water's edge. She was smoking a cigarette, and her expression was sad. She would not meet Cissie's eyes.

"Hello," she said. The waves splashed up around her feet, and over her dress, but she appeared not to notice.

"You'll catch your death," said Cissie. She was crying: she could feel the tears on her cheeks, but she did not feel sad. She did not feel anything, in fact. It was as if she was the ghost, and the wind passed through her, and the spray passed through her: she was insubstantial. She was a child again, she noticed, and her body her own. "Why did you do it?"

Now Kagan turned to look at her. "You know. You didn't then, but you do now." She tossed her cigarette into the water, which seemed to rise to catch it.

"Grandma turned odd after that, you know. And dad..."

"Serves her right. She should have kept more of an eye out for me. And dad? Well." She looked away again. "I see them sometimes, in the distance, but I daren't speak to them. There are shadows, you see. Shadows cling to them."

"I missed you so much." Cissie corrected herself. "I miss you."

"That was the only thing. I shouldn't have done it, not with you there. I wasn't thinking clearly, you see. And impulse, it's terrible when you give in to that. You know that too."

"Yes," said Cissie. "Yes, I do know that."

"I have to go now."

"Yes."

"Are you coming?"

"Yes." More firmly. "Yes."

Cissie climbed onto the railings, clinging to the wet bars. She put her arms around Kagan, who was substantial and warm, just as she remembered her being. It was such a comforting feeling.

"I never did marry Dave, but then I always knew I wouldn't."

She laughed, and Cissie smiled, and they leapt and they fell and descended down and down into the green, engulfing depths.

EIGHT

A snap and a pull and a push and a shove and a shove and a shove and a snap and a flush, and down the toilet he went, trailing wisps of protein behind him. Poor old Johnny Condom.

There was porcelain white then gelatinous brown and green: the passage of toilet bend and waste pipe with its tattered fronds of decay lifting and separating and sometimes torn free in untidy fragments, each flake of waste a spiralling island through which he travelled, propelled by the water's rush and surge, down into a deeper darkness, into colder depths from which all light was driven, so there was only the awareness of his own form carried forward, ballooning, to a destination he was unaware of, and could not even imagine.

In time his passage slowed, and light began to return, leaking from above, a dim artificial glow reflected and broken by the water into strands. On either side he was aware of other objects that bobbed and swivelled: guttering webs of tissue paper; smoothed, elongated turds; syringe needles; daubed sanitary towels; masticated, regurgitated food; snags and clumps of hair; cigarette ends; plastic wrappers; and other, less identifiable items.

Eventually, he was carried onto a jutting slab of stone that rose from the water and he clung there, vacillating in the thin wash that flowed over his form. He was, he saw, in a tunnel. It was a large tunnel, constructed of brick, with enclosed strips of lighting spaced evenly along the walls, like stitching. A narrow walkway flanked the water travelling down the tunnel's centre.

"You're new here, aren't you?"

He saw he was draped alongside a gelid goldfish, its one exposed, pearlised eye staring towards the ceiling, its body partially ravaged so bones had begun to poke through.

"It's peaceful around these parts. I like listening to the water running. It reminds me of the old days, swimming around all the time." The voice paused, sighed. "I wonder what the others are doing now? Maybe they don't even remember me."

The voice seemed to be coming from nowhere. The fish – the only creature near to him – lay unmoving.

"Not very talkative, are you? Here. Beside you. Are you blind?" The fish wiggled its tail, or perhaps it was only movement caused by the water's passage.

"I'm sorry. I just hadn't expected a goldfish to speak."

"That's a bit rich coming from a condom. A used condom, come to that. At least I've a mouth to speak with. Here... I hope you're not planning on leaving behind something infectious on my rock and then swimming off downstream again."

"No, no, I assure you. I'll be terribly well behaved."

"And I would hope so too. Around here there are repercussions, see? If you don't behave, like."

"I'll be as quiet as anything, lying here. Don't you mind me. I'll be as quiet as a mouse."

"Mouse? Condom? Make your mind up, what are you?"

"A condom, I suppose."

"A condom, I *suppose*. Dirty, dirty creatures, condoms. Who knows where you've been. Did you take a journey into the fish pie then? Into the tasty fish and cheese filling?" The goldfish chuckled filthily to itself, admiring its own joke. "Maybe you even had a bit of chutney along the way. Some people are partial to a bit of chutney, you know."

"I don't really remember. It was all so quick."

"Oh I bet you did. Up the stinky brown passage. You look the type."

The fish sniggered again, then added, "I'm only joshing, lad. You'll get used to me. We'll be good pals, sitting here together. I'll enjoy the company, I admit. And even if what I said is true, there's nothing wrong with taking a visit to the unmentionables. Well, not when you've had a good clean in the water afterwards, anyway."

"Have you been here long?"

"Nearly three weeks now. You're the first person I've talked to in all that time."

"It must get awfully lonely."

"I sit here and watch all the things floating past. You'll be amazed what people get rid of that ends up down here. There was a cat went past the other day."

"Cats? Did someone say cats?" The voice came from above, high-pitched and ghosting through the tunnel's vault. "They're not around here, I hope. This is one of the last havens we have from the foul creatures. Rip you apart as soon as look at you, I swear."

A rat, sleek grey and glistening, leapt down alongside them. The stone on which they lay rocked and splashed.

"Here, watch what you're doing. You'll have us all in the water if you're not more careful." The goldfish's tone was agitated.

"Rats can swim. *You* can swim, surely."

"I've taken a liking to dry land. And I've seen what goes floating past. Cats are the least of it. You don't want to end up in that water, believe me."

"The term 'like a fish out of water' suddenly takes on a whole new meaning." The rat circled the stone's visible perimeter, sniffed at the condom lying there. "You're a strange one. Not edible, that's for sure."

"I wouldn't bet on that one." The goldfish snickered to itself.

The rat circled the goldfish now. "You, on the other hand…you certainly are edible. Fish. I'm familiar with fish."

He bit into the goldfish's tail and hoisted it in his mouth.

"Here. What are you doing?"

"Survival of the fittest and all that." The rat munched on the fish, holding it between its claws. "Most delectable too."

"Not fair! Murderer! Thief! Scum!"

"Everything is meat," explained the rat. "Or fish."

He lunged into the water, carrying the goldfish with him.

"No, not the water! No the wat –"

They disappeared from view, and the vibrations of their plunge dislodged the condom so he too slid off the rock. Carried down by the current, he saw, briefly, the rat clamber up the walkway at the sewer's edge, the goldfish still dangling from its mouth, and then the water's intensity increased, its break and flow turning into something resembling rapids, and the force carried him downwards, down and down into the swirling, silted depths so nothing was visible any longer, and all that existed was the increasing speed of his passage while, somewhere, a vibration shuddered and shook and rumbled until the very elements around him seemed to break and spindle.

In time, the darkness began to diminish, replaced by a white luminescence visible but distant, ghostly in the way it folded in the water's weft, and then intensifying, as the vibration also intensified, turning into noise, thudding and banging and roaring with a continual, erratic beat. The current was so fast he no longer knew where he was, whether he faced up or down, or sideways, the ridged latex of his body twisting around as he rushed with a horrifying propulsion to the looming whiteness ahead.

Something happened then. The noise ceased, suddenly and unexpectedly. The waters slowed, then stilled. He found himself caught around the bars of a metal grille, a green-slimed gateway into deeper, darker territory. A white, concrete wall held the grille in place, and it was also the source of the frightening blankness he had been heading towards.

"You know, with all that white, I thought I'd died and gone to heaven." A hand, barely formed and translucent, waved in front of him. Blue veins traced below skin the colour of milk-clouded water. "But I was wrong. It's hard to make decisions when you're so young, isn't it? I mean, at one point I thought I was a boy, but now I've decided I'm a girl. What do you think?"

The remainder of the body floated into view. It was an oversized foetus, its body not quite defined, its features amorphous. A raggle of umbilical cord was still attached. Its banded arms and legs made little swimming motions in the water.

"It's hard to tell. I don't blame you for being confused."

"My mother always said I would be a girl. So I've made my mind up: a girl is what I am." She spoke in a high, fluting voice, the words not easily distinguishable when they emerged from her mouth, which was little more than a permanently open O. "I was looking for a dress, in fact, but so far there's been nothing that's come down this way. There was a shoe, but it was a man's shoe, and it was so large I could have snuggled down inside it quite easily. For the moment I'm as naked as the day I was born. Though maybe born isn't quite the right word to use. It is embarrassing though. You don't mind, do you?"

"Not at all. Where are we anyway? Do you have any idea?"

"Somewhere. I'm not sure where. I'm not even sure what's up and what's down any more, to be honest. I do know - " she indicated the white wall before them - "if you go in there you don't come out again. Not in one piece anyway."

"It was quite frightening being pulled down towards it like that."

"It'll start up again soon, you'll see. I think there's some sort of pump system that drags everything in, but I really don't know what it does after that. I hold onto the bars with this -" she waved the length of umbilical cord - "and that's enough to protect me."

"There are so many dangers down here. There was a rat earlier on, and he certainly wasn't nice. He ate a friend I'd just made. Though to be honest, I wasn't particularly keen on the friend either."

"Oh, you'll see rats everywhere here. I've lost count of how many I've seen. You get good ones and bad ones, same as anywhere else. They've never harmed me anyway. Maybe I just confuse them too much." She floated down alongside him, hovering in the water. "Anyway, what about you? You must have some stories to tell."

"I haven't been here long. I remember there was a pushing and a pushing and a snap and a flush, and then I went down into water. I met the goldfish I told you about, but it was eaten by a rat. And then I met you."

"Well, that must have been you being born. I had the same experience, you know, almost exactly the same. I think that makes us soul mates."

"That would be nice."

There was a low, deep whirring sound and the water began to vibrate.

"That's the pumps switching on again. Quick. Down this way. The current doesn't reach this spot." She pulled him down to the base of the white stone wall where there was a fissure, enough of a crevice for them to swim into. A small purple-shelled crab already occupied it, but it shifted sideways to allow them room to enter.

"It's near the sea," she explained, indicating the crab. "You see them all the over the place here. Horrid things. They eat all the muck of the day."

The crab glowered at them, but said nothing.

"That's what my mother used to say," she continued. " 'I'm eating all the muck of the day.' I can still hear her saying that."

"You sound as though you miss her."

"She was going to dress me in pink booties, she said, and I'd have a crib with a crocheted blanket and a little spinning mobile with stars and crescent moons." She sighed. "I never did get those pink booties."

They sat silently for several minutes. The pumps had begun again and their throbbing, dissonant impact would have made speech impossible anyway. He noticed the foetus staring at him oddly.

When the pumps stopped, she said, "You know, you're sort of a pink colour aren't you?"

"Am I?"

"Don't you even know what colour you are? Yes, you're pink. And you're shaped like a sock. I think, in fact, that I've found my first bootie."

With that, she lifted him and slipped him over her foot, before he had even time to protest. Her fingers were soft and felt boneless. Pulled to his full length, he reached up to her knee.

"Hm. Not a bootie, really, more of a stocking. Oh well, I've skipped the stage of lovable infancy and have instead become a full-blown harlot." She laughed at her own witticism. "Not saying anything? Oh, I suppose you can't, really. That's another thing my mother used to say, 'Don't talk with your mouth full.' I don't know who she was speaking to when she said that. Maybe it was my brother, or my sister…strange to think I might have a brother or sister out there, somewhere. Don't you think?"

"He can't reply. Why do you keep on asking him questions? You're just being vindictive, that's what it is."

It was the crab who spoke, although he didn't move from the position in which he sat, or even look in her direction.

"Who asked you, you horrible little CRAB?" She knelt down beside him, and prodded his shell with her fingers. "My mother used to eat crabs, you know. She'd pop them in a pan of boiling water and they'd go screeeeeeee while they were being boiled alive."

"If your mother produced such a loathsome offspring as yourself, then I'm not surprised she did things like that. It must be passed down through the genes."

The crab scuttled sideways, away from her reach, and into a recess of stone where she could not follow.

"That won't protect you." She pushed her baby moon face as close towards the crab as she could. "I can wait. I can wait forever, in fact. Just watch me."

She sat down on the rock and waited, staring at the crab with an embittered intensity. The crab rolled its long-stalked eyes, but otherwise said nothing.

The scene grew silent, or as silent as it could be with the constant passage of water, and the on-off concussion of pumps beating, though by that point the condom had become accustomed to their continual presence and no longer heard the noise. The foetus dangled her legs over the edge of the fissure and kicked them aimlessly, dislodging dirt and air bubbles. The water pushed forward and back, back and forward in constant repetition. Threads of silt wavered and spun through the water.

Gradually, the motion slowed, then stopped altogether. A regular shudder ran through the foetus' body, suggesting she had fallen asleep. The crab, taking advantage of this, crawled down from the fissure, clinging to the white, grained surface.

"Sound asleep," he confided as he passed. "Sleeping like a baby, in fact. Heh." He giggled a little at his own joke. "I'd try to free you, but these - " he waved a claw towards him - "are probably not the best things to grab you with."

The crab continued on down, towards murkier waters, where he could barely be seen. "Good luck," he called from below. "And if you do escape, head to the side of the building. There's a passageway there that'll take you straight out to sea."

Then, with that, he was gone.

There was a lull then, pleasant and timeless, where the condom was little more than his surroundings. A salt tang to the water suggested the sea was very near. A stray wisp of weed collided with and wrapped itself around his body, then loosened itself and whipped free again. A gape-mouthed kitten drifted past and waved in greeting.

"Take me with you," he wanted to call, but was unable to.

After a while, he too slept, or perhaps he only hypnotised himself into a dulled stupor. What woke or stirred him was the foetus moving. More than that, the foetus *screaming*.

"He's gone! You must have seen him go too, you obnoxious, pathetic little object. Why didn't you warn me? I wanted to crush that purple shell of his to a paste, and him with it. Now he's disappeared and I'll never find him. All these crabs look alike to me. Which way did he go?"

He was, of course, unable to answer.

"Well?"

No answer.

"Oh for God's sake. Do I have to do everything around here?"

She leant down and pulled him from her leg in one easy movement. His body felt stretched and flaccid, and dangled weakly from her almost-formed hand.

"I've decided I don't like you anymore. I can find other, better clothes out there. It's a woman's prerogative to change her mind."

She cast him out into the larger expanse of water where he floated, spinning, caught in a small eddy, before heading downwards, the fluid catching and distending his body.

Above, he could see her swimming away, presumably still hunting for the crab that had escaped.

"I never thought you looked like a girl anyway," he called, before catching a cool, salt stream that slipped though the water like a promise, following it to its larger, colder, more frightening source.

The stream led him down the side of the building, through the narrowest of passages. Below him was a graveyard of the forgotten, silted over, objects that had lost their purpose and form. They called to him in passing, and each cry was a hurt, but he was the current's property now, and it took him further and further into its depths. Then there was only brine and a terrible chill, and he knew he must have travelled out into the expanses of the sea.

It took time to get used to the ocean. Light impacted on waves then spread and filtered downwards, creating splintered pillars of luminescence to travel through. Huge, darkened shapes sailed above him, and beside him, and below him, shapes with sails and fins and with mouths opened wide enough to swallow, it seemed, the entire sea's contents. Down in the murkiest depths, strange lights blinked and shone with an internal radiance. Plants grew up with waving, shaking tendrils that reached almost to the ocean's surface. He saw all these things and was amazed: because he was such an insignificant thing, floating amidst all the vastness. He was more comfortable when the current carried him to shallower waters, the ocean bed – igneous rocks and invading drifts of sand - below him.

Other creatures were here: evasive fish; gasping mussels; jellyfish floating past, pulsing and ghostly; and objects too – a discarded bicycle wheel; plastic carrier bags sailing much as he did in the current; bottles protruding from the bed like a promise of hidden treasure. There was sunlight, and the curtained weft of shadows thrown and tangled through the water to pattern the ocean floor.

This felt a good place; and he was glad when he was washed onto a shallow bed, an object of brief curiosity for the creatures that came to investigate whether this latest visitor was in any way edible, or dangerous. The water was warmer, the sun's heat reflected and magnified. As he floated there, the tide drew back, leaving only a draining wash that salted white. There was a subtle lapping still at the end of his body but he was back on land, more or less.

Something pulled him back into the colder ocean. One moment sun; the next receding light, and a constellation of air bubbles to track his decent.

"You don't want to do that! Not lie in the sun. Good lord, man, you'll dry out and all that'll be left of you is a rubberised smear."

A severed hand appeared in front of him. It was - or had been - a man's hand. The sea had turned it wrinkled and somewhat bloated. A mast of fractured bone poked through the tear of skin that once joined onto a wrist. It scuttled around the rocky bed as though excited, using all five of its digits to walk.

"I hadn't thought. It was just so nice to be warm again."

"Well, you should have thought. Warmth is your enemy now, the same as it's my enemy and the enemy of everything that's found its way down here. I tell all the newcomers that and they thank me for it, each and every one." The hand raised its index finger to emphasise this point. "Each-and-every-one!"

"I suppose I'd better thank you as well, in that case."

" 'I suppose?' Oh dear me, you are green around the gills, aren't you? I *suppose?* Oh dearie, dearie me." The hand quivered and danced around with a particularly unjolly mirth. "I tell you, my lad, you'll need to shape up fast out here. There's not many you can call friends in this place, and those you do find are precious indeed."

"I've met people, but none of them have been very friendly. In fact, they've all been a little strange. Or so it seems to me, anyway. Maybe it's normal to be strange around here."

"If we were all normal, we wouldn't be here, would we? This is the place where all the unwanted things go. Out there - " the hand gestured at the sky and land beyond the water - "if you're out there, you're one of the lucky ones."

"I don't remember much about that. All I know is there was a pushing and a pushing and a shoving and a warmth and a snap and a flush, and then I was going down and down through a passageway. I met a goldfish who was eaten by a rat, and a foetus who wore me as a piece of clothing, and a crab who told me how to get here. Now there's you. I was wondering...when you talk, where are you talking from? I mean, I don't see a mouth."

"Ho, that's rich, coming from a tube of rubber, isn't it? How do I talk? *I* don't know. How do birds fly? Why does the ocean not fall into the air when the world tilts on its axis? Why does toast always end up butter side down? If I knew the answers to those sort of things, I wouldn't be here, would I? I'd be lording it over the entire universe, rather than rescuing an ungrateful discard from the rays of the sun."

"I am grateful. Really, I am."

"I'm not one to hold grudges anyway. Everyone will tell you that."

The hand travelled further down the rocky incline and pointed to a ridge, beyond which the water turned murkily black, and the ocean floor could no longer be seen.

"As long as you stay in this area you'll be safe. Down there though, it's different. There are boats that were sunken before I was born, and the bones of whales that fish have turned into a playground, and huge tentacled creatures that won't care you're not edible because they'll eat you anyway. Come look."

The hand nipped him between two fingers and took him to the edge of the rock shelf. The water turned suddenly intensely, icily cold.

"Up here, it's not so bad. We're three steps from God is how I see it. The first step is the sky, and then there's land. We're close to land, so we must be step three. Do you remember that song? Three steps to heaven?" The hand did an unexpected, sashaying little dance, singing along to itself, then stopped and indicated the chill blackness. "That's step four. That's hell, or as close as you can get to hell in this place."

Further down in the water, vague shapes could be distinguished, moving through the dark.

"It doesn't look so inviting."

"That's an understatement, if ever there was. What you need to do, lad, is stick close by me. I'll see you all right."

He lifted the condom and headed back up the rock shelf. They settled amongst an untidy swirl of vegetation. Green, threaded fronds swayed and wavered in the current.

"Lesson number one: never stay out in the open. They're out to get you, and they will, if you're not careful." The hand extended one finger. "Lesson number two: never leave my side." A second finger extended. "Lesson number three: everything ends up here eventually, in one form or another." A third finger extended. Then the hand lifted a flat stone at the base of the vegetation. "See?"

Below the stone was a small hoard of rusting coins, a length of chain, a red, beaded necklace, and three gold rings, one embedded with rubies.

"My little treasure trove. For the days when I get back up there again." He lifted and slipped the ruby ring on his little finger. "It's worth a small fortune, this piece."

"Up there? I thought you said it was dangerous in the sun."

"For the moment, yes, but the day will come. The day will come and all the abandoned things will rise and they'll walk the land again, and I'll be there amongst them. You'd want something then, wouldn't you? To beautify yourself. To make yourself pretty or handsome as you once were. As I once was."

"How do you know all of these things?"

"I listen, see? I listen to the plants and the way their fronds beat in the current. I listen to the waves when they're crashing on the rocks overhead. They tell me things. There, don't you hear?"

The condom listened. There was the drowned pounding of water fighting itself. There was a muted rush as a fish swam between the tendrils of the seaweed they hid amongst.

"There. Clear as day... You heard that didn't you?"

"I think I heard something."

"It takes practice, my boy. Give it time though, and you'll hear those voices as plain as I do."

The hand stopped, crouched and then sprung on a passing fish, which it swiftly dismembered, gouging eyes, eviscerating gills, reducing its body to bloodied gobbets and a dangerous, exposed spine. The remnants caught and carried in the water's current, and were pushed over and down into the blackness below, beyond the rock's edge.

The hand returned, trailing residues of flesh and blood.

"You have to take them unawares, you know."

"I don't understand. Why did you do that? That fish wasn't going to harm us, was it?"

"The voices demand their sacrifices. It makes them powerful. And the more powerful they are, the closer the day of resurrection. There's a strong tradition of that you know, sacrificing. To the gods."

"But the pieces went down there. You said it was dangerous down there."

"That's where they live, see? That's what makes it dangerous."

"I understand." The condom allowed himself to be carried away a little by the current. "Can I ask, all those other people you befriended…what happened to them?"

"I forget." The hand turned around and around on itself. "They must have run away, or became careless or something."

"Uh-huh…" Floating further and further back, away from the hand's cage.

"Or maybe they decided they didn't want to be with me any longer, and there were other purposes they could serve. Do you know what I mean?"

"Of course…" Reaching for that strong whip of current he could feel tickling his back end.

"Is something wrong? You seem a little - I must say - *nervous.*"

"Not at all, I assure you..."

Then the current had him in its grasp, and it whisked him away from the hand which at that very moment leapt, resembling a particularly large and threatening spider. He was gone though, faster than the hand could follow, and the pull led him away from the hand, away from the rock and into the murk, the bitter, unilluminated pit he had been warned so severely to avoid, to never enter, because that way led to hell, in literal or metaphorical fashion.

At first there was still light, but gradually it dissipated, cracks and foils of brightness escaping in the dark like shoals, elusive as he passed, his inevitable descent, the passage of waves too large or too distant to be truly evident, and he spun downwards, ever down, down, a spiralling intensity that was also stasis because by this point light was almost entirely gone. He fell through blackness, with the bulk of creatures unseen around him, large at times beyond comprehension, or filament small, little more than guttering threads, brief scratches with their own internal illumination, so faint it might almost not be there; and then a deepening pressure came that folded him in on himself; and still he fell, and it seemed as though he would never stop.

In time, other creatures appeared. He dared not even call them fish, their forms were so outlandish: globular and spiked and wide-eyed, their expressions that of constant surprise. They had barbed teeth and carried their own lights above them, rising out of their bodies and hung like lanterns. As he fell, they hovered above him like a predatory constellation of stars, but there were still more below, guttering fires he would pass in turn.

Finally, he reached the ocean floor. It was fissured and barren, gas vents throwing out a cumulation of bubbles, rising in constant, unsteady columns. The fish gathered here, throwing out enough light to see, though the ground had its own radiance, distant between the earth's cracks. The sea water had grown warm again too.

He drifted between formations of strange, molten rocks. They were fired black, and pitted. At their heart was a hollow, leading down to a sandy, silted bed. There was movement in the hollow, a swaying from side to side. This was where he finally settled. He lay there, and the sensation of falling was carried with him still, as though the descent had been and was endless. There was a crushed can alongside him, its colour long faded, its words unintelligible. There was a wooden chest, covered in vegetation that in turn had died. There was glass, worn to a pebble smoothness, green and white, gathered together like treasures.

If this is hell, he thought, *it isn't so bad.*

Something drifted past him. It was another condom, bleached of all colour, almost shapeless from the length of time it had spent in the water.

"Hello," he called. "Hello?"

There was no reply. The condom floated over and disappeared behind a haft of iron that had been something once but now was unrecognisable. He allowed the water's shift to carry him in that direction, a journey in gradations, until he too mounted and vaulted the iron mountain.

Behind it was an entire world of condoms. There were pink ones and red ones and green ones and orange ones. They were extra-thick and they were ribbed and they were textured and they were flavoured. They floated and they drifted or they lay there atop one another. There was light that bathed them in lustre, chintzy cocktail music played, and there was the sound of laughter, a woman's, far off, like distantly heard conversation. They mingled and locked and danced in streamers of illumination that came from somewhere, far above, striking them like spotlights.

"Welcome," they said. "We've been waiting for you."

And he knew at that moment, and knew it to be true: this wasn't hell. It was heaven.

NINE

She was leaving her apartment, the first time he saw her. In tow, a bodyguard, his occupation unmistakable, body beyond stochastic, knuckles actually scraping off the marble lobby floor and heavy-browed eyes set so far back they intruded into another era. The bodyguard stood between her and a cabal of fans waiting, autograph books, posters, hands thrust forward, some of which she signed in an absent fashion, speaking a few words in answer to shouted-out questions, before stepping into a car with blacked out windows. She had long blonde hair - it had to be blonde - and wore a white dress, tightly fitted. Her face was familiar, but he could not place her name.

The fans solved that problem: "Callie!" they screamed, all reserve lost, betraying their pubescent fantasies in voice as well as appearance, dreams dredged up through endless, sleepless nights, daytime reveries, images replayed from movies watched over and over. If he did not recognise the name, then he was familiar with her expression, the one that looked through him, and past him, for he was another transient on London's streets, clothes dirt-oiled, a little madness in his eyes hinting of possible danger or older, transforming traumas.

From the very first, he was transfixed.

She lived in a newly built apartment block, incongruous in that place of Georgian grandeur, rising high above the other buildings, so those at the top could look at those below and find them reduced to something less than human, to dots and smears, to a beaded pattern of movement.

It was an area he passed through most mornings, never stopping, because the rich were untouchable and, he found, often uncaring. In comparison, the streets beyond were lucrative and populous, a place where there were faces and not only traffic, there were shops and restaurants; and it was here he scavenged his existence as he had for...how many years? Too many to count. He no longer even knew his precise age.

That first day, he stood there stupidly, long after she had gone, and the fans had gone, gazing up at the apartments. They all looked the same, blankly secretive, and all vacated by mid-morning. Across from the apartment a house sat, part renovated, scaffolding in place, plastic over the windows, a half-full skip in front. A further block of houses separated it from a large parkland area. He sometimes slept in the park, curled at the foot of a tree in summer, or under cover of its central pavilion in winter. He thought then, even after the first encounter, that he should move somewhere closer to the woman's apartment. You could say it was a calling, although precisely who was calling whom was unclear.

After that, he waited for her departure each morning. He made his home in the building opposite, which was easy to enter: there were no doors, and the upper storey was partially demolished, exposed to the elements. It was here, rather than on the more sheltered lower level, that he made a bed for himself, protection from the floorboards and the elements provided by a length of clear tarpaulin once used to cover planks, then sheets of newspaper laid beneath to guard against the rising chill. No work appeared to be taking place on the house; had not been for months, from what he could recall. From this spot he could watch, ghosted behind polythene, his vantage point dark enough so no-one could see him.

She resided, he saw, in the top floor apartment (absurd to think it would be anything less) and he could look up to where she lived, or he could look down onto the street to see the hurried flow of passers-by.

Her morning routine: she left at precisely eight thirty, normally accompanied by her bodyguard, and she would disappear inside her car's enclosure, her driver waiting impatient and reckless, always speeding, and she would be taken someplace not-there, a place he could not imagine, where she remained until late evening. There were times when fans lay in wait, and times they did not. His own startled, unwitting attention was constant. There was something ferrous in his desire, one that did not allow his own day to properly begin until he had seen her depart.

Abandoned during daylight hours, her apartment was lit throughout the night, brash as an advertisement. It was as though she never slept, or slept and kept the lights on to drive away unguessed-at fears. He could see her shadow as she crossed the room, and it was tautened, folded, multiplied. Sometimes she came to the window to look over the city, traced and stitched in electric, while he looked up at her, often in full view, though she never seemed to see him, or made no indication if she did. Then he would retreat to his bed of tarpaulin, crawling between its folds, pulling it over his head to retain warmth. If it was raining, he lay and listened to the drops blown inwards, striking hard against exposed wood and brick. The impact sounded almost Biblical, yet even in the heaviest downpours he could still see her in her apartment, staring out, reduced to wash, and it was as if she orchestrated the great, booming storm that descended on the city.

Night unified them. In the day she left for that destination he could only poorly visualise, while he in turn walked the distance to the high street, to beg.

As a beggar he supposed he was successful. In part, this was because people and crowds made him frantic. The crush of bodies and the contact of eyes were antagonisms. People sensed this and gave him money, just so he would leave them alone. He never changed his clothes, or washed, unless it was an involuntary shower standing in the rain, his odour so pungent even other homeless people shunned him. He avoided them anyway, especially at night: they favoured sleeping in underpasses and doorways, with their attraction of life-saving heat, but the very thought of living so close to the city's heart made him nauseous. Only distance guaranteed safety, no disturbing intrusions, no unpredictability, and he found this in the building he called home. Here there was safety and isolation and, yes, for all his misanthropy, loneliness.

He knew what misanthropy was, he was educated, he had knowledge. Once, he had trained to be an estate agent. How long ago that seemed, and what a different person he had been.

The woman was his opposite. She dressed, he could tell even from a distance, with care, as if she desired attention, as if she knew and expected to be observed. Dresses white or black (she favoured classic, simple cuts), and in the evening a shawl thrown over her shoulders, worn when she opened the window to gaze out or, sometimes, stepped onto the balcony, with its impossible drop, one even he, accustomed to the exposed heights of his dwelling, dared not have ventured on.

Birds - he was unsure what variety - nested in the eaves above her apartment. When she stood on the balcony, they swept down, frantic, sweeping and dive bombing. Protecting their young, he imagined. She ignored them, did not even acknowledge them, but remained holding onto the railings, looking ahead, imperilled surely in the wind that must be ever-present so high up. Did she look out to the city, its grids and enclaves, its modern towers and relics, or did she look past it, to whatever lay beyond, whatever could be seen from those heights? Her face gave nothing away. It was as indifferent as his was continually impassioned. She would stand there, for minutes, half an hour, an hour; and then she returned indoors, the window shut and, often, the blinds drawn.

The loneliness in those moments was terrible. He wondered at those times if he was, in fact, a little in love with her.

His morning routine: rise, and piss in the ruin of the bathroom sink (the toilet having been stripped out), one eye on the balcony, feeling his cock harden a little at the thought that perhaps she watched him, stepped back from the window's reveal. Eat breakfast: biscuits, bread, sometimes the remains of someone's abandoned takeaway. A drink of bottled water, filled the night before (always water, although everyone who saw him assumed he was an alcoholic). Wait for the dark to lift, and the light to bring Callie's arrival. After she left the building, he wandered into the street, with its continual dangers and annoyances, to distress passers-by with the wildness of his eyes, his odour, his demands which hovered somewhere between pleading and threat. Sometimes a police officer appeared, and then he ran, having been arrested before: the police cell was not unknown to him, with its collection of drunks and drug addicts and multitudinous crazies, of which, he supposed in his more lucid moments, he was one. And what was the point? The next day he would be released, and would head back to the very spot he had been arrested, which was defiance or stupidity, or both.

He watched her but she never looked at him, he knew that. Once - only once - she waved, standing on the balcony, but it was not to him, but instead to someone she recognised, someone passing in the street. For a moment he had dared hope. Her arms were almost anorexic, her skin so leeched it looked as though she seldom saw daylight. As perhaps she did not; perhaps she travelled through an endless succession of rooms and cars and further rooms.

"A good, hot meal, that's what she needs." That's what his grandmother would have said. Why did he think about his grandmother? He barely remembered her face. Maybe she was still alive out there, in the frightening green expanses of his upbringing, as terrifying as the crowds, and as inescapable.

Sometimes crowds talked in glossalalia. Sometimes complete strangers looked directly at him and uttered commands he did not understand, but which were clearly harmful, to him or others, as though the very words were weighted.

A demon hid in every person. Perhaps there was a demon hiding in himself. The woman though? No, she was a goddess.

He was intelligent enough to realise his objectification. She was so distant she could be anything. But who else was she trying to impress, dressed and as perfect as a model, alone in her apartment with no-one else to see? Her hair lifted and tumbled to one side in loose curls. She wore dangerously high-heeled shoes and stockings, and her dresses were surely couture. She dressed for him and him alone.

Either that or she was a tart.

Her face, he discovered, adorned the front covers of magazines. She was a rising film star. Callie Hale. There was a pleasing similarity to his own name, which was Callum, though hers was surely a stage name used to keep her own secret, away from the appropriations of fans. Photographed close up - closer than he had ever dared see her in the flesh - she seemed shorn of imperfections. It was as though the nearer he approached, the more faultless she became. Even from a distance she radiated power. Her face was not only on magazines. It appeared multiplied and synchronous on TV screens in shop windows. Her photoshopped likeness stared from movie posters. Rooting for food in the refuse bins, he found newspapers with her image grained in black and white. He removed these pages, and at night sometimes slept with her features pressed against his skin, while he masturbated with a furious, determined heat, thinking of the warmth of her flesh, so unlike the concrete floor on which he slept, offering her a hot jolt that would seep and meld her image so it impastoed on his belly. That was closest he ever came to her.

In the mornings, her car arrived, its windows blacked out. They were the colour of obsidian, so she could see out but no-one could look in. Not him standing there on the pavement with his look of (...what? Madness? Longing? Envy?), or the rush hour traffic penetrating even the richest enclaves of the city, traffic lights bringing her momentarily to a standstill, buses and cyclists alongside, looking, wondering who travelled in such auspicious fashion, especially in these times of austerity. What did she see, if she looked at all? A frieze, flattened and dimmed, as though it was a spool of one of her own films, unravelled, laid out for her to view. He could not pretend he was anything more than an extra.

Secrets of the stars. Thirty day diet. The shocking truth about. How easily her features fitted amongst those headlines. He squatted on street corners that were invariably cold, and often wet, because that was the city's nature, it drew the gloom down into the pavements, so she could better shine, and he breathed its exhaust fumes, he eyed enviously the moneyed drawn to the stores with their electric allure, and he gathered coins hurriedly scattered, wordless, at his feet. These were his offerings. He was the obverse god of the city, grabbing its foul depths, the tunnels of sewage on which the city was built, its horrid waters, the refuse gathered in back doorways, the ones he frequented, that provided his meals, the cold, congealed takeaways and scraped offcuts of meat on the turn, and really, truly, he did not even need money. He had refuge, he had food, he had the cruel shelter of isolation, even amongst crowds. And he had her, before him, because he ensured she was before him, in some form or other, flesh or image, or simply thought, if even the images failed, though they seldom did, because she was everywhere.

Often she held parties. The music drifted down, caught on currents of draught, to where he lay, intruding and waking, even though the sound was faint. Shadowed figures crossed or pressed against the windows, stood on the balcony, smoking, the faint start of their cigarettes, laughter and sometimes shrieks, and the laughter was imbalanced. He felt a sympathy with that sound, and imagined himself amongst them, in that high, lit palace, and this thought was both thrilling and terrible.

One evening, a woman fell from the balcony to the street below. He saw it happen, though it occurred so unexpectedly he at first was not certain what had taken place. The screams began then, after what seemed an unnaturally long silence, and he could see the body lying there, amid the stalled traffic. His first, overwhelming thought was that it was her.

He registered the white dress, now blooded. The cross of her legs and the way her hair (long, blonde, like Callie's, as though it was a necessary accoutrement to wealth) splayed. Passersby clustered around her, and there were sirens, already, distant but growing closer. Above, on the balcony, guests peered with vertiginous dismay at the scene below. Some wept, there were cries of shock, they held each other, to still their trembling. Finally, Callie too arrived, and dared look. His own relief then, that it was not her lying there, and he thought: what if it was me, what if it was me down there, would she look at me in that same way? Would, finally, there be recognition?

The scene lasted the whole long night and onwards into morning. There were police in the apartment, and, below, paparazzi, the shutter of their camera flashes as the guests left, subdued now, faces captured for the following day's newspapers. There were television cameras, reporters repeating the same phrases in different forms, the curious stopping to stare, to find themselves cast as unwary ghouls homing in on disaster, immortalised somewhere thereafter, bound to the magnetic groove of storage drives, digitised for future generations to feast on what will by then have become trivia, names, faces no-one remembers...

When the police left, and then the onlookers - nothing new to see - he emerged onto the street to find it empty, a section taped off, and no-one around except one last cameraman, remnant of a day when the news was otherwise slow, one final broadcast to make, and he was caught on film with the apartment behind him, the disturbance of his presence apparent even through the distance of lens, the crazy man in the background that others avoided, his image there for others to discover, one day when this was all done, the piece of the puzzle that may or not be linked to her forever.

Those were the hardest days, those days of absence. Her face was only seen in discarded newspapers, the lined image on television screens, while the apartment remained in darkness, its emptiness reverberating across the entire city, in which his activity was only a distraction, as each day melded into the next, and the next, its repetition numbing, or more numbing than ever. The madness, those tics and squalid thoughts, overwhelmed then. He hid, because if he was taken (and all the city's inhabitants were threatening, their danger suggestive), he would be locked away and would never see her again. He knew that, recognised the sickness inside himself, just as he saw the sickness in others, for there was a cunning lucidity to his fevered paranoia that kept him safe, even during the worst times.

When she returned, the accident old news by then, for newer, more dreadful events had come and gone in her absence, there was a greater radiance in her than ever. If she dared venture out (the visitors had mostly gone, there were no more parties), he had to shield his eyes from the light. How did no-one else see? It was brighter than the sun's glare caught on the windows of her apartment, its intensity white and crippling, the very bones in his hand illuminated, the surge and pulse of blood, and when she returned indoors there was the ghost of her image carried in his eyes for minutes, sometimes hours, afterwards.

He wondered whether he would go blind if he stared at her too long.

When did the idea come to him? He could not say precisely when, but once it had arrived he could not dislodge it from his brain: *he had to be up there*. Not down on the street, the source of so much dismay, nor in the building where he lived, which was neither up nor down, limbo, or purgatory, or whatever it may represent, but up there, with her. He wondered what it was like. He imagined soft lighting and living space stretched to infinity, tastefully furnished with modernist chic, a minimalist ethos unforgiving of clutter. White spaces, cream and beige walls, all functionality hidden away in cupboards. Chrome kitchen appliances. Air conditioned even in winter, holding seasons in stasis. Glass panelled bathroom (or bathrooms). A bedroom resisting imagination, he dared not think of that, the unbidden thoughts it brought.

At the same time, access seemed impossible. A security guard stood in constant attendance, vigilant, aware of the dangers accompanying wealth. Doorways were (he had seen, looking from a distance) opened by swipe cards. The CCTV cameras were alive, not ornamentation as with so many buildings, their swivelling accompanied by alarms and locks. Still, the very thought filled him with trembling, with desire: he must, he *would* be there with her. He wondered what she looked like up close, not the manipulated image in magazines, and decided she would be as fragile and porcelain as a Victorian doll. She would talk with a clipped, cold accent, the sort that reminded him of his childhood, with its central figure: the authoritarian grandmother. That image was deceptive though, there were deeper forces at work, the spark, the fire accompanying fame and power....

If he ever had the opportunity, he would throw himself before her, a sacrifice.

Desperation provided inspiration. From the skip at the back of a charity shop he salvaged a suit, archaic enough to be almost chic. Someone had vomited on the left lower leg, and what appeared to the greasy remains of a takeaway curry stained the lapel, but he considered it added a little colour, looked at in a certain light. A matching shirt he stole from a stall in Portobello market, one so lurid the stallholder could not even muster enough indignation to chase him, watching his unravelling, lurching body push through crowds that parted because, well...no-one wanted to go near *that*, he might be infectious. Expensive, overpolished shoes were appropriated from a drunk fallen by the roadside on a Saturday night, and his socks too, so the man would be woken by the police and find himself barefoot, but with wallet and watch intact. Thieves sure are selective these days...

He washed in the showers of Paddington station and the dirt rimed beneath his feet, the slough of accumulated dead skin, and it felt good, the striking heat, the ingrained dirt washed from his face, the steam risen so thick it seemed to coalesce, revealing the features of people he had known long ago, different places and different times, almost forgotten....

A shave (disposable blade, leaving his chin bleeding) and a haircut (scissors — the shop assistant he bought them from gave him the strangest look, as though he suspected a more sinister motive behind their purchase) left him looking, well, almost presentable. Washed, newly dressed, he studied himself in reflective surfaces and felt and looked reborn, a baptism he hoped would give him access to that unreachable place, high above, where she lived, and waited.

His plan was this: the parties she held had resumed, and so he would tailgate in behind a group of drunken revellers. He saw them often enough, laughing and unsteady, designer clothes slipping along with their posture, arriving in the wee hours, Friday and Saturday, often Sunday too, squeezing those last moments from the weekend before the dull labours of the working week arrived; if they worked at all, that is, for their wealth suggested a life beyond such mundanities.

The very next weekend, the opportunity arrived. He stood togged and ready on the cold London streets, enough people around for him to become, if not exactly inconspicuous, then not too obviously adrift during this time of induced hilarity and aggression, just one more face among so many faces, the backdrop of shouts and sirens, traffic running a little too fast now the roads had started to empty, daring someone, anyone, to step off the pavement and get in their way...

At two in the morning a group arrived, the riot of their behaviour, emerging from two taxis drawn up in front of the apartment block, giggles and stumbling, voices raised too loud as they struggled with the effects of drunkenness, the odd shriek or two at some imagined witticism. He stepped in behind them, affecting his most proper manner, one of the group even said hello in a surprised and amused fashion, the scent of perfume and youth came from her, and he was following them, the door held open, you could always count on good old British politeness, and he was through, he was inside, he was that one step closer to...

"Excuse me, sir, where do you think you're going?"

From nowhere, so it seemed, the doorman appeared, a mass of brawn fitting barely into his suit, eyes thickset, a snarl only just suppressed, and almost a hint of intelligence in the far, far recesses of those eyes. Hands like - not hams but *whole haunches*- seized him, ever so politely, ever so forcefully, at least until he was escorted out of sight, out the door, down the steps, and pushed facefirst onto the pavement.

"You dare fucking come round here again, you fucking freak, I'll break your fucking head in." A kick in the ribs for good measure, just to emphasise the point.

So that was the end of that then. There was nothing to do but limp back to his dwelling, the empty floorspace suddenly both intimidating and inviting, a place to sit and look up despairingly...

And there she was, at the window, silhouetted, and was it, was it is possible, *did she look down at him....?*

The next day, in a moment of inspiration, he decided to write her a letter. Contact by proxy, enthralled by the thought HER hands could touch, HER eyes could read his words. Maybe that would be enough. Maybe she would descend her tower, maybe she would seek him out and find him and they would talk, and then, and then...he dared not think. It was enough to smooth a sheet of paper and hold a pen (how many years was it since he had held a pen?), writing phrases he found difficult to articulate, feelings that inhibited and aroused him. He spent hours, days, hunched over, writing into the failing light, until he found the words, or an approximation of the words that strung helix-like, that came to him even when he slept, forming his attenuated handwriting, his style rigidly upright, suppressed loops, letters afraid to touch: that had never changed. It was not a love letter, not exactly, more an expression of awe, of her untouchability (though, of course, he would dearly love to touch...), and it said much less than he would have liked to say. He was afraid to scare her away with that intensity. When he posted the letter (address not exactly specified, but enough to get there, he was certain), all his hopes went with it, his longing. Then he waited.

At first he expected to see her the very next day, but knew that expectation was unrealistic. Would it be the day after, or the day after that? He looked to her window to see if she would give a sign, some sort of clue, but there was nothing. Nothing but her reflection in glass, her to-ing and fro-ing; but perhaps she too was anxious, perhaps she too mentally composed what to say, decided what to wear.

A week passed, and still there was nothing. He wrote another letter. Maybe she did not receive his first? Did she have secret concerns of her own? She need not worry: anything, any sort of recognition, a look, the slightest touch of her hand, that would be sufficient, even if he hoped for so much more.

That too was posted, and again he waited, and again there was nothing.

A third letter followed, pleading. No reply.

His fourth letter was full of hate. He threatened to rape and kill her, he detailed the blackness crowded into his brain, the words came easily that time, the images, the language very specific. He posted it in a rage, and was immediately full of remorse, and so another letter followed, articulating his regret. When there was no reply, not to any of them, he wrote another letter of hate, more incoherent than before, and he knew even as he composed it that he was fracturing, the pieces were falling apart, and he would soon be dispersed by the winds of his madness. Yet he could not stop himself, it was his compulsion, and only she could make him whole.

And still, and still, nothing.

What did he expect to gain from it, this bile, this acid, the terror his words must have brought? A reaction, chemical surely, something to reconfigure the lines of his days into something less certain, more abstract, as though he was in the presence of someone divine, someone to rescue him from the street's slop and grime and a future seemingly fixed and inevitable.

But there was only emptiness, a void. Was this how the ancients felt, when their illusions of godhood were shattered, when the intricate mechanics of science began to supplant that divine presence? The falling away, the meaninglessness, the vacuum left by His (or Her) vacation? And nothing rushed in to take its place, leaving only a corrosion of hate, eating away at itself.

One morning, he saw her on the street. She stood across the road, looking in a shop window, dull in the sun's heat, as though she had lost her inner light. Was that his doing? Separating them, traffic travelled dense and unending, it was only just past rush hour, seemingly intent on preventing him from crossing. She was already moving on, some new attraction to catch her eye, disappearing into the crowds of tourists, early morning shoppers, the idle who already appeared on the pavements, hoping to find some distraction, some way to fill the day. He could not let her go.

In the end he cut across traffic's push, ignoring the glares of drivers, the careening bulks of metal on the way to their slow extinction, that threatened his own extinction, although he barely noticed, because his quarry was fast disappearing. Quick, quick, no time to lose....

As he approached her, the sky darkened. Clouds pulled in, curdling, wind sprang up, it had an undead moan, the litter on streets went scuffling, it was horror film territory all of a sudden, the beautiful girl and the approach of the maniac, high shot just above the girl's head, looking back to a figure that could be heard but not seen, feet tripping faster and faster...

Except she dawdled, turned back, shielding her eyes from the whipped up dust, something Saharan in its rising, and others around her did the same, exclaiming, "Goodness, where did that come from!" Still that touch of reserve in public, it had never been lost, echoes of older times when diffidence was all.

He had almost reached her, hurrying, enough for others to look in alarm, a distraction beyond the sudden rising of wind, and he held out his hand out to her, but she did not see him, something had got in her eye and she was rubbing it and...and...

It was not her at all. It *looked* like her and from a distance, and even up close, you would think she was a professional lookalike, certainly an option to consider, but it was not her. There was a smallness to her features, a lack of lustre to her hair which was dyed blonde and showed black at the roots. She had a chipped front tooth, her clothes were designer lookalikes, last season's, bought cheaply from the supermarket sales, a knockdown price, fifty pounds reduced to thirty to ten, the falling figures of attractiveness, glamour at third or fourth remove. She looked up, just as he was almost upon her, as he realised his mistake. He rushed past her and, yes, he began crying, bawling in fact, an atavism of his infancy, and the dreams he had inherited, that occupied him, that reduced him and elevated him, sometimes at the same time, they had come to nothing, nothing at all. Maybe the wind, falling now, marked their passing...

He returned, dog-whipped, to the security of the building site. What he felt was not even numbness. It had grown dark but the blinds in her apartment were drawn, the lights extinguished. Something dreadful was happening to him, and he did not know what. It was as if he had lost what little control remained in his life, so even the city seemed ordered by comparison, its cries and maladies hiding behind its bright veneer.

Sleep, when it came, was an agitated respite, because she infiltrated even his dreams. Her face, her presence, was everywhere, as if she now inhabited the city, testing its sinews from above, its muscle and bone, and finding no resistance, none at all.

The following day he returned to the spot where he had seen the woman, but she was not there. Nor was she the following day; but she did return the day after that. How obvious, now he knew, that it was not the same person. The difference lay not in her looks, which were similar but tarnished, but in aura, as though her pallid life seeped and infected the air around her.

She worked in a pound shop, which seemed oddly appropriate, a store of cheap replicas masquerading as something better, trying to attain something they could not be. Irons and suitcases, bedding and ornaments that could only be called tawdry. The women she worked with had a similarly vulgar look, they were too thin or too fat, and they laughed too loudly, in a way he thought obvious. He watched her that day, and the day after, and the day after that, with a growing sense of resentment. Did she spot him, standing there, waiting on the opposite side of the road? Did she see the way passers-by avoided him? No. She saw nothing. She was blind. Sometimes he thought he was the only one who could truly see.

The lives of the two women, Callie and her imposter, were paralleled in ways quite apart from their looks. They appeared at roughly the same time of the morning, Callie in her car, the imposter on the streets, for she evidently walked part way to work. Callie was escorted by her bodyguard. Similarly, the woman arrived accompanied her workmates, and from their conversation he learnt her name: Cassy. Callie. Cassy. So similar in sound, just as they were so similar in looks. Perhaps, he wondered, might they be related in some way? Though it was hard to imagine the possibility as, despite their resemblance, one was the inverse of the other.

He began to follow Cassie, daring the crush and whine of the underground where, even during rush hour, he was afforded space. She lived in the East End, in a tower block overlooking a park. It had been built in the 1960s, its architecture Brutalist. Most of the occupants seemed to be immigrants. Each day she travelled by tube to the nearest station, then walked the remaining distance to her workplace. Usually she was accompanied by one of the other shop assistants, a woman, and from their talk he learned she had difficulty paying her bills, that she had a husband and four children. On her feet she wore pumps that had started to split at the seams. Her voice had a raw, untutored quality, with an accent he could not place. Once, as he stood near to the shop where she worked, she gave him fifty pence, but he would not touch it, as if to do so would be some sort of betrayal.

Once a day, the lives of the two women intersected. A section of road had subsided, and traffic was diverted along side streets. Temporary traffic lights halted vehicles just along from the pound shop, so Callie's car would often idle there, and he briefly had both in his sight, the actress and the imposter, the precious metal and the clinker. Their combined proximity gave him an unexpected thrill, as though the experience was transgressive.

Now he rose even earlier, and did not even wait for the actress's departure; instead he travelled streets still dark, and waited close to the shop, in the cold morning chill. There was no-one else around at that time of the day, apart from vans making their early morning deliveries, road sweepers with their constant, intrusive whine, party-goers returning home from a night of enviable debauchery, a chemical light still in their eyes. Gradually, the neighbourhood came to life. Then he would wait for those minutes or seconds when he would see the two together, before departing, waiting for the evening to come, the actress's arrival home, when he could glimpse her radiance as she stepped from the car to enter the building. The eclipse of her exit left him gasping because it felt as a part of himself had been taken.

At times he woke in the middle of the night and looked up at the building, feeling the fever of her presence; and he imagined the other woman, with her dreary corruption, lying asleep in her bed, her surely brutish husband curled close, and it was as if something twisted within him, so he could not return to sleep until he had attended to the pain of his ferocious erection.

The staff from the pound shop began to recognise him, and avoided him, as all avoided him, because his strangeness had become even more evident. He kept his distance, mostly sheltering in the doorway of a building a few doors along, he had that cunning, and if they still looked, he would walk to the street corner, the one where vehicles accelerated after being held in stasis by the traffic lights, and he would grow light-headed from the speed of their departure.

Did he always have the plan? Perhaps. Perhaps he did, even if he did not realise it. Perhaps it had been formulated on the day of that first encounter. He had long ago stopped trying to unravel his mind's unreliable workings. Perhaps it was not a plan at all, only opportunism.

On that day, the last day, he arrived early, even earlier than normal. It was winter and the ground was covered with a hard slush, the air icy enough to hurt his lungs. Cassie was the first to appear, alone, and she stood in the shop doorway, huddled against the cold, waiting for the manageress to arrive. He sat two doors down, in the entrance of a now empty store, its LAST CHANCE and FINAL SALE banners the only things remaining. He had stuffed newspapers inside his clothing for warmth.

A second member of staff arrived, a man this time, and he and Callie complained about the weather, and the manageress' late arrival. They stood far back from the kerb, in order to avoid wet thrown up by the traffic. He watched the two of them and felt inexplicably jealous.

They were joined by a third, a woman. They looked at their watches, they laughed, and complained. The third woman took her mobile out of her bag and called someone, perhaps the manageress, but there was no answer. Around them, other shops had begun to open.

He watched all this. He watched the traffic. He rose, because the cold pushed into his body, and found he was numb. He rose and he waited.

Callie's car approached at the end of the road. There was a bottleneck in front of it, and despite the driver's manoeuvrings, it failed to pass the vehicles ahead. Its windows a blankness, as always.

He began to walk, slowly at first, then more quickly. The streets were almost empty: few were foolish enough to be out in this weather, sleet starting to fall heavily now. The three were pushed tight into the grilled doorway. The third woman to arrive had an umbrella, and they all sheltered, unsuccessfully, beneath it.

The traffic pushed ahead, little by little, Callie's car amongst it. He imagined her inside, impatient perhaps, or maybe indifferent to the events around her. She would be reading a magazine, one with her own image on front, or a script, mouthing the words she would have to say, or she would be talking with the driver, who inclined his head, as though listening. Her bodyguard would be mute and unthinking. The car stopped at the traffic lights. He began to walk rapidly, towards the shop.

He pushed into the three standing there, all recoiling at his approach He did not say anything. His mind was a bright determination. Cassie was held in his arms, and at first she did not say anything either, too shocked perhaps, and it was only when he dragged her onto the pavement that she began to call and, yes, to scream, yet still the others did not move, their fear an inertia. The woman took out her mobile phone, but dropped it, she shook so. The man did nothing. In the adjoining shops and businesses, people looked out, to see what was happening.

It was difficult to hold on to Cassie, the way she struggled, pulling from him, biting, punching him: but he was strong. To survive on the streets you had to be strong. He was half-running now, he still had her. It was only a short distance to the end of the road, where the traffic accelerated. Not far at all.

Did she see what was happening, there inside the car? Was the sleet too heavy, did it obscure her vision so she was unaware of what was taking place until the very last minute? Or was she too absorbed in what she was doing? The traffic lights were very near. It took two minutes for them to change, he had counted the delay often. If only the woman would stop struggling; and so he punched her, with great force, in the face, and then she was still. Only, that was a mistake, because then she became dead weight. Her nose was bleeding, and one of her eyes. He lifted her in his arms, and ran.

The traffic lights were changing. Red, amber, green. The vehicles sped, impatient with the delay, Callie's amongst them. He ran towards them and between them, traffic swerving and making sudden stops: but not Callie's car. He knew the driver too well, his impatience, his petulance. No, her car accelerated: and he ran directly, deliberately, into the path of it.

TEN

On the fourteenth day, we found the temple. By that time only Abbott, myself and Kenda, our untrustworthy guide, were left alive. The rest were dead, or mad, having fled into the depths of the jungle. In truth, we edged towards madness ourselves.

The temple resembled a Mayan pyramid and rose in tall, level tiers – too high and sheer for any person to easily climb – and was so overcome by foliage only patches of stone escaped the crawling lianas, the inevitable bloom of mosses, the trees and flowers taken root in solid stone; and so the entire structure seemed an animate, living thing. It was so vast the upper levels were concealed by cloud.

Around the temple were the remains of fallen statues. Stone-hewn, almost cubist in appearance, each had the features of an animal or bird, grafted onto a human body. I lifted a decapitated head, a panther at one time, it seemed, and a rain of ants poured from its pulminate eyesocket.

"Were they gods, do you think?"

No-one answered. Abbott crouched, reloading his pistol, and Kenda was somewhere behind me, soundless, as always. Perhaps they were unable to hear, for the click and burr of insects had grown almost intolerably loud, disturbed by our arrival. Nobody came here, not any longer, not even the natives who, from the moment we entered the rainforest, watched us with such tense anticipation.

"I hope the bitch hasn't led us into a trap." Abbott rose, and several times fired his gun into the trees, for no reason I could see. There was a sudden shrieking of birds, and animals cried, their calls echoing each other.

He must have seen my expression. "Haven't you noticed? She's gone. That'll give her something to run from."

And indeed, there was no sign of Kenda, who had escaped, choosing our moment of exhaustion and elation to disappear into the foliage, the intensity of green that had swallowed us so completely that our previous civilised, decent lives now seemed increasingly unreal.

I waited for the sound to subside before replying.

"We don't need her any more, do we? She's done her job, let her go. You know how superstitious the locals are. You saw them: making the sign of the evil eye when we passed. Kenda said they thought we were ghosts. I'm not convinced *she* didn't think we were ghosts."

"Fucking savages." Abbott pushed his gun into his back pocket and strode towards the temple. "I suppose we should think ourselves lucky they didn't eat us."

*

Kenda had skin darker than the darkest bitumen. Her dropsical body gave her the appearance of a lambent goddess, conjured from the jungle's most exotic, most fabulous reaches. In actuality, she came from a fly-blown village in which even to breathe seemed an effort. She spoke a rudimentary form of English taught to her by a missionary who fell victim (she claimed) to a cannibalistic neighbouring tribe, but she said this in a sly, knowing fashion that suggested he met his fate not quite so far from her village. His pocket watch hung around her neck, like a totem. I was more than a little afraid of her. Abbott, by comparison, was contemptuous; I thought this foolish. She was the only one who dared take us here, to the temple all the natives seemed to know of, if only by reputation.

Now she was gone and our chances of finding our way back through the torturous vegetation were at best slim. We had found the fabulous, the legendary temple, although perhaps no-one would learn of our discovery.

It may be we were in denial, or the realisation of our predicament was secondary, but we spent the morning investigating the grounds around the structure. There appeared to be no entrance. The huge, carved blocks had weathered and crushed together until the entire building appeared seamless.

"Maybe there's no interior," I suggested.

Abbott grunted, looking upwards. "There's always a way in," he said.

His face had three spectacular weals where he had been bitten by insects. It says something of his determination that he appeared not to notice them.

The insects had been the most difficult thing at first, with the realisation the ground underfoot, the branches overhead, the very air we passed through, contained a dizzying colony of creatures that would sting, nip, or weld themselves to your skin, invulnerable in their multitudes. He ignored them, or was indifferent to them, I was never sure which.

He pointed towards the temple's summit. "That's the way to go. There's nothing here, so it's the only possibility."

I looked up at the sheer, the seemingly unending ascent. "I can't," I said. "That's beyond me."

"Now you're being defeatist. I won't let anything beat me. When we reach the top, then..."

He left the sentence unfinished, gesturing at the temple's topmost visible levels, and I knew he had no more idea than I did about what we would do when we reached our destination.

We began to climb. Each step of the ziggurat was tall and sheer, and even with the handholds afforded by the vegetation, it proved difficult to move from one level to the next.

"Whoever built this, they must have been giants." I looked down on Abbott, who had slid and fallen while attempting to clamber up to the level on which I stood. Fortunately, he landed on a layer of leaf mould and loam, and in this way saved himself from injury. "Wouldn't it make more sense," I continued, "to keep on looking around the base? There must be an entrance of some sort that leads to the top."

"We could spend days searching and never find anything. Also, I don't trust the savages. Who's to say they haven't been secretly following us all the way here? If we're at the top we have a vantage point, and we can look for a way inside. They said there was a way inside."

He found handholds in the ruined stone and twisted roots, and pulled himself up, both determined and hesitant. His face was a fierce red, and slicked with sweat. I supposed mine was no different.

"Can we believe them though? How long has it been since anyone was really here last? They were afraid of this place. I don't think any of them would have dared come."

"Race memories, that's what it is." He was alongside me, wheezing, our journey having stolen both our energy and health. "How many bodies came tumbling down these steps? I'd bet if we tore some of this vegetation away, you'd still see blood stained on the stone. Down there –" he pointed to the land around the temple – "it must have fed on the dead."

We sat resting for a while. Our climb had taken most of the afternoon, and still we were only a third of the way to the top.

"It'll be dark soon," I said. "We should get some sort of shelter arranged. Besides, I don't know if I have the strength to go any further today. If only Kane hadn't left with our supplies..."

We made a makeshift shelter from a sheet of polythene I carried in my backpack, tying it to a tendril of vine, weighing it down with stones, then lying beneath it, our hammocks spread over the ground to act as some form of protection. Abbott shot and skinned a monkey that wandered too close to our temporary camp, and cooked it over a fire that oiled black from the humidity, so the meat we ate tasted of smoke and little else.

From where we sat, the jungle spread in all directions. There was the glint of a river in the far distance, but otherwise all we could see was the canopy of trees, spreading with a determined uniformity that belied the frightening diversity of the rain forest.

"You see?" Abbott gestured at the landscape. "Anybody could be hiding out there. At least we have the advantage of being able to see anyone that approaches."

"Or anything." Kenda had claimed one of our party had been killed by a jaguar, and although we were sceptical of this explanation – his belongings had also vanished – there had been paw marks nearby, and certainly there had been a killing. We later found the dismembered corpse, rendered in such a way it indeed suggested some sort of animal was responsible.

That had caused the first of the arguments, a week into the expedition, but by that time we were so far removed from civilisation it was pointless to go back, although it also sapped our determination to go forward. Abbott was the one who made the decision though; you couldn't argue with him. It was his expedition, his obsession, his discovery, and we all followed in his wake like the wayward flotilla we had become. Now though, now only the two of us remained, he seemed more cautious, as if the diminution of our numbers also lessened his power. Perhaps his aggrandisement was in fact the result of our real, very palpable fear.

Lying there, trying to find comfort in the lumpen mattress of our bedding, he looked old, and not a little worn. His features were lined and had gained the shapeless quality afflicting the elderly, even though he was, to the best of my knowledge, only a little past middle age. I saw too how his hand shook when he lit the fire. Tiredness was overwhelming him, as it had overwhelmed us all.

As night drew in, and we curled into an uncomfortable sleep, he wrapped his arm around me, touching my breasts. At first, I feared it was an unwanted sexual advance, but his face had the slack contentment of a child's, so I could not be certain. When later I woke, because rain had started to fall, striking the plastic sheet with a sharp fury, he slept still, but I imagined the ghost of the monkey's features hovered around his own, shrieking in terror and fury as it met its fate. At that very moment, the cries of primates rose from the trees around us, something had woken then from their own sleep, so the very air seemed a distillation of fear, catching and holding us at its centre.

*

As a child, I dreamed of the jungle. I imagined myself in pith helmet and blouse and khaki jodhpurs, much like the adventurers I saw in black on white films on TV, or read of in books. There would be scuffles with wild animals and perhaps long-lost creatures from a prehistoric age, along with the obligatory romance with the handsome leader of the expedition. There would be an erupting volcano and a hidden treasure and a final, daring escape from a scene of peril. When Abbott first proposed our expedition, these were the images that came to mind, even though I attempted to temper them with reality.

By the time we spent the night on the temple, none of those illusions remained. The jungle was an oppressive, frightening place, alive with danger, real or imagined. The smell was not of green, growing things, but of decay. The creatures inhabiting it were not exotic, fabulous beasts but were hidden, identifiable mostly by sound, everywhere, all around us, clicks and whirrs and screams that sounded oddly human. Even at night: I woke often, and there was always something out there, somewhere, crashing through the undergrowth or skittling through the branches, while the wind rose as darkness fell, so the trees softly soughed and cracked and sent objects, always unseen, crashing to the floor of the rainforest. I imagined a journey full of wonder and curiosity; the reality was one filled with desperation and fear. I understood superstition at those times; it was so easy to surrender to its irrationality.

None of these emotions seemed to infect Abbott, at least not outwardly. He slept soundly, and almost unmoving. My own sleep was broken. I woke at one point to a feverish terror, and the conviction someone was climbing the temple, a slow grapple up the route we had ourselves followed, motionless when I strained to hear their advance, and only daring to move again when I temporarily relaxed, telling myself it was simply imagination. By the time dawn came, with its welcoming mists and tracery of red, I had been awake for hours.

*

That was when I discovered Abbott was dead. He lay, still curled in a curious position of insecurity, one hand tucked beneath his cheek, the other cupped between his legs. His eyes were open, his mouth slightly agape, and insects had already started to colonise his skin. The body was stiff, and terribly cold; everything indicated his death had happened hours before. I had probably been awake at the time, looking out, locating nothing more than my own fears. There had been no sign, no sound, and now, in the daylight, no clue to indicate what had happened to him.

Hysteria might have been an appropriate response, or at least crushing desperation. Instead, I sat beside him, silent, knees drawn up, staring at his body, as though I might be mistaken, and it was only the deepest sleep he had fallen into. It was shock, I suppose.

How long did I sit that way? Long enough for the morning mists to dissipate and the sun to regain its ferocity. Long enough for his skin to turn a sullen purple and the stench from his body to overwhelm the jungle's own natural scent of loam. Time enough for me to formulate any number of ways out of my predicament, however impractical. In truth, I do not remember thinking of anything.

I grew clinical then, stripping the body of objects that might prove useful: pistol, pocket knife, lighter, cigarettes; his wallet, with its collection of redundant notes and credit cards; iodine tablets; a bottle which I filled with water that had gathered in the plastic sheet; his mobile phone, which still carried a charge but which was completely useless in this place that evaded the advances of modern technology. I took his backpack, and his gun. Then I dragged his body away from the tarpaulin, along the stone plain of the temple. It was difficult work, and I came to know the meaning of the term 'dead weight'; but I have always been stubborn and determined, and even though I had to at times push his body by sitting on the ground and shoving it with both feet, I eventually managed to move it to the perimeter of the ledge. Then I kicked it over, afraid for a moment I would follow.

My plan had been for it for continue down, following the temple's incline, until it landed in the jungle, but it only crumpled on the ledge below, in the most ridiculous position, landing chest down, lodged against the wall with legs upright, arms splayed, head turned so it looked back towards me.

*

After that, the decision to continue climbing, and not to descend, was an easy one. It was his eyes: they now seemed to accuse me.

The temple rose in steps towards the clouds, or so it seemed. It was only a matter of climbing those steps, one level at a time, finding handholds amongst the tangle of vines and the twist of palms embedded in the very stone. There were over a hundred tiers, each at least thirty feet in height. It looked as though it had indeed been designed for giants, a race long extinct, and recalled only in the trace of memory handed down from tribal generation to generation. Kenda had said the temple's creators were not human, but we dismissed her claims as superstition. Now, looking down at the building's expanse, at the sheer size that brought it above the tree tops, breaking into the sky, I was almost inclined to believe her.

By the time I scaled three quarters of the temple's height, it had grown silent and cold and damp, because now it was under permanent cloud cover. I carried nothing but my backpack, but even this smallest of weights seemed to drag me downwards, to make the most meagre advance the greatest of efforts. The mist was so impenetrable, anything could have hidden in its murk, although there appeared to be nothing: it was absolutely still, with no sign even of the primates that so jealously guarded the temple's lower levels. The clamour of the rainforest was frightening; but the quiet was more frightening still. I thought of Abbott somewhere far below, no longer even in view, a colony for insects in the humidity and heat, and felt a little surge of triumph in knowing I had come this far and he had not, and that I would reach our goal, though our goal had been, and continued to be, ill-defined.

There had always been an unspoken rivalry between the two of us. I was the only woman in our expedition, and his attitude to women was, at best, protean. Yet I had money, while he was impoverished; I had social status, while he was considered something of an amusing, possibly dangerous, joke. Those demons he claimed to have materialised in Tibet? Popular opinion was that they had been conjured from a bottle, or something more narcotic, the fibrillous dream of opiates. The serpent seen in the Congo, its breadth greater than a man's height, it length indeterminate but receding into the depths of the jungle, was exposed as a hoax, and it suggested the blurred, vapid footage of leopards roaming the English countryside was similarly faked. Yet these speculations did not bother me, for I knew how insubstantial the dividing line between visionary and charlatan could be. What he offered was the opportunity for adventure, the dream of something more exotic than my suffocating, stilted, socialite lifestyle in which money counted for nothing and possibilities, being endless, lost their allure.

When he told me then about the temple, of course I was in thrall. It had been glimpsed once, no twice, from a plane, in an area of rainforest, its location nebulous, as the story itself was. He had been attempting to impress my wretched brother, whose ambitions went no further than using our family's considerable fortune in the pursuit of men who, once his object had been attained, he discarded. Abbott was drunk, as usual, and he played court jester to our gathering. His clothing had superficial respectability, but had clearly been obtained from the dusty recesses of a junk shop. The damp patch on his trouser leg was either spilled drink or, more likely, vomit. Only the desperate would have granted him credibility, but I was indeed desperate. How galling for him that I was the one to take his story seriously, to provide the funding to chase this most elusive of dreams; and how ironic that I would be the only one to see the fulfilment of that dream, which the summit of the temple, hidden as always amongst cloud, represented.

*

It took a further five hours to reach the top: the climb was more difficult now and, because I could no longer see clearly, there was an added danger in the ascension of those forbidding, impossible walls of stone, in the vegetation threatening to give way under my weight, as indeed it sometimes did. Even the perimeters of the ledges were difficult to see; if I had fallen, even down to the next level, no-one would ever find me. This was a forgotten temple, in a lost location, on a dangerous continent. Decades might pass before anyone ever came this way again. Indeed, had we not prided ourselves with the thought that we were pioneers?

At first it was not even apparent I had reached my goal, though the narrowing area of each tier of the temple had given some indication. There was nothing to see or hear, beyond the ghost of my own body in the cloud, the breathing that closed in with such intensity it was difficult to realise it was my own.

There was little at the summit to signify what had taken place there at one time, if indeed anything had. Perhaps its only purpose was to reach into the sky. The stone had accumulated a heavy covering of moss which was sodden with moisture. There was a frighteningly small area on which to walk, and I circumnavigated this by lying on my stomach and feeling around the perimeter with my hands. Beyond that, there appeared to be nothing, no entranceway to the temple I could see. I celebrated by crying, frustrated, exhausted tears, exacerbated by hunger and, finally, shock, the realisation I had found nothing, and that no-one would ever find me. Foolishly I even tried to call for help on Abbot's mobile phone, but there was no signal in the rainforest; of course there was not. We had travelled far, far from civilisation; and that was what I had longed for, but how foolish that now seemed.

I lay there, and in time I slept. The sleep was deep, and engulfing.

I woke and it was nearing sunset, but the cloud had cleared. I could again see the tops of the trees, below me now, dwarfed. I could hear once more the jungle's unending chatter, its cries. Far off, something crashed through undergrowth, and roared. It sounded positively prehistoric.

Below my feet was a passageway, previously hidden by cloud. Its entrance had grown clogged with rubble and moss which would take a full day's work to remove. I could see though, in the dying light, that the tunnel penetrated far, far down and, although it was initially in darkness, this gave way to a curiously golden luminescence. There were noises too, almost like children's voices. I am certain I heard babies crying, and music.

I had stepped into the pages of one of my adventure novels. I would rest, then in the morning I would carry on, as I must carry on, and I would be taken on endless exploits, lurid perils and excitements that would closely resemble the events of Technicolor movies. It was the life I had always desired. I lay on my back, in the high, cold mists, in the thin air that made my head spin, though that was also exhaustion. I lay and I dreamt, in that terrifying, familiar way in which dreams have more substance than reality. I dreamt; and in my dreams I stepped inside.

ELEVEN

At the side of the road. Sleeping under a pile of rubbish, isn't that sad?

No, no-one knows her name.

The dirt, it was awful. But when it was washed away, she looked about the same age as I am. How could someone let themselves get into a state like that?

Needles and white, white tablets.

Can you speak, dear?

*

The first time I died, I was decapitated with a chainsaw. In an attempt at frivolity, the chainsaw had been decorated with fairy lights. It slashed and roared and my head flew a-tumbling through the air to land on a settee where it remained, wearing a poorly approximated expression of astonishment. Strange to see my features there, tongue a-jut, eyes lolled back, a widening leakage of blood seeping into the cushion's fabric. I felt a little hysterical at that, I can tell you.

Near to my head lay the body of my boyfriend. We had been having overenthusiastic sex, right up to the moment the killer pierced him through the heart with a barbeque skewer. Rather cruelly, his death had coincided with the moment of climax, a Freudian subtext that was surely unintentional. I have trouble placing his face now, much less his name which was probably Brad or Cody or some such wannabe cute boy appellation. I do remember his total lifespan was three minutes and twenty seven seconds, whereas mine was precisely five. Those sort of details stay with you.

I cannot say it was the most memorable of appearances, and if there is any spark to my contribution which, in truth, veers on the unctuous, it is probably due to the vicious enthusiasm with which I approached my task. My hair was dyed blonde (it shrieked bimbo by virtue of its unclassy brassiness) and I had a practiced, affected giggle. My lifespan - all five minutes - had been procured by that most classic and venal of procedures, the casting couch. The producer had a toupee and emphysema, and enjoyed having newly lit cigarettes stubbed out on his chest. All along his skin, a cratered wreckage recorded the history of his tortured, libidinous desires.

On the screen, amplified, I was a goddess. Forget the acting. Forget the stilted dialogue. Forget the movie itself because, frankly, I have. What was the name again? **Slay Ride** or some such. My head ended up in a sack and eventually decorated a Christmas tree as a ghoulish bauble. I didn't care. I had those moments of power, those brief minutes when I shone and the camera, cliché though it may be, loved me.

Not that the critics saw it that way. *A lamentable, sadistic juxtaposition of sex and mutilation that lacks the redeeming feature of being the slightest bit frightening* was one of the kinder reviews. *You'll be horrified at how dreadfully inept this routine teenager slash and stalk flick is* was another. The comments, bowdlerised, were stolen for the advertising campaign: *Sex...Mutilation...You'll be horrified*, it promised.

Not that I disagreed with the critics' overall assessment. As debuts go, it was hardly the most auspicious. Still, I hoped some would be perceptive enough to recognise how clearly my abilities stood above the rest. As it was, the only favourable response to the movie came in the form of fan mail to the leading actress, and only because of her ridiculous, prosthetically-enhanced mammaries. I wish I could say she was welcome to those fanboy, suspiciously stained missals, most of which optimistically supplied phone numbers and home addresses, but truthfully I was more than a little jealous. How unfair, how unjust, that she should receive the attention, and not me. *Hi Madison* the letters began or, more obsequiously, *Dear Madison, I hope you don't mind me writing to you this way...* It should have been my name on those envelopes, my name the pathetic, acne-scarred, never-had-sex geeks wrote at the beginning of letters. *Dear Chelle*, it should have said, yes that, *Dear Chelle*, not *Dear Madison*, not *Madison*, never, never *Madison*.

I'm sorry. I lost my temper there. I have a tendency to do that sometimes. People tell me these days I am positively fearful.

I digress. Things were very different on the day of the film's premier. I wore a tight-fitting silver, mottled dress, a last minute, credit-stretching acquisition from one of the high street stores (I would return it the following day, hoping the second-hand smell of smoke and alcohol would not be noticed. The wages I had received for my role were minuscule). Accompanying me was my friend Harris, waspish, who in public affected a persona camper than camp, and who shrieked with delight at the moment of my onscreen decapitation.

"Darling, you were *fab-u-lous!*" he announced, in a voice loud enough for all around us to hear. "You've made dying a real art."

At which I giggled, blushing, simultaneously proud of my achievements, and embarrassed by his behaviour.

Of course, the joke was that he was not like that at all.

We made an attractive couple, I must say. His Italianate hair rose in tight, mahogany waves and kinks, and his skin similarly had a touch of dusk that made you suppose he was, at the very least, of Mediterranean origin; but when he spoke it was in a broad Scottish accent even I could barely decipher.

"Don't you be deceived by the appearance. I spent most of my life not even seeing the sun. We saw it weekdays when we were at school, a wee watery thing that gave light but no heat. Then, at the weekends the heavens would open, so you'd need to an ark to travel one end of the village to the next.

Once, one of the fishing boats came loose from the harbour, and there it was sitting in the middle of the street the next morning, the water had risen so high."

He said this whilst looking out the window of the flat we shared with what appeared to be half the population of London, his back towards me. But then he turned to face me, for his timing was immaculate.

"Aye, I may have never seen sun, but there's a lot to be said for fake tan and hair dye."

I wondered if his accent was a similar affectation, for he lost it easily when he assumed the persona of camp, mincing window-dresser. It was his revenge, I think, on a world that prejudged his sexuality and occupation; and so he pandered to those expectations, while secretly mocking them.

And so it was at the premiere. That I giggled all evening was his doing, although I was, admittedly, a little tipsy. It was far from a proper opening night. Those days lay ahead, with their red carpets and sycophantic, antagonistic paparazzi, but this instead resembled a cast party with pretensions. There were drinks (champagne supposedly: in actuality, cheap, fizzy wine), and a meagre finger buffet. Film crew, investors and a few invited friends filled the cinema, so naturally we applauded, of course we gave a standing ovation as it spooled to its predictable conclusion.

Up there, magnified, every gesture an enormity, I felt myself in thrall to my own image. What spiralled through my body was a carnal thrill, a fizzing, exploding excitement that made me feel more than human. We emerged from the darkness and it was as if I generated my own light, so bright was its glow.

Thinking back, that was the first indication. At the party I wafted from person to person, less and less sober, increasingly incoherent. The music made it impossible to hear what anyone said, and faces and names grew blurred. Inevitably, I humiliated myself, though perhaps no more so than anyone else present. I'd grown giddy with the anticipation of fame. Well, that and the alcoholic rush and the wrap in the toilet cubicle that provided me with confidence to match all the other fixated gazes. I had the indiscreet pebbling of a nose bleed along one powdered cheek.

Wherever I went, Harris accompanied me, his remarks unsubtle and cutting. It was duplicity on his part, for he played his role as successfully as I played mine. In reality he was ambitious and analytical and, without his support I imagine I would not be in the position I occupy today.

Slay Ride limped around as a limited release and then found rightful oblivion on video three months later. In later years it gained something of a cult following, thanks to its sheer awfulness. *It's so bad it's good* was the common consensus. People can be quite unaware of the banality of their observations sometimes.

For me, the glory was facile and short lived. The following day I went back to waitressing six nights a week, returning in the small hours to a flat I shared both with Harris and five other equally determined would-be actresses. The flat was damp and cold, and permanently smelt of cigarette smoke and makeup. I was not disheartened: I had obtained my taste of fame, and never once did I doubt the inevitability of my own success.

How deluded we can be in our aspirations. What I had found was not fame: it was sugar glass. One night of ersatz glamour provided not celebrity, or recognition, or even enough money to pay my monthly rent, but a padded mouth, a day-after tremor, and a nose with the lining ripped raw.

Harris met me for coffee. Or, more accurately, I served him coffee in the cafe in which I waitressed. One look at me:

"I see they've resurrected the corpse of Norma Jean."

He never less than dry. That day, admittedly, I failed to appreciate his wit.

Harris was the first friend I had made on arriving in the city. The bus that carried me there travelled past the grandest of houses set behind gated walls, their gardens artificially green, and I imagined it would all be like that, wealth and fame determined by geographical location and little else. Instead, I arrived at the city's dirty heart. Every person stepping down into that station must have felt the same withering of dreams. Blued petrol fumes substituted for air, while around me were the borderline psychotics drawn inevitably to places of arrival and departure. There was danger there, in that spot, but it lacked the sanitised glamour of its depiction on the cinema screen. There was no cameraman tracking movement, no director ready to call *cut!* at the first precisely captured expression of emotion.

I must have looked a sight, wearing the only clothes I possessed, and my carefully spiked hair crushed to the side of my head. I had no belongings. Others retrieved their cases, they hurried to catch their connection, or excitedly embraced those who came to meet them. I stood paralysed in the cold, echoing station and looked at the signs overhead, the place names which meant nothing to me, and I must have looked exactly what I was, a bewildered girl who had fled to a place existing only in her imagination, only to be confronted by the much crueller reality.

That evening my only meal was a part-eaten sandwich someone had thrown into a bin. I dared to leave the terminus only briefly, for at that moment the heavens opened and drove me back indoors, forcing me to sleep propped upright on one of the waiting room benches, while the station filled and emptied, and the robotic announcements faded out of focus. I was not the only one to do that, no, not at all. The terminus was a gathering place for the transient. I had no money, I knew no-one, and I had arrived with the nebulous desire to become an actress, even though the only experience I possessed was a role in a castrated school production of The Tempest, after which my father had praised my acting. What conclusions might be drawn from that, you may ask, and well you might.

When they make the story of my life, the unauthorised version, always so much more entertaining than the official, sanitised tale, it will tell the bittersweet story of a girl from the country who arrives in the city, chasing a dream, the true nature of which she is unaware, and who is, in the process, transformed. It can be my apocrypha, the account everyone prefers, but which cannot be proven. In my world, no-one is interested in certainties; rumour and speculation are the true sources of power. Throw them a morsel and they rise like goldfish to the top of their bowl, in a feeding frenzy.

Of course, now you are wondering how I managed to get from that first, frightening arrival to where I am now. Suffice to say I was approached by a very sympathetic older man, the first of many such sympathetic men, who offered me a moment of security. It was my first introduction to the entertainment industry, in a way. Please, don't feign shock. I found myself somewhere safe, comfortable and warm, in the company of someone not entirely repulsive, who only asked I dress in a schoolgirl uniform and call him daddy while I smacked his bottom until it bled; and as I did this, he would masturbate with his one good hand and come feebly over his scented bedsheets.

That was how I met Harris. Harris, who was in art college at the time, and not above supplementing his income by hanging around the very same places I soon frequented, the railway and bus stations, the popular tourists spots, under the gaze of Eros, or Nelson, with his frighteningly blank eyes watching the none-too-surreptitious gatherings around the base of his column, the place where we stood in sunshine and rain, waiting for the approach of this man, or that, for it was always men, always. I had gained a certain reputation and dressed to match, which in any case was my natural inclination: ripped fishnet stockings, high heeled shoes black and polished. My hair was an elaborate Mohican, my makeup the palest foundation, my lipstick a nightshade purple. My chosen name was Cordelia, in part because it sounded exotic, but mostly as a form of protection. If I withheld my true name, the one people call now in veneration, then it was not me performing these actions, not me that bound and whipped and ground and beat her clients, and spat and shit upon them, that sent yellowed sprays into their willing mouths, or forced them headfirst into toilet bowls to lick the rheumy contents. All this before I was even eighteen. How hard the city makes you, how willing you become to do anything in order to survive, to even take an unwitting pleasure from it. If my ascension seems limitless, it is only because my descent had been so terrible. Though in doing so, at least my income was not inconsiderable, at least I did not live the astringent life I would encounter when I first decided to make concrete my dreams, as opposed to the dreams of others.

We had made a pact, Harris and I: we would leave the business together. He abandoned college, having found employment as a window dresser, while I took advantage of one of my clients, a film director, and persuaded him to cast me in a non-speaking role in a TV commercial he was creating. I use the term "persuaded" with a certain amount of irony, of course.

*

Such terrible bedsores she has. There's nothing to her but skin and bone. Not long for this world surely. Does she know where she is do you think?

I hope to God not.

Coughing throughout the night, somewhere in the room's dark.

A curtain to the left, always drawn.

The room has a sour smell. It smells of sick.

*

"I think," said Harris, "you should start up a wee fan club."

I had been reading a film magazine someone had left behind in the cafe, and looked up, only half-listening.

"Who for?" I said.

"For you, you daft gowk. Who else?"

He was joking, surely? I failed to appreciate his prescience; for he understood a person's fame is not necessarily based on their abilities. He saw that if you say you are famous, and behave as though you are famous, then it will often happen by a mysterious process of osmosis. Remember, this was before everyone had an internet connection and self-publicity had not yet become commonplace.

He set about organising the club in his usual methodical fashion, advertising at first in science fiction and horror fanzines, and then the classifieds in film magazines, paying for these out of his own pocket. Sometimes the advertisements were accompanied by a grained black and white picture showing me in a state of semi-undress. Those who enquired were sent a scrappy mimeographed newsletter, along with a photograph in which I wore strategically ripped clothing, a flash of breasts thrust upright, held in place by strips of unseen parcel tape. My lips, close up, looked as though they had feasted on overripe berries.

'The new scream queen'. That was my tagline. What is it about women in terror? Does it encourage fantasies of valiant acts? Does it conjure images of the sort most would never confess to? Those were questions I could barely comprehend in those days, much less answer. I could certainly scream though. During that first shoot I screamed so loudly I talked in a hoarse, broken whisper for days afterwards.

My fan club was a domain for geeks, before the term became fashionable, a haunt of unhealthily introverted adolescents and grown men with personality deficiencies. These were the obsessives, the people who spent an inordinate amount of time and money on something - or someone - they had convinced themselves was special, who was exclusively theirs. It would not be long before some found out my address and stood in the street looking up, trying to work out which apartment I was in. I found this both exciting and disturbing.

He was clever, Harris, in a way I then was not. He launched outrageous rumours which circulated in fanzines, suggesting I was in the running for major roles which somehow, miraculously, never materialised and which, in fact, often never even existed. This did not seem to matter - even the suggestion of their existence gave them a solidity, a reality in that most unreal of worlds. Letters began to arrive, their creators even more socially inept than the writers of the hand-written missals I had seen delivered to Madison, my great rival. Sometimes they enclosed their photograph, and in all the photographs they averted their eyes, as though to look at me, even by proxy, would be their undoing.

What fantasies they had in their heads. Of course, they were fantasies we had planted there. The reality was the grim waitressing nightshifts, which I continued with, even though Harris now had a full-time job as a window dresser and earned enough money to keep the two of us. I felt the need to contribute somehow, no matter how meagre the offering.

Occasionally, there were auditions. I tried my best, but somehow the producers never saw what I already knew, which was the inevitability of my own greatness. Sitting there in a line with all the other girls was a situation as unglamorous as any job interview, and we would all try and convince ourselves that this was the one, this was the moment to propel us upwards into the overbright constellation in which Tom and Julia and Michelle dwelt.

Sometimes I saw Madison at the same auditions. She always greeted me with a hug, coupled with a smile of evident insincerity, even as she professed delight and her words, which emerged through perfect, capped, whitened teeth, wished me good luck.

I wanted to kill her, I really did. When she won a role in The Awakening, and I did not, I wanted to kill her even more. We had all been on the casting couch but, believe me, she was the casting couch. Half of Britain's film industry must have ended up sitting on her at some point. It certainly was not talent that won her all those roles, nor which tainted her breath sulphurous.

Harris rented a flat of his own, in a not undesirable district, and I moved in with him. Success came to him much more easily than it eventually did for me: his window dressings became known for their glittering, gaudy displays that were never more than kitsch, but which nevertheless generated their own sense of luminescence. He had quickly been courted by several companies, and had accepted an offer both lucrative and prestigious.

Our ex-flatmates said their farewells, tinged with envy, as though my departure took me one step closer to the fame I - and they - desired. There were whispers, ludicrous of course, that we were lovers. Later, we would capitalise on this confusion.

It may be the rumours emerged from the way Harris worshipped me, perhaps in displaced compensation for his own lack of anything resembling a sex life: he played a character too camp, too much a cliché to appeal to any man for long. His was the solitary fuck, the inevitable question, "Can I see you again?" and its equally inevitable veiled refusal. In fact, his adoration of me may have been part of the character he played, the gay man who venerates the hard, determined woman. If I was not yet that person, than he must have seen the potential, long before it emerged in any concrete form.

I have never forgotten how much I owe him. If not for him, there were times I would not have had the conviction to carry on. When you are overlooked, when you are forgotten, when no-one remembers your name, you find yourself stretched to a thinness, a friable gauze that threatens to unravel with each small puncturing hurt. If it had continued for much longer, I might have faded away altogether.

Certainly the news of Madison's success (her second starring role, the fifth of her screen appearances) did nothing to halt my diminishing sense of worth. Harris, when he learned of the news, was livid, oh absolutely livid, I can tell you.

"What do they see in that daft bint? You're the one with the talent. Anyone can understand that." He fretted at the ignominy, strutting around the flat in a manner suggesting his sensibilities had been offended, not mine. "Mind you, she's one with biggest mouth." As though that settled the matter.

I was beyond caring. While I slept, an exhausted, weighted sleep, he stayed awake, scheming, hatching fantastical plans of improbable ambition. Perhaps realising their impracticality, he decided instead to organise a campaign that generated fourteen semi-literate emails from my adoring fans to film's producers.

Perhaps this, in conjunction with what happened next, did indeed have an effect: it is easy to sneer at such a whimpering, pleading following, which managed to be both priapic and innocent at the same time.

Every aspiring actor or actress can tell the story about their lucky break, the moment from which they can pinpoint their ascent to stardom. Mine came through the acid gossip that formed the small talk of those who waited in line at each audition. *Did you hear...?* they'd begin, and with those words you would know you were, at the very least, about to be told something positively salacious. The exploits of Clara Bow were as nothing to some of the tales that came to me that way, I can tell you.

I suppose this ritual made us feel more virtuous, or at least not so belittled, knowing even the famous had to beg and fawn and carry out unspeakable acts in order to win the roles they performed. Whether these tales were true or not is quite another matter. I imagine these days they say the same about me, though they will do so in whispers, in voices below even a whisper. My wrath is terrible, I assure you.

I have wandered from the topic a little. Did you notice that? I do not even want to contemplate her name. Madison. Such a superficial, ugly, spit-in-the-dust name. What else could it be, when not once but twice she had taken the role rightfully mine.

It cannot even recall the part I was auditioning for, but I do remember this: as I sat there, waiting in line, I was told Madison had been found face down in a refuse bin, her legs a-jut from the top, cut belly to throat so she emptied out like an over-ripe fruit. Imagine my barely-withheld glee! Of course I expressed dismay: I may even have managed to evince a few thin tears. In sympathy, an actress whose name I never learned (nor, to be truthful ever wished to learn) gave me a consoling hug, though in her arms I sensed the same faux passion I expressed. Secretly she was delighted, as was I. The misfortune of others was always such a psychological boon. Yes, I claimed to be upset, but frankly I wanted to celebrate. I wanted to dance and sing and proclaim my satisfaction to anyone willing to listen.

The murder had taken place just a few streets from where I lived, so the thrilling, sordid details of her demise were readily available. Hardened police officers had been violently sick at the sight of her body, or so the story went.

The strange thing was, I already knew. When I had woken that morning, I was not dispirited at the thought of the coming audition. I did not feel exhausted from my labours of the night before. No, I felt strong, alive, more robust than I had in years. A shrill brightness seemed to spark through me. Everyone noticed it. "What is it that's changed about you today?" people would say. "Because you look, well...*different* somehow." That was about as specific as they could be, because in fact nothing had altered. Take a photograph of me from one day to the next, and the camera would record the same person. Strap me into a machine that shimmered and probed down to a molecular level and all would remain unchanged. Still, they knew, I knew. There had been a shift of power.

Naturally, I said all the right things. "How awful," and "Who would do a thing like that?" My acting skills have never been greater than in those moments. You see, it seemed right somehow. No, it seemed *just*. That is the word I am after.

Here is the thing though: when I saw her photograph in the paper, beneath the suitably lurid headlines, I could see we bore a strong resemblance to each other. How strange that I had not noticed that before.

My satisfaction grew was when I was called in to re-audition for the role Madison left vacant. I did not get the part, but there was a re-evaluation: this time they were evidently impressed. My reward was to come not bottom of the bill, but second bottom, the second to get hacked, flayed, dismembered. I call that progress of a sort. Moreover, this time my lifespan was a full twelve minutes and seven seconds.

It occurs to me this talk of lifespans and screen time is misleading. In reality, it is a type of immortality. Long after you are gone, my image will still be there on the cinema screen, or TV screen, or whatever sort of technology may yet emerge. That is my face, enlarged, more than human, that people see. That is my voice escaping through the speakers. Is that not amazing? Does that not make you feel small as you edge your pathetic way to worm fodder and ashes? Is that why you gaze with more than longing at celebrity pictures in magazines and ape their clothing and hairstyles? It is sympathetic magic, it is the ointment you rub on your body to rescue yourself from the grave.

The Awakening had a little magic of its own. Released at a time when the box office was in the doldrums, it managed to creep its way to number four in the box office charts, and created a sizeable return for its producers. None of which found its way to me, of course, but I did not care. For now I had been in a profitable movie, and the movie business loves success, it drinks and thrives on it, much as you do. As much as I do.

Perhaps Madison's murder contributed something of a frisson to the movie's release. The papers were full of scandalous chitter-chatter that talked of links to possible cults and the actress's sordid yet unsurprising past. It was rumoured her boyfriend was connected to organised crime. It was rumoured she was a lesbian. There were suggestions of an extravagant lifestyle, fuelled by unpaid debts. As each story surfaced, mention would also be made of the film she had been about to star in. How ironic, they said, that this film would have propelled her to greater recognition. She would have been a celebrity. This, also ironically, is what she became after her death.

Harris would sit and read the news stories out loud in his most affected manner and we would be consumed by laughter. This may sound unnecessarily cruel, but the laughter was really a form of release, softening the realisation of fate's capricious workings. There was no doubt her misfortune had been to my benefit. I was certain people started to look at me on the street, sly, sideways glances of almost-recognition. This in a place where the famous are commonplace. My star, as they say, was evidently in the ascendant.

Not that producers saw it that way. I had been told, with the certitude always accompanying those who rely on hearsay, that it would grow easier now I had made The Breakthrough. Except I had not made The Breakthrough. In reality I had played a small part in the sort of movie in which the roles and those that occupied them were virtually interchangeable. I was not famous, I was not in the ascendant. No, I was deluded. The only people who did not think so were the growing numbers of my witless, fawning fans. Requests would arrive for photographs almost daily, and of course the paltry earnings from my waitressing job would not allow me to fulfil their requests.

It was Harris who suggested I sell signed photographs, for the not unreasonable sum of five pounds apiece. It proved to be a successful ploy, to the degree I sometimes found myself at the end of the week with some money that had not been eaten up by bills and the barest necessities of life. These days, of course, the photographs are beyond desirable. That is, if their owners dared sell them. Still, I expected more: not an overnight transformation, but still I wanted, no I *demanded* more from my career than that.

I relied on Harris for so many things. It occurs to me this too fits a role, that of the heroine who is nonetheless subservient to her male co-star, or stars. How obvious that seems now, but it did not seem so apparent at the time. Yes, Harris comes to the rescue of Chelle yet again.

In fact, my third acting part directly arose from the fact that he serviced some ghastly old queen he met in a bar one night. It turned out this man was the casting director for a new film in the process of carrying out auditions. If Harris were to agree to some 'special needs' the casting director enjoyed indulging in, then a minor role would be virtually guaranteed.

I never found out what these special needs were – and if Harris, (who normally regaled his meagre sexual conquests in vivid detail) did not disclose them, then they must have been special indeed – but the role was definitely mine, though it was barely a role at all.

Here is the film's opening scene: a woman is running along a pavement, with a man in pursuit. The man is carrying a large, blood-encrusted knife. He is almost upon her, when they come to a gated park. Frantically, she starts to climb the railings, but slips, and is impaled on the metal spikes. Cue opening credits.

That was my part. I emphasise *was*. I was grateful to get it, of course, but also a little disheartened. What I pictured was endless years of nearlys and near misses, leading to the eventual combustion of my dreams. I would have to find a proper job, too old by then to even return to my previous specialised services, and this would be followed by a bitter life in which I reflected on what might have been, one in which I came to the sour realisation I simply was not good enough.

Cue the death of another actress. No, cue the death of two. Yes, once again they were in the same film as I was. This time they were found bound together with duct tape, with a metal rod gashed through both their bodies, right through their hearts. The news outlets began to talk of a serial killer, one obsessed with horror films, although at this point there was little evidence of that.

Two points occurred to me: was it not a little bit coincidental that actresses associated with two out of the three films in which I had appeared were murdered? Moreover, was not the method of death in this particular instance a little too close to the impalement my character was to suffer in the opening scenes?

I did not discuss any of this with Harris, afraid my conjecture had no more foundation than my growing paranoia; for did I not fear, at that time, for my own life? Besides, he seemed so pleased when each new opportunity presented itself, caught in a little rapture of glee as he accompanied me back to audition for the roles which now needed recast.

"It'll be different this time, you'll see," he said.

I did not voice my doubts.

Yet he was correct, things were different. Now the casting director no longer even recognised me. I had grown sleek and powerful, and there was a side to my character that was a little bit wild.

"My dear," he said, "you're almost feral."

I made them weep that time, as they shared the terror of the scene I acted out. You could see their faces caught in the moment, as I invested the leaden dialogue with an intensity they – and I – had not thought possible. At the end, they applauded. "You're wasted, simply wasted," I was assured and not one but two of those watching chose to slip me the number of agents better placed to promote my skills.

That was my first starring role. From bottom of the bill to the top, just like that! I could barely believe it myself, and Harris celebrated by taking me to a nightclub where we consumed two bottles of champagne and three wraps of cocaine in the space of an hour, so the world became a buzzing, tingling place. On the dance floor I turned heads; there were little glances of admiration, perhaps even awe. I don't think it was simply the effects of the cocaine. No: I know it was not the effects of the cocaine.

The film was released to generally indifferent reviews, but the notices I received were ecstatic: *A real find, whose talent far outclasses the mediocre film she is starring in; Chelle Stewart is a revelation – a star in the making; Mark my words, Chelle Stewart is a name to watch. It's just a shame you have to watch her in this particular film.* I started to keep a scrapbook, with each notice carefully pasted in. At night, before I went to sleep, I would leaf through the reviews, reading and re-reading them, until my fingers grew black from the newsprint and I memorised every word. Now of course, whole books have been devoted to me, and these too are just as carefully read and memorised, but this time it is others who make that inner pilgrimage, who silently mouth their words of devotion.

I found a new agent, not one of the names passed to me after the audition, but one of many who now professed a sudden and deep interest in my career's progress. When agents come to you, and not you to them, you know you have power.

Within a few months I had not one, not two but three parts in movies of the sort I had never dreamed – no, that's not true, I had dreamed, I always dreamed – of featuring in. These were major roles, in films with budgets that would keep a small third world country afloat for a year. My agent told me the parts would be good for me; but it was Harris's advice I valued.

"Aye, you have to chase the money just now. Talent's grand and all that, but there's not much artistry in the film business and they'll not keep paying attention unless they think you can deliver the goods. Though keep one of the parts personal. That's the sort you win awards for."

Which is exactly what I did.

We moved, Harris and I, to a much grander apartment, one I paid for this time. Of course I took him with me: we were inseparable and, besides, he was my totem. Our roles were reversed, for now I was the one recognised, I was the one lauded; his own achievements palled in comparison. It is to his credit that he seemed to bear no resentment, happily relinquishing his own position to settle in to his new role of paid helper. Not only that, but my interior designer too.

The first thing he did was to decorate the walls with framed copies of my publicity photographs. So many poses: pouting, reflective, severe, knowing, wry. I have to say that even I felt a little in awe of those images.

"It looks like a shrine," was my only remark.

"Well, it's not a home, is it?"

It was only later I appreciated his wisdom. The life I had chosen was all about appearances. You projected the image and lived the life to match the image. In the process you became something else altogether. Certainly I was changing, I could feel it.

*

Our mystery woman spoke today.

What did she say?

Nothing that made sense to me anyway.

If I end up like that, shoot me.

*

How distanced from reality life became. I had told myself fame would not change me, that I would remain grounded. How naïve that supposition proved to be. I found myself on a film set as large as a town, in which it was possible to become lost amongst the ersatz streets, as if the frieze of propped-up, painted skyscrapers were indeed limitless in height and not truncated at the third storey; and if I were to open the plywood doorways I would find myself facing not hardboard fasciae but the chaotic, hop-laden, smoke-filled bars I was supposed to frequent. For did I not play a lady of the night? Yes, the Tart With a Heart, the foil for which Our Hero (hard drinking, overworked cop, family problems, yada yada yada) eventually falls. Predictably, (for nothing in this movie was less than predictable) I came to a bloody end. Cue bittersweet music, with the cop staring out across the East River with the Brooklyn Bridge distant. And yes, I had been butchered by a serial killer, so in some respects my latest role had not changed dramatically from the very first.

Then I was a spy, one who was a master of disguise. Her world was one of sheened glass and metal; and I discovered how unfit I had become, or had always been, even with the assistance of a stunt double made up to look exactly like me. It was an eerie feeling, to encounter yourself on set, dressed to the exact same detail, and if the hair (a wig) did not exactly fit, then it was not noticeable as she leapt from tall buildings, raced between traffic, and hauled herself up a Papier Mache rockface, representative of some anonymous mountainside in Kabul. At which point the camera would cut to me as I reached the top, or came to a standstill, or landed and rolled on the conveniently soft contents of a conveniently placed dumpster, all the while still grasping my pistol and with barely a gloss of sweat to show I had been in motion at all.

The third role was that of an isolated fisher-lass in an unnamed Scottish village. "It's all herring guts and angst," I had been promised, script at that point unseen. It was indeed mordant in its depiction of a girl crushed by social expectations and circumstance. By the time it came to the scene in which the girl was abused by her father, I could no longer tell fantasy from reality, and fled from the set, weeping hot, endless tears.

"You were magnificent," the director told me.

As, naturally, I was. But I did not know any longer who I was, not really, and questioned if I had ever known in the first place.

Of course, that was the role that would go on to win me my first Oscar.

All the dreams in the world are not enough to prepare you for the moment when you are taken from nothing, from less-than-nothing, to a life in which your defining quality is not your talent, or your looks, or your personality, but rather your fame, and only your fame.

I had not even left the country before, and now that I did, it was to see it reduced to patchwork and serrations and drifts of cloud and light. It was hotel rooms and restaurants and film sets. It was press interviews and talk shows in which I was so tired I could barely compose a coherent answer. And the questions! All of them tiringly unoriginal, repeated over and over until my answers, too, became rote.

I had imagined being accosted by fans (proper fans, not the squealing, impotent creatures I relied on previously), had already received their letters, and met some of them in person; but I had not anticipated the late night telephone calls which came even though I changed my number, made it ex-directory. Nor the fans who slept on the street, awaiting my departure or arrival, standing close or at a distance to stare in a manner awed or threatening. I had posed for publicity shots, but had not expected the intrusive paparazzi who sat in cars to record my movements with telephoto lens, leaving me paranoid, overly self-aware.

That was when I realised the true nature of obsession, that it was something sharp and unreliable, edged with hate as much as admiration. If I fed on my admirers, then they too fed on me.

Every moment of my life became a performance. I had longed so intently for success that when it arrived I did what so many of the newly famous do: I crumbled.

As a waitress, life had been exhausting, it had been dispiriting, its rewards had been scant. Still, it had normality. Stardom, *true* stardom was so far divorced from everyday life, it was beyond imagining. Of course I wanted that, for how banal it would be to inhabit a commonplace existence. But my new life was a void. It was as though I fell, and continued to fall, into a world increasingly dark; and in the dark hid the brittle pleasures brought to me by my changing lifestyle. These possessed the power to lacerate.

Now everything was a facade, from the carefully applied makeup I wore, even indoors, to articles in newspapers and magazines that were not even distorted truths. Reading these stories was like looking at another person, someone who possessed my name and image but who existed independently, doing things I would never do, saying things I would never say.

How unreal and how mundane this new life became. My little army of sycophants grew, some of them more than willing to provide the inevitable dusting of nose powder that left me startled, gravityless, and unable to sleep. So I was awake to answer those calls that arrived in the middle of the night, the ones that came from fans so shocked by the sound of my voice they in turn were robbed of theirs, and I spoke to an asphyxiated breathing that sounded as though they were doing something unspeakable at the other end of the line. Perhaps they were.

At first Harris accompanied me everywhere, to and from the studio, on location, jetting from country to country, always at my side. He looked at the world I gained entrance to with the same mixture of awe and intimidation I did, but his confidence grew quickly. He became my 'personal assistant' which in the movie world is normally a euphemism for whoever you happen to be sleeping with at the time.

We turned this confusion to our advantage, staying in the same hotels and posing for photographs together at press junkets. No-one appeared to question the assumption we were a couple, an arrangement beneficial to us both. For me, it was both a protection against unwanted advances and a diversion. People were less likely to notice my sudden nose bleeds and advancing paranoia if I was accompanied by someone who represented a potential romantic interest. How absurd, you say. And yes; how absurd.

For Harris, it was an affirmation of his masculinity. He lost the camp affectations, and became instead its opposite, a parody of traditional manhood in power dresser suits, checked shirts and jeans and (a step too far) leather jackets. He was my protector. Or he was until the day he fell in love.

Our faux relationship was a facade, in an industry composed of nothing more than facades.

Back in the days when I obsessively leafed through old copies of Photoplay, an inheritance from my mother, it always fascinated me to realise the extent to which the famous live a life of artifice. The real person lay behind the carefully posed or stolen images, the vetted questions, the contrived publicity romances which, miraculously, flowered to coincide with a movie's release. I would press my finger to the photographs so hard the paper threatened to burst, as if by doing so I would somehow touch the person beneath.

When I became one of the elect, naturally I heard stories only hinted at before, and I was shocked, truly I was. I was so unprepared for fame that it was like the day I had arrived at the bus station all over again, but this time to another, even more hostile environment. At the same time, I was thrilled. How liberating it is to be privy to the world's dirty little secrets. Yet, how disorienting too.

I had Harris to ground me, even though my existence had become like helium. Other than him, I saw no-one I previously knew. The streets I once walked were now seen only through car windows, tinted, so the world seemed permanently shrouded. I no longer bought anything for myself - Harris or a minder would do that for me. No, what I saw was film set after film set, and hotels, and the interiors of cars and planes and trains; so I saw the world but did not see it, because the world viewed behind glass seemed as artificial as the one created on celluloid.

Away from observation, in a toilet cubicle somewhere, the only place where I could guarantee not to be observed, I wept and wanted to dig out my eyes, so I could no longer see what I had become. At the time I did not understand, you see: it was the trauma of transformation.

Locked in this hermetic, stifling existence, somewhere in that slippage of personality, I felt as though I lost my sanity. I grew gaunt. I felt like a piece of string that is being stretched to the point of snapping.

Rumours circulated. I was 'unwell' in the most favourable reports, anorexic and psychotic in the less generous. There were hints of drug use, which of course there was, but the powerful are litigious and there was never more than coded stories in the press.

I felt as though I was fading. I was acclaimed, I was famous, I was powerful; but I was also nothing, less than nothing. It seemed my image on the screen had more reality and substance than I did.

For my fans, I became an icon. They wore what I wore, they aped my makeup, and so obsessively reported the details of my existence in fan magazines, it grew to be the way I tracked moments of my life I had forgotten.

On the street, in restaurants, in stores and airports, they stared, they nudged each other and whispered. At film premiers they screamed, waving autograph books, and took photographs in which I appeared red-eyed and pallid, as though I was something undead, animated by a power that directed and shaped my life and over which I had little or no control. I was scraped to a translucence finer than the finest of rice paper. I tell you, you could have taken me and crumpled me and tossed me aside like waste.

When a woman threw herself and a passer-by in front of my limousine one morning, not long after I left my apartment, there was screaming and blood and I felt the world collapse inward with an unreal gravity.

*

A permanently cold light. A tube, for feeding. Clipped footsteps, or the squeak of sneakers on the floor. Air that carries the ghost of Lysol.

My nan said. Here, I'll sort that to make you more comfortable. It was such a shock. Do you know what happened the other day?

*

That was the worst moment, the absolute worst. The newspapers carried the story, of course, and the news reports. The woman was a down-and-out; no-one even knew her name, not until the police discovered letters she had sent to me. 'I'll be in your biographies and the film of your life,' the last one had read. I had never even opened it.

"There's no such thing as bad publicity," Harris was fond of saying. I was not so certain. Hers was not the only death, after all.

There was the fan who videoed herself recreated scenes from my films, dressed as I was, mimicking my

235

actions and repeating my lines perfectly; at the end of which she sat down and blew the top of her head off with a shotgun. I did not see it, but I heard of it, because the police came to question me.

Then, during one of the parties I felt obliged to hold, one of the guests fell from the balcony and was killed. When I looked down at her, stretched and blooded on the street, I saw she had mimicked my way of dress, and the cut of my hair, so it was as if I looked down at myself. The police questioned me about that too. Afterwards, one of the policemen asked for my autograph.

At least they did not suspect any involvement with the actress found dead from an overdose of barbiturates outside the studio in which I was filming, or with the mother who murdered her prematurely born child and disposed of it in the sewers. Afterwards, she settled down to watch a DVD of Aftermath.

Women again. Do you notice that? Always women.

None of this affected my career. It was sad, but there were crazy fans out there, everyone accepted that. And who was more entitled to have the craziest, the most outré fans, than me? I was on the way to becoming one of the biggest stars on the planet.

The night I won the Oscar was confirmation. My acceptance speech was famed for its brevity and feigned humility which, in a ceremony in which the unctuous were common, was in itself enough to create headlines. I dedicated the statuette to Harris, "for his unending support," and the cameras zoomed in on his face, so I could see brimming tears. Then my own face in turn, which was undeniably beautiful.

For the ceremony we had chosen to wear matching rings, ostensibly to symbolise our working partnership, but in reality we knew it would generate speculation in the press. That had been Harris' idea. Again. The more we denied our relationship was anything other than platonic, the more it was seen as a confirmation. When you are famous, you enter a world of mirror logic. Nothing is as it seems. I thought of that afterwards, holding the statuette. It was heavier than I had imagined, but its gold remained gilt.

We moulded our own lives to match this artifice. We both had our teeth whitened and straightened. Harris had hair implants, for he was balding early. I bought a mansion in the Hollywood hills, a totem of my success, and nothing else. I certainly did not have time to stay there, nor the inclination. Harris found it more to his liking, but returned after a month.

"I was longing for a bit of cold and rain," was his only comment.

That was the first time we had been apart for any length of time, but not the last. We were drifting apart, you see, although I did not at first realise it. I was too busy staying in the lurching sequence of near-identical hotel rooms, flying to countries I would be unable to locate on a map.

In time, Harris did not accompany me at all. He remained at home and attended to my business affairs. Without his steadying influence I became lost in the series of roles I played, the wealth I earned, and the adulation I garnered. Yes, I was lost, and I realised it, and could do nothing about it.

By that point, we seldom saw each other, our only communication by email, or telephone. When we did meet, our conversation was stilted and the silences uncomfortable. We were becoming strangers again, so it was as if the years we spent together were undone. Neither of us dared say it, of course, but we had become employer and employee.

During one of our increasingly infrequent meetings, he confided he had fallen in love, news he broached with the fervour of an evangelical. His partner (as, for once, the passion was not one-sided, but reciprocal) was a carpenter. Their first encounter had been on the set of one of my films. I met his partner a few times. He was bearded, heavy-set and did not say a great deal. He smoked roll ups constantly. Their love was evident though, in that slightly nauseating manner of the newly infatuated.

Had we thought clearly, it would have been obvious this new relationship would cause problems. Were we not, after all A Power Couple in the eyes of the world? But I was too busy, and Harris too distracted by his romance.

It was not a surprise when Harris moved out of my apartment and into his partner's house, an ex-council property in a less than desirable part of the city. Its combined rooms were, I was told, smaller than a single room in my residence. Yes, he had gone downmarket. Not that he complained, for, after all, he could have bought an apartment of his own, had he chosen.

"It's cosy," he said. "Like a real home."

The implication being, my own was ersatz. In that he may have been correct. I sometimes think all Harris was ever looking for was someone to love, and I was only a displaced substitute.

His departure did not go unnoticed. There were articles in the press, with headlines such as 'What's up with Chelle?', invariably featuring an unflattering photograph of myself, at some moment when I had been caught unawares. There was talk of my 'mysterious relationship' with Harris. That we did not confirm or deny these stories was another miscalculation. We should have issued a statement to the effect that our relationship was over, but that we remained good friends and would continue to work together. It would have been the obvious move, an unremarkable, and, since no rancour was involved, rather dull story. Then it would have been forgotten.

Instead, what happened instead was this: Harris was photographed kissing his partner in public. The following day, it was on the front page of one of the tabloids, and gossip, both true and untrue, circulated around internet newsgroups. The day after, all the papers carried the story. *Chelle scorned. Chelle's heartbreak. Chelle's sham marriage.* This last despite the fact that we were not, had never claimed to be married. It was the rings, I suppose. It appeared in magazines. The same photograph, over and over. It had gone viral, long before the term was created. The accompanying stories carried barely concealed scorn, resentment and glee, borne, no doubt, by the way we had controlled the press, and my apparently unassailable rise to fame.

He telephoned me the day the photograph first made its appearance and, truthfully, I was not unduly concerned.

"It's a flash in a pan," I told him. Told myself. "There's no such thing as bad publicity, you always said so."

The story would not go away. It did what the deaths had not done: it tainted me. We kept our silence, then issued a curt press release stating it was a private matter. That did not make any difference. It was the silly season, news was scant, and our supposed breakup offered titillation. Worse than that, tales began to leak out about my background. Innocuous enough tales, but you could tell reporters were digging for dirt. Of course, my life was full of dirt, I had pulled myself up from it, I had clawed my way to the very top. That was the first inkling. The second was when I was turned down for not one part, but two, and with no explanation. That was when I knew: Harris had to go.

I cannot say he was not bitter. I cannot say he did not shout and swear and accuse me of betrayal. And it was betrayal, it's true, but I did not need him any longer, he had become a liability. So I fired him. I fired him and let it be known to the press I had fired him. From that moment the number of articles about me - us - grew greater than ever. Now though, the tone had changed: they were sympathetic, they talked of my terrible ordeal, of my despair, and then used the story to talk about other suspect showbusiness relationships, of which there were, and are, many. Now I was the trouper, the one who would not let it get me down, I would soldier on. Surely that explained my sometimes strained appearance.

I paid Harris a substantial sum, enough so he need never work again, but it was hush money. He knew too many secrets. I relied too on his remaining loyalty, and the fact he was in love.

Six months later he was dead. He had gone missing at first, in itself a warning. Then, weeks later, he was found at the foot of a bridge in his hometown, the place he always talked about so disparagingly. He must have travelled there especially to carry out the act. That is what I think, anyway.

It was suicide, of course, although there was no proof, no note left behind. I attended his funeral, but kept my distance, a veil drawn over my face so there would be less chance I would be recognised. Which of course I was. It would have been foolish to think otherwise. His partner was also present, standing by the graveside, looking grey and drawn. Later I found he had terminal cancer.

So all of it, the whole scandal, was just another death, or two deaths, to add to the tally. I sometimes wonder: did I wish them all dead? Perhaps. Perhaps I did. Did I blame myself? Naturally. I am not a monster, despite what people may say.

*

She's fading. It'll be a blessing in a way.

Do you think she hears us? She's smiling.

I wonder what's she's thinking? If she's thinking at all. There can't be much left of her left with the morphine.

You know what they say. Your life flashes before your eyes.

It'll be some life she's imagining, then, the amount of drugs being pumped into her. Here, don't you think she looks like someone? Someone famous?

*

Two weeks after I learnt of Harris' death, the voices began. His was the final sacrifice, you see.

I heard them in a restaurant, where I had been meeting my agent. I was in the toilet at the time. At first I imagined someone was in the cubicle alongside me, making conversation. There were five voices, and the voices were male. I was panicked by this, stupidly imagining I had somehow wandered into the men's toilets by mistake. But two women had been leaving as I entered and, as further confirmation, there was a sanitary towel bin alongside the toilet bowl. Then I thought perhaps they were workmen, but their talk was strange, and it overlapped, as though they were all speaking at once, but not to each other. Moreover, I could not make out what they were saying. Their voices seemed muffled, as if I was listening to a conversation in another room. At the same time they were there, most certainly.

When I hurried to finish my business though, and left the cubicle, the toilet was empty, there was no-one else there.

I ought to make the nature of my business clear here, for it involved rolled notes and white powder, and the jolting, chemical numbness that followed. So, although I imagined phantoms, or perverts, or crazed fans who had somehow followed me into the rest room, I told myself it was, in reality, a hallucination raised by my drug-addled mind.

"Are you all right?" my agent asked on my return. "You look as though you've seen a ghost."

Three days later it happened again, but this time I was in my own apartment, in my own bed. There was a man lying beside me. I could not see him or feel him, but I could hear him. Then a child's voice, a girl's. Once more I could not make out what was said, but the girl was crying. Do you remember my first role, the one in which I screamed so loudly? Well, true terror is nothing like that. It robs you of your voice, and your ability to move, so I could only lie there, listening to the whispers which receded, as though they and I were being pulled apart. Then one final word, clear as anything: "Daddy."

I could not sleep the rest of the night, so I rose and stood at the window, the one providing a panoramic view of the city, traced in sodium and dark. I slid the window back a crack to allow the night air to enter, and the noise and odours of the city, the rush of its cars, the slightly sour smell of fumes and the river, was a comfort. Since Harris had left, my apartment had seemed too big, too empty, no matter how often I held the parties for which I was famous but which, somehow, I never enjoyed. Out there in the city, like stray radio signals, came voices, snatches of phrases, solitary words, faint at first but increasing in strength, and I realised these were the city's voices, which I heard not with my ears but with my mind. And I knew too then that I was mad: that part seemed more than evident.

I was not mad. I was changing. Think of transmigrating souls, or chrysalides. Think of burnt offerings. Think of worship and jealous gods. Then think why you cannot turn your face to me, lest you be burnt by my cruel light.

It was only later I realised the voices were the thoughts of the people who loved me, or loathed me, who worshipped me or, sometimes, only knew of me. I was not yet at that time the most famous actress on the planet, but I had begun my ascent. While I was at first frightened, I grew to love those whispers that played out in the dark, those evasive thoughts I learned to dredge and untangle. For were they not companionship of a sort?

It is true that the higher you rise, the more rarefied you become. I fed on those emotions which contained their secrets, their fears, their sad expressions of love, and of hate; and I thought back to when I was like them, and how I had ascended beyond them. Did I not say I had grown terrible? Did I not say people worshipped me? And from their fear, from their worship, did I not grow greater, and stronger?

At a movie premier I willed the audience to stand up and applaud at the end, which they did – they rose, they clapped and they cheered. Their clapping grew more frenzied when I appeared, to acknowledge their applause. I was only partially human, almost floating across the cinema stage to take my bows. There was no lighting, but I stood as if caught in a spotlight: I cast my own radiance, you see.

That was the first true intimation of my power.

Whilst visiting a hospital (film crew in tow, one of those PR exercises designed to show how in touch you are with the common people), I raised a woman from the dead. Or, more accurately, I raised her from a coma. She had been found, homeless, on the roadside, and had been mistaken for a bundle of rags. She was not an old woman, but she was dying of cancer. I touched my fingers to her forehead and spoke her name, after which she opened her eyes and looked up to me, then rose and embraced me. The word miracle was uttered, more than once. I saw the awed and fearful way people looked. It was the strangest thing though: when I looked at her face, it was my own features that looked back, as though I stared into a mirror.

I grew bloated with power. When I walked, there were blue, flashing sparks of static. I had only to think, and it would be done. I had only to talk and people would listen. The world became something I could prod and manipulate, like the all-seeing gods toying with humans in those awful sword and sandals movies from the 1950s.

You know how it goes from there. You cannot fail to know.

One day, for reasons I still do not fully comprehend, I made a pilgrimage to the area where Harris had leapt to his death. He had not exaggerated when he spoke of the bleakness of the village in which he had grown up. It was remote and cold and so far from the lifestyle I now lived, it seemed alien; and yet at the same time it felt like home. I recalled the boat he had fancifully said had been beached in the centre of the village, but the village was far from the harbour and it would have required a flood of diluvial proportions to carry it there. At the time he had told me, I half-believed him.

It was only a small bridge, but it spanned a dizzying drop. My driver took me there and then I dismissed him, so I was alone. By way of tribute I carried a small bouquet of flowers and placed them on the wall of the bridge. The wind caught them and I watched them fall to the ground far below.

It had been nearly six months since Harris had died, and so much had changed since then. I stood there and looked around about. There were high, steep hills, and trees that somehow found a way to cling to their sides. A trickle of water – it could not be called a river – was visible below. A bird landed right alongside me. It was a crow. It perched there on the wall of the bridge and looked at me. I wondered for a moment if it controlled my actions, just as I controlled those of others, for I was filled with the sudden impulse to clamber up on the wall, to teeter at the top and launch myself into the air. Yet I would not fall, I would not. The air would support me, and the wind, so strong in this place. Death was beyond me now.

Death was for humans. And had I not become a goddess?

TWELVE

As a child, Harry often dreamt he was sitting on the summit of a tall pillar of rock. It was a stack eroded from the mainland, so it now stood alone in the sea, a home to gulls and guillemots which circled and shrieked incessantly around the crevices that hid their nests. The rock was real: children often dared each other to climb to the top, but it was too far from the mainland, it was too high and dangerous, and the water too deep, so no-one ever accepted the dare. Or they did, but found some excuse not to carry it out. Yet here he was, perched on the very top, with a fierce wind whipping past his ears and the sea far below crashing white against the rock's base.

"It all sounds very phallic to me," said his sister, when told about it. She had a better idea of where things were going than he did, though he at least had professed innocence on his side. "You'll see," she said. "I'm right. Just wait until your balls drop."

He did not argue with her. She had turned fierce in her teenage years, and dyed her hair impossible colours. She wore fishnet tights and black leather ballet pumps, and a hip-hugging skirt barely reaching her midriff. Everything was black with her, except her clarted-on makeup, which was white, and her lipstick, a blaring purple.

"My wee lass has turned into Elsa-fucking-Lanchester," was her father's sole comment.

Harry inherited none of her rebellion. As a teenager he grew quieter, more introverted, and wore clothes best worn by a middle aged man. That was his grandmother's influence: she had always been clingy to him, the youngest of the family.

"Don't let her bully you," Cathy had said. "You're too soft, that's your problem. There's not always going to be someone to stand up for you, you know."

In retrospect, he wondered if that had been a coded warning, because the very next day she ran away, off on some bus or other, away from the village, or she had hitched a lift somewhere, from an unfamiliar car, down the west coast, or into the cities, or even another country: she had the stamina for that.

In time, he would follow, though less dramatically, and found himself in a guarded life far from the one he imagined. He sometimes wondered if her life had also attenuated so radically, into routine.

"When I grow up I'm going to be a Hollywood actress," she had often said.

The first time she told him, he was too young to know what a Hollywood actress was, so he replied, "I'm going to be one too," and she had teased him, though at the time he had not known why. Odd, how he remembered that scene, out on the lawn playing with Cathy, while Kathleen lay stretched flat on the grass, barefoot, laughing at them each in turn.

"I hope you'll remember your favourite sister when you become a star. And you'll introduce me to the most famous actors in Hollywood."

Kathleen had the most beautiful long blonde hair, he remembered that. He remembered that, and her hands that would lift him, but oddly, he could not recall her face, and later in life there was not even a photograph to remind him. His grandmother would have all those, he supposed.

Yes, poor Kathleen. Those dreams certainly had not come true for her. Nor had his, were he truthful.

In Israel, there is a pillar near Mount Sodom, said to be Lot's wife. It stands high up, looking down on a landscape heat-blasted and barren, leading down to the Dead Sea. The pillar is made of salt, that most sterile yet most necessary of substances. From certain angles it resembles a woman dressed in robes, her arms at her sides and her head tilted slightly, as if caught in the act of turning. It overlooks the saline sweat of the sea, its creator. Yes, it looks like a woman, but seen from a different perspective it resembles nothing more than a misshapen lump of rock. Its territory is barren and dangerous, but also beautiful.

Cathy had a passion for eyeliner. He sat alongside her in the bedroom while she took the stubby kohl pencils and drew a heavy rim around her eyes, sharp at the corners.

"Geisha eyes," she said.

Once she kohled his eyes too and the two of them went out, giggling, down the village street, even though there were disappointingly few people to see them. Their grandmother did though, when they returned, and she made him wash his eyes with soap until every trace of the makeup had gone and they were instead red-rimmed and bloodshot.

"That's no way for a boy to behave," she had said, and stood there with her arms folded, wearing an expression of disapproval that did not allow for any argument.

"You look like a fish that's been taken out of the water." Cathy found the whole affair enormously amusing and he wondered whether she had done it deliberately. She had taken up smoking and hung out her bedroom window, blowing grey jets into the night air. Her habit of nervously flicking her cigarette sent brief sparks into the dark.

He lay back on the carpet and spread out his arms and pretended he could feel the whole world spinning.

"Eight hundred miles an hour."

He had not meant to say it out loud.

"What?"

"Eight hundred miles an hour. That's how fast the world spins. I read it at school today." He was silent for a moment. "How fast does dad's train go?"

"It's not his train, silly. It's the railway's. But that old heap of shit? Sixty miles an hour, if it's lucky."

"It seems really fast though. It seems sometimes like the whole train's going to come apart, it's so quick. And that's only sixty miles an hour, Cathy. If the world's spinning at eight hundred miles an hour, why don't we fall off?"

"Oh, I fell off years ago. You will too, if you've any sense."

In summer, when the weather was good, and his father was not working, the whole family would go down to the beach. It was formed of shingle, so they took blankets to sit on, or perched instead on outcrops of stone. They took sandwiches and lemonade in glass bottles and a can or two of beer for his father. Harry and Cathy stripped down to their bathing clothes, and ran out into the water, leaving Kathleen to watch. The sea was always bitter, even on the hottest days, so mostly Harry paddled in the shallows: further out waited clumps of seaweed unpleasant to wade through, and beyond the seaweed the water became much deeper, and was much too cold and dangerous to swim in.

"Maybe when you're older," his grandmother said. "But the tide's too strong for a young boy like you. The sea could sweep you right out, just like that. I've seen it happen."

He looked at the deepening water, the sudden lurch from green to black, and never felt the temptation to go out there. He knew his grandmother was telling the truth. That did not stop Cathy though: she would swim above the seaweed, and kick out beyond, swimming as far as she could go, until her grandmother or father or sister saw her, and shouted to her to come back in.

"You'll get yourself killed, lass," his father would say, but there was almost a note of pride in his voice when he said that. Harry always wondered if he should follow her one day, out into the expanse where the sea grew choppy, but he was too afraid. He had been out on boats, and looked down into the water, its depth making him giddy, and felt he would fall. Given the opportunity, his sister would have stripped to her knickers and plunged right in.

After the accident, or at least that was how they referred to it, they did not go down to the beach at all, at least not as a family: sometimes he and Cathy went, but there was always that memory before them, and they would talk in a muted fashion, or too loudly, and once Cathy ran along the beach calling her sister's name, as though she would somehow answer through the beat and crash of the waves. In later years, she often had her boyfriend in tow, so it was different, even though she never discouraged him from following, and he felt the difference in their ages keenly: he had not yet made the leap towards adulthood she had.

One day, he went alone to the beach, removed his clothes and swam in the sea. It was early morning and the day was cool, the water glacial, but he did not stop. He swam towards and over the barrier of seaweed, to the water beyond. The tides pulled and were strong, but he continued on. He swam out until he could no longer feel his body and a terrible pain rose and filled his head; then he grew afraid and returned to shore, standing juddering on the wet stones, looking out at how far he had gone. It was not far at all.

That night he dreamed he was atop the pillar of rock again, and he did not dare look down, in case he would fall.

He left the village on a bus, his few belongings stowed in a suitcase in the hold. He could have taken the train, but his father was the ticket collector, and his resolve would crumble if his father was there: he would have to say goodbye to him at the station, before heading for the next connection. Although he had said he did not want anyone to see him off, Edward had been waiting, still dull-eyed from their drinking session the night before. They hugged a little too long, and they saw the bus driver watching.

"You take care of yourself. And keep in touch."

Those had been Edward's parting words, and then he did not wait for the bus to drive off, but only stood until Harry had found his seat by the window, before turning away quickly. The bus revved as it pulled free from the stop, stalling at first, and then the village streets were drawn past him and he looked at them with a numbed longing. He did not want to leave. He did not ever want to return.

The journey would take five hours and then there was another fifteen hours after that, one terminus to the next. The seat beside him was empty, so he spread out the contents of his bag. A book; two sandwiches; cans of lemonade; an apple and a banana. It struck him he had packed the same provisions he would have taken for a day out on the beach.

"You're Andy's lad, aren't you?"

A woman leaned across the aisle towards him. He recognised her, dimly: a wizened, puckered face, and sharp blue eyes.

"Aye that's right."

"I thought I knew you. My, how you've grown. It's not so long ago you were just this wee thing in shorts, running around the streets with the other laddies." She did not introduce herself. "Off on a holiday, is it?"

"A bit longer than that. I've a job in Weybridge, and this is me heading on down there. I'll not be seeing the village for a long while."

"Och, that'll be grand for you. Though it's terrible how all the young ones are heading away now. Just your dad and nan left now, is it? They'll miss you, they will."

"It's not so bad. I'll keep in touch, and there's the phone too, I'll call them regular to let them know how I'm getting on."

"Aye, aye." She leaned back and hauled out ball of wool impaled by two knitting needles. "The world's not as big as it used to be."

He looked back at the village, but could not see it at all now.

"It's still big enough," he said, and there was a sickish feeling in his stomach as he said it.

He remembered being dandled on his mother's lap, the pattern of her dress and bare knees, and her hands and arms that lifted him, pale even in the hottest weather, as though her skin refracted the sun. He remembered that, and did not think it imagination, although Cathy told him it was.

"That's just silly. Who can remember that far back? It's something you've made up and told yourself it's real."

Later, he would realise the hostility in her tone was really directed at their mother, for having dared leave them orphaned, or as good as, anyway. It was only in retrospect he understood the true reason for his mother's pallor, the sickness that was never far away, and was never named.

"She always had one foot in the other world." Who had said that? He could hear the voice but not place the face. That had been at his mother's wake. He and Cathy had not been allowed to go to the funeral, but he remembered all the people gathered in the house afterwards, the smoke and smell of drink in the air, and how his father had passed out at the back door, found lying face down in the coal scuttle.

"Aye, she'd always a bit of the ghost in her, she did. Not so much when she was young, but later you could see it coming through. I think having the bairns fair took it out her."

The strangeness of that moment, with the sadness in the air and scraps of her life revealed in conversation. He went up to his bedroom and Cathy came with him and they looked through old picture books they had been given, drawn into the warmth and surety of an earlier time. Their mother was dead but she was not dead, her memory a living presence in the rooms and the objects they contained, in her clothes which still hung in the wardrobe, as though she would one day come to claim them.

"You look like your mother," he was told. And sometimes, it was true, when he saw his reflection, there was the echo of his mother's face there.

Cathy was watching at the moment of his first proper kiss, standing high on the braes and hidden, so she could look down, but they could not easily see her. It was almost a chaste kiss, because their fear prevented anything more. When it was done, they drew apart, and they were flushed, and Harry found himself shaking, and he had an erection. That was when he saw her, far above, hands on hips, almost hidden amongst the yellowed gorse, but it was too distant to see the expression on her face clearly. They drew quickly apart, and it was an admission of their guilt.

On the way home she said, "You might have given him a decent snog at least. That's the sort of peck you'd give your aunty when she was visiting."

He did not say anything. It had begun to rain and the rain had turned heavy, and they were walking back along the track through the field to their house, which had turned to mud. They did not have coats, so the rain soaked them right through. Cathy had started wearing her hair in spikes, reinforced with gel, and the rain made them wilt and fall down her face. Her makeup ran and left black streaks down her cheeks.

"You know the first lad I kissed? It was Davie. We'd been drinking cider up the river and I was a wee bit tipsy." She paused, ruminative. "Don't you ever touch drink, Harry. It's a terrible thing and makes the ugliest of laddies seem attractive."

"Davie? Really?" Intrigued, despite his reticence.

"Aye. He offered me a pound too, if he could put his hand down my pants, but I wasn't *that* drunk."

She ran on ahead, and splashed through puddles, like the child she really was. "There, that's made you laugh. You've a face on you like a horse this afternoon." She turned and walked back to hug him. "Don't worry. I won't tell. Though maybe next time it's better not do it on a hillside in full view of everyone, eh?"

The last day, the day before she left, or ran away, or disappeared, or whatever had happened to her, she had been crying. He asked what was wrong.

"Go away," she said. "I don't want you to see me like this."

In other words, she did not want him to see she was weak, to see the façade behind the made-up, snarled veneer.

That was the last he saw of her.

"I'm going to get married one day," he once said; and he did. "And I'm going to have three children, two girls and a boy," and he did. Cathy had laughed when he told her that. He lived with his wife and children in a red-stoned Georgian house that cost more money than he had ever dreamed he would earn and he had his own business which, if not thriving, was enough to allow him and his family to comfortably survive. He loved his wife in a way. He had grown used to the town with its lack of green spaces, and the noise that never quite subsided, and the heat that grew unbearable during the summer months. His accent had softened, and had grown proper, so people imagined he had been born in the area, and were surprised when told where he had originally come from.

Often at night he dreamt he was stranded on the tall pillar of rock again, with the sea far below, its crash and engulfing roar. He woke shaking, his wife asleep alongside him, and he was thinking of Cathy. He was thinking of the village. He was thinking of his father and mother, of Kathleen, and his grandmother. He was thinking, above all, about Edward; and he was filled unexpectedly with a terrible, terrible longing to return to the place he had once called home.

THIRTEEN

Three years to the day after my mother died, the kittens were born: five in all, firstborn to runt, each one clarted with viscous, yellowed slime. They had the alarming frailness common to all newly born creatures, eyes glued shut and their thin, matted legs reaching upwards when Missy, their mother, cleaned them. She cleaned them until they squealed, and they began to resemble the fluffed, helpless creatures we had anticipated. When, exhausted, she lay back and bared her teats, the kittens hauled themselves forward towards her, catching on the blanket on which she had given birth, following a pre-programmed instinct we all marvelled at. Suckling temporarily halted their cries, which were sharp and distressed, and which cut the silence of the house, which that day was fragile.

Despite the excitement of the births, our grandmother forced us to follow her determined, humdrum routines. She had greyed hair and large, knotted hands that had begun to twist with arthritis. In later years, I remembered those hands and thought them a perfect expression of her personality. She talked constantly about the past, and embarrassed my father by telling us what he had done when he was younger. None of the tales recounted were flattering. "One eye in the present, one in past," was my father's description of her.

Now she was trying to remember how many kittens had been in the first litter she had seen born.

"There was the tortoiseshell one...and the black one...two ginger ones. One of those was Hound. We had him for nearly twenty years. He was such a lovely cat." She trailed off, having forgotten what she was talking about in the first place. "What was I saying?" She pushed her glasses back onto the ridge of her nose, as was her habit.

"You were talking about Hound. Why did you call him that?" Kyrie, my sister, was good at feigning interest she seldom felt.

"Oh, he hounded us. Never left us alone. He was one of those cats that is very insecure. Though you'd never think it to see him at first, he was all front. A bit like you, in fact."

My grandmother's mind may have started to wander, but she was always a good judge of character.

"What happened to the rest?" That was my question, because I was determined not to let Kyrie get all the attention. It was our constant game.

"My mother drowned them all, apart from one. There were nine of them, and it was such a strain on the mother. I cried and cried for days. She killed my favourite one, you know, the lovely little tortoiseshell."

I don't know if she realised she'd answered the question that had started her train of thought in the first place.

"That's horrible," I said.

"It was after the war, and we couldn't afford to keep them. Nobody had any money then. The one that was left, she was a little black and white one. We called her Lucky."

Kyrie looked up from where she was lying on her floor, on her stomach. "Because she was the lucky one. She'd survived."

"She was killed I remember. Hit by a car."

"That's so morbid." Kyrie giggled a little. "You're always talking morbid, granny."

Henry, our younger brother, began to cry.

"Cry baby." Kyrie pushed him to the floor, where he landed with an ungainly and painful thump. "That'll give you something to cry about."

That was one of our father's phrases.

"Ssh." My grandmother said, lifting and hugging him. "It was a long time ago. And you, Kyrie, don't be so spiteful. Just look, look at the lovely kittens we have now."

We watched them, all of us, Kyrie, myself, Henry, and my father, watching in silence. I rubbed my eyes and found with surprise I too had been crying. None of us imagined that six weeks later all the kittens would be dead.

It started with a cough, one of those thin, sharp coughs cats have. Then it spread to a fever, first one kitten, then two, then all five curled up in their basket, all of them rheumy, fur matted, clinging to each other for a warmth they seemed unable to generate themselves. They shivered.

"They're going to die, aren't they?" Kyrie stood watching them, at a distance, as though their illness was catching.

"They're very ill, but they're strong creatures, cats. It's only the first of their nine lives. You'll see, they'll be all right". My grandmother wiped yellowed pus from the eyes of one of the kittens with a wetted tissue.

Kyrie looked unconvinced. You could always tell, because she made an exaggerated, lopsided droop with her mouth, which was intentional, and she played with her long, blonde pigtails, which was not.

"If they're still like this tomorrow, we'll take them to the vet." My grandmother threw the balled paper into the fire, where it hissed and sizzled. "Don't worry so much. You and your sister, you're standing there with faces like it's the end of the world."

It seemed like the end of the world. We had watched their eyes open, watched them grow, had watched their personalities emerge - timid, boisterous, bullying, attention seeking - and had chosen names to suit.

"I wish dad was here," I said. "He'd take them to the vet straight away."

Our father was away a great deal, leaving our grandmother in charge.

"It's late now – see how dark it is outside? You just can't turn up on the vet's doorstep, not at night-time."

We lived in the country, a long way from anywhere else. From our house, the lights in the village looked as distant as stars.

Seeing my expression, my grandmother added, "Your father would say the same thing. Go to bed, get a good sleep, and in the morning everything will be fine, you'll see."

We did as we were told. In the morning, they were dead, all five of them. Their bodies, still bundled together, had gathered into a hard, congealed lump. They had traces of vomit and blood around their mouths, and their bodies (which we were afraid to touch) had grown entirely cold.

"It was meant to be," our grandmother told us. "They had a happy life for the time they were here. Think of them all playing away in heaven."

Except I didn't believe in heaven. What's more, she had said almost the same thing when our mother had died. Was heaven so big that they could fit everyone in there?

"It'll be like the slums of Calcutta," Kryie said, "what with all those people crammed in."

She had seen a TV programme about Calcutta once, and was obsessed with the city.

Although we were upset about the kittens, we giggled, the two us, at the irreverence of the remark.

The kittens were placed in a cardboard box and buried at the foot of an apple tree at the bottom of the garden. We took turns digging the hole, because my grandmother said she didn't have the strength. Henry made a cross from two sticks bound with a length of string and we planted this on the kittens' grave while my grandmother said a mawkish prayer. Henry kept on crying and I could see Kyrie was shaking a little. I didn't feel anything, really, because I refused to let it affect me. Then it began to rain, those big, heavy drops that come in summer, and that drove us inside, back to the shelter of the house which now seemed disproportionately empty.

That was in the autumn. Browning leaves fell and covered the grave, leaving only the frail cross to act as a marker. For a while, we superstitiously avoided the spot, with its uneven ground the grass had not yet covered, clods of earth roughly battered down. Kyrie would go there sometimes, standing at a distance, to watch. She had an abstracted look at those moments, not unhappy, but remote. I wondered what she was thinking, but never asked. The Kyrie I knew was sardonic and cutting and a little bit fragile. I didn't understand the dreamy, abstract person she was becoming.

That was Kyrie. I just avoided the place altogether. Henry was always there, but that was because he forgot. "Henry!" we would shout when he went too near the grave. "The kittens!" Then he would come running back, chastened, and a little frightened. He flapped his arms when he ran, like wings. I sometimes wondered if he was a bit soft.

Autumn turned to winter. The permafrosted ground lessened the threat somehow, made the area less untouchable. When it snowed, you would hardly know there was anything there at all. One time we were in the garden, Kyrie and me, hurling snowballs at each other. A near-miss made me slide and I landed on top of the cross, which cracked beneath my weight. I barely noticed, too intent on rising to my feet, clothes crusted white along my underside, determined to avenge myself on my sister. She had braided blue taffeta through her pigtails, the cold had brought a brash colour to her cheeks, and she was laughing. My grandmother stood in the doorway, watching us, too afraid to risk the treachery of the slippery ground, but she laughed as well, and it was genuine laughter, which was rare for her.

That moment felt like a breakthrough somehow. There was very little to distract us in that place, which was so far from anywhere. We only had each other and, once that unity had been broken, it felt as though we had nothing.

I loved those clear, starry winter nights. One time, when Henry had been upset, I pointed up to the stars and told him that's where the kittens were, up in the sky. "See them twinkling? That's them saying hello."

"I liked the kittens," he said. "I miss them."

"It was just their time, that's all. See how happy they are. They're so sparkly and bright."

I felt very grown up saying these things. Though the thing is, once I'd said it, I could almost see it, half believed it: up from the ground to sky, forming playful configurations.

That was the winter. By the time summer came around again, the kittens were a painless memory. It was something that had happened a long time ago. Grass grew to cover the grave's disturbed earth and the apple trees flowered, fragile, momentary blooms that would turn in time to small, hard fruits we would leave to fall and feed the birds. That year, when they arrived, the apples were covered with a greyish blight and they dropped to the ground unripened, as if even the tree could not bear to hold them any longer.

"Your mother was the gardener," my grandmother said, "she would have known what to do about this. Though the tree itself looks healthy enough." She stood on her tiptoes and pulled down one of the lower branches, looking for an infestation that may have caused the problem. "Maybe it's just one of those things. It's been a miserable summer."

As indeed it had, overcast most days when it had not been actively raining.

"It's going to be a bad winter, you mark my words. Bad summer, bad winter, they go hand in hand. Always have done. I'll get your father to make sure you have plenty of warm clothes stocked up."

We saw more presents from our father than we saw him: a parcel would arrive every few weeks, from some exotic location I had never heard of. "He's visited every country in the world, you know," Kyrie once boasted to one of the few friends she had made. Truthfully, we seldom knew where he was exactly – the names on the cards and the words spoken on telephone calls were phantoms, and we could not mentally match them to the places we saw on maps.

Even the birds refused to touch those apples. They lay there and browned and softened and collapsed inwards. My grandmother gathered them all up with a spade and deposited them beside the wall at the back of the garden, a spot overgrown with docks and nettles. No-one went there, not even Kyrie and me in our expeditions of play exploration. That was the place of stinging things, the part of the garden where wasps built their nests and there were sudden, frightening movements in the long grass. The movements (I suspected with an unvoiced horror) may have been rats attracted to the thin stream of water that ran past our garden's boundaries. There, spiders built arcing webs to catch the many fat, somnolent bluebottles that gathered and bred in thick clusters. I avoided that area if I could. We all avoided that area. It seemed cursed.

One day, as the second winter was drawing in, Missy went missing. Mainly a house cat, she never ventured far, too fond of the house's warmth and companionship. She was one of those cats who doted on attention, stretching out to get her white, heavily furred tummy rubbed, or that special spot that induced dribbles of ecstasy, right behind her ears. Three weeks she was missing. We searched the garden, calling. We checked places where she might have been locked in – the empty garage, the spare room where all the junk was stored, the old stables at the side of the house that our father promised one day would be renovated, but which were gradually collapsing inwards, dangerously.

"Don't worry," our grandmother said. "She's probably off hunting. Cats do that sometimes, they get a scent of the wild, and forget they're domesticated."

This only made me worry more. Our grandmother's reassurances always made us think about the very things we were trying to forget. When our mother had grown ill, she had told us everything would be all right and just from that simple statement we knew her illness was very serious indeed. So it was with Missy. I would wake at night and look out my bedroom window, to see the grass frosted, and imagined her out there somewhere, in the cold.

One morning I woke and thought I had heard her crying: it must have been imagination, because on waking there was nothing to be heard, apart from the sound of the sea, which carried inland on the coldest nights. Still, I rose, while the others slept, wrapped myself up in my thick parka to keep the numbing air at bay, and walked into the garden with its hardened ground, a chill mist hanging low, and searched and called for Missy. It didn't seem quite real, in that place, at that time, barely light, bitter enough to keep all other life hidden.

"Missy," whispered at first, and then realising the others were unlikely to hear, "Missy! Missy!"

I found her at the bottom of the garden, at the spot we avoided. She walked out of the sculpted grass, strangely cowed and a little afraid of me when I moved. It was as though she had forgotten who I was. I lifted her, and she growled at first, then settled in my arms as though resigned.

"Ssh," I said. "It's all right, you silly cat. What are you doing out here all alone?"

She answered by burying her head in the folds of my jacket. She was shivering, but I wasn't sure if something had scared her, or if it was the cold.

"Did you have something here? Were you hunting, is that what it is?"

I brushed aside the grass with my foot. It made the sound of paper being crushed.

There, in the grass, were bones. Hundreds of bones, all delicately thin, and white. There were leg bones and thin skulls and collapsed lines of vertebrae. There were scraps of what looked like long perished fur, ground up with once mudded earth, now frozen.

"Have you been hunting mice, is that it? Or rats?"

She answered by burrowing further into the folds of my coat.

"It's all right now, we're going home."

I kicked aside the bones and fur. The fur was ginger and black and white and grey.

"Giving us all a scare like that."

We headed back to the house where warmth, then later a scolding, awaited the two of us.

"Fancy going out into the garden in the middle of the night," my grandmother said. "You'll catch your death, carrying on like that."

I didn't mind the telling off. I was glad to have Missy back. We all were, because the unspoken assumption had been she was lost forever.

Only afterwards did it occur to me the bones I found may have been the kittens'. Maybe something had dug them up. Maybe some freakish movement of the ground had made them resurface elsewhere. What I couldn't shake was the idea that they had been absorbed into the tree, into the spoiled fruits and, when they had fallen, they released the bones to sink once again into the soil. I never told anyone that, not even Kyrie. I was afraid she would laugh at me, though, thinking about it now, it was probably the sort of idea she would have approved of. Like me, she was always that way inclined.

Those cold, frosted mornings marked the start of the winter. It was the worst any of us could remember. Even my grandmother said she had known nothing like it. Snow fell so heavily it accumulated to a level where it completely blocked the back door, where it had drifted. The front door was still passable, but when we went out into the garden, it was to sink deep to our waists in a soft, powdery accumulation. Usually snow arrived as a thin scuff over the ground: we had never seen it fall in such quantities. It was exciting at first; and we spent hours outdoors, all of us, wrapped up well as protection against the cold. I say all of us, but my father was away, as usual, and my grandmother peeked anxiously out the doorway, too afraid to venture out, in case she fell.

"Once upon a time I would have. These days I'm too afraid to risk it."

Her fear must have been feigned, for I cannot think of anyone of my grandmother's age more physically capable.

The roads were blocked, and the schools closed. It was exciting, and it was liberating. When the phone lines went down and the television went off the air, we discovered tedium: then when the electricity failed, the days became endless, and unending. The snow stopped falling, the sky became the bitterest blue, and the temperatures fell and fell until it hurt to even venture outdoors, because the air stabbed and scraped at our lungs. We had coal and wood, so there was still warmth, but it did not radiate beyond the room in which the fire was burning. There was food, because our grandmother stockpiled tinned and dried supplies for just this sort of eventuality. Any frozen food we buried outdoors, into the snow, where it was so cold it remained frozen, because the sun had no warmth, even though it shone. We wore double layers of clothing and discovered ways to pass the time: I Spy and Hide and Seek. We found old, boxed games hidden in cupboards. We rediscovered conversation. Kyrie wrote a play, which we performed, the three of us, for my grandmother's entertainment. And finally, finally, we submitted once again to boredom.

"It's like being in the war," my grandmother remarked, but did not elaborate further, as though we somehow shared her childhood memory of those years.

Boredom drove us to irritation, small squabbles that led to fights, and then sulking, so we took refuge in our individual bedrooms where even the chill was preferable to the bickering and studied indifference I knew would take place in each other's company.

"Will you children calm down?" said my grandmother. But separation was the only way to calm us. It was as if the winter had woken an unsuspected frenzy: we wanted to go out, but it was too cold out. It was too cold in. I would curl up in bed, only the tips of my fingers poking out, enough to hold a book, to read, until that too became a source of boredom.

My response, our response, was to sleep. We slept a great deal, all of us. We were captive to the winter and the lack of warmth and the dark: it was no longer a novelty. Instead it was misery. (That was my grandmother's word, "misery", all thoughts of wartime-like camaraderie now forgotten). Even sleep provided no real escape. I would wake in the dark, in the middle of the night, and lay there, too chilled to rise, but unable to rest. Sometimes I called out for Missy and she would come, slipping from one bedroom to the next, crawling beneath the bedcovers to curl up tight beside me, purring, stealing some of the heat from my body.

It was on one of these nights I first heard the scratching. The still, frozen air carried sound from miles away – as it would have to, because we were miles from anywhere – and at first I imagined this the source of the noise. I could think of no explanation for its occurrence though: it was too inhospitable, surely, for anything to venture out. When we had gone to bed the thermometer had registered a temperature of minus twenty five.

"That's never right," my grandmother said, "surely not."

Except it was: you could tell from the leeched glow of the landscape, a bluish luminescence that corroded the darkness, even with the absolute absence of obvious light.

So no, nothing would be out in that. But still. Scratch. Scratch. Scrabble.

My bedroom door opened.

"Do you hear that?" It was Kyrie, sneaking into my bedroom with studied caution, a blanket wrapped around her body for warmth, though she still went barefoot. "It woke me up."

"I was awake anyway."

We spoke in whispers, alarmed and giggling, animosity forgotten. Why we were giggling, neither of us could have said.

"I think it might be rats."

"Here? In the house?" Kyrie said this not with alarm, but enthusiasm.

"No. It's outside. Or I think it's outside."

We listened to the sounds, faint but distinct.

"Poor things, out there in the cold." We looked out my bedroom garden, out into the garden, but nothing appeared to be moving.

"Let's go downstairs," Kyrie suggested

We didn't even discuss the matter. Boredom, as I say. We descended the stairs with a deliberate theatricality, aware of each creak and crack, our breath suspended between each footfall. The house shifted, it sighed, protesting against the drop in temperature which grew greater as we descended, so we shivered uncontrollably by the time we entered the living room.

The source of cold came in large part from wide glass windows that had been fitted in the room, the sort that slide aside to let in the warm light of summer, a prospect that seemed as distant as my grandmother's nostalgic memories. Now the windows were sealed by a rim of ice formed around the metal frame, thawed a little in the daylight and then refrozen, so it created an elaborate, deadly frieze.

Through the glass the garden was blue-white and it seemed to generate its own luminescence, even though there was only starlight, so many stars, more than I had ever seen before, poking through the sky's blackness.

Kyrie pressed her face to the glass, then withdrew it quickly. "That's freezing," she said, "it made my skin stick to it."

There was the imprint of her features on the glass, slowly fading.

"Did you see anything?"

"Nothing. There's nothing out there."

I peered through the glass as well, but at a distance, eager not to make my sister's mistake. The garden was still, and silent. "Let's wait for a little while. Maybe the noise will come again."

We curled up together, under the blanket Kyrie had carried down with her. The quiet was alarming but exciting too. I wrapped my arms around my sister. There was nothing to her, all angular bone with a thin layer of flesh.

"That's nice," she said. "I feel almost warm."

As she said this, for a moment, from the corner of my eye, I thought I saw a movement, something darting across the snow.

"No, I didn't see anything," said Kyrie, anticipating my question.

"I thought I saw..."

"But I did have my eyes closed." She curled up into a tight foetal knot inside the blanket. "I could sleep. If it wasn't so cold. I'm tired of the cold."

We pressed together, for the warmth of each other's bodies, and remained that way, in silence.

"Do you ever think about mum?" Kyrie's voice, barely a whisper.

"Sometimes. I think about when she was well. I like to remember her that way."

"I think about her all the time. I *really* miss her. I miss her coming to bed to kiss me goodnight, and in the morning I almost expect her to be there when I come downstairs."

"She's our mum. We're always going to miss her. Even after nearly five years."

"It was so horrible what happened."

"She's in a better place now. She'll be up there in heaven." I remembered my conversation with Henry, and the lie it had seemed.

"I don't believe in heaven" said Kyrie, flatly.

"I'm not sure I believe in it either. She'll be there though, if there is one."

Kyrie began to cry, although there were no tears. Her whole body trembled. It wasn't just the chill that did it.

"Ssh. Let it all out." Another second hand phrase.

"I miss her. I wish I was with her."

"Ssh."

I held her until she fell asleep, and then I fell asleep too. Later, we woke in the darkness, heading up to our rooms before the others rose.

"Wake up."

It was the following night. Kyrie stood by my bed, shaking me. She had an alarmed, slightly bewildered expression.

"What is it?"

"Don't you hear?"

Yes, I did hear. It was faint but clear, the sound of cats mewling.

"It's not Missy, is it?" Because we kept Missy in at night, after the time she went missing; and besides it was too inhospitable for any animal to go out. We had seen the litter of birds that lay frozen on the ground in the morning.

"No, she's in my bedroom, under the covers."

I rose. There it was again: definitely a cat meowling. A cat or perhaps even cats? Was that two calls I heard, simultaneously?

"Poor creatures." Kyrie peered out my bedroom window, which overlooked the garden, to see if she could see anything outside. She had done the same thing the previous night, and I had a giddying sense of déjà vu.

We took it for granted we would descend the stairs together once again, equally fearful of being discovered, too aware of the creak of floorboards and the house's distress as it weathered the arctic temperatures. The living room was brighter than the night before: a sliver of moon lit the snow as brilliantly as if it was daylight.

Kyrie had gone a little ahead of me. When I entered the room, she was staring, she was pointing, she was crying.

"Look," she said. "They've come back." She pointed through the glass. "The kittens," she said. "The *kittens*."

There was nothing. There was light and snow and a still, terrifying chill. But there was no movement whatsoever.

"You're imagining things," I said. Then, with less certainty, "Where?"

She pointed through the window. "Stop pretending, Cinth. You can see them. You *can*." She shook, and began to cry. "There's the little black and white one. She's coming up to the window. Let her in, she must be so cold."

There was the snow's still silence. There was ice, traced around the edges of the window.

"Poor things. Poor, poor things."

"Kyrie, you're scaring me."

"And there's the ginger one, running through the snow after her."

I didn't see anything. Perhaps I was afraid something would be there.

"Why don't you *look!*"

I did, I swear. I told Kyrie I was looking, that I saw nothing.

"Help me open the window. Come ON!"

I drew back, though. I retreated into the room's shadows, away from the window. I was scared, you see, by the possibility.

"Don't," I said. "It might be dangerous."

"Dangerous?" her voice rose. "How can it be dangerous? They're kittens. They're *our* kittens."

"Our kittens are dead, Kyrie. We buried them. You were there."

"But they're back. If you'd look, you would see."

Did I hear scratching on the glass? Did I hear a meow, almost inaudible? In retrospect, I almost imagine I did.

"Come back to bed. You're tired. You're not thinking straight."

Kyrie shook her head. "I want to watch them. You go. I'll be ok." There was a calm determination in her voice now.

"Kyrie, please – "

"I'll be fine. Leave me alone."

To my shame, I did.

How did I sleep after that? I can only think it was to escape. You can do that, sometimes. I was freezing, I was tired and I was bewildered. I have never mentioned what happened that night, not to my family. Not to anyone. It's not that I worry about being believed. It was the guilt and the blame. I have to live with the former, but the blame, I couldn't live with that as well.

It was my brother who made the discovery in the morning. He had risen while the rest of us slept, and saw the hummocked shape in the garden. The living room was beyond frigid: the door had been slid aside, somehow, and had been left open. There were no footsteps in the snow: it was too solid to register any passage of movement. The day was bright and still, and silent. Nothing living dared go out in that. My brother did though, drawn by curiosity. I would have remained indoors; I would have guessed and would not have dared. I try not to imagine the scene, though it always comes: him, curious, shivering, shielding his eyes from the cruel, reckless sun which turned everything overbright and deadly.

Kyrie lay beneath the rowan tree. She still had her pyjamas on, and a blanket wrapped around her thin body. Her face – I hope this was true – was smiling. Her skin was blue and, in places, edged with black.

"She could have been sleeping" my grandmother said. "She could have been, yes, lying there on her side. She looked so peaceful. I thought at first, I thought maybe she was."

In private, I hear her skin had torn when they had to prise her from the ground. Her clothes had welded to the ice and to her body. The cold disoriented her, they said, and she had wandered out. It was a tragedy. Perhaps that was true. Perhaps, then, I have only myself to blame. I cling to one hope though: all around her there were bones, thin and white and fragile. There were bones, and she was holding on to them, and they said she must have unearthed them somehow, dug them up from the earth with her hands, even though

284

the ground was so hard even a spade would not have broken it. There were bones, and she was smiling, and that is the thing that haunts me, that I can't forget.

That house, it was a house of memories. I was glad when I left it, and what remained of my family, and left the village forever.

FOURTEEN

The men gathered on the railway platform, five in all, in boilersuits and station uniform: Lewis, Davie, Lechie, Iain and Tavis. They smoked cigarettes, spat, chewed sandwiches meant for lunch, read the sports pages of the papers, or examined the page three girl with clinical appreciation.

"Her tits are lopsided. See?" Lewis angled the newspaper to allow Lechie a clearer look.

"She was on Wogan last night. I'm telling you, she's a looker. Not the brightest though."

"Aye, says mister Albert-fucking-Einstein there."

"And she'd be talking with her mouth full?"

"You're a dirty minded cunt, Lechie."

It was still early morning, the sun barely risen, and a chill remained in the air.

"Hurry the fuck up, will you?"

Davie said this to no-one in particular, but instead to the empty length of track ahead. It led from the station, under a bridge and then into the density of trees.

"It'll come when it comes. That's the problem with you young ones, you want everything now. It's the instant-fucking-gratification generation, isn't it?" Lewis hunkered down alongside Davie, who sat on his kit bag. He pointed down the railway track. "Here he is now, walking down the middle of the line as usual. It's just as well the train's not behind him."

"Is he sober?"

"It'll be a first if he is. You didn't see him the other morning, he could hardly fucking stand."

The sight silenced the group, who watched the man's slow lumber, his heavy limp and bowed head as he watched where he placed his feet on the tracks. When he reached the concrete platform, he stopped to light a cigarette, then stepped onto the ramp and continued down the platform towards them.

"Lads."

"Aidan."

He carried on into the station, and emerged some time later, holding a ticket machine in his one good hand.

"Though I don't know why I bother. It's not exactly crowded, is it?" Aidan gestured with his other arm. He had no hand, only a rounded stump that stopped just above where his wrist would have been.

"Aye, not a soul. Peak season too. We'll not fucking last long at this fucking rate." Lewis stood up. "I can hear her coming, lads."

The train rounded the corner, and settled at the platform. Its arrival startled crows which had built a nest in the station rafters, so they swooped and cawed above the men's heads.

"I told you we should have shot the bloody things, I could still manage it now, I reckon." Aidan looked up and stepped back to avoid a heavy gobbet of bird shit that landed by his feet. The men had moved ahead, none of them listening.

On the train, they settled as a group at the table nearest the front door of the first carriage. There was a woman at the far end, but otherwise it was empty. Aidan followed, and left his ticket machine sitting on their table, alongside their tool bags, and headed into the driver's cabin.

"Christ, he stinks today." Lewis scratched his thin, grey beard resignedly. "He's a fucking embarrassment, that one."

"Come on, he's had a hard life. You wouldn't wish that on anyone."

"You grew up with him, Lechie, you give him more slack than he deserves."

"What's this?"

"Ach, he's right, Davie," Lewis said. "You're too young to remember all that happened. I mean, a man has his share of fucking misfortune right enough, but he's had a lifetime of it. I'll tell you sometime, when he's not around."

The train pulled out of the station, past the junction, and into the trees. The men sat in silence and watched the land slope away down to the riverside, before it levelled out to fields on either side, sheep scattering at the train's approach.

"So what's on today then?" Lewis turned away from the window, back to the men.

"Still repairing that track up at the junction. Man, that last heavy rain fairly screwed it. We're talking weeks yet before it's fixed properly." Tavis spoke while picking at the hard skin on his hands, which were red and chapped.

"Aye, it's a tough job that one. And it'll not long be fixed before the next thing'll come along. That's fucking life for you, one thing after another." Iain pushed back in his seat, looked in his shirt pocket, counting the number of cigarettes he had left. He and Tavis were twins, but they did not look in the least bit alike.

"You're fair cheering me up today, you shower of miserable bastards." Do you want to know what I did last night? I met this girl Carol down at The Sharpies - "

The men cheered

"- and fair fit she was. She had this long blond hair, and her chest – man, it was out to *here* – "

"Is this one of your stories with a dirty ending, Davie?"

"Aye, well, maybe..."

"Here, my sister's family's up visiting, and my niece Carol was down at The Sharpies last night. I hope it wasn't her you were doing your wicked way with."

Davie looked at Lechie, aghast.

"I'm kidding man, no, my sister's not even up visiting at the moment. She does have a daughter Carol though, so..."

"Ach, you're not getting me twice like that. Once is enough. Though it was a good one, fair enough."

The train began to slow at the approach to a platform ahead. It was a plain concrete embankment on the sidings, with a structure that resembled a bus shelter for people to wait in.

"That'll be Mrs Taggart. I'd best go help her on." Lewis stood up to look out the window. "Because that cunt Aidan'll not see fit to do it."

"Aye, she's there, and two young lassies too. Backpackers by the look of it." Lechie peered out the window to get a better look.

"One doesn't have blonde hair, does she?"

"You're safe enough, Davie. They're not even legal, by the looks."

"Aye, well. I've not stooped that low. Here, you've got it wrong, here's Aidan now."

Aidan emerged from the driver's cabin. A smell of fresh tobacco smoke followed him. He picked up his ticket machine from the table then turned back to stand by the door.

The train drew to a halt. Aidan opened the door and stepped out.

"I'll still need to help Mrs Taggart." Lewis followed Aidan.

Lechie, seeing Davie's questioning look: "He's got an eye for the young girls, does Aidan"

"Aw, that's just sick, a man his age. He's old enough to be their grandfather, almost."

They watched him through the train window, offering to carry the girls' backpacks.

"Come off it man, you're barely fit to carry yourself, never mind those lassies' bags." Iain put his hands over his eyes in mock horror, then removed them again so he could have a proper look.

Lewis was on first, helping Mrs Taggart up the steps. She was a small woman, frail, her body bowed and shaking with a continual tremor. The two girls waited behind, then lost patience and walked the platform to the door at the other end of the carriage.

"Oh dear, I'm holding things up." Mrs Taggart shuffled past the men, Lewis leading, steadying her with his hand.

"Set yourself down there, Mrs Taggart. I'll get your bags for you."

He left her at a seat with a table, then reappeared carrying a tartan suitcase which he placed in the luggage rack.

"Going somewhere nice?"

"I'm off to see my son in Surrey. It's nearly two years last since I saw him last."

"That'll be a grand trip for you. It's a lovely place down there, I hear."

"Oh, I hope so. I'll maybe even see a bit of sun, eh?" She laughed at her own suggestion, looking up at him with dropsical eyes.

"Aye, that'll be a change. Well, you have a good holiday and say hello to Hugo for me. Have you someone meeting you at the connecting train?"

She shook her head.

"Leave it with me, I'll get something sorted for you."

"You're an awful good man, Lewis."

He walked into the driver's cabin, then reappeared a few minutes later to talk to Mrs Taggart, before returning to the table.

"Barry's going to radio ahead and get someone to help her at the other end. No point asking that useless cunt." He gestured at Aidan. "Look at him, trying to chat up those two lassies. He'll maybe get his finger out and collect the tickets at some point before we arrive."

"Calm yourself, man, mind your blood pressure. Here, have a look at the paper."

Lechie pushed a copy of the Record over the table towards him.

"Aye maybe."

He sat and lifted the paper, but kept peering over the top of it to see what Aidan was doing.

"There he goes, collecting the tickets now. He's maybe seen you glaring at him." Lechie was turned round in his seat, watching Aidan hurple down the aisle. "You'll notice he's not spending any time with any of the others. Here: he didn't even talk to Mrs Taggart when he took her ticket."

"I'm not fucking looking. You lads are just winding me up."

Aidan passed them, not speaking, and disappeared into the driver's cabin again.

The train sped through the countryside, its dull clatter and clack, rain falling heavily now, accompanied by a sharp squall. Lewis had folded the paper and was staring at his own reflection in the window. Davie opened his toolbag and was raking through it, intent.

Tavis announced, loud enough for the whole carriage to hear, "I could do with a shite."

Lewis had to rise to let him out, while at the same time the driver's cabin door opened, so Aidan stood behind them both, waiting to pass.

"It's as well I'm in no hurry," he said.

Lewis turned round to face him. "Aye, that'd be a first."

"You're not my boss, Lewis."

"That's easily seen. Here, just get on past, get out of my fucking –"

***

"It's a damn shame, that's what it is."

Lechie nodded at the gathered crowd. The men stood at the front of the graveside, apart from the rest of the mourners. They had just laid a wreath formed of carnations, in the shape of a train. The head office had sent it over.

"They've a fucking sense of humour, whoever thought of that one." Davie spat a wad of chewing gum down by his feet, along with a sizeable coating of phlegm.

"Here, mind your manners. It's a funeral we're at, not a night down at Sharpie's bar."

"I can't help it, Lechie. I'm gagging for a fag and we're stuck here in the fucking cold, and wet in our uniforms the chiefs said we had to wear, and there's no sign of the service even starting yet."

"I feel sorry for his mother. You don't expect to outlive your son, do you?"

"Don't you worry about her, Davie. Most of the family's a screw loose, you ask me, but she's hard with it. See, even after she had that win? She'd Bob's men do the house up before she moved into it, and she haggled them down so fucking low they were near making a loss. Aye, don't worry about that one, she can cope."

"Hold your tongue, Lewis. She'll be hearing you."

A large crowd had gathered with, further back, a few members of the press, their cameras ready. The story had made headlines in the Record and the P&J, and would again the following day, less prominently, on the inner pages, a black and white photograph taken from a distance, along with a few lines of text.

"Here Lewis, is that Aidan's laddie? He's fair spruced himself up if it is."

"Aye, that's Hugh. He came back up for the funeral. No sign of the lassie though."

"Och, that one, she was fair weird anyhow with her makeup and thon clothes she used to wear. Though, mind you, all the lassies dress like that these days. Aye, anyhow, you'll not be seeing her, I mean, who's to say she's even still alive?" Lechie scanned the crowd, as though she would suddenly appear, doubting his own words.

"Did you not hear, Iain thought he saw her on the telly?" said Tavis.

"What, on the news, picked up for soliciting?"

"No, genuine like. He was watching some late night programme, and she'd this wee part in it. He's sure it was her. Is that not right, Iain?"

"Aye, right enough. I mind her for sure. Her or her fucking double. She'd didn't speak or anything, but you could tell it was her."

"Shush. There's the minister."

They listened to him talk, and when he was done they each took turns to walk forward and throw a handful of dirt onto the coffin. Then, when the service was finished, they stood with false stoicism while the rest of the crowd dispersed and the rain grew heavier.

Lechie had taken his car, and all the men piled into it, Lewis on the back seat, along with Iain and Tavis, the twins.

"Here, move over, Lewis. Your arse is so fat there's no room for us two."

"Less of that, Tavis, you cheeky bastard. Aye, at your age, I'd never have thought to speak to my elders and betters like that."

"That'll be fucking right. It's the pub then, lads?"

"Aye. Since the company didn't see fit to arrange a wee gathering afterwards. And even if I hated the fucking cunt."

"Christ, Lewis, the man's barely in his grave."

"Aye, well, he'll not be worrying what I'm saying about him, will he?"

The car passed the railway station, which was closed, the track still impassable further down the line. Buses had been laid on temporarily to take passengers further south. The men all agreed that this was it, the station had come to an end.

They carried on to the pub and bundled inside to satisfy their collective thirst.

"They'll wait a few days, so as not to seem disrespectful, like, and then they'll start complaining about the cost. And there'll be some delay, then another one and another, and by that time they'll say it's not economic to repair the line. Aye, and it'll come no surprise to anyone either."

Lechie was waving his glass around so animatedly that Lewis had to stay his arm. "I'm not wanting your rum in my good whisky," he said.

"It's not so bad for me, I'm near retiring age anyway, but I feel sorry for the young ones. There's precious little for them here as it is"

"I'm not worried," said Iain. "I'll get my payoff, and then I'll head off down the line. I've been saying it for years, that's what we should do. And Alanna and the wee one with me."

"Aye, you're the sensible type. Not like that wee cunt you call your brother, he'll have the redundancy spent on drink and women and things I don't even want to think about, and all before the weekend's out." Lewis raised his voice. "You hearing that, Tavis?"

"Aye, I'm hearing you. Notice I'm not disagreeing?"

"Proud of it too. Fuck me, the youth of today." Lewis winked at Iain.

The pub was filled with mourners, the voices getting louder, and there was a little air to be had amongst the cigarette smoke. Davie stood chatting to a girl he had seen at the funeral, while the rest sat at a corner table, glasses multiplying around them.

"Here, see who's just come in?" Iain pointed towards the bar, where Hugh was standing, ordering a drink. Iain rose, walked over to talk to Hugh, and brought him back to the table, pulling over a chair for him to sit on.

"Here, I'm sorry about your dad. Terrible thing." Lewis looked down into his drink as he said this. There was a trace of whisky at the bottom.

"Aye. We were all fair shocked by it. Everyone else walked out without even a scratch." Lechie lit a cigarette and offered one to Hugh, who shook his head. "You always were the bright one. How're you doing?"

"It's a bit unreal. Not just the funeral, but all the people I haven't seen in years. There were so many there, and there were faces I recognised, but I couldn't remember their names."

"Aye, it was a big affair. An accident like that happening in a wee place like this...well, everyone knew your dad. How's your gran doing?"

"She's not too bad. Shocked, like. There's people up at the house, but it's an all woman thing. I know when I'm not wanted."

"Aye. You're better off here, with the lads. You getting the next round in, Lewis?"

"Fucking bolshy crowd you've fallen in with, Hugh. Though it's my turn right enough." He stood and headed for the bar, taking a handful of empty glasses with him.

"You in England, then?" Iain drained the last of his glass and handed it to Lewis as he was leaving.

"Weybridge. Been there seven years now."

"You've picked up a bit of the accent."

"I've always been one for fitting in. My partner says I'm more English than her these days."

"Any bairns?"

"The one and another on the way. That's why my other half's not up with me. Only three weeks to go, and it's a long journey."

"I was saying, maybe Alanna and me will do the same, head on off. Not out the country mind, but Glasgow or Edinburgh, something like that."

"It's a big change, city life. People say where I live is small, but it's big compared to this place."

"What's fucking not. It'll be grand to have a bit of life around us."

Lewis returned with the drinks, placing them in front of each man in turn. He sat and raised his glass. "Here's to your dad. To Aidan."

The rest of the group raised their glasses too.

"Aye, to Aidan."

The sun was rising by the time the men left the pub. There had been a lock-in and they were amongst the last to go.

"Man, I'm fair buckled." Lewis stopped in the pub doorway to steady himself.

Lechie was alongside him, lighting his eternal cigarette. "I'm heading home. The wife will be ready to kill me." He searched in his pockets for his car keys.

"You're not fucking taking your fucking car." Lewis made to stop him, but Lechie pushed him away.

"It's only a wee distance, and there's none to see."

Lechie lived at the top end of the village. He found his keys, lurched for the car, dropped the keys, picked them up again after considerable effort, and with further difficulty opened the car door.

"Any of you lads coming? I can drop you off and then head on back."

"That's all right, Lechie. I'm walking home with this crew." Hugh gestured to the men. "It'll clear my head."

"And I'm not fucking risking my life driving with you in that fucking state," said Lewis.

"Aye, well, please yourselves. I'll see you later in the day lads, if any of us is fit. My wife will be wanting to take me to church in a few hours time. God help us right enough."

They watched Lechie slowly drive off, creeping along the empty road.

"That'll be another fucking funeral in a few days time then." Lewis said. "Daft cunt that he is."

They turned in the opposite direction, to the bottom of the village, where all five lived.

"It fair hits you when you get to the fresh air." Iain had to stop for a moment, steadying himself by holding onto Hugh's arm. "You've held your drink well. For someone who's half English these days."

"It's in the genes, isn't it? The amount my old man put away and was still walking, I must have a fair tolerance built in."

"Aye, he was a character, your dad."

"I wish I'd kept in touch more. This is only the second time I've been back. And it's only my nan left now, so I'll probably only be making the one trip here again." He looked around the village. "Jesus, this place is bleak."

"It's not so bad. It depends what you're looking for, doesn't it? I'll be sorry to see the back of it when we eventually go. It's a grand place to bring up the kids. Kid." He corrected himself. "Kids, in time. I want a wee laddie next."

"Are you two fucking abandoning us then?" Lewis shouted back at them. He, Tavis and Davie had gone on ahead, and now they stood, waiting for the two of them to catch up. "Fucking yapping. Christ, you pair are worse than a pair of women."

"You do not a bad job yourself," Tavis said.

"Ach, you're just sticking up for your brother."

The five of them walked down the village astride.

"It's like we're in a western." Hugh hummed a burst of music to himself. "Dum-dum-de-dum-de-dum-dum. What's that?"

"One of thon Clint Eastwood ones. The Good the Bad and the Ugly. Or A Few Dollars More. A fine set of cowboys we'd make. Though, right enough, I feel the need to get my shooter out." Davie wandered to the roadside, unzipped his fly, and let off a fierce stream of piss.

"Your shooter, is that what you call it? Fuck me." Lewis wandered over to join him, followed by Hugh, Tavis and Iain, and all five of them stood pissing.

A car appeared from the bottom of the village, a woman driving. Davie waved at it as it passed.

"Another lassie that's seen my cock. There can't be many in the village who haven't now."

"You're a dirty cunt, man." Lewis shook the last few drops and tucked himself away. "Ach, I'd done the same at your age. Make the most of it, laddie." He looked ahead. "Fuck, I'm just outside my house anyway. You daft cunts, could you not have told me?"

"Aye, and is that your wife looking out the window to see what you've been up to?"

Lewis looked up, laughed. "You nearly had me there. She'll be in her bed asleep, and I'll be heading for the couch when I go in, so as not to wake her."

"That's a good one. I'll need to learn that trick." Hugh shook Lewis's hand. "It was good to meet you again. I'll be about for a few days more, so I'll maybe see you around, eh?"

"Aye, and grand meeting you too. Mind how you go with these three, they'll lead anyone astray."

He stottered up the path towards his house and they watched as he opened the door, then disappeared inside.

"So then there were four." Davie fished in his pocket for a cigarette, found and lit the last in the packet, then crushed and threw the packet into the grass. "You'll be heading off now yourself, eh, Hugh?"

From where they stood, the road branched. One route led to the left, past the tail end of the village, and then there was a long track to Hugh's grandmother's house. The path to the right led to the harbour where the other three lived. Iain and Tavis stayed alongside each other, while Davie was further down still.

"I'll follow you lads down to your houses. Then I can cut across the fields to my place. It'll clear my head maybe."

They walked down the steep road leading to the harbour. It dipped and twisted and the majority of the dwellings fell away until there was only the occasional house dotted at the roadside, on shelves cut into the sides of the braes. The bracken was in full bloom, and the wet ground filled the air with the heavy odour of soil.

Hugh pointed to the tops of the braes. "Remember we used to go up there when we were kids? And we'd slide all the way to the bottom. Or roll. Sometimes we'd roll."

"I mind that. You look now at how steep some of them are and it's a wonder no-one was killed," said Iain. "Is that not right, Tavis?"

"Ach, we were hardier than kids are these days. They'll not head to school, some of them, without their mum or their dad in tow."

"It's worse down south. Some won't let their children out onto the street, they think it's too dangerous." Hugh paused, stopped. "I'm a bit like that myself, mind. It's a different country down there."

They walked in silence then, around the bend where they could see the harbour and the high bridge leading down to it. The sun was starting to warm the ground now, so the roads and hills began to steam.

"That'll be thick before long. Are you fit to go that way, Hugh? Those slopes can be fucking treacherous when you can't see what's in front of you."

"As long as I can see my feet on the path and not wander over the cliff edge, I'll be fine, Davie."

They approached the bridge. Iain's house was on the hillside beyond, a low, whitewashed building. Above it, in a building of similar style, Tavis stayed with his parents.

The bridge was made of stone. It crossed a high gorge, and a burn twisted far below.

"Mind when were kids, we'd stop and keek over the edge?" Tavis gestured at a memory only he saw. "Now it gives me the shakes just crossing over."

"Aye, I've seen him walk across with his eyes closed, so he can't see over the edge. I torment him sometimes by looking over the sides." Iain approached the thick stone walls bounding the bridge.

"Don't! You'll make me boak."

"Have you not considered, Tavis, that, actually, walking along a road with your eyes closed might be a little more unsafe than looking where you're going? I'm sure walking into the path of a speeding car is considerably more dangerous than the view of the drop over the side of a bridge."

"Ach, you don't understand what it's like, Hugh. See, when I get a house of my own, it'll be nowhere near this bloody place." Tavis began to edge across the bridge, as though it was in danger of crumbling.

"Here. This is what you want to do." Hugh walked to the left, to the stone wall, which reached to the middle of his chest, then hoisted himself up. At this point he was still at the start of the bridge, with the slope of the bank alongside him.

"Ah man, you're a crazy cunt." Tavis covered his eyes with his hands.

"Then you walk, like this." Hugh stretched out his arms, for balance. "One end to the other."

He walked slowly, wavering across the wall. The men grew silent, watching him.

"Don't be daft, man," said Davie. "You've had a fair fill and you'll fall."

"I won't fall." As he said this, Hugh swayed, but steadied himself. "It's a wide wall. It's like walking along a narrow path and the only difference is you're aware of the long drop down one side. The trick is, don't look down. Just place one foot in front of the other. Easy as anything."

He walked slowly, if not entirely steadily, until he was in the centre of the bridge. Tavis had sunk to the road and had wrapped his arms in front of his eyes.

"See? Half way there already." Hugh made a pretend jump, up and down.

"Stop it man, you've lost your head." Iain made to move towards him.

"When you grow older, you should lose your fear of things. Unnecessary fears, anyway." Hugh measured his words carefully, with his steps. "Maybe, in fact, coming back here makes you realise how small those fears were." He stopped, looked down deliberately, over the edge. "It's a small village, in a small county, in the middle of nowhere. And my father's in a box in a grave where no-one can hurt him, and he can't hurt anyone else." He looked back up again and walked rapidly, deliberately, to the end of the bridge. There he jumped down to the road. "You can look up now," he shouted to Tavis.

"You're fucking mental, man. What if you'd fallen?"

"But I didn't fall. I'm here, in one piece, and the sun is rising above us, and all is well." He stopped, turned to Davie. "But I'll take a fag off you, if you have one."

Davie reached in his pocket for his cigarettes, found a new packet, removed the cellophane, and handed the packet and lighter to Hugh. "It's the whole lot you'll be needing, after that."

Hugh lit a cigarette, coughed harshly and handed the packet and lighter back.

Ian was helping Tavis across the bridge. He was so weak-kneed he had to lean on Iain's arm.

"Sorry, I didn't mean to freak you out." Hugh inhaled deeply on the cigarette, blew out blue-grey smoke. "It's the strangest feeling, that. As though I'd done it before." He shrugged, tossed the cigarette half-smoked down into the burn. "Right lads," he said. "Time to head for home."

Hugh left them then. The twins staggered to their houses, while Davie had that bit further to go, down to the harbour. Hugh followed a footpath that descended the braes, steep and slippery, hidden in the rising mist. It bottomed off to a footbridge below, spanning where the burn turned, before heading out to sea. Here, the air had the dense smell of bracken.

He slid down the path, tripped on a lurk in the ground, steadied himself and carried on. The sun sparked off the ocean, making it difficult to see, so he shielded his eyes with his hands. The mist was at his knees and it was as though he was being slowly erased. By the time he reached the footbridge, the whole landscape around him was hidden.

"Hoy!" Davie calling him from far away

"Hoy!" he called back.

Nothing after that though: it was a shout of recognition, or a check he was still safe. From here the path carried on up the braes, steep enough to make him breathless and his knees ache.

The mist began to lift, further up. He could look back the way he had come, over to the bridge, the road that had led him there. There was a light on in one of the rooms in Iain's house, he saw.

"Tavis, man, what a state." Said out loud, the name by association.

Ahead, the land flattened into fields. He startled a flock of sheep which ran in the opposite direction, then ignored him. Beyond that was a field of wheat, part grown, green and clinging. He skirted the edges so as not to damage the crops. After that there was another field, then another, and by that time the sun had risen high enough to make him sweat. He removed his jacket and tied it around his waist. The wet rose blackly up his trousers legs.

One last field – cattle this time, stares poignant, as though aware of their fate – and then he was on the track to his grandmother's house, now gravelled and potholed, because it was so seldom used.

"One day, all this will be yours." This said aloud, to no-one but himself. Then, as he turned the driveway, the house came into view, sleeping, shadowed, pooled by trees: home.

FIFTEEN

First off, she wasn't an old woman, she was a young girl. Sixteen, I think she said, all raging hormones and goth gloom. Budding breasts and a fondness for lurid, purple lipstick. Purple, to match her hair. Her habits: smoking thirty Marlboro Lights a day with a determined ferocity; self harming, so her arms were a crisscross of fresh wounds and mottled scars. She laughed a great deal, even when there was nothing amusing to laugh at, a humourless laugh intended to display the ennui only teenagers think is attractive. There were friends, of a similar ilk, uniformly dressed in black and with skin that seldom saw daylight. A sometimes-boyfriend too, three years older, speed-addicted thin, a backroom job with the Co-op supermarket to waste away the days, and nights to fill with a helpless debauchery. She was of a type, I suppose. You'd pass her on the street in some provincial, nowhere village, the sort she was brought up in, and you'd think *she's a weird sort* and maybe be a bit afraid: that is, if you were seventy, and wore one of those heavy, quilted coats, and carried a reusable shopping bag with flowers on the front, full of your messages for the week. The place she lived was full of those sorts of people. It wasn't much fun if you were young, and you'd maybe think someone like her would feel trapped in that sort of place and would want to get out of there at the earliest opportunity. Which she planned to do. Which she did.

Her name was Elsa. Not her given name, you understand, which was the much plainer and unglamorous Chrissy, but it was the name she used, and the name her friends called her. Even her father and grandmother (father: drunkard. Grandmother: brittle-tempered) had become used to it. She took the name from Elsa Lanchester, and specifically Elsa Lanchester as she appeared in Bride of Frankenstein, with that iconic hairdo and the outraged mouth that, even in black and white, you imagined as a red, gaping slash.

Yes, sixteen. Sulky, impetuous, self-important, self-hating. An existence that was a circuit of school and street corners and the protective enclosure of her bedroom. You wouldn't think her life would be modelled on a nonsensical rhyme, deliberately or otherwise, but that's how it is sometimes, it's full of strange coincidences and even stranger behaviours. I shouldn't have to tell you that: you know that sort of thing as well as I.

The fly visited her one night as she slept. It crawled inside her ear, and whispered her name, softly at first and then insistently, with its horrid buzzing voice, and then she woke, frightened, into the darkness of her bedroom and, far, far off, the sound of a lone car racing down the main street, much too fast.

"Hellllllo," said the fly. "Chrrrriiisie."

Something horrible happened after that, but she wouldn't tell me what. No, no matter how much I insisted, or pleaded. I always think that's the key. If I knew what happened then, I'd understand what came after. But I don't, and you don't, so it'll have to stay a mystery. I know she swallowed the fly though, to shut it up, to stop its persistent, endless wheedling, its insinuations, its dreadful buZZZZZZ. Down those lips with their ghost of lipstick and into her gullet with a single swallow, her hand over her mouth to stop the

314

gagging, the other one free to wipe the tears, and a ringing in her ears that kept her awake the rest of the night. Even if she could have thought of sleeping, even if she had dared sleep, because the fly was in her belly now, and it still buzzed, it still spoke, it still whispered her name, and shouted her name, and demanded her attention. She had to keep her hand over her mouth because otherwise she would vomit and the fly would be free again, or she would scream, or both.

In school the next day, the fly's buzzing accompanied her words whenever she spoke. No-one else seemed to hear it, but she did, and she imagined they looked strangely at her, all of her classmates and schoolteachers, to hear the continual buZZZZZZZZZZZZZZZZZZZZZZZZZ that followed her around through the classrooms and school grounds, and into the toilet where finally she was sick; but now it was too late for the fly to reappear, to be sicked out, it had burrowed deep into her, and had no intention of emerging.

It was only John, her boyfriend, that she could talk to about it, which she did that night, amid mumbled hysteria and snot and tears, but he was even less coherent than usual because he'd just been paid, so the world sped past him in an amphetamine judder, and at first all he could do was grind his teeth and speak at great length about how much he hated his boss at work, the fat wanker, power mad, he hated him so much. The fly was vibrating down inside her, fracturing her words so they fell out in shards as she curled against him, the two of them in pieces, for different reasons, under the harsh, unshielded light of his bedsit which smelt of stale food and cigarette smoke and uncirculated air.

They found the spider on the kitchen floor, amongst the dust and crumbs of mouldering food fallen down the side of the cooker. It scurried then curled when Elsa scooped it up with her hand. It was very small and brown and she imagined she could see its multitude of eyes looking at her with horror and resignation as she opened her mouth and tossed it to the back of her throat, swallowing quickly, decisively. Then she washed it down with a glassful of water that tasted of must, because it stood there unwashed from a week before. There were more tears and unsatisfactory sex and cans of cider, at the end of which they both fell asleep on the third-hand carpet, half-undressed, listening to a hard, banging music that reflected exactly the emotions dominating their lives.

In the morning, the buzzing was gone, replaced by a terrible wriggling, tickling sensation. It filled her body, from to her feet to the nape of her neck. John lay asleep alongside her still, unmoving even when she rose, his shirt half-removed to reveal the trap of his spine through his skin. There were six text messages from her father on her phone, and three missed calls. She turned the phone off. In the bathroom the light was too bright and her face seen in the mirror was a mess of smeared lipstick and mascara, while the pancaked foundation had flaked, revealing irritated, acned skin beneath. Something squirmed and roiled in her stomach.

"Spider," she said to herself.

The spider answered by crawling up her windpipe. She swallowed, hard.

John was still asleep when she left. It was early morning. Cold, with a cold light. John's flat was on a steep slope and from there she could see down onto the main street which was a horrid grey, slicked by overnight rain. She followed the road to the end of the village, which took her twenty minutes to reach, head down, trying not to make eye contact with the few people out at this hour, as if by reading her eyes they could also read her intentions.

At the end of the village, the road forked, and here she hitched a lift from a truck driver who looked wonderingly or desirously at her outfit of black mesh stockings and almost-skirt, the high-heeled shoes she barely balanced on. For some reason she felt vaguely ashamed and wrapped herself tight in the length of her ankle-length coat (also black: always black). The heating inside the cab was turned on high and made her feel sleepy.

"How are old are you?" the driver asked.

"Sixteen. Seventeen in a month's time. Old enough."

The driver shook his head. He had a kind, amorphous face, the sort you see then forget as soon as it's out of sight.

"I've a daughter your age," he said. "I left her asleep and tucked up in bed, and she was holding a cuddly lion in her arms. Kids these days." He stopped, wonderingly. "Kids these days, they try and grow up too fast."

She didn't answer that one, and pressed her head against the side window, looking at the concrete parade of towns they drove through, with their out-of-town shopping centres and 99p stores and fast food outlets, all of them still closed, the truck's passing a ripple of shadow over the shuttered windows, the grilled doors. Watching them, she was suddenly aware she was ravenous, it was an ache of hunger inside her. Aware too it was not her hunger, but the spider's. She tried to ignore it, tried to make it go away. If she ignored it, perhaps the spider would starve to death. She examined her purple, chipped fingernails, listened to the forced chatter on morning radio.

"It's like they've got Tourette's," she said.

The driver laughed. "Too bright for you in the morning, is it? Or too late from the night before, eh? I miss that, I must admit, the energy you have when you're young."

He swung into a truck stop, and bought her breakfast in a cafe.

"A proper fry up, that's what you need. Keep you warm. There's no sense in you, running around dressed like that, in weather like this."

The other diners stared at them, older man and young girl together around the Formica table, suspicious perhaps of something not quite right, newspaper headlines replayed of teenagers abducted or murdered or, more prosaically, simply of having run away from home. No talk: these were solitary diners, caught between the here and there, the roadmap of memory and signs. In this setting, their voices were overloud.

"I never asked. Where are you heading?" He placed the breakfast tray on the table, two cholesterol-ridden plates of meat and carbohydrate, accompanied by cans of diet coke to mitigate the guilt of the calorie intake.

"Friends. I'm staying with friends. They're not far from here."

"Do they know you're coming?"

She nodded, mouth full of food.

"You're wolfing that down, like you haven't eaten for a month. I don't want to pry, but..."

"I'll be fine. I'm able to take care of myself."

That was the end of *that* conversation, which was followed by one of those uncomfortable silences in which any words seem like an intrusion. Cue the scrape of fork and knife on plate, evasive eye contact, an awareness of the strip light's fluttering overhead, its static hum.

It was Elsa that broke the silence. "That was good. Thank you."

Her gratitude was genuine. When she ate, the spider was still, its hunger abated. She imagined it grown monstrous with all that food, so that her belly would swell, as though she were pregnant.

"You needed it. You want to put a bit of meat on that body of yours, take care of yourself."

She stood and the room swayed and she suddenly felt very tired. "I need some fresh air. You'll wait for me? Just for a bit."

Outside, the day was cold and damp, and the wind had risen. Trees surrounded the cafe's boundaries, and they trembled, soughing. Smoking a cigarette, her back to the cafe, she could see diners reflected in the car windows, watching her with more than a little curiosity, the only thing of interest in this place with its sad routines and banal pleasantries. She moved out of sight, around the corner, the place where discarded wrappers and dead vegetation were gathered, pinned and spinning.

Then she ran.

She ran across the car park, and over the wall, and into the trees behind, a place of leafy greenness smelling of wet and mould that concentrated the cold in its shade. There were paths between the trees, thin mud tracks for hikers or dog walkers to follow. She avoided these and charged instead into the undergrowth, the sharp whip of branches and coiling bramble, the sky broken overhead, grey snapped where the tree canopy allowed visibility, a shake of accumulated rainwater falling down with the disturbance of her passage.

Somewhere, far back, the driver was calling for her. He called her "girl" because he did not know her name. When she had run far enough, she could not hear his voice any longer.

She came to a clearing and for a moment, with the cloud's breakage, there was sun and a kind of warmth, because the trees provided shelter from the wind. Birds chirruped, as if in celebration of her arrival. Stopping there, breathless, the spider started to writhe again, its movements somewhere between a tickle and a sharp pain, willing her on.

"No," she said, "I'm too tired". Talking to no-one but herself.

She lay on the grass. It was damp, but she was exhausted and beyond caring. There was an accumulation of dead and disturbed vegetation on her coat, and the heel of one of her shoes had cracked. It was nice, the warmth. She wanted to curl up and sleep, to imagine she was still in the enclosure of the lorry's cab, the heat of the hot air blower rising over her, the look of protection in the driver's eyes.

The thing was, she didn't even know why she had run. Too late to think of that now, anyway. That was half an hour back, and he'd be long gone, wondering about the strange girl who had spent a few hours in his company, so different in manner from his daughter.

Thinking of that reminded her she still carried her mobile phone. They could track phones, couldn't they? She remembered seeing that on the news.

She threw it into the undergrowth, and in the process startled a flock of birds.

One of the birds came to her. Was it a sparrow? A young bird anyway, feathers fluffed fat and cheeping, the burr of its wings as it demanded food. She opened her mouth wide.

Did it sense the spider? In any case, it flew excitedly into her mouth, its feathered body almost weightless, forcing itself down her oesophagus, bulky and as difficult to swallow as a dry mouthful of food, and then it travelled further down, down into her gut. There was a brief writhing in her stomach, then it was still, the wriggling stopped. Afterwards she slept, even though it turned colder, even though it was damp, even though she worried someone might have followed her, even this far away from designated paths. She slept and there was a stillness in the air, only the toil of vegetation to provide any sound, and she felt safe there, alone, with no-one to see her.

When she woke, it was almost dark again. Two things woke her: the fluttering in her stomach, the bird's frantic movement. Then there was the cat; already halfway down her gullet, only enough time to see the flash of its ginger tail before it slipped down into her stomach. There was a minute of frantic thrashing, followed, once more, by stillness. She burped, and then the evidence: a blooded feather ejected from her mouth, followed by the faintest of meows.

When she had run into the woods, she had done so unthinkingly, because her only thought had been of escape. Now it was dark and she had no idea which way she had come. Still, she somehow managed to retrace her steps, aware of the crushed tilt of grasses here, the weft of disturbed branches there. Night birds called, high, unworldly shrieks, and their cries seemed amplified in the stillness. She wondered if she had picked up some of the cat's sense of direction, or if it guided her in some way. It sat in a heavy lump in her stomach, purring and occasionally kneading the lining of her gut.

Returning to the car park, she found it deserted. The cafe was shut and the roads almost empty, apart from the occasional lone car, speeding, lights set to dazzle, a flicker of cat's eyes ahead, and some lonely driver, intent on a destination that could only be far away, fighting a sleepy heaviness, windows wound down to let in the night air, which had turned unnaturally warm. Clouds of insects hung and spiralled. Caught in car headlights, they looked like trails of smoke.

At the back of the cafe there were wheelie bins; and in the wheelie bins there were black plastic refuse bags. When she clawed at these, a treasure of half-eaten food fell out: chips and congealed eggs, pies and sausage rolls, the remnants of cakes and biscuits. She ate them, ravenous, then drank from a puddle of water that had collected in the car park. The water tasted of mud, and petrol. She thought longingly of home, that place of warmth and familiarity, but something drove her forward, something in the night air had its own allure, sharp with sounds and scents. Everything seemed heightened somehow, as though she had taken one of John's pills, that secret cache he stored beneath the settee and removed and depleted every night. Maybe she had. Maybe she had and had forgotten about it. Maybe that's all it was, all of these things, something drug-enhanced, illusory, increasingly unreal.

She avoided the road, walking instead along the grassy embankments. Cars passed occasionally, slowing sometimes to gaze at her with curiosity, but none of them stopped. She didn't want them to stop. She walked barefoot, having at some point lost her shoes. The grass was wet and cold beneath her feet, and eventually she was unable to feel her feet altogether. She felt the vibration from her stomach though, the cat purring, its steady state, the metronome propelling her forward, one step, two step, three step, four. Forward, forward. There were street lights in the distance, a gathering of some sort, houses and maybe shops, though they would all be dead at this time of night, or early morning, she was uncertain which because her watch had stopped. Maybe it had been damaged when she had run through the trees. She was crying too, she could tell, because her face was wet, and the tears dripped down onto her T-shirt, but she didn't feel sad, she didn't know why she was crying, there was only the impulse to continue, towards and past the lights, and on again, to a destination she was unable to name or even quantify. She would know when she arrived there though. She would feel it in her bones, and the whole jagged knot of nerves that pushed her onwards would cease and there would be peace, peace for the first time in days.

The police found her lying on the road. She had been spotted by the driver of a passing car which swerved to avoid her, for she had fallen off the grass verge and onto the tarmac. Her body was covered with bruises, and her clothes were torn. When asked, she was unable to explain how that had happened; the memory of that moment had gone. The police suspected it was self-inflicted.

She was sent home again, via a detour to the local hospital where she stayed for she didn't know how many days. There were tubes and examinations and the steadying beat of monitoring machines, along with brightly coloured tablets, administered by a nurse who handed them to her in a small plastic dispenser. When she was sent home, she continued to take the pills and they made her lethargic, they dulled her mind to a blunt ache. They made the cat sleepy too, its purr a drawn out bass, so loud she found it impossible others did not hear.

At home, her grandmother fussed around her a great deal, but it was annoying rather than helpful. Never emotionally equipped to deal with anything beyond practicalities, her attempts at comfort were characteristically laboured. Not that this prevented her: her energy was such you thought that if she ever stopped, then she would stop altogether, like the clockwork mechanism of a windup toy which had spiralled to the end of its life. "Chrissy," she would say and "Chrissy," and "Chrissy," as if with each sentence she had to be reminded of her granddaughter's specific, unglamorous existence. Her father was away a great deal, which was a relief. Either that, or drunk. As for her brother, he was sympathetic but too young to fully understand the change that had taken place.

John came to see her, but Elsa only looked at him dumbly most of the time, and if she did speak, it was as if a heavy syrup spilled from her mouth. His visits became less frequent and after a while they stopped altogether.

That was it, apart from the occasional visit from friends, but eventually they ended too. She had lost her febrile immediacy, so visitors found themselves sitting in silence.

"She's like a slug," two of her friends said, right in front of her, as if she was unable to hear. "So fat and slow." It was true, she had become fat or, rather, bloated. So much of her time was spent sitting in her room, alone, unmoving, spacing, thoughts so abstract they would not coalesce, lulled by the cat's unstoppable purr and the occasional shifting as it moved from one comfortable spot to another in her belly. The sound was there when she fell asleep, and it was there when she woke, and even her dreams were underscored by the steady vibration, that expression of contented laziness.

Eventually they encouraged her to go out, grandmother or sometimes father or brother in tow.

She wore loose clothing now, baggy jogging trousers and T-shirts that tented and hung. Sometimes she caught sight of herself in shop windows and an alien creature stared back, pasty-faced and lumbering, an expression in which the light had dimmed, and which receded further with each day, each glance.

"How's she doing?" people would sometimes ask her grandmother, always her grandmother, not her, as if she didn't exist any longer. "It's so sad what's happened. She doesn't look at all well."

Her grandmother would nod, and look anxious, and would reply in a faux whisper which she somehow imagined her granddaughter would not hear. "She's still poorly," or "We're awfully worried, she's not getting better at all."

Then they would go home, and she would return to her room and stare into space, watching the light's gradation.

Purr, went the cat. *Purr*.

Perhaps that's the way it would have stayed, perhaps the rest of her life would have been one long, Mogadoned slur, if it hadn't been for the man with the Rottweiler.

Elsa would see him sometimes, on days when she was taken outdoors, to be led dully down the dull village street. His face was familiar, a distant flashback to that other life *she* sometimes thought about, dreamily, recalling events that seemed as though they had happened to another person. He reminded her of John in some ways, but older, skin drawn and worn, too many cigarettes and too much alcohol, too much of who knows what else. His clothes: the rebel garments of another generation, battered leather jackets and dirtied jeans, winklepicker shoes. Fine when you're twenty, not so much when you're fifty and still pretending to be the hard man. Place him in a fight and he'd be vicious and taunting, but that body couldn't stand up to much these days. Still, he had the dog to compensate, black and solid, tongue constantly hanging out, devoted to his master who took him everywhere, or who the dog took everywhere. Who was to tell who really was the dominant figure in this symbiotic relationship of audacity and power, the way people avoided them on the street, crossed sides, took detours, avoided eye contact. No-one to talk to: it's a lonely life being a hard man. He wasn't local either, so add distrust into the equation; people commented how the neighbourhood had gone downhill, how you wouldn't have seen that twenty years ago, forgetting their own youthful follies, the things they did once upon a time before respectability beckoned.

Elsa remembered though. Maybe the sight flickered something of the old life in her, made her nostalgic for the person she had been months, almost a year, before. Maybe that's what made her tread so carefully downstairs, so her grandmother would not hear her, and down the driveway, across the street and to the place where the man stood on the pavement. He watched expectant at her approach, attempting to stare her out, to stare her down, but she did not avert her eyes so that – could it be possible? – he even looked a little afraid of her, this bloated, pasty girl with her hair hung in tatters, her mouth a little slack, and eyes both muted and filled with a fire, an invitation almost.

Is that what made the dog attack her? The huge pull of his bulk, this heavy blackness that barked and leapt and threw her to the ground, at which point it became apparent that, no, it wasn't after her, but what was within her, the thing that arched and hissed and spat and clawed in anticipation as the dog's wattled head pushed into her mouth, her jawbones dislocating out of place, and she tried to scream but could not. There was a hugeness inside her, an expansion, a swallowing that fought against her gag reflex, the pain, and there was a terror in her stomach, mercifully brief, and after the heaviness, a terrible heaviness within.

She must have passed out, because when she woke he was kicking her, the man, and he was screaming, "What have you done with my dog?" and her grandmother was there, emerging from their house, and neighbours, all afluster, attracted by the noise. Elsa was crying, involuntarily, and there was more commotion, people were trying to pull him off her, and there were police.

After that everything was more confused than ever, she didn't know who did what or when, but she did know she ended back up in hospital with lacerations and heavy bruising, her attacker on the front page of the local newspaper that very week, a bit of excitement to enliven the village's tedium, its routine. The headline: LOCAL GIRL SAVAGELY ATTACKED. There was a photo of the man, and of her (pre-slothed, in her slim, attractive days). Of the dog though, there was no mention.

In the hospital, at night, she took to baying at the moon. She rose from her bedcovers, stiff, still finding it difficult to move, and began to howl, incessantly. She barked at nurses and doctors who came to quieten her, and bared her teeth, until they backed away, uncertain, more than a little afraid of the savagery in her expression, the way she pawed and shivered and snarled. Even under sedation she yapped, the power of speech temporarily lost, showing her gums, limbs jerking, running, dreaming of chasing rabbits or perhaps of some larger prey. Her very face seemed lupine and animated with an angry vigour. Even for the non-superstitious, she was frightening. Some of the staff refused to go near her at all. At first, when she had been admitted, the comments had been: "It's so sad, a young girl like that"; "I don't know what the world's coming to"; "It's a tragedy, it really is". No one made those comments now. They avoided her. They were afraid of her, catching something atavistic in her eyes, avoiding her teeth which lunged and snapped. Always at night, that was the thing.

That lasted a month. A month of coaxing and wheedling, demand and fear, but there was always the same response: a dull nullity in the daytime, the fierce antagonism at night. She was moved to a private room, then a secure ward, and finally she was taken to 'an institution' (the words deliberately ambiguous, although everyone knew what they meant: her family, her friends, the staff who heard the news with undisguised relief). Bundled ungraciously into the back of a van, the straightjacket holding her powerless, even though she was docile, even though she looked at her captors with a mute expression, even though they had pumped her with enough drugs to, as one doctor said, "stun a bull elephant"; because you never knew; better to be safe than sorry; she could turn just like that; she wasn't entirely human.

They took her to a house that was white (because such buildings are always white) with barred windows and a wide, lush, high-walled garden that stopped others from getting in and, more importantly, helped prevent patients from getting out. I know, because I spent fourteen years of my life there. That was where I met Elsa.

*

You heard her before you saw her, the howl amongst the demented night-time chatter, the tics and cries and outbursts from our own neuroses and delusions. It was paper-thin sanity that life had scored too hard, or some genetic defect that left an imbalance of chemicals crawling amidst the dendrons, misfiring neurons, shaping a world invariably fearful. Nothing was more fearful that that nightly howl, bestial, and the cries of the staff who attempted to contain her and who suffered bites and scratched limbs and bruised faces and bodies.

Yet when I saw her during the daytime, she was nothing; less than nothing. A young girl, once attractive, pasty now, though that was the drugs. They also made her face pallid and gave her spots and turned her hair lank, as though it was seldom washed. If I spoke to her (and I spoke to everyone, even if they or I did not always make sense), the words rattled around her skull, you could almost hear the revolution until they settled, and there would be a reply, a few words if I was lucky.

Sometimes there was nothing but the blankest of stares. You expected that in there; she wasn't the only one. After all, none of us would have been in that place if we had been able to offer sensible, rational conversation.

As weeks passed though, and months, she began to change. We would meet in the smoking room and at first it was only little things: asking for a light, asking how I was. Then details of her life emerged; where she had lived, the sort of person she had been and would be again, she hoped. She recognised she was ill, you see, and that recognition is always the first road to recovery. That's my experience at least.

On good days, we walked in the garden, its scissored lawns and symmetric flower beds, tended by patients as part of their therapy, because there was something healing in the process of watching things grow and flourish under your control.

I suppose we had become friends or, at the very least, confessors. I told her things I told no-one else and she did the same. It was like an emetic, confession, secrets kept on coming out and out until there was very little else to tell.

Some secrets though, as I previously mentioned, were never told.

But I found her name was really Chrissy, her middle name Mary, and her taste in music was for singers and bands I had never heard of. I learnt she had liked dressing in provocative clothing and all about her home, and how dreary and constricting she found everything to be, and how she had longed to run away to something brighter, more glamorous, more enticing.

"So I did," she said, "but I didn't expect to end up here."

Then she told me about the fly and the spider and the bird and the cat and the dog. She had never heard of the rhyme (or is it a song? I don't really know), and thought I was joshing when I told her about it. Ignorant and mad: that's some combination. Though that's a cruel judgement, for I liked her really, especially when you could see a bit of the old fire creeping back, the flash of her eyes, a sardonic upturn to her mouth, the lipstick she had taken to wearing again, harlot red. She was getting better, she said. Even the staff said it, they could see the difference too, puzzling away at the ravel of her brain, although I don't know if they ever really did too much. Instead, it was whatever disaster had overtaken her was in the process of receding.

I knew though, I'd been around long enough to see: madness was like a tide. It could recede, but also return, it could come back stronger than ever.

It came in the form of a snake. The snake had a scaled head and forking tongue, but walked on two legs. It had eyes so blue they were like cut glass. It came into her room where she lay, still bound at night, still sedated enough to make reality waver, its cold reptilian heft. The coiling of its body around hers and the wickedness of its tail. The wide unhinging of its jaw that threatened to engulf her, top to toe.

So she ate it instead. It wasn't as it she didn't have practice. Headfirst, all the way down, a little swallowing of her own. Her body lurched, and flailed, and then was still, aside from the seething knot in her tummy.

The snake was followed by a pig. It too walked on two legs, its eyes glittered red, it snuffled and squealed and crushed her with its heavy, porcine body. It had red, swollen teats and its trotters were sharp and scraped and drew blood. She opened her mouth as wide as she dared and consumed the creature.

The goat came last. It had horns and smelt of a heavy musk. It had distempered eyes and foul breath, and yellowed teeth. It leapt on her and pummelled her with its hooves and drew deep, livid bruises. She cried and screamed and tried to push it away, but it held on to her with a randy persistence, urinating over her sheets, chewing at her hair, until she was forced to, had to, swallow it as well.

Then it was dreadfully still, with only the night mutterings, the movements and growls and tears of the deranged to keep her company. A stillness full of fear, in which she dared not move or cry for help, not until the morning, the light that normally brought relief but which left her as paralysed with terror as ever.

The nurses found her, blooded and bruised, a mute hysteria in her eyes, her voice refusing to work, her pyjamas ripped, lacerations on her skin. She whimpered and cried, then huddled against the nurses as though she was an upset child, something not far removed from the truth.

There were investigations, of course. Who was responsible, and why had no-one heard? Not the staff, not the patients. Had she somehow done this to herself? Stranger things happen in *that* sort of place, you begin to expect them, anticipate them almost.

But no, one-one had seen or heard anything, not that they would confess to, so we shared a mute responsibility. I had seen. I had heard. It was a ward full of patients: I could not have been the only one. When she began to spit like a snake, or squeal like a pig, or bleat like a goat, I knew why. I had seen them, their rough violations, and I knew where they had taken refuge, deep down in her very gut so she spoke in tongues, as though possessed. Even the staff, long hardened, long indifferent, those that considered themselves unshockable, even they were perturbed. She was taken out of the ward and into a separate room again, but still we heard her, and saw her through the gridded window, we forced ourselves to look when we heard the screaming. I would like to think there was very little of her left, mentally, very little to comprehend what had happened to her, and continued to happen to her.

Or, as one of the nurses said in passing, "It's like living with the bloody girl in the Exorcist. Next all we'll be needing is the revolving head and the pea green vomit and we'll be right inside the fucking movie."

You did think that, that there was something otherworldly at work. Snake; pig; goat: what else are these creatures but symbols of the demonic?

I was the one who helped her escape. Or perhaps escape is too strong a word: I stole a nurse's pass and opened the door to let Elsa out, still in her night clothes, out into the darkness of the garden in which something dreadful stirred, rippling at the sky's edges and gusting through the trees, and into which she disappeared with a maniac determination impelled perhaps by fear, which these days seemed the only constant in her life. The hospital was no place for her, not at that age, less than a third of mine. Her only obstacles were garden and wall: this was not a prison, after all. She didn't even look back, not once, not even a thank you, that's how glad she was to be leaving. What remained: a room that smelt of sulphur; soiled clothing; staff that pretended not to notice her absence until she was long gone, off onto the moors somewhere, the barren landscape that housed nothing but its own eerie insularity, sodden ground and rock scree, the bones of murdered children and suicides.

No-one saw her after that, although there were searches, there were news items, her face static on the TV screens we all watched passively. I thought of her often, and imagined her the source of the rumours we shared, the news of the outside world that was brought second, third hand: of the flayed carcass of a cow; the disgorged remains of a donkey, fur and hooves retched up and left for some unsuspecting farmer to discover. I'll hear of her again one day, I imagine, when it's least expected, found here or somewhere distant, my poor Elsa, feral by now surely, barely recognisable as being the person I knew, lying there dead, unloved, alone, alongside the half-digested body of a horse.

SIXTEEN

Howard knows the cubicle is haunted. Its ghosts come not with a clanking of chains and woeful moans but instead with a hungry eye and muted whispers. They leave behind blood and semen and tears and an engulfing terror. Sometimes he wonders if he is going mad, if he is not mad already.

Visiting the public toilets is a routine, worn so deeply into his life he barely remembers a time it did not exist. The lavatory block is old, Victorian, with heavy brick walls, frosted glass windows and a chill even the warmest day cannot penetrate. When he first moved to this town it sat at the end of a row of shops, but these have been demolished and turned into a car park. This ensures people enter and leave at all times of the day.

There are three stalls. He habitually sits in the one furthest from the entrance, with his trousers around his ankles, his cock in his hand, and one eye focussed on the peephole drilled into the dividing wall. Every few months the peephole is covered up, but someone always bores through it again. He always wonders who has the forethought to come prepared with whatever implement is used to create the hole.

Each evening he arrives and remains for an hour, no more and no less. It helps, he finds, to stick to an established routine. At one time he did not have long to wait for someone to come and sit in the adjoining stall, communicating by the established ritual of shadows and coughs and sly glances. Sometimes in the course of the hour there would be two or three or four or, on one memorable occasion, six. Now he sits and often no-one arrives. It is the times, the times have changed. These days there are only ghosts, and his patient, desperate waiting.

There is the old man with the walking stick. He has a bald head and skin patterned with thread veins. One side of his mouth droops, perhaps the result of a stroke or Bell's palsy. He did not always look this way. He always had the walking stick though, to correct the limp that causes one foot to hang heavily. It made, and makes, the sound of his arrival distinctive: tok tok tok on the tiled floor. Tok tok tok. He thinks the man's name is James, though those first encounters were so long ago he can no longer remember. Mentally, that is what he calls him anyway.

James always wore an overabundance of cologne, with an undercurrent of alcohol. He leaked loneliness like another scent, that clinging, slightly unnerving musk accompanying isolation. Howard recognises it on himself sometimes, though at least he has Jean and the children. It is a love of sorts. Without that there is the void. If he looks towards the man, if their eyes meet, he sees what he might have become. The man's expression carries the same intensity he remembers from years before. There is still the scent of cologne.

Often James stands at the urinal, waiting for Howard to leave, which he only does because to stay any longer would raise suspicion. Howard does not dare speak, or stop. The emotion he feels is so intense it seems to rise and rise from the core of his body, until he feels dizzy and he struggles to breathe while he hurries out of the toilet, not looking back, in case the act of looking is an invitation for the man to follow.

When not at the urinal, James sits in the stall alongside. Howard can see movement through the peephole, the flash of uncovered flesh, the man's face turned to look towards him; but then he is gone. There has been no sound of his departure. At other times there is only the echo of footsteps, the tap of a cane, and no-one is to be seen.

Years ago, James was his first. They met not here, but in another place, one that looked remarkably similar to the one he visits daily now. He remembers the encounter as being characterised by combined desire and revulsion. There was the sly touch of the man's hand, and his own frantic unbuttoning of his trousers. At the time he was fourteen, or fifteen: like the man's name, this too has become uncertain. He remembers he would not let the man kiss him, and the hurt, repeated comment: "What's the matter? Don't you like me?" He remembers the man's smile too, his shy affection, and the way he took out his false teeth to suck him off. He is dead now. He is certain to be dead: those encounters were over forty years ago. He has to be a ghost.

He cannot meet the eye that stares through the peephole.

When he arrives home each night, Jean always has the dinner ready. She works part time, has done ever since they had children, and she is always in the house before him. Boredom drives her to keep the place pristine, to act the role of the perfect housewife. He supposes both their lives are spent occupying roles of sorts.

"Hard day at the office?"

It is their standing joke: the dutiful wife and the successful businessman. They occupy a stereotypical dream. He kisses her and sometimes his breath carries a taint of semen, or his pants are wet from the dribbling residue of someone's cum. She smells of perfume, and her red hair is carefully cropped and styled. It makes her look like an older version of Mia Farrow in Rosemary's Baby.

"You don't think it makes me too mannish, do you?" she asked, when she first had it done.

"Don't be silly. Of course you don't look too mannish."

Two of the children have left home now, and the third is at university, so the house feels empty. They fill it with chatter. Howard works in real estate, and knows of the impending marriages, the couplings, the births, break ups and deaths. She works in a lawyer's office, and knows even deeper secrets. They can talk about such things, now there is no one around to hear. It is one of their shared passions. Theirs is a small town, on the commuter belt, and it is difficult to keep privacies in a place that size. He has learnt though: people are foolish with their secrets. He is not foolish.

There is the teenager with lacerated wrists. He pushes them under the partition wall and blood leaks onto the tiles. The youth is another resurrected memory, another face pulled from the past. He used to stand at the latrines and watch men come and go, until one made eye contact, and then they would disappear into the stalls together. Howard always made eye contact.

He knows this ghost's name. It is Jason. Years ago, when he had been carrying out interviews for a position in his company, the teenager had walked into the interview room. Neither of them acknowledged they knew each other, but the interview was brittle and uncomfortable.

At the end Jason had said, "It's like a scene from a porn film, isn't it?"

Howard did not dare give him the job; but then he worried that he could not. The side of his life he had for so many years kept secret suddenly felt in danger of exposure.

In the end, the youth withdrew his application, calling the following day to say he was no longer interested. What had caused him to change his mind? He did not say. He still waited for Howard's arrival each Thursday evening though, but now sat in the stall alongside and reached beneath the walls to wank him off. Sometimes, while Howard was shopping with Jean, they would meet in the supermarket, and they would both smile in recognition.

"Who was that?" Jean once asked, and his answer was only a half-deceit: he had interviewed the lad for a position in his company.

Jason's visits stopped suddenly. That happened sometimes. People moved away, or settled down, or found a way to suppress desires they could barely admit to themselves. It did not matter. A week, a month later, someone else would come along to take their place. Such varied people, and yet such unvaried needs.

Yet these lacerated wrists provide the answer. They have been cut so deeply the tendons have severed, so they are cruelly limp-wristed in the most literal fashion. The blood is congealing but is still liquid enough to splash the brightest red over the bathroom tiles, which are a darker maroon. He can see the shiver of a face reflected in the tiles too, and it wears a pleading expression. That sight is dreadful, but the weeping is worse. It is soft, intermittent – no theatrical show of despair here – and on hearing it he feels as though he has intruded on a deeply personal moment. What he experiences then is not fear but something worse. It is embarrassment, coupled with guilt, as though he has intruded on the youth's final moments. When the wrists have been withdrawn, the blood remains, before it too fades, and the weeping begins. Often he cannot sleep at night because he still hears that sound, reflected by memory, until it has grown huge and overwhelming, as do all early morning terrors, dispersing only when the sun begins to rise.

In the toilets, there is a code to be followed. He cannot remember how he learnt the code. It is a Morse composed of tapped feet, glances, shadowed hand gestures, coughs and sniffs. He has become expert in its communication. The smell of stale piss and bleach is one he has come to associate with desire and even love. It is always cold in there, but he seldom even notices now.

He has only loved twice in his life, once as a teenager, and then again in his thirties. Neither instance involved his wife. Jean was the first, and the only, woman he dated. People said they were meant for each other, their relationship almost like the closest of friends rather than the binding, polarising heat of lovers. It was not an act calculated to quell suspicion, no, it was following expectations, and avoiding fears. The desire for men would be a phase, something he would grow out of, or at least overcome. Marriage would change it all.

The path of their life together seemed laid out for them, and there was never opportunity to veer off that path; no excuse seemed adequate. Within two years Ben, his son, was born. Emily followed, two years after that. That was when they decided to get married. None of Howard's family were at the ceremony. As he had said, they were either all dead, mad, or missing.

"Look what I'm marrying into," Jean had laughed, and then had kissed him.

No, it was not love, it was affection and companionship and a securing of their lives. But it was not love.

There was a gap of thirteen years before the birth of Susan, their third and final child. Her conception had taken place one evening when he had been drunk, and Jean had been drunk, and the alcohol had reignited a desire they had thought forgotten. Throughout, Howard fantasised he was being buggered by Liam, a monosyllabic builder he encountered on a regular basis.

Liam had the blackest of beards, a body unnaturally hairy, and an expression that always seemed on the edge of desperation. They met many times and their couplings had a reckless intensity that was more than lust. Once, Howard dared take him back to his house, while Jean and the children were away on a weekend outing: he had feigned a stomach bug. That was the only time they spent more than a few furtive moments together, and he declared his love for this man whose surname he did not at the time know, who he had spent no more than a few days with in total. Accreted days, and accreted desire. Liam was also married; ritually, he would remove his wedding ring before they had sex.

It was not true love, of course. It never gained the opportunity to mature to that level. It was infatuation, and desperation, it was the might have been, the what if, the possibility that, in another place, another time, in different circumstances, things could have been different. On the evening Susan was conceived, the ghost of Liam was in that bedroom, the touch of his calloused hands, his body that carried at all times the scent of cheap aftershave and smoke.

Liam died only a year after that, of lung cancer. *So young*, people said. His wife contacted Howard shortly after, to put the house on the market. She had left her husband for another man, when Liam's cancer had been diagnosed. She did not look a hard woman, she did not look uncaring, but still she had been able to do that.

He surveyed the building himself, alone. All its contents were intact and the rooms still carried the odour he knew so well, along with the less welcome evidence of illness. In a drawer he found a photograph, showing Liam working on a building site, bare chested, looking up and smiling at the camera. Yes, smiling for once. He stole it and keeps it still in his drawer at work, but he cannot look at it, it lies face down. What he is afraid of is this: he will look at it and he will feel nothing.

Liam is another of the ghosts. Howard has never seen him, but his presence is unmistakably there. It comes in the form of sound and scent, the aroma that remained on his skin after they parted, and that he would catch himself smelling, aroused, when he was alone, not daring even to wash his clothes in case he lost the trace that followed him after their brief moments together. Now it has returned, the slight must of sweat that clung to Liam's body, and stale tobacco, and he recognises too the sighs, the tread of feet, the sly tap on the cubicle walls. And once, only once, the sound of a voice: "Howard." What he feels then is a heartbreaking nostalgia, and a forgotten longing, along with a sense of grief that threatens to overwhelm, but which he will never submit to. He thinks if he starts crying he will never stop.

He always considered himself to be a pragmatic man and supposed that ghosts were hallucinations, the invention of the over-imaginative, or the opportunistic. Yet, from his first experience, he had no doubt.

Years ago, not long after he was married, a man had started to arrive at the lavatories. Howard never saw his face, and only recognised him by signal: three definite sniffs, in quick succession, before a hand reached beneath the wall. It was an older man's hand, with dirt engrained in the fingernails, scrubbed oil in the crevices in his palms. He smelt of grease and petrol.

Howard always wondered who the man was. Each time he stopped at a local garage, or at a petrol station - the two almost always interchangeable in those days - he tried to spot who it might be. Yet he only had sound as a means of identification, the sight of the hands. It could have been any of the mechanics he saw or spoke to. As with so many he encountered, the man's visits became less and less frequent, and then stopped altogether.

That evening though, a winter's evening in which the world had that still, frosted quality that drove most people home to warmth, he heard it again. Sniff. Sniff. Sniff. In quick succession. The stench of motor grease was almost choking. The only sound came from outside: the labour of cars slowly crunching through ice and snow, the plumbing with its perpetual burst and drain of water. He had been sitting there for over half an hour and no-one had entered, he was certain. But still. That sound. That odour. Unmistakable. To be certain, he looked but there was no-one, the stall doors were ajar, and any footprints left on the tiled floor were long dry, the most recent being his own.

The following day at work, he sat on the internet and read up about ghosts. They seemed overly fond of old, baronial mansions, of underground passages and battlefields, and the closest experience he could find to his own was of a poltergeist fond of flushing toilets in a council house. This made him even more convinced of his experience's authenticity. It was not something he had read somewhere, or a story half overheard. That sound: it cut through thirty years of his lifetime.

Even with that knowledge, the event itself was not frightening. It carried with it an element of the unreal. Unreal, even though he was positive, he was certain it had taken place. For weeks afterwards, he waited for it to occur again, but it did not. The others came though. He wonders why these ones, out of the hundreds or perhaps thousands of anonymous encounters, and why it is him they come to.

It is a small town, with little in the way of secrets. He has always lived in fear that Jean will find out, or the children. Fear and sometimes a kind of hope. He is careful always to walk from his offices, which are only a short distance away, and he always leaves the light on at work, but locks the door: it is his business, and he is always the last to leave. His telephone is diverted to his mobile, just in case Jean calls, which she sometimes does. He wonders if the echoing acoustics give him away. Once she called while a man (encountered once, never seen again) was giving him a blow job. He answered anyway, and that deception was an extra thrill. Sometimes he wonders if that is the real addiction at work here, the thrill of transgression, now his sex drive is far diminished from what it was, after years of overwork, and overeating. He has joined the ranks of fat, stressed, unhealthy businessmen.

Once she called when Jason pushed his severed wrists towards him, and he dared not answer then, he dared not speak. If he did, he would surely scream. The youth has only appeared three times and each appearance has been far apart. What makes him arrive when he does, he wonders. Why that evening, why that moment? The first two encounters produced the most sheer, the most absolute terror, but the last time it occurred, he began to feel a sense of sympathy, to wonder what had driven Jason to kill himself. Was it shame? There had been low moments in his own life, but they had never been *that* low.

The first time he saw him (the second of the ghosts, the second of five), he was so disturbed he talked in his sleep, he woke with night sweats, he gained a look that could only be described as haunted. When Jean had asked, he ascribed it to overwork. What else could he say? The whole, complicated ravel of his life would have sounded insane in that context. Perhaps it was insane.

There are two more ghosts. One is a tramp. Or he thinks it is a tramp: maybe it is only someone old, and dirty and (from the expression on the face) possibly unbalanced. His eyes have a slightly crazed look. Another face from the past. Howard never dared touch him and instead only stared while the tramp wanked in front of the peephole, the foreskin pulled back and forth, back and forth, until there was the inevitable discharge. It was never exciting, more horridly fascinating, and he could not look away. The tramp had scabs on his penis, and when he left, the stench of stale, ingrained sweat remained. Howard had not seen him for years, and the first time and only time he reappeared he was not sure if it was a person alive or dead. But he was there; and then he was not, and there were no footsteps, there was no opening and closing of doors.

A ghost then, like the others.

The last is the worst. This man wears a suit, just as Howard does. It is a pinstripe suit, in an unfamiliar style. He is bald on top and his face wears the scores of age, even though there cannot be much of an age difference between the two of them. He had never seen the man before, but he appears and disappears as the others do, without warning. The two men could be brothers.

"Howard," he says. "Howard, let me in." He raps on the wall, and on the toilet door. He can see the toes of overpolished shoes below the door.

How does he know his name? Has someone told him who he is?

Rap. Rap. Rap.

This man scares him more than all the ghosts, more even than the youth with severed wrists. He cannot say why. He lifts his legs so they cannot be seen, he blocks the peephole with toilet paper, but still the knocking continues. They knocks grow so loud the whole cubicle vibrates. When they stop, always when he least suspects, he dares not venture out. Perhaps the man is waiting for him out there, silently. When he does finally emerge, it is only when someone else has come into the lavatory. It is safety in numbers. Even then he cannot help but run, to attract unwanted attention, but it is the fear, it is so great.

Each time he vows he will not return, but the memory of the terror fades, he gains rationality as a shield, and he is back the following evening, or the evening after that, sitting there, waiting. It is, he realises, an addiction. It is, he realises, the pattern of his life marked out in minutes, accumulated hours of desperately listening for the right sound, looking for the right movement, the fleeting contact that is so excitingly intense.

Although the ghosts seem to want to communicate with him, he has never dared make any sort of response back. Besides; maybe they do not even realise he is there at all. Maybe they are acting out a memory, performing actions carried out so many times they are engrained in the thick, stone walls, like the moisture settled there, like the mould formed on the ceiling. He does not know which is less comforting, to think that all we may be is the result of our actions, or that any afterlife may be one of thwarted, endless desire. Do others see them, or do they appear to him alone? Do they want something from him? Are they trying convey a message? He cannot talk about it with anyone, because this is the deepest secret, the one he can never confess.

He has started to have a recurring dream. In his dream all the ghosts have arrived at once. They gather outside the cubicle and he hears them talk in low whispers amongst themselves. Although the door is closed, he can somehow see them. The man with the limp is there, and Jason, his wrists bleeding. There is Liam, who coughs (the same cough he once knew, so telling in retrospect), and he stands alongside the man with oiled hands (an old man, he sees now, in his sixties, thin, unremarkable). They look at the man in the business suit, as though seeking guidance. Then they begin to call. They call his name, softly at first, then louder, and they rap on the door and on the walls of the adjoining stalls, they bend and peer through the peephole, and they crouch and push their faces below the partition, their hands reaching out towards him.

"Howard," they say, as the man in the business suit always says, "Let us in."

He is in a place beyond fear in these moments and there is a dread that rises and numbs his thoughts. He sweats so intensely and his heart beats so rapidly he imagines he will die; but still they do not stop. They call and they call and they batter against the cubicle walls with such fervour it begins so shake, to bow inwards a little. He stands and retreats into the far corner, and he wants to cry out, but cannot, for someone will hear, he will be discovered, he is certain.

"Howard," and again, "Howard".

He advances a little, slowly, for his body trembles so, he can barely find it in him to walk, he looks straight ahead so he cannot see the reflection of their longing, desperate faces on the floor; and he reaches out, he pulls back the catch on the door, and he lets them in. He lets them in.

SEVENTEEN

They stood on the shore, watching the boat flounder. Caitlin wore a cagoule and waterproof trousers, and her father an all body waterproof cape reaching down to his feet. Rain ran down from the hood onto her chest and back, and she held onto her father's arm to steady herself.

"Look on," said her father, "you'll not see the like of this again in your lifetime."

He was a sturdy man, but the storm was so fierce she could feel his body buckle against the harsh gusts. The sea churned to foam beneath a sky more than black.

As she watched, a lance of lightning reached down and hit the boat's cabin, and there was a sharp explosion of fire.

"Oh." The word said involuntarily, as though stolen from her.

On deck, they could see men, almost hidden by the rise of the waves. They slipped and slid from one end of the deck to the other.

"Will they be all right?" Her voice small, made smaller by the events they watched.

"Everything will turn all right in the end. Doesn't it always?"

As her father said this, the wind grew greater still, the waves higher than she had ever seen, and the ship keeled, all in one movement, so the men disappeared into the bleak, dangerous water.

"Daddy!"

With that, in the whole terrible, exciting, overwhelming moment, the cold overcame her, and she fell down onto the shingled shore, the waves only inches from her head, as though the sea was trying to reclaim her.

Her father lifted her and carried her further back, to the shelter of an abandoned smokehouse standing just above the shoreline, the place they called home. The cries of the men followed them, proof of life for the moment anyway, and the stones on the beach rose and smacked together like the cracking of innumerable bones.

In the shed, he covered her with a blanket. It stunk of dried fish and woodsmoke, as everything in there did.

"Is she sleeping?"

The speaker, a boy, stood in the doorway. He could have been the man's son, so similar was their appearance. Cusped on adulthood, his face had not yet lost its softness. Similarly, his voice was suspended somewhere between child and adult.

"She fainted. It was too much for her, watching." Her father nodded, thoughtfully. "I'd have done the same at her age. Come in."

"The rain won't hurt me."

It was true: it seemed to fall through him, as though he lacked substance. He did not even wear a coat, and was dressed only in a thin t-shirt and shorts. He was barefoot. Behind him the sea whipped and the sky lanced down rain so heavily it threatened to drown out even the sound of the wind.

"Please yourself."

"I'm half way to freedom now, even you can't deny me that."

"You'll be away when you've the chance, just like everyone else. I'm glad I have my wee girl still for company." Then: "What's happened to the men?"

"They're ashore, the waves washed them here. Not there's much to see beyond their broken bodies. The sea's stripped even their clothes from them."

"There's none alive?"

"None I've seen."

"Away to look then, and tell me if there's any." He turned his back, as though done.

"You're not forgetting?" The boy's voice turned plaintive.

"No, I'm not forgetting. Do this and you'll have your blasted freedom." He turned to the doorway again. "We'll all have our freedom."

Then the boy was gone, as though he had never been there.

When Caitlin awoke, her father was sitting alongside her, smoking his pipe, its drawn fire the only visible light in the room. He had pulled their wooden table in front of him, and was sorting dried mushrooms and blue petals into hessian pouches. These were his objects of power and their magic made him lord of the island. His spells only worked with their aid.

"How long have I been asleep?" She raised herself up on one elbow. It was dark outdoors, and still.

"A few hours. I shouldn't have taken you out in that storm, it was too much for a lass like you."

"It's stopped though." Then: "What happened to the boat? I remember it overturned..."

"You'll see what's left of it when we go outdoors. Bits of wood thrown up on the shoreline and not much else."

"But the men...?"

"They maybe survived and they maybe didn't." He turned to her, touched her arm. "Life at sea is cruel, you know that." He rose and headed for the stove. "I've made some soup. It'll heat you."

They sat around the table, hands leeching warmth from the bowls.

"Feeling better?"

Caitlin nodded. "Still cold though. That wind's chilled me through."

"I'll get you a blanket."

"Don't be daft, I'm cold, not an invalid. I'll soon warm up when I get moving again." She stood and took the bowls to the basin, washed them in cold water. "There." As if that proved the point.

Her father stood by the doorway, looking out. "It was a storm like that on the night we arrived here."

"You've said."

"Six of us then. You were just a baby."

"You said."

"And now there's just the two of us, on an island even the wind wants to pass over."

"You're getting morbid, father."

"And you know what? It was them bastards on the boat did it, I recognised their craft as soon as it came into view, and there was a bit of me fair rejoiced when it tipped those cunts into the sea. Them as stole my life from me. My hand."

He lifted his arm and thrust it towards her, as though she had not seen the severed, scarred stump before.

"That'll not be right, you're thinking of long ago, and those men were not the lucky ones. They got nothing but the sea; at least we've the shelter of the island. It's past, father, and you've to leave it there."

"Aye, maybe."

"The sun will be up soon. When it comes, let's go for a walk and clear our heads. It'll do us both good."

"You're growing fast." He held her to him "I don't know what I'd do without you. My wee one."

Rising sun tinted the beach the colour of washed blood. Debris from the boat covered the shore: fractured beams, gutted sails, the sundries of everyday life, clothing. Bodies too, caught in the rocks, stripped naked, or almost naked.

"The sea's cruel," her father said, "but it's bountiful as well. Give me a hand with this will you?"

Together they pulled a sack of potatoes that had somehow survived intact, dragging it further up the shoreline.

"Aye, Caitlin, we'll get it out of sight before the beast gets her hands on it."

They retrieved what they could from the wreckage. Further out to sea, the boat's hull, or what remained of it, arced from the water.

"It's so still now, you wouldn't think there'd been a storm at all." Caitlin lifted a shirt from clothing they had gathered. "This one would fit me, maybe?"

"It's a dress you're needing, not some dead man's cast-offs"

"Beggars can't be choosers."

"Aye, I'm the poorest king ever to rule an island. And you're the poorest princess."

"There's none that would fight us for our titles, is there?"

They covered the scavengings with driftwood and stones.

"It's not perfect, but it'll do," her father said. "You'd not know it was there unless you were looking. We'll collect it on the way back, after we've seen if there's any more to be had."

Ahead the beach turned to rock and they clambered slippery stone. The island curved here and the sea had worked its way into the tall cliffs, creating cavities feeding back inland. A body was caught in the rock, water bloated, face upwards, eyes still open.

"He's only young." Caitlin knelt and examined his face. "He'll not have been expecting to end up like this. He'll have been expecting adventure and money and some woman in a port somewhere, waiting for him."

She was talking to herself though: her father was further off, pulling a wooden chest from the water.

"Come see this," he shouted.

The rocks were covered with dulce and it was difficult to keep her balance. Near to where her father stood, the ground fell away, and the sea churning around the edge of the rock was deep and cold. The water's extra weight made the chest difficult to move, and they both had to pull with both hands, straining to see what it contained.

"We'll live for a year on our findings." Her father had a clarity to him she seldom saw. Too often a darkness came over him, and those were the worst times.

"At least –" She slid, and reached to catch herself, but the rock rushed towards her, faster than she could respond, and the chest slipped from her, down into the water, something bright and glinting in its interior. There was a most terrible pain, and then, briefly, there was nothing.

Something pulled at her legs, so she was dragged over rock, blood drawn in the process.

"You witless bitch. Let her go!"

Caitlin lifted her head back and saw her father hauling a thin, scrawny figure from her. The girl was nearly naked, with hair grown long and matted. Her skin was scabbed with dirt and sores. The beast, of course: no failing to recognise that one.

Standing, still shaken, she saw blood falling from her nose onto her cagoule. Her trousers were ripped at the knees, skinned beneath, and her hands bruised and punctured.

The beast was twisting and had almost wrested free from her father's grasp. Caitlin fell on her, punching, pulling at the girl's hair, bashing her against the rock, so she howled like the creature she truly was.

"Why did you do that? Why did you do that?" A fury filled Caitlin, fuelled by pain.

The beast looked up, directly at her, said, "It was mine! I saw that before you did!" She pulled free and crawled back, crying and fierce at the same time. "I saw it. From my cave. You've enough, and I've nothing."

"You don't deserve anything!" She kicked the beast, who slid backwards again, and cried as stone caught at her back. Her whole body was blooded, sharp cuts on every part. "You're not even human!"

It was her father that stopped her.

"Don't blame the creature. She's not right in the head, you know that."

All three stood now, unmoving.

Finally, the beast's tears turned to real tears, not of fury now, but of self-pity. "You hurt me. I was only hungry. I'm so, so hungry." She held her arm which hung loose, already ripening with bruises.

Caitlin's father spoke to the beast.

"You don't deserve food. You want to be back in your cave where no-one can see you. You're happy in your cave, aren't you?"

The girl nodded, beyond words now.

"Fetch us some wood for a fire and we'll fetch you some food. Is that fair exchange?"

The beast nodded again.

"Go then, and meet us back here."

She hurpled away over the rock, as steady as they were unsteady.

Caitlin's father turned to her. "Pinch the bridge of your nose, that's best for stopping a nose bleed. You're not too badly hurt?"

Caitlin shook her head, close to tears now herself.

"You mustn't judge her. She's wild that one and what little she knows is what we've taught her. She has no more morals than the birds you see in the sky, or the fish in the sea."

"She frightens me." She turned to look at the water. "The chest's gone now, and it's her fault. We'll never know what was in there."

"There'll be more treasures. Maybe even that one again, if the tide throws it back."

Ahead, the beast was climbing the cliff, the damage to her arm apparently forgotten. She clambered with ease, her movements practiced and alien. At the top, she turned and waved at them, then picked and tossed a rock which, even at this distance, was thrown with enough force and enough accuracy to crack and shatter at their feet.

They walked on, Caitlin lagging behind her father. The coast curved inward, leading to a small shingle beach, completely inaccessible unless the tide pulled far out, as it had at that moment. The sun was stronger, but it was a cold sun, and the wind had risen again, robbing even that little warmth. Gaining sight of the beach, Caitlin's father broke into a clumsy run.

"What have you seen?" Caitlin found it difficult to keep up, because she was tired, and the girl's attack had left her sore. She shouted to her father but her words whipped back to her. Perhaps that is why he did not stop to wait, or turn, or reply.

Near to the beach, on the rocks, a group of seals lolled, eyes curious but unafraid. They had nothing to be frightened of here, though it seemed to her they looked at her strangely, their expressions more than curious. They ignored her father.

"Stop, wait for me," she called, but he was far ahead now, and she could not reach him.

There was a man on the beach; her father could see that clearly. He stood, apparently unharmed, although he must have been washed from the ship. He wore fisherman's oilskins, yellow and orange, which somehow, miraculously, remained intact.

"Ho!" He waved his arms. "Ho!"

The man waved back, but did not move, watching Caitlin's father approach instead, as though to stand was effort enough. He did not speak, even when Caitlin's father embraced him.

"We thought there were no survivors, but you've the luck, or strength, to have bested the sea."

The man did not reply, but looked straight ahead, his eyes strange and distant. He was looking in Caitlin's direction.

"Are you mute? Or, no, it's the shock will have stolen the words from you. You understand me though?"

The man nodded.

"We'll take you back to shelter, until aid comes. There's no others beyond you?"

This time a shake of the head, but he kept his eyes fixed on the girl.

"Aye, that's my daughter. She's a bonny lass. The sea's not stolen that sense from you, eh?"

Caitlin was running up the beach, towards them.

When Caitlin saw her father, he stood on the beach talking to himself.

"Father, who are you speaking to?" She looked around, as though someone might be hidden amongst the high pilings of shingle, and the tossed, grey pebbles.

"Please. Don't jest like that. You belittle our guest, the prince. I'm not wrong am I? You *are* a prince?"

The man nodded, still mute.

"He says he's a prince!" Her father turned to her, and there was a wild, almost ecstatic look on his face.

She held back from him, afraid. He stood on the beach and he talked and he gestured, but he gestured at nothing.

"Father, you're scaring me. I swear, there's no-one there."

There was real dismay on her father's face when she said this.

"Don't insult our guest. Or is it your head? You didn't hit it when you were attacked by the beast, did you? It's you that's not well, if you can't see what's clearly here before you."

"No. I swear. Here." She approached her father, and walked full circle around him. "See? Am I walking through him, father? Is he speaking to me? We need to go back, you've grown stressed with the storm. Or is it the mushrooms? Did you have them in your soup? Is that's what making you see and hear what isn't there?"

The prince, still silent.

Her father knelt down in front of him. "Say something. Let her know you're there."

The prince sat, mute.

"Has her bonniness taken the words from you, is that it, eh? Here." Her father clutched the man's wrist. "Is that anything less than skin and bone I'm touching? If you can't see him, there's some other explanation." He looked up to his daughter. "You swear? You see no-one?"

"There's no-one there father. You're scaring me, behaving like this. Here, let's head back. We've food enough for a good meal, and it's maybe what you're needing."

"It's the beast then. She's put some sort of spell on you, and you can't see what a treasure has been brought to us. There's a man here, Caitlin, a prince, and he's maybe the only the only survivor of the boat. We'll make him our guest, until help arrives."

"He'll be waiting a long time then." She looked to the way they had come. "We need to go back. The tide's changing, and we'll need to hurry."

He father watched her turn, then helped the man rise.

Caitlin walked far ahead, her pace rapid. She called. "Quick," she said, "we need to get home, or we'll be victims of the sea too."

She arrived back to the hut and banked the stove with the remaining wood. The wind had begun to intensify, and the sky darkened once more. Rain busied the roof with its intrusive language. Her father did not appear. She occupied herself by peeling potatoes, gathered from the spot where they had been hidden earlier, though she did not have the strength to take the entire sack with her. Periodically she looked out to the beach. It had grown so gloomy it could be evening, it was difficult to see clearly through the rainfall, and there was no sign of her father.

Perhaps her father was flying. Sometimes, when he took the mushrooms, he flew. Once, he had made her take the mushrooms too, but she fell down and down, and it seemed she would never stop.

After that she would not touch them, although their magic still returned sometimes, in a fizz and spark at the edge of her vision, or in the sculpture of clouds, or leafed tree branches that seemed beyond real, as though they possessed a greater weight than other objects around her.

"Once you've had the magic, there's no turning back," was her father's only comment.

She lay down on her bed of straw and hessian, and closed her eyes. If she slept, he would be there when she woke. It is what had always happened before.

There was little firewood to be found. The beast had gathered a few broken branches, but that was all. The island was flat and scoured and little grew that survived the winds. There were stunted bushes, turned backwards, and trees that managed to find shelter where the land dipped into hollows, but that was all. It was cold, and although she had a blanket wrapped around her for warmth, the chill penetrated it easily. The storm, which had receded, was pushing back inland again. The entire island grew dark. Abandoning her task, she found shelter under a crop of rock and pulled the blanket over her body. Rain started to fall, heavy and drumming.

She lay in that way, silent, the waiting an endurance, alive to sounds of the land and the sea. Gradually, she became aware of approaching footsteps. She did not look to see who it was and sat, hoping the footsteps would pass.

They did not pass. The blanket lifted, and the man crawled below the blanket with her. He was wet and he smelled of drink. She was too frightened to speak.

"I've found you," he said. "Dirty, dirty beast."

When she woke, her father was in the hut, but from the look of him he had not been there long. He was removing his clothing, sodden, because the rain had soaked it through, and he replaced it with his cape, which was the only other item of clothing he owned. He draped the wet clothing on the pipe above the stove, so water dripped and spat and sizzled on the hot surface.

"You're awake then," he said.

He knew somehow, even though he had not turned to face her. She imagined it magic, but in truth he saw her movements reflected in the metal of the pot placed on the stove.

"You worried me, going off like that, and talking nonsense about a man who was not there."

"Oh, he's there all right, if you've the wit to see him." He turned to her then, and she saw his eyes had not lost their manic quality.

"The magic's still in you then."

"The magic never leaves you." He tapped at his head. "It's in here, see? If you'd sense enough you'd find the way to use it." He knelt alongside her and gripped her arms. "The prince has agreed you are to be his wife." He shook her. "His wife!"

She stood and pulled away from him, but he held on so tightly he tore the sleeve of her shirt.

"There's more. We are to be rich and will live in fine palaces. We will have servants and the finest food and everyone will marvel at your beauty."

"Don't."

"I tell you, he is in love!"

"Father, you are mad."

When he held her again, she began to cry and then to scream. "Don't. Leave me alone! You have lost your mind, you scare me."

He hit her. The force of his blow sent her falling to the ground and she knocked her head.

"Don't."

He held her pinned. His anger was so great, he could barely even speak. "He loves you and you defy me and doubt the words of your own father." He hit her again, so her nose began to bleed, for the second time that day. "Your mind is closed and you cannot see."

She lay there, stunned, and he rose and fetched a potion from the shelf. It was dark and pieces of twig and leaf and fungus floated in its muddied waters.

"This will cure it. Drink." He pinched her nose and forced open her mouth and poured the liquid down.

She coughed, choking on the debris.

He held her down, sitting on her chest. "It will calm you. It's you the madness has taken; it has spread into you like a disease. You will sleep and you will see."

Already her features slackened.

"Sleep." More gentle now. "You will see what I see now, and you will believe."

Caitlin felt nauseous. That always happened after drinking one of her father's potions. She already could feel herself growing drowsy, but it was a deep and frightening drowsiness that drew her ever downwards, as though she was pulled into one of those powerful and unpredictable rip tides around the shoreline. Her father was there, still in the room, making conversation with someone who did not exist.

Except...was there someone else there? Kneeling down to her. He wore a gold spun cape and there was a haze of dusk around his skin.

"Caitlin," he said, "we are to be married."

This was surely hallucination. He ran his finger over her lips and his taste was salt, he still carried the sea with him. His eyes were brown, and to look at them was indeed to fall, and how ridiculous, to fall into the depths of her own teenage fantasies...

Someone was singing, an old song, one she knew from long ago. A man's voice. She tried to raise her head to look up, but could not.

"Who...?"

"Don't speak." The prince kissed her, brutally. Was it her imagination, or did he resemble her father? His aquiline nose, his long face.

The room must have grown larger, for it seemed it had turned the length of the island. Something wet fell on her face and she had to close her eyes, then when she looked again there was no roof but only sky, the storm's force abating, and through blackened clouds, a rainbow. There were fields around her, full of ripening wheat, caught by the wind. There, in the field, was her mother. How long since she had thought of her?

She came to Caitlin and she could smell her, she had forgotten that smell, the warmth and comfort of long ago. "My only wish is your happiness and a life free from pain."

There were people in the fields, dancing. No, they were cutting the harvest. They had sickles and scythes and they cut the wheat; and the wheat fell under sun that had broken through cloud. The harvesting of the wheat let a blackness in though, it seeped from the edges, it pushed in and in, and there was pain, so she cried out, she could not contain her silence any longer.

Then everything was still.

She could see the light of the hut in the distance, fevered, even through the rain, which fell with such force she was half-blinded. She was bleeding, having fallen into a gorse bush and then the cruel marram grass on the sand dunes. Still, she continued, through pain and exhaustion, spurred by hate, by fear, and a determination for revenge. She carried a sharp length of flint, shaped like a dagger. The beach seemed very long and, in the dark, threatening. The sea's voice was warning or admonition, she could not decide which.

As she came closer, she could see the father through the open doorway. He was naked, singing, and dancing around the room. The girl lay behind him, on the floor. She felt sorry for the girl, even though she was cruel. She knew why the girl was cruel; the lacerations on her own body were testament to that. She crouched down, close to the doorway, and remained there, unable to move. The desire for revenge which had taken her so far did not give her the courage to take those final steps into the building.

The father had stopped dancing and now was talking, but he talked to no-one. He gestured, and he smiled, but he could not be speaking to his daughter, who was unconscious, or dead. Suddenly, his expression changed, and he turned and looked out at the beach, directly at her.

Had she made a noise? It would have been impossible to have heard it in any case, not over the sound of wind and sea, but he knew somehow. He stood in the doorway, frail, but his frailty was deceptive, she was aware of that. He looked out, and he looked straight at her.

*"The beast," he said, and he came right to her. She was so
scared she could not move, and he took her into the hut.*

The air in the hut was full of fumes. He had thrown
herbs on the fire, blue flowers and leaves curling and
sparking. She saw creatures crawl and leap from the
corners of the room, but when she turned her head she
saw it was only clothing. Yet then they were beasts
again, terrible beasts that whispered to her, and she wet
herself from fear, the hot trickle down her legs, and the
man was laughing, as though he could not stop. She
was being drawn down an endless, angular tunnel and
there was a sense she was being watched, quite apart
from the beasts (ethereal now, dissipating) and the man
who laughed, whose name she could not remember, if
she had ever known it at all.

At some point, the visions dissipated and she found
herself lying on the floor. She was covered by a cape
which she recognised as being the one the father
normally wore.

The man was leaning over her, but she did not feel
any hate for him. Everything felt unreal and
disconnected.

"You have come at a time when I have lost my
daughter," he said, yet he smiled as he said this. "And
for this I forgive you your trespass."

His daughter lay only feet away from her, but she was
still. Her face was tinged blue.

"She is to be married, to a prince." He stopped, as
though confused. "Though where has he gone? Do you
see him?"

She nodded. "He said he was going to fetch a present for your daughter."

"Odd...I did not see him. He thought to make it a surprise, perhaps." He smiled, brightened, then his expression darkened again. "You must remove those clothes. They are for my daughter's wedding."

She stood, still unsteady, and removed what little clothing she wore. Her body was slicked with sweat.

"Naked as the day you came into the world. It's not a bad thing to be naked, is it? Before your creator. A party will come to rescue the prince, you know, and we shall go with them. We shall go where it is warm and the people rich, and we shall be crowned high nobles. And then..." He turned to face her. "and then, this island will be yours."

He looked up. "You've returned." He spoke to no-one she could see. "Calm the storm. Then you will have your freedom."

He stood, listening. "You see? It is calm. My spells are undone and I grow weak. I cannot flee without forgiveness; and that is only yours to give."

She could not tell if he addressed her, or his daughter, or some other.

"I only sought to give pleasure, you know. Now I throw myself on your mercy and that will guide me far from here, from my crimes, across the sea, stilled now."

The wild blew more ferociously than ever, the rain clattered madly on the wood of the hut.

"Forgive me."

At that she rose, and she fled, out into the storm, which was brutal and frightening, but more comforting by far than this madness.

EIGHTEEN

Up in the chair-o-plane, a clear night sky and the lights spun past them, scored on the edge of the retina, someone screaming above or was it below, hard to tell in the ride's tilt and spin.

— Get that hand from under my skirt, Al. You'll be getting me in the family way.

— You'll not get that from a wee fumble.

— It's what your hand has been touching before that worries me.

Giggly, because he had made her swig from a half bottle of whisky he carried in his pocket, the taste that burnt her throat and made her cough and cough and swear *never again how can you drink that stuff*, though she took a second swig to prove she was not the weak sort, and maybe that was why everything around her spun so, it was not just the ride, and she snuggled close and let his hand prise its way into her cunt, despite everything she said, riding his fingers with the in and out of her breath, and his too, as she pressed down on the fly of his trousers, rubbing. He came with a judder and the wet stain was there on his trousers all evening, a sight that made her blush at her boldness.

—You're a fly one, Maggie, making me come like that.

Later that night, her head in a fever of the sideshow's fake glamour, the words spoken he knew she wanted to hear, and she did want it anyway, she did, it was an ache somewhere deep inside her, she took his cock too, it was inevitable after the smoky fever of their kisses, his hands that found their way beneath the folds of her clothing, and that time he did get her in the family way, he did, and that was the end of it, or the start, depending how you looked at it.

That was still the future, *and you never*, the very thought of what she had done made her giddy, the ride slowing and descending, the ground lurching when they stood on it, the motion carried still in their bodies, pushing through crowds eager to take their place.

—You're a one.

There was a ghosting to his face, the emotions came twisting to the surface, and she wondered if he had really done it before, even though he said he had, but men were like that, all mouth and no trousers, all her girl friends said.

—You would have complained enough if I hadn't.

Lighting his cigarette for him, so he squinted against the rising blue smoke, letting it hang from his lips the way he had seen it done in the movies. She looked almost afraid to the patch on his trousers and there was a smell on her hand where it had got wet, it had a stale, metallic smell, old pennies or something. Screams above them now, the chair-o-plane spinning, rising, where they had been minutes before, an excuse for other couples to clasp together in fear, skirts pulled tight and hair askumble, while she and he went on, deeper into the crowds, it was a busy night, smells of cooked food, sausages and beefburgers mixed in with the taint of oil, petrol fumes, generators revved past their natural lifespan. Hours yet, they had hours.

—There's Ted. I'm needing a word with him.

He left her there while he talked with his friend, one she did not know, not attractive anyway, overweight and with one of those acned faces that would go pock-scarred and leave him branded all his life, he would have to settle for some second rate girl, if he got a girl at all. They were laughing together, and the boy was looking over, so they were talking about her, what she had done, would do. She reapplied her lipstick, pink blush, watching them in her compact mirror. Two other boys had joined, they were passing the half bottle round, it would be near done, and their voices got louder and louder, though she still could not make out what they were saying.

—I'm not talking to you, she said when he returned, turning away when he tried to manhandle her, give her a kiss, his mates watching all the while. She would not give him that satisfaction, so their laughter turned to jeers and she was glad. She stalked away, pushing past crowds, found, surprised, that she was crying, though she would not let him see.

—Aw, don't be like that.

Chasing after her, trying to hold her, calm her, but she would not, she would not. Head down and pushing on, through people that refused to let her past, caught up in the noise, the distraction of each other's company, the stalls never less than gaudy, the pulling cries of barkers.

—What's wrong?

Then:

—I'm sorry,

He said this in such a way it suggested he did not know what he was being sorry for. Maggie did not reply, not looking back or sideways, swerving to avoid him when he danced in front of her, no real concern in his expression, it was a game to him.

—You were laughing at me, I saw you.

Looking up now, and there were more tears, but they were tears of anger, the mascara running, too heavy to begin with, she had not learned that confidence.

—Don't be daft. Listen to me.

—Well I'm daft now am I? You get away Al, I should never have done.

When he stood in front of her, not moving, she screamed *Get away!* so loud everyone stared, and he looked almost afraid, his bravado gone now.

—I wasn't laughing at you, really I wasn't. We were just getting the crack, honest. I wouldn't do that to you, you're my girl.

And the interest moving on, just a teenage squabble. She let him put his hand on her shoulder, pull her towards him. He kissed the top of her head, her hair with its lacquered smell and

—Don't you worry, I'm not the bad one.

Rocking her body, as though she was a baby needing comforting, and she let him, the two of them standing there, not saying anything, just standing, holding each other, until she could feel the hardness as he pressed into her, and she pulled back, laughing now, saying

—Al, you dirty bugger.

Later, they passed the hall of mirrors, tentflaps opened wide, a full length mirror at the entranceway, and a bored teenager, not much older than they were, standing there taking the threepence admission. Al stopped.

—Have you been in one of those before? When I was wee, I went once with me mam, it makes you fair dizzy.

They looked inside, but it was set like a maze, with the mirrors angled away from them, so they could not see their reflections from a distance.

—Only thruppence, said the lad, You'll not regret. His accent heavy, north England somewhere.

—Thruppence? That's a quarter of packet of fags, that is.

—You'll not remember having smoked them in a year's time, but you'll remember this.

—I'll buy, she said. I've a bit of my pay left yet.

—I'll be marrying a rich girl then?

—You'll be marrying no-one, unless you stop your cheek. Turning to him: Is that a proposal?

—It might be. What would you say if it was?

But she just laughed

—Let's go in.

Leading him by the hand.

Inside it was half lit, not enough power from the lights set hanging on the canvas walls to see clearly. Their shadows spilt two and four onto the grass beneath. There were wooden arrow signs set into the ground, showing the way.

Al pointed to the first mirror they came to.

—You look like a dwarf in that one.

Their bodies shrunk down, squat and rounded.

—Fat too. He lit a cigarette and offered one to her, and the flare of the shared match lit the mirror as though it burnt from its interior.

—My mother would say it's for the better. She's always telling me I'm too thin.

—Och, she's talking nonsense. You're grand, you are.

The next mirror drew them tall, stretched out far above their natural height.

—See, I'm taller than yon Lennie. I'll tell him, when we're back on the boats.

Reaching up, so his arms threw tall shadows, taller even than the mirror's reach.

—It don't half make us look wicked, she said.

Beyond, they saw themselves rounded into obesity and, beyond that, their bodies pulled into fine threads.

In the final section, the mirrors surrounded them with their reflections, not distorted now, but multiplied, and in the dark and that setting it was difficult to tell what was image and what reality.

—Oh, I don't like that, that's strange, that is.

—It's only tricks.

But his voice told her he found it unsettling too.

After that, a passageway led them back the way they had come.

—Well, said the lad. Was it worth your thruppence?

—Aye, it was grand. I feel a wee bit dizzy now, though.

The ground seemed unsettled below her feet

—Lean on me, I'll see you right.

Al winked at the lad as he said this.

Beyond the hall of mirrors was a rifle range, the sort where people shot at moving cards to win a prize. There were other couples there, as intimate as they, the night and noise brought them together.

—I fancy a go at that. I ought to be a crack, all that practice shooting crows with me dad.

—There's a bracelet there. You could win me that. It's a shame though, shooting them birds. What harm did they ever do you?

—They're cruel. You don't see what they do, you just see them noisy and flapping in the trees and think they're a grand backdrop to an evening's walk.

—Well, I think you're the cruel one.

Biting her lip and frowning.

—You don't complain about the fish I give you, do you? And what harm did they ever do?

When a space was available, he handed over money to the man at the stall, and sighted and aimed at the cards. The cards were mounted on posts which revolved on a pulley system, jolting unsteadily forward. The gun went crack and then crack and then crack, loud even against the background music. Maggie jumped a little with each sharp detonation, she could not help it. He took three shots in all, but none of the cards were hit.

—I'll take another round.

—I thought you'd no money? she said.

—A wee bit stashed away.

Again the sound, his aim more careful now, but he only hit the back of the tent, the slugs impacting into the cork board there, joining all the other missed shots. The ground at the base was grey with pellets where they had fallen.

—It's fixed, I swear.

He handed the rifle back.

—I'll have a go.

Reaching into her purse and fishing out a few coins.

—You'll never. When have you ever shot a gun?

Then, to the stallholder:

—Mind and duck!

She lifted the rifle, positioning it as she had seen Al and the others do. The trick was to shoot just before the card reached the rifle sights, it stood to reason.

She pressed the trigger, one, two, three times.

Two cards out of three flipped over. She shrieked.

—You've a right Annie Oakley there, son.

The stall holder waited until the rest of the shots had been fired by the other couples, then went to pick up the cards.

—Two shots, two prizes.

He handed her a bag of puff candy and a goldfish, swimming in a plastic bag.

She held the fish up to examine it. The fairground light caught it and made it spark as it flipped side to side in the water.

—We'll need to get it in fresh water once we're home. Isn't it bonny?

But he was not listening.

—Beginner's luck, he said.

He ate the candy though, the two of them sat on the ground beside one of the tents, dipping their fingers into the bag and lifting the friable, caramelised pieces, getting their fingers sticky, laughing, trying to touch each other on the face with their tacky hands.

—Beginner's luck, that's what it was.

—Aye, keep on trying to convince yourself. It needed a little thought, is all.

Looking at him, seeing his expression occupied, licking fragments from his fingers, his face already reddened from his days at sea.

—Did you mean it, what you said earlier on? About getting married?

—Aye, one day. We'll have a grand house, and fill it full of kids, and I'll have a boat of me own to pay for it all.

—That'll be right. Still...

She sighed, shifted.

—My bum's getting wet on the grass.

—Do what I'm doing and sit on the edge of the canvas.

She moved closer to him, and scrunched up the bag, empty now, stuffing it under the tent's edge. The bag containing the goldfish sat, sagged, between the spread of her feet. She lifted it and the fish fluttered, disturbed.

—What do you suppose it thinks about, swimming away in there? In that wee plastic bag with hardly any air, when it should be out in the rivers.

—It'll not be imagining anything. It'll not have come from the wild, they'll have got it born in some fishbowl somewhere. You'll not miss what you've never had. It'd be like we were born in that big house on the hill, we wouldn't think anything different.

—You wouldn't complain about that though. You'd be a proper toff and speak all la-dee-dah like they do. My mother's always wanted that house. In your dreams I say.

—Mine and all. I like my wee council house though, it's grand. I've my own room and my mam to cook my dinner. I'll bet them on the hill have flagstone on their kitchen floor too, and rooms with wee patches of mould on the ceiling, like we have. It's not so different a life as you'd think.

—It's fine having a room of your own. I'd not have that if I'd brothers and sisters.

—Aye, a room, but it's a house I'll be needing soon. I put my name on the council list.

—My mother wouldn't stand for me doing that, not unless I'm married off first. Besides, I couldn't afford it, not on the pay I get at the biscuit factory.

—Aye, it needs two. That's gets you up the council list as well.

He removed the half of whisky from his pocket, not yet empty, its contents turned dark by shadow.

—You want another swig of this?

She shook her head.

He unscrewed the top and tipped the last down his throat, finishing it off with a contented *Ah!* He slid the bottle under the canvas edge, alongside the sweetie bag she had pushed there earlier. They stood and he lit a cigarette for her and then for himself, the pulse of the coal as he inhaled. She still held the goldfish in her other hand.

—You smell good, he said.

—What do I smell of?

He inhaled, theatrically.

—Perfume and smoke and hairspray. And your skin, I can smell your skin.

—You smell of fish still. Though I'm not complaining. You'll never be rid of that, not with your job. It's like my mother, when she used to gut the fish for a living. Aye, there's worse things than working in the factory.

—And all thon broken Rich Teas you come home with too.

—You'll soon get sick of those. I can't look at the things any more.

They started walking again, almost at the edge of the sideshows now, with only fields beyond, the clod of cattle standing by the fences watching, eyes lit by the show's light.

—We should be going back, she said. It's late and I've work tomorrow, early shift.

—The night's young. Come on back with me. We can sneak up to my room and sit a while. My mam'll be in bed by now.

—If it's only a wee while. You promise?

—I promise.

They walked out onto a side road that led from the town, down to a farm. It was unpaved, and she stumbled, almost falling.

—Walk on the roadside, it's safer. Mind the ditches though.

Al led and she followed, holding onto his hand. There was no light, except for those from the sideshows and farm lights in the distance, and they were walking in the opposite direction to those.

—There's a dip just ahead. You'll need to be careful.

—I'm not worried for me, it's the fish if I fall.

They walked in silence after that. The air was still and they could hear waves breaking onto the beach, far away, then the drag on the shingle.

—The tide's coming in, you hear it doing that, he said.

—We'll maybe go there a walk tomorrow night, if the weather holds.

—Aye, maybe.

They reached the end of the road. From there it forked and led down into the village. There were other couples ahead and behind, their conversation equally muted, and groups of boys jostling and shouting.

Behind them, the music from the sideshows stopped, and the lights started turning off, one by one.

Al lived in a street near the edge of the village, his the last house in a terrace. It was an area with a rough reputation, but there was no-one out on the street that night, the only sound their own footsteps. The lights were off in the house when they arrived. Al had a key, and he opened the door as quietly as he could, stepping inside with exaggerated stealth.

—Al? Is that you?

His mother's voice calling from down the stairs.

—Aye, it's me. You go back to sleep, mam.

—You'd a good time then? I heard the music.

—It was grand. I'm tired now though.

He started climbing the stairs, and motioned to her to follow.

—Come and give us a kiss before you go into your room. Come and see your old mam.

—I'm not a bairn now. You go on back to sleep.

He turned, whispered

—She's had a dram, you can tell.

Maggie held back at the top of the stairs, in case the mother appeared, or maybe some man was with her, but there was no-one, and Al waved her on. His bedroom was to the left, at the top of the landing. His mother's bedroom was straight ahead. The sound of someone snoring issued from it, very loudly.

She walked, trying to match his measured footsteps so they became a single sound. There was no carpet on the stairs and their footfalls sounded extraordinarily intrusive.

In his room she whispered

—We should maybe have stayed downstairs.

—And have me mam walk in on us if she decides to get a top up from the bottle? No thanks. We can stay here and we'll be quiet. She'll not come in, even if she does get up.

His room was sparse with little in it beyond a bed, a bedside table, a chest of drawers and a wardrobe. On the wall was a photograph of the boat on which he worked, the whole crew lined up, smiling, fags in hands, stuck in gobs, hoisting boxes full of fish, fishing nets, filleting knives. Alongside the photograph was a poster of a train travelling by night, windows lit and steam ripped above the carriage; stolen from the station, by the looks of it.

—Boats and trains. That's such a laddie thing. You don't get lassies with those pinned to their walls.

—And you'll be getting rid of your poster of the Everly Brothers?

—That's different. That's people.

They sat down on the edge of the bed and she removed her shoes, aware of each creak of the bed frame. It was an old fold-down bed, its mattress so thin she could feel the metal struts beneath.

—I've a drop more whisky, hidden away.

He got up, pulled a part-drunk half bottle from the rear of a drawer.

—Are you not allowed to drink in your own room, when you've to hide it like that?

—Nah, it's in case my mam finds it and drinks it herself.

—You'll end up like her, if you keep this up. Soused every night.

391

—No fear. I'm smarter than that.

He took a pint glass from below the bed, emptying it upside down first and giving it a shake.

—I'm not wanting any beasties in my good whisky.

He poured a heavy-handed slosh into the glass for her and took three good swigs from the bottle himself. To match him, she poured her drink straight down her throat.

—Come here.

He pulled her towards him, and she let him, the two of them collapsing back onto the mattress with a sound that seemed alarmingly loud.

—I thought it was just to talk.

She did not let him answer and kissed him.

—You'll not make a noise? she said.

—I'll not.

He began to unbutton her cardigan, and then push down the straps of her dress below it. She helped him, and saw he was shaking. She was shaking. He saw her looking.

—I want it so bad.

—I'm wanting it too.

She whispered into his ear, surprised by the sound in her voice, its desperation.

—You'll not hurt me?

He shook his head.

—I would never hurt you, you know that.

She finished removing the dress herself, letting it fall to the floor, but kept on her bra and knickers. He removed his own clothes then, unbuckling his trousers, fumbling with the buttons on his shirt which would not respond to his fingers, all the while not daring to look away from her, her body thin and pale, as though she was still a child.

—You've a fine body.

She touched his stomach with its dark covering of hair. He did not speak.

—Oh, she said. Wait a minute. Where's the bathroom?

—Out opposite. You're not leaving?

—Dressed like this? That'll be right.

She disappeared out the door, taking the glass with her. He sat and listened, hearing the toilet flush and then the tap run. There was no other sound in the house. She returned, holding the pint glass, filled now with water.

—For the fish. The poor thing'll suffocate if it's left in the bag like that.

Lifting the bag from where it was placed on the dresser, she untied it, and tipped the fish into the glass. It began to swim around and around.

—You're not half the Good Samaritan.

He came up behind her, cupping his hands awkwardly around her almost-breasts. His cock was pressed hard into the small of her back. She reached behind to touch it.

—Don't. I'll come if you do that.

—Is that not the idea?

—In you though. I'm wanting in you.

She turned around to face him and pulled him tight against her, and they lowered themselves down onto the floor. There was a thin mat to lie on. He pushed down her knickers and was in her, and she kissed him. She twisted her hips and he roared, he could not stop himself.

—Ah fuck, I've come. I didn't mean to.

He pulled away from her.

—Ah fuck fuck fuck. Don't tell the lads. Tell no-one.

—I'm not going to stand to stand on a street corner and say, see that Al? He shot his load right in me. You're being daft. Come here.

She pulled him back to her, so the two of them lay there on the mat, shaking still.

—You've not to worry. There's nothing to be embarrassed about, it was grand.

She woke at four in the morning, the time signalled by the bedside clock's luminous hands, green in the darkness. Al was already awake, curled beside her.

—I didn't mean to fall asleep.

She pulled herself upright, still naked, shivering with the cold. They lay on top, not beneath, the bedcovers.

—I fell asleep a bit myself. I didn't want to wake you, you were sound.

—It was grand snuggled into you. But I'll need to go, they'll be wondering at home what's happened.

—They'll be asleep, same as here. Don't worry.

—Your mother's not up?

—Snoring goodstyle. Sleep through a thunderstorm, that one. She'll not see you go.

She dressed quickly, in part to keep warm. The window had been opened to let out the cigarette smoke, and it had turned cold, the sound of the waves sharper than before.

—I swear to God there's been a frost. I'll get jittered heading home.

They both looked out at the studded, crystalline sky.

—I'll give you my jacket, it'll keep you warm.

He fetched his heavy donkey jacket from the cupboard, smelling still of grease and fish.

—It's the warmest one I have.

—I'll give it back to you tomorrow. No, today. I'm getting confused with it being so late.

—Give us a kiss. Mind on the goldfish. Take the glass, I'll get it back with the jacket.

—Tonight.

—Aye, tonight.

It seemed to take forever to go down the stairs, step and stop, step and stop. They talked in whispers, kissed too long in the doorway, the cold seeping in, until she fled when his mother shifted upstairs, bedsprings creaking.

It was a mile to her own house, the streets empty. The only sound came from two cats yowling in someone's back garden, the wheep of a night bird off somewhere, in the fields or over the roofs of houses. Then her home in view and the relief to see it in darkness.

She did not go to bed but curled in the living room, on a chair, a blanket thrown over her. The world had changed somehow; she had changed in that moment of contact, and could not sleep. Already the sun was cracking the lid of the darkness. There would be the milk float soon, and a few lorries passing in the distance, their headlight's flare on the horizon. In an hour's time she would have to go to work.

Later, she made herself some toast, not worrying about the noise now - she would have been up anyway -

and sat with a cup of tea in the kitchen, looking out the window over the village. Her house was on a hill, and she could see the whole town spread out including, far off, the outline of the sideshows. She warmed her hands, wrapping them around the cup, and looked out at them, remembering.

She checked on the fish before she left for work, but it was lying belly up in the water. They never lasted, the fairground fish, never. She flushed it down the toilet and watched its gold, limp body swirl down with the water, heading to the pipes and sewers.

NINETEEN

After the miscarriage, Carra returned to the village she had imagined she would never see again. She arrived by bus, and the driver stared at her as though he recognised her; and she in turn thought she recognised him, but could not be certain. By that point she was the only remaining passenger, her journey having taken almost a full day, and when the bus drove away, she was left looking down onto the village's long, narrow main street which was made grey and mean by a thin covering of slush and ice. It was early morning, and a Sunday, and no-one appeared to have risen yet, or at least no-one foolish enough to venture out, the wind's cut hard and driving. She had forgotten how cold it could be. Standing there with her small blue suitcase beside her, she looked down into the village and wished she had not come.

There was no taxi service in the village, so she began to walk down the road, case trundling behind her.

The place did not seem to have changed a great deal: there was the church, there the playing fields, there the pub, one windowpane cracked and held together with sheets of cardboard and parcel tape. There was a small grocery store, and a post office that doubled as a newsagents, both of which she remembered from her childhood. A corner shop sold baby clothing: that was new, but she could not recall what had stood there before. She examined the window display with its pink and blue crocheted baby jackets, its babygrows and knitted slippers, blankets embroidered with yellow ducks and Thomas the Tank Engines. The glass held her own reflection and a sodium sky behind her. She felt nothing.

A car drove past, slowly, because the road had not been gritted, crunching over the ice. She looked to see if she recognised the driver and, as she looked, the car stopped and reversed.

The window wound down and a man stuck his head out.

"Are you needing a lift?"

She lifted her case, and hurried to the car.

"Drop it in the boot. Just push anything else in there out the way."

The boot had nothing in it though, apart from a spare tyre and an empty shopping bag.

"Thank you," she said, once she was inside.

"It's no morning for walking. Where are you heading?" The driver was around her own age, dressed in suit and tie. The car smelt of pine. An air freshener hung from the dashboard, in the shape of a fir tree.

She gave her grandmother's address.

"Aye, I thought that might be it. It's Carra, isn't it?"

She looked at the man more closely.

"Do you not recognise me? You've not changed, I'll tell you that much, though you're not so keen on the goth clothing these days, eh?"

"It is Euan? It's never, is it?"

"See, you do remember! And you know, it's odd, I was thinking about you and Hamish the other day, the crack we used to have."

"Aye, those were some days. Though I'll confess, I'm not sorry for leaving."

"You fair caused a stir with that one. It was the talk of the village for weeks after. You've not been back since?"

She shook her head. "Anyhow, what are you doing with yourself now?"

"Ach, I've a wee salesman's job that takes me from place to place. It's not great, but there's not much better out there at the moment. You're quite the famous one though, I hear?"

"A few shitey commercials is not famous. I keep hoping though."

"It's better than most manage. You're looking tired, if you don't mind me saying."

"It's a long journey. And I've not been well this last while."

They turned the bend at the bottom of the village and there in the distance her grandmother's house stood on the hill.

"It's not changed."

"Nothing round here changes, Carra. You made the right decision, getting out."

They continued towards the house, up the long gravel path, where Euan stopped then helped her with her case. "I'll maybe see you around, eh?"

"That'd be good. You've got your phone number on you?"

"Better than that." He handed her his business card. "Give us a ring when you've a chance." He turned to go, stopped, turned back. "Here, do you ever hear from Hamish, how he's doing?"

She shook her head. "I don't even know where he's living now. My gran might."

"If you find out, let me know? I think about him a lot." He smiled. "You know how it is."

"Aye, I know. Thanks for that, Euan, and I'll be in touch." She looked to the house. "You know? I'm crapping myself at the thought of seeing them."

She gave him a hug before he left, then watched him drive away.

She had thought someone would come to meet her, but there was no sign. She stood at the front door and rang the doorbell. The paint on the door was flaking, so the weathered wood beneath showed through. She found she was shaking. When there was no answer, she rang again, then opened the door and entered the house.

"Hello? Dad? Nan? It's Carra."

There was no reply, but a light was showing from the kitchen ahead. When she entered, her grandmother was sitting at the kitchen table. She was eating her way through a whole Battenberg cake which she had placed before her, neatly sliced.

"Oh, it's yourself." As though it had been hours and not years since they had seen each other last. Her grandmother looked up, her expression accusatory. "You might have said you were coming."

"You changed the telephone number, it's ex-directory. But I sent a letter. Did you get it?"

"Was that the one addressed to your father? It's sitting over there still." She gestured to the kitchen worktop where her letter sat on top of several others, all unopened.

"Is he away?" Carra looked about as though he might be hidden in the kitchen somewhere.

Her grandmother looked at her. "My dear, didn't you know? He's dead. Died nearly four years ago now."

She seemed to smile as she said this.

"So that was my grand entrance. Now you see why I wanted to get away. No, that's not fair, she's getting dottled, you can see it in the way she moves and talks. She's still hard though."

Carra sat with Euan in the seating area of the village cafe, with its yellowed Formica tables that surely had lived through the 1960s, if not before, and tubular metal chairs that scraped across the floor when someone shifted their weight.

"I wondered. Just that you said you were nervous about meeting *them*, and I thought, does she know, but then I thought you must do."

"It's my own fault. I shouldn't have run off like I did. For all they knew I could have been dead myself. Aye," she sighed, "I'd such grand dreams. Now she's acting like I've never been away, and she's so wandered maybe she thinks I haven't been away. She'll never last up there on her own, Euan, not the way she's going. And the house, you should see it, it's falling down around her ears."

"There's a reason they say you should never go back."

"I just thought, closure, you know? Going back to confront old ghosts and all the rest of that shite. But now? Now I've no idea what to think."

"It's a shock for yourself as well."

"I don't think I've taken it in, really. I keep on thinking I should feel sad, but I don't. That makes me seem such a heartless bitch. Mind, it's my fault for not keeping in touch."

403

She looked out the window. It was midday, but the streets were almost empty. In the post office on the opposite side of the road, the clerk was staring out the window towards Carra, who stared back.

"Put your eyes back on their stalks, why don't you?" she said.

"You'll mind the reason for not coming back here soon enough. It's no fun when you're young. I waited too long, and now I've bought myself a wee place that looks down over the harbour and I'll never move. Don't blame yourself, you did the right thing getting out when you did."

They finished their coffee and headed out in Euan's car to his house. His was amongst three new bungalows built, one alongside the other, on what had once been farmland.

"See?" He pointed to his neighbour who watched at the window when the car drew up. "They'll be saying to each other, 'Euan's got himself a fancy woman now.' It'll be all round the village this time tomorrow."

"That'll come as a shock then."

"Och. I'm just an eccentric bachelor lad to them, too busy with his work to worry too much about lassies and suchlike. They've barely got their heads round the birds and the bees, some of these old ones, much less the bees and the bees and the birds and the birds."

"You're not seeing anyone then?"

"I was for a while, someone out west, but it got complicated." He was silent for a moment. "You know how it is."

"Well, I think you're a catch. They can spread all the rumours they like."

They stepped out the car onto the gravelled driveway. Braes rose above the house, frosted still, while below was the road to the harbour. She could see the beach from there, and the lighthouse.

"You've a grand view. All I see from my flat is other apartment blocks."

"You'd not be saying that when the wind blows in from the north sea."

He opened the door, and they both went inside. For a modern bungalow, it was surprisingly dark, and the rooms overcluttered.

"Mind the mess. I'm away so much I never seem to get time to tidy up. I'll make us another cup." He gestured at the sofa. "Settle down and make yourself comfortable. Switch the telly on: you might see yourself."

"I see myself every time I look in a mirror, I don't need the TV for that." She sat down on the couch. The springs had gone so it slumped beneath her. "It's not anything like as glamorous as you might think. And it's not a business as will make you rich."

"You must have seen some sights though." His voice, disembodied, coming from direction of the kitchen.

"Aye, but they're not always bonny sights, Euan. It's not a bonny business, really."

He appeared carrying two mugs of coffee, one for her, one for himself. A skinny ginger tom followed him, meowing, getting in the way of his legs.

"Ach, away. You're not long fed." He handed the cup to Carra. "He's a bottomless pit, that one. Not that you'd think it to look at him."

"I miss my cats. We always had them in the house, mind? I should maybe get one now, it'd be a bit of company in the evenings."

"That makes you sound lonely."

"It can be a bit. It's not like here, Euan. Big cities swallow you up and most people don't even know you're there." She held the mug in both hands, for warmth. "Here puss, puss."

The cat turned and ran out the living room.

"He's contrary like that." He sat down opposite her. "Are you up for long?"

"I don't know. It's not been a good time for me this last while, but I'm not sure living in that old house is going to help any."

"You're welcome to stay here, you know. I'll be coming and going over the next few days, but not far. It's a bit more central too, and you'll see meet some others you recognise. Though there's not many of them now. Most did what you did and got out as quickly as possible."

"It'd not be fair to my gran. I feel sorry for her, up there all on her own. Though she's the cats too, mind you. She's a bit scary now. You look at her and there's something come loose, you can tell from the expression."

"She always was a bit scary, your nan."

"It was when she had the win, and then she stopped drinking. I mind someone saying that, how it had made her sour. Here," she stood up suddenly, "we could take a walk down to the harbour. I've not seen it since I arrived." She moved to the window and looked out.

"Aye, there's a bit of sunshine now and the walk'll keep us warm. Do you fancy it?"

"Sure. If that's what you want."

The sun had slipped behind a layer of grey, uniform cloud by the time they arrived, and a bitter wind pushed in from the ocean. They stood on the sea wall that divided the harbour from the beach and looked out to the water.

Carra had borrowed one on Euan's coats, which hung too large around her body. "I'd forgotten how cold it was here. There's no escaping that wind, is there?"

"You've grown soft living in the south."

Two fishermen passed on the way to their vessel, a small creel boat docked by the harbour. They wore yellow, fluorescent waterproofs that looked unnaturally garish in the stark light. One of them waved to Euan, who waved back.

"The rumour grows," he said.

They walked to the far end of the sea wall, which stretched beyond the beach and into the sea. The hand rails that ran on either side had come loose and, in some places, were missing. When they reached the end, Carra lifted a pebble by her feet and threw it into the water, where it skipped across the waves.

"I've not lost that touch," she said.

They stood there, watching the surge of the ocean, which pushed inwards, breaking against the wall and throwing spray up so it spattered them. Far off, sun broke through the cloud and lit a section of the water, which glittered.

"So that's where the sun went." Carra leaned over the railing and pointed. "Far, far away."

The waves threw white spume around her feet.

"We'll need to go back," Euan said. "The tide's coming in."

"I will, in a minute."

She stood looking down into the sea, which pushed inwards. One of the waves rose and broke full against her legs, but she did not move.

"Really," said Euan. "We'll have to go."

He grasped her hand and took her back to the steps that led from the wall down onto the shore. From there, they trudged up the shingled beach to where it met the road.

"Are you all right?" Euan walked alongside her, though he had let go her hand by that point. "I was a wee bit worried about you there."

"Aye. I'm fine. I'd forgotten how many memories this place holds, and they're not pleasant, some of them."

"I wondered." He hugged her. "I don't know if it's a good idea, you coming back here."

"It's fine. Honest it is." She looked up to him and he saw she was crying. "Oh, Euan," she said. "What's happening to me?"

Her grandmother was watching through the window when Euan dropped her home.

"Like everyone here," he said. "Addicted to windows."

"I'll call you later. I hope I haven't been too much of a downer."

"Of course not. Of course you haven't."

She stayed in the same bedroom she had as a child, but it had been stripped of all of her belongings. Now there was only the bed and nothing more. Out the window, the trees were fuller than she remembered, but they had turned bare. Crows still sheltered in the branches, against the wind, which had grown stronger.

She did not go out for the remainder of the day. Her grandmother watched television, while she played with her mobile phone, trying to get reception.

"It'll do you no good, it's not a fancy city life you're leading here," her grandmother warned, and she was right.

On the television, a hospital drama was showing, and one of the doctors had just delivered a baby. Carra had to run to her bedroom, where she lay on the bed, crying.

"I got Hamish's address for you. My gran had it still."

She handed him a slip of paper with the address written on it. They were in the car, sitting in a side road, looking on to fielded braes and, beyond that, the ocean.

"That's grand. I've not heard from him since he left. He came for your dad's funeral, but I was away. He's doing well for himself, I'm hearing. His own business now, and a wife and a bairn. In fact, two bairns at least: there was another one on the way when he was here last."

"He said that, he'd get married one day. I didn't believe him. You'll not get your hopes up too much, eh?"

"There's plenty that are married, Carra. Sometimes it's just for show. Playing the part, aye?"

"It runs in the family then." She pointed to a small fishing boat, far off in the water. "There's not many of them now. I noticed that yesterday."

"It's a hard life, you know that. People have become softer, Carra. They want their jobs in the office, or the shops. There's not jobs of any sort here. You can see the place dying around you, especially since the railway closed." He paused. "The crash was only an excuse though. They'd wanted to close the line for years."

"I mind my dad saying that. 'Its time's running out,' he said. Well, he was right about something."

Euan was examining the address.

"Will you contact him?"

"Maybe. But sometimes it's better to leave the past alone, you know?" He folded the paper and put it in his wallet. "Have you anyone, Carra?"

She shook her head. "Not really. Ambition's a terrible thing Euan. It eats away at you and doesn't leave time for anything else. Yes, I've imagined myself married, and with a few wee bairns of my own, and sometimes I think there'd be nothing better, and sometimes there'd be nothing worse."

"It's not like our parents though, on the scrapheap by the time you're twenty if you haven't met someone. There's time."

"Aye, maybe." She bent forward and tears fell from her face to her lap. "Oh Euan, I've done such awful things."

"No you haven't. It's all in your mind, Carra. You're like your mam, she always looked on the black side too."

He tried to pull her towards him, to hug her, but she pushed him away and opened the door with such force she fell out onto the tarmac, and she ran down the adjoining field, towards the sea.

Euan caught up with her down by the wire fence dividing one field from the next. She was curled up tight, pressed against the wire. Her clothes were sodden from sweat and from the wet of the grass. She was crying still. He helped her up and led her back to his car.

"Where did you think you were going?"

She looked at him, and there was despair in her face. "Hamish, what's happening to me?"

"It's Euan, not Hamish. You're all confused, Carra. Promise me, you'll go see a doctor?"

But she only looked at him, as though she did not recognise who he was.

She woke to find a hand over her mouth. It was translucent and wet and she could see the blue veins traced below the skin. An almost-child sat astride her. It had wide yellow eyes like a cat's and it straddled her chest, looking down into her face, and it wore an expression somewhere between hatred and despair.

"Mummy", it said, "Mummy." Over and over, without variation.

She found she could not move: her arms seemed paralysed by her sides, and neither would her legs respond. It was difficult to breathe, for the hand pressed against her mouth seemed considerably larger than a child's. A harsh, stale smell filled the room.

A few doors away, she could hear her grandmother moving around, talking to herself, but the words were indistinct. It seemed impossible she could not hear the child, who was calling with ever greater volume and urgency. A wash of light came through the bedroom window, its curtains drawn back, a habit she had retained since her childhood. The light filtering through was the stark colour of snow and stars. Carra wet herself, so the sheets beneath her thighs became at first hot and then uncomfortably cold.

The child's words grew increasingly frantic so they began to run into each other. Mummymummymummy! It pushed its body against her own and clung to her with a tight ferocity. She could not scream, not out loud, but inside something crumpled and withered and pieces began to fall away, so the scene became even more unreal. She felt a terrible pain, it was a violation, but there was only the child pressed to her, its grip so tight it was agonizing. She could feel herself sinking and sinking, as if tumbling down in the deepest sea, and she carried the child and her hurt with her, welcoming the blackness that lay waiting on the ocean bed.

When Carra did not call, Euan drove to see her. Overnight there had been a heavy fall of snow and he had to leave his car at the end of the driveway, which was blocked, and walk to the house. The drift came up to his knees. He had not seen a fall like that since he was a child, and they used to slide down the braes, using empty plastic feed sacks. The white of the snow, unmarked apart from a few bird tracks, made the house look even more dilapidated than usual.

It was the grandmother who answered the door. She had wrapped a thick coat around her body, even though he could feel the heat radiating from indoors. It struck him that he did not know her name or, if he once had, then he had forgotten. She looked at him, but did not invite him in. Behind her, he could see all the lights had been turned on, but the hallway still managed to seem gloomy.

"Is Carra in?" He would have said this as a child.

She looked at him and then through him. "She's away," she said. "Last night or this morning, I don't know when."

"Didn't she say she was going?"

The wind, rising, sent a spray of white around his feet.

"No. She's off like the last time, without a goodbye to anyone. That girl." This last as if to herself.

"Are you sure she's all right? She didn't say she was leaving, and she was a bit upset last night when I was speaking to her."

"She took her clothes with her, if that's what you mean. If she intends any harm to herself, she'll do it well-dressed." She leant towards him. There was a smell from her breath, slightly sweet and unpleasant. It smelt like custard power that had gone off. "And you know what else? I'm glad she's gone. Coming back where's she's not wanted, and stirring up things that should have been left alone."

"Will you get her to call me then, if she's in touch?"

She turned away from him though, shuffling. She wore pink, furred slippers shaped like rabbits. She closed the door, with such force snow fell from the eaves.

A moment later, it opened again.

"Euan," she said. So she knew his name, even if he did not know hers.

She leant forward again, and spat full in his face, then closed the door quickly, leaving him standing there bemused, alone in the snow.

TWENTY

They should not have left her alone they should not, the house all empty and the children gone, their father too - her son - and only the cats wandering up and down the hallways, their soft tread, curled at her feet at night then waking her in the morning, their insistent purr, different from contentment, and she would put on her slippers, the sort that flipped and flopped, the pink fur across her toes, the nightdress pink as well, the nylon static on her skin, she must have looked a sight coming down the stairs into the cold kitchen, the cats gathering around her legs, wailing, while she reached up into the cupboard for their food, opening the tin and forking the strong smelling meat into their dish, watching the battle between them all when the dish was placed on the floor, before she returned to bed, it was still too cold, autumn cusping to winter and the fire dead in the hearth and no coal in the scuttle, she would have to go out to fetch some more but it was still early, the house was dark and she was afraid, the central heating had never been fixed, she cursed the day she had the winnings for she missed her old council house, its cosy rooms, its view over neighbours' gardens and the noise in the street no matter the time of day, traffic passing and children playing and her friends out for shopping, carrying their bags with the Co-op label, filled with loaves of bread and packets of fishfingers, a pint of milk maybe, but here it was so far from anywhere, only trees and fields to look out on, and neighbours were far off and not the sort she would talk to anyway, so the isolation of the house pushed in, its noises unexpected even after years of listening, so unlike the noises in the past, the sounds of life to deflect the ones that scared her so, as if the house was not truly deserted, as if there were others in there with her unseen, and who was to say there was not, the number of people who must have lived there over the years, the tracks of their passing melted into the walls, and even in her bedroom, the covers she slipped under, it did not feel safe, it was as if someone watched her, the room's shadows more definite in the growing light, and which was worse all dark or part dark she did not know, she wished someone was there to keep her company, even the knowledge of their presence would be a comfort, and on the roof a scuffing that would be birds, the crows that gathered when they left their treetops, vaults of nests in the branches, they were cruel birds, they were, they would get the lambs, she saw it when she was little, they would go for their eyes, no she did not like them, except maybe it was not crows, maybe the noises came from the attic, she had never been there, her legs would not take her up the ladder, it was a strange land that place, she had never seen it, she imagined it as you would imagine a foreign country, a shadowed place with hidden dangers, she had never gone abroad for that reason, everyone had said she should, but she bought the house and that was most of the money gone, knowing what was left would see her into old age if she was careful, though she had not thought at the time how far those years would stretch, with their isolation, yes, she had always looked at the house and admired it and wanted it, she wanted the envy in people's eyes when she passed, but the house was gloomy, its shadows seeped in and infected her mind and now she was the only one and it would be the grandchildren's when she was gone, wherever they might be, and she would be another ghost to haunt the corridors, the long passageways with their dun light, that never seemed bright even when the sun shone, and she wondered who lived here before, the house was old, three hundred years, generations come and gone, and sometimes she thought she saw someone at the end of the corridor, where it turned to the back bedrooms, the glimpse of a foot, barefoot, perhaps the whisk of a skirt, but she could be mistaken because it could not be her, it could not, but it looked like her, the same, the very same, the one that used to walk barefoot around the house in winter, her feet blue with cold but she would not wear socks never mind shoes, even when she was scolded about it, and when the girl stubbed her toe and the nail came loose, she told her serves you right, not without satisfaction, she was ashamed of that later for the girl was only a child and children had their own ways, and she was a peculiar child as well, both the girls were strange, it must have come from their mother, she was a wayward, fey thing, always so sickly, that pallor would frighten the dead, and she was the first to go, it was no surprise really, you would have said it was expected, she remembered how, after they moved in, her daughter-in-law was so delighted she wandered the garden and cupped her hands and held them up as though she was catching the light, and all the time there was the strangest look on her face, she was only half-there sometimes, it was the children that had done it, she was too frail to bear that burden, you could see it in her face and her body that seemed to collapse into itself, and maybe it was her and not the granddaughter in the corridor, the one she would not enter at night, unless she switched all the lights on and carried a cat in her arms, even though she really needed both hands to climb the stairs, it was like taking a canary into a mine, though sometimes the cats would spook her, they would be lying in the living room and they would look up and stare, seeing something she could not, they say animals can see things that we cannot, ghosts, yes, animals and children can do that, their minds not yet formed, and she would feel chill then, it was only her mind, she knew, but something passed her by, she felt it near, it was her imagination, it was her imagination, it was her imagination and oh what about the singing that time, it was only the wind, the way it whistled through the trees, except it was not, and she had been in the kitchen, the same place her cats led her in the morning, and there was a man's voice singing low, she could not make out the words but it was clear in the ever so still, it could not be the wind, and besides it was close to her, it could have come from the same room, but the sound was muffled as if heard through a wall, she wondered at first if it was voices from the television in the living room but it was not, and then it had suddenly become ever so cold, even though it had been a summer's day, it was cold enough to see her breath and that was not her imagination, no, so she ran from the kitchen, she could not help it, into the living room, and she slammed the door tight but then remembered the cats, she could not leave the cats in there, so she opened it again and there was a terrible fear, it rose and rose through her body, freezing and electric at the same time, she knew then what it was to be paralysed by terror, she did, even though there was nothing there and nothing had happened and it was only her imagination, you had to expect that, an old woman in a big house all alone with no-one to talk to or confide in or share her worries, because she sometimes wet herself during the night and did not know why, and there was the top room she would not go into, the one with the green wallpaper that made the room close in on itself, it was so claustrophobic, the girls' belongings stored in there, they had never been thrown away, old dresses and dolls and games still boxed, some counters missing, scores written on notepaper and the youngest had always won, she remembered that, and that was the problem, the house was crowded with memories, she could not escape them, so the present seemed less substantial than the past and the hours between rising in the morning and turning to sleep at night were the flimsiest of things, they were tissue paper, while events from fifty years ago had the clarity of water she paddled in as a child, down there on the shore, only warm in the shallows that lapped over her toes, the sand and pebbles underneath, and it was so hot her shoulders would burn and peel, her mother watching further back on the beach, though she would sometimes join her, the two of them wading through the shallows, those were happy times, she had taken her own son there and the grandchildren too, though she could not go there now, even if she was able, those memories had soured, and she wondered again about the figure barefoot upstairs, the one she may or may not have seen slipping past the corner at the edge of the passageway, and sometimes she had the urge to follow her, to run and to shout, but these days she could not run, she could only shuffle, her legs barely carried her, and she wondered what she would do if they gave up altogether, she could not live in the house then, but she would not leave either, no she would curl up and die rather than go into one of those nursing homes where they treated you like children, although maybe it was better than this, the loneliness and fear, the only people she saw were the postie and the coal man and the man who delivered the groceries, she would sit at the window waiting for them to come, watching for the vehicle to drive up the long track road, then the excitement as it turned into the driveway so there was maybe a word or two with the postman, because she would order things that had to be signed for, it gave her the opportunity to speak, or the groceries had to be taken into the house and unpacked, and to have someone there made such a difference; but then she was alone again and sometimes what she had ordered would go straight into the bin, clothes she did not want or need, she sometimes thought she should get someone in to help, because that would be company, but she did not trust a stranger in the house and besides, it filled the hours, polishing and polishing ornaments and the pictures on the walls, although she had to take the pictures down in the hallway because she passed them and saw her reflection, and she was always afraid she would see another figure there, wan in the glass, a man or woman or girl or boy following her, only part substantial, and would it be worse if it was them or not, she had not heard from the girl or boy for many years, they could be alive, they could be dead, yes, who knows, she had outlived all the others, her friends too, and that was the problem, yes, it was the house, it was alive with their ghosts, and the boy had sat in his room with his friend, the one who had talked and looked like a girl, and she had wondered what was going on behind the closed doors, the soft giggles that came, and once she had tried to look through the keyhole but could not see anything, only the rounded, blurred shape of the lock itself and the light beyond, so she sometimes entered under the pretence she had come to clean his room and did not know they were there, or did they want something to eat, but they were never doing anything, only sitting on the edge of the bed looking at the backs of LP covers or at comics, or they were seated on the ground talking ever so softly, so maybe they did not dare but she knew they did, they were careful, they were clever, and even to the boy's father it was evident, although he did not say, and he hit the bottle so hard he did not care anyway, she wondered if there was talk, that still mattered to her then, and she felt ashamed to speak to people she met, people now surely dead, and she sometimes wondered if she would ever join them, or if death would flutter continually at her shoulder without ever descending, she was so afraid it would land, she was so afraid it would not, that was how it was, and when she settled into bed at night with the cold, still house so evident around her, she wondered if she would wake or if this was the final day, if the cats would still press around her when she was gone, hot clumps around her cold body, and who would look after them then, who would even notice she was gone, it might be weeks or months before someone raised the alarm, she had read of stories like that, the body discovered husked years later, forgotten not only in death but in life, and she wondered if the boy and girl would mourn her, or if they ever even thought of her, they were living a new life somewhere, one she could not even guess at, and her so alone with only the shadows and unsettling sounds to keep her company, she ought to visit the graves of the others someday, but would she even be able to find them, no one else would visit them now, they would be untended, not even flowers to fade and wither, the names strange to those who wandered the graveyards, not even the anchor of memory, and maybe is that why they came, if it was them, if they caused the knocks and creaks and bumps and sighs that were even more evident at night so she could not at first sleep for fear, it crawled alongside her, an unwelcome bed-mate, there was the terrible apprehension that eventually turned to a sense of unreality, and then sleep came in fits and starts, an exhausted sleep, and maybe one day she would scare herself to death, but until that day she would continue to lie there, sometimes daring to close her eyes, she scrunched them tight, as though whatever was there would go away, if it was there, and it did, it did, it eventually did, but only when daylight came, the light chased the worst away and the circle began again, so she trod down the stairs to feed the cats and the house was cold and the fire was dead in the hearth, and she returned to bed until it was warmer, yes, it felt as though her entire life was caught in a loop, that was how it felt, and she would look outside the window but not feel tempted to go outside, though maybe she should, especially on the warmer days, but the garden was alive with insects and birds and the distant sound of the sea, and maybe an aeroplane overhead scoring the sky, and that only served to make the house's silence all the more evident, at least in the few rooms she limited herself to, there were bedrooms that were empty, she had not entered them for years, the doors were shut, no need to go in them any longer, and who knew what she would find were she to open them, the rooms maybe smelling a little of damp, the windows failing to let in much light, dirt-grained, she could picture it exactly in her mind, and it was so different years ago, all the children had their own room and her son and his strange, wayward wife, she thought of her now and was certain there was something a little bit stray there, it had come loose after the first bad illness, the one where the family gathered at her hospital bedside certain she would die, the fever biting deep and the pallor of her skin so grey, she would never recover any colour, though she had little enough to begin with, you could see her ribs and the cut of her shoulder blades when she turned, and how she would get lost in her memories, and then in the evenings, when she was tired, she would talk animatedly of people and places she had known, and no-one would pay attention, they knew the routine, but she carried on talking anyway, before eventually heading to bed to fall into the deepest sleep, it carried her far into the morning, through the noise of the children rising and their father rising even earlier to head for work, a time not fully light even in summer, yes, and in the winter they would not see him in daylight at all, it seemed he stayed away as long as he could, especially after his

425

wife's death, and the event on the beach, the one she still saw replayed, and the horror never lessened, the family seemed to fall apart after that, no wonder the two remaining turned out so odd, taking after their mother, the youngest girl even had the same illness as a child, yes, they took after their mother not their father, though god knows he had his faults, and they were her own too, though now she did not even have the enthusiasm for those failings, she felt herself stretched transparent, and soon something would give, she knew that, yes she did, and maybe that was why she clung to the disagreeable past now, why she hunted out old photographs, age-curled, the family posed with stilted smiles, the artificial poses, the early ones so often at the beach but not the later ones, that would be unthinkable, the faces she had problems remembering without the photos to aid her, and even then she had difficulty placing them in memory, she remembered details, what they wore, the way they moved, the things they owned, but when she tried to visualise them it was the photographs she mentally saw, their awkward poses, and would it be like that for her too when she was gone, though did anyone truly remember her, or did others look through their old photographs and wonder who she was, there would not be many left who recalled her, and if she was to turn the corner, if she was to face what waited there, if she did look up in the kitchen, would she recognise who stood before her, would it be the son or daughter-in-law or granddaughter, would she know who they were, and would they recognise her, she ought to build up courage, they were only phantoms as disembodied as the voices on the telephone, the ones that called and tried to sell her things, they were the only people who rang now, even though she was ex-directory, it was that or wrong numbers, like the voiceless call at two in the morning, the one that used to alarm her but which now did not, because who was there to worry about, no-one, that was the truth, they would only be images like the ones on her TV screen, made up of lines, it was just an illusion, all you were really looking at was light that acted and moved as though it was human, yes, that was it, it was a memory, it was an echo, it might even be her own memory escaped and taken form, it would be like looking in a mirror from another time, if only she had the courage, if only she had, and she told herself it was imagination, but could not convince herself and that was not because of what she had heard in the kitchen, not what she had seen at the end of the passageway, nor sensed in the empty bedroom, no, it was because of the garden and truly that was why she was afraid to go out, because there were figures amongst the trees, she saw them from a distance, between the tree trunks, the crack of twigs, the crush of leaves, and a phantom would not do that, they were surely real, and sometimes they spoke, she recognised the voices though she could not say with certainty it was them, the voices had faded like the faces, and once she was alone outside, it was a summer's night and she was sitting on the doorstep, and one of them called to her, it said her name, it was not a stray word, it talked to her, it was a girl's voice, maybe it was *her* voice, and she stood and for a moment was in an earlier time, the years had fallen back, they split for her like shed skin, and she found herself walking down the driveway and over the grass, towards the trees, she was beyond thinking, and someone stood there, shadowed, calling to her, and she walked towards the figure and it was as though she was younger again, she was not an old woman, there was the smell of heat in the air, as it was when the children had played in the garden, yes, she had been the one to look after them once the mother was gone, they were truly her children, they were, and she tried to protect them but the world was so fast moving and strange, and moreover there was always something unspoken in the air, something that passed between them, the girls and the boy, but she never found out what, she had even tried to bully it from them but they would not say, it was their shared secret and their source of power, and the tension she felt in the air then, it was there again that evening amongst the trees, her name called softly, and it was the girl, it was surely the girl, the one she could almost see, standing there, shadowed, and the figure held out a hand and she held out her own, it was if she was in a dream, as if she was hypnotised, and what would have happened if they touched, if she had held out her hand and had felt fingers warm or cold, that would be unthinkable, and so she hurried back to the house, but age caught her again, her legs gave way, she fell and she was crying, she was like a child once more, and she looked back certain someone would be there advancing, but there was no-one, only a high, terrified roar in her ears, and when she returned indoors she shook and shook and the trembling would not leave her, and has never left her since.

She knows one day she will climb the stairs, she will walk without hesitation down the corridor, around the corner and past the rooms that have lain untouched for years, the ones she will open to find only memories, there are too many of those, and she will walk below the hatch for the attic, the one she never opens, and she will walk to the very end, to the room with the green wallpaper, the one that is locked, that is always locked, she will have taken the key where it hangs on the kitchen wall and she will turn it in the lock, and the lock will be stiff but it *will* turn, she will have to use both hands, it will grind then click, and she will push open the door which will be rigid with dirt, stepping into the interior which will be dark, the light will have been banished from that room, the curtains pulled for years, more years than she can remember, and it will be silent, but she will step inside and there will be sounds, faint at first then louder, there will be footsteps and voices, and then when her eyes have adjusted to the dim she will see them, emerging from the corners, they will come to her and they will hold out their hands to her and she will not be scared, she will not, and they will touch her and she will let them, and she will be gathered into their arms and the darkness will take her and engulf her and then there will be nothing.

TWENTY ONE

They approached the island with a storm pushing behind. Where they were, the sea was unnaturally still, the only sound that of the boat's engine as it cut through water. The island was green and flat and unfamiliar, even though they had sailed that way many times before.

"It's going to be a monster." Iain turned back from his position at the helm to look at high, curdled cloud, ferociously black and streaked with grey. Beyond, it was still blue sky and sun, but the dark rose and overtook it faster than the boat could travel.

"Aye. We'll be lucky to reach land before it hits. Though thon island's not going to be much of a help by the looks of it anyway." Jock had taken the wheel from him temporarily. "It's the lad I feel sorry for. See him? White as a sheet. He'll not have seen a storm like this before."

He pointed at Artie who stood at the stern, looking out, unmoving, watching the sky's advance.

"We'll maybe none of us have seen a storm like this, the way it's looking. You feel that breeze that's starting up? It's almost tropical."

"I wouldnae know, Iain. It's not all of us that's served in Africa like you have. I spent most mine in a raw and dirty barracks Aberdeen way."

"These lads today, they have it made and they don't know it. A bit of national service never did anyone any harm."

"That's when I met Jessie. She's done plenty harm over the years, the way she spends money."

Both men laughed, memories turned inward. "We'll maybe get him here," Iain said. "It'll do him no good staring like that. That's rabbit in the headlights, if ever." He shouted to Artie. "Here man, get yourself up here and give us a hand."

He had to call twice before Artie responded and only then with reluctance. He turned and his face had a fearful, distracted look.

"It'll not kill you. Come up, help Jock keep an eye out for rocks. His eyesight's not what it was." He winked at Jock, while Artie trod uncertainly towards them, feet unsteady on the deck. He was small for his age, his twentieth birthday coming up, and had not yet gained the bulk to compensate.

"You're fair looking green. You'll get used to the storms, and be all the more glad to return home when it's over." Jock lit himself a cigarette and let the smoke plume around his features. "Head up top and keep watch. I've been this way before and there's less depth than there appears. Give us a shout if you see anything."

Artie nodded and left without speaking, leaning over the boat's edge and looking into the water. The cloud had nearly caught up with them, and so the water appeared black, and grew choppy.

"Do you think we'll make it before it hits?" Iain had lit a cigarette of his own and was lashing down the creels and nets as best as he was able.

"You wouldnae be doing that if you thought we would, would you? Aye, we'll all be green about the gills before the day's over."

From the side of the boat came the sound of Artie spewing.

"And the wind's not even caught us yet." Jock pointed to his head. "It's all in here. I mind my first time too, I fair shit my pants before the storm was even on us. They were some waves, it was a right wall of water in front of us and we were just like this wee bit of wood being tossed about. Aye, I willnae forget that one in a hurry." He shook his head, remembering.

Iain looked skywards. "The gulls are beating us to it."

A thick flock of birds, white caught in grey, were descending on the island, which was still in sunlight. The same light had gone from around the boat and the sea began to swell.

"Ah Christ, it's catching us sooner than I'd thought. We'll need our wits now. Best get the lad."

The wind rose and water splashed over the sides, a strangeness in its scent, as though it had been pulled from the depths.

Jock called to Artie "Here, get back here where it's safe."

Artie turned, then slipped and slid his distance to the cabin door, when the craft tilted. Iain reached and pulled him in, the three of them tight in there, afraid but unwilling to admit it. The boat rose and rose on ever growing waves and the sky was a colour almost soured.

"Cheer up, Artie. There's not a storm we haven't come through yet," said Jock.

The boat, climbing, began to fall. It fell and as it fell, the water seemed to part on either side to welcome it.

*

There was the cold, salt touch of water and, above, the boat capsized and fragmented. Someone spun close to him, but he could not see whether it was Iain or Jock; the water held them and pushed them down and further down, further than he could see. There was not even time to be afraid, with the whole crashing, muffled, violent sea around him, the blackest of black, and to even attempt to fight against its weight was hopeless. He was beyond sight and beyond touch and felt nothing but the chill reaching into his body, its intensity. His life did not flash before him, no blinding lights appeared at the end of tunnels, with his ancestors paraded beyond, waiting to greet him; no, there was only cold and there was only dark and then there was nothing.

He woke to sunlight, on a shingle beach, and the sea had ripped the clothes from him, so he was naked. Around about lay shards of wood from the boat, along with great clagged mounds of kelp, water still held in redded fronds. He was aware of that, of light, and especially of pain. He could not move for the pain, for his body was wealed as though someone had whipped him, livid lashes and bruises already yellowed and purpled. A black headed gull was beside him, picking at his face, and did not even pay attention to him when he moved and groaned and attempted to wave it away.

He saw then his hand had gone and all that was left at the wrist was a ragged stump, congealed and sand-encrusted. He did more than stare at death at the moment; he welcomed it, and wished the whole damn world away, the beach, the numbing, surging water, the too-blue sky, and the bitter, constant wind that whipped around his ears and sounded at times like someone crying. But death did not come.

The men found him a full day later, by chance. He could not remember any of that except, perhaps, a transitory moment in which he was carried in someone's arms, his face pressed against an orange lifejacket, but he could not be certain this was not something imagined in retrospect. He was certain he dreamt Mary, his wife, had come to visit him on the beach, standing there as pale and wan as always, just standing there, sad and looking down at him while the waves crept close enough to almost touch his body. That would have been the ultimate irony, if the sea had first saved him and disfigured him, but then had chosen to draw him back out into its weighted, unknowable depths. Years later, he asked her, had she dreamt she had seen him lying there, but she only smiled and shook her head with that withdrawn expression she had come to wear so often, and he pulled her to him, lying there in bed, her body frail as a bird's, and he was afraid she would crack if he held her too tightly.

They never found Iain, or Jock, and he did not ever dare to return to the fishing.

As a child he had gone to the harbour, and sometimes one of the fishermen would take him out in the boat, while he helped them lower and lift their creels with the brown crabs and lobsters caught inside. It had seemed such an idyllic life then, there could be none better, and it was all he dreamed of throughout childhood, in the stifling classrooms. People would ask him what he wanted to be when he grew up, and he always said a fisherman; it was always the same answer. He had not thought of the danger, even though people had warned him; and now there was only danger, he could not think past that.

He was fitted with a prosthetic hand, but it lay stiffly on his wrist and its inanimacy seemed a worse disfigurement that the sight of his reddened, scarred stump, so one day he removed it and never wore it again. It lay in a drawer, undiscovered, long after his wife had died and he had died. It was his own mother who found it, and she stared at it as though it was an alien thing, because she could not even remember him having worn it, and by then she was lost in the confusion of her own memories anyway, could no longer distinguish past from present, or even realise there was any difference between the two.

"Artie?"

He was on the boat again. The sea rose and fell, and the wind was mounting and lifted the waves over the prow in a hard, fierce spray. He slid on the slick deck, unable to keep his footing. Iain and Jock were there too, but the waves caught them and they slipped past him as the deck tilted. He reached for them, and they held out their arms, but all he had was a stump for a hand and he could not grasp them.

"Artie?"

His wife shook his shoulder, lightly at first, then more forcefully, but she could not raise him. He had been calling out and the sound had woken her. Though he was quiet now and at least he had not disturbed the rest of the house.

It was growing light. She lay for a while, trying to get back to sleep, but the brightness was intrusive, even when she pulled the covers over her face to block it out. Artie smelt of whisky.

Eventually she rose and stared out the bedroom window. It was a fine, clear morning, and the rising sun shone through the tops of the trees, wakening crows that roosted there. They rose and spun in the sky, which had not yet gained colour. From where she stood, she saw the window open in Crissy's bedroom, and her daughter's head poked out, watching, as she did, the birds pulling free from the treetops. After a while, she became aware of her mother looking at her, and waved to her.

Mary padded out of the room and towards her daughter's bedroom. She only wore a thin nightdress, and shivered, even though the morning was not cold.

Crissy was still looking out of the window when her mother entered her bedroom.

"Go back to bed," Mary said. "It's still early."

"But you're awake. And I couldn't sleep."

"Your dad woke me. He was having one of his dreams."

"Is he all right?"

"You're too young to be worrying about things like that. Go to sleep."

She curled up beside her daughter on the bed, and held her, and sleep did eventually come.

The two of them were in the street, talking, Jock's wife, and Iain's. Jock's wife stood in the doorway of her daughter's house, which she had moved to after her husband's death. She was frail now, and had to hold herself upright with aid of a walking frame. Iain's wife had her children in tow, the four of them, well-dressed, because she had remarried quickly, out of necessity. Her new husband was a bastard, everyone said so, and she sometimes walked through the streets with dark glasses on, even on overcast days.

Artie avoided them. They had not spoken since the memorial service, the one where everyone stared at him with pity, or with accusation, and he could not speak or think or hear the entire day. When he thought of that time, all he could recall was the loud, loud ringing in his ears and his static, unfocussed vision. It only occurred to him afterwards he had been on the edge of collapse the whole time. When it was over, a terrible emptiness took its place.

"You're so lucky to be alive."

How many times had he heard that? But he was never convinced by the statement.

That day though, he was too late to avoid them, and the women saw him, both nodding in recognition. He nodded back, then crossed to the opposite side of the street, as if that was the direction he was heading. His deception must have been obvious, him in his station uniform and the afternoon shift about to start. He took the long way round to his work, and he had difficulty breathing, he felt giddy, and was it like the day of the service all over again.

When his mother won the pools and then she bought the house, people said, "Things are changing for you at last," but he did not believe them. His mother was as hard as sin and he had to work the trains each day, same as before. Passengers would stare at the stump he used to hold the ticket machine in place while he operated the buttons with his one good hand.

One day Iain's wife was on the train and so he did not collect any tickets at all, hiding in the guard's van instead, recognising each unseen stop from the train's clatter and rattle, knowing when it would turn the bends and when not, and when its speed would increase and when it would slow. He said he was ill, and he was, but the illness was the fear that buzzed around his head each time he was forced to remember his past. He kept a bottle hidden in a corner under a pile of work jackets, and he kept a half bottle in his uniform pocket too. By the time the train reached its destination he was stinking drunk and had to open the door of the guard van to be sick on the railroad tracks. Nevertheless, he went to the station bar and drank through his hour's break, so they had to carry him on the train and call his wife to meet him at the station when the train arrived back.

"There are worse off than you, you know," she had said, the following day, when the chill of her emotion had decided to break.

Still he could not bring himself to tell her why, and besides, he could not fully say himself, except he dreamed nightly of the rising, blackened sea, and of his hand cast somewhere deep into its waters.

When his son was born he was afraid to hold him. When his wife died, he could barely help carry the coffin, and when he did, it tilted to one side, so a man from amongst the mourners had to rush to help him, in case it fell. He did not recognise the man, and never learned his name.

"She's better off where she is," he was told, "she's not been a well woman." That and, "It must be a relief in a way, now it's over."

This said in such a way as to indicate they knew it was not only physical illness that had taken her, and that this was worse somehow than the gnawing onset of cancer or the flip-flop-stop of a heart attack. It was true, it was a relief in a way, because sometimes she had looked at him the way she would a stranger, but still the bed was empty and cold, and the silences were silences of absence even the children's sounds could not fill, their laughing and shrieks and squabbles sounding dwarfed and empty, as though they played in an vast and unfriendly hall. He wondered if he had been responsible in some way, as he descended deeper and deeper into some place he had no name for, and could not escape. It was not that his life was without its pleasures, but these pleasures were reflexive and indulged in with a sense of shame, and he could not stop himself.

It was worse living outside the village, because there was only the family around him, his mother and daughters and son, and he missed someone to speak to, someone he knew in passing, or who was an old mate, or who he worked with. If he did not have to work, he would have chosen to anyway, because at least it got him out of the house.

More and more often he found himself staying away, leaving for his early shift and returning late at night, often when everyone was in bed. At least in the village he drank in company and there was laughter and the crack, and faces he had grown up with, or people who had become drinking buddies in the village's sole bar, the smell of malt and smoke following as they lurched out onto the street, closing time or later, if there was a lock-in.

He would walk the long path back to the house, clear night or no, the fuzz of his mind beyond emotion. The sky would be clouded or lucid or unleashing its armoury of rain, or hail, and he did not mind this, or anything. No, not even his arm that waved its taunting stump as he attempted to steady himself when he entered the house and climbed the stairs, trying to make as little noise as possible, as though he was a teenager again, and sneaking in long past his bedtime.

Then the shakes in the morning, his body trembling as he tried to steady the ticket machine, and everyone thought it was his hand, or lack of hand; or at least they did if they did not know him, or smell the stale alcohol sweat on his skin. Yet it was not the lack of his hand at all, perhaps none of it was the lack of his hand, or even the memories, even though they came to him nightly. Time did not heal, that was the lie. It returned and produced fresh scarring, even though that day had been long ago, two decades now.

It was only once he returned to sea. Once, with his family, on a boat decked with bunting and a crew dressed as pirates: it was the village gala day, and the boat was taking people on trips, out onto the water. The decoration did not disguise the smell of fish, infused into the very decking. Artie was there with his family, and his children were taken below deck where they hid in one of the cabin rooms, pretending they were slaves, taken captive by the pirates. It was a calm day, and the skies were grey and airless, a heat trying to break through.

He stood with his wife, looking over the edge of the boat, down into the deep, lapping waters.

"Are you ok?" she said.

"I'm fine. It'll not kill me, a wee trip like this. How's the stomach?"

"It's been better. But I'll be fine too." She took his arm and the both of them looked at the sea's break and surge. "It's not all a bad thing, you know, what happened. Not in some ways. Oh, I know, poor Iain and Jock, and you've all those nightmares, but if you were still doing this, going out to sea, in all sorts of weather, I'd never settle. I don't know how they do it, those other families. You'd be home reeking of fish, and you'd be sleeping for days after coming home."

"There's that."

"And I know, there's your hand, and you fret about it all the time. But better that than one day the children don't have a father."

"There's that too."

She smiled, touched his face. "You don't look convinced."

444

"It's not gone the way it should have done, has it?"

"Does it ever? Maybe it would have gone the same way anyway. You can't tell these things."

They watched the boat's wake and the waters lapping.

"Do you ever wonder," she said, "where it's gone? Down there somewhere, where you can't see it."

"There'll be nothing of it now, anyway."

"The fish'll have got it, or the gulls, and the bones'll be caught in the sea bed, or they'll be washed up on a beach somewhere. Do you not find that strange? There's a bit of you come loose and it's out there in the world someplace." She looked at him and there was a distressed, unfocussed look in her eyes.

"You're upsetting yourself now. No use worrying over spilt milk. That's the thing to do, isn't it? Aye, you worry too much. And I know, I brood too much. We're a fine pair, aren't we?"

She half-smiled at that, and pulled him to her. The boat's motor gave a roar, picking up speed as it turned around, the sea spray sharp, and it headed back towards shore.

TWENTY TWO

"Fuckface!"

Hearne turned to look up towards Eamon, who was at the very top of the brae. To come here, he must have walked over the moorlands with their treacherous, frozen bogs, and then across the fields. He carried an empty polythene feed sack, folded beneath one arm. It was orange coloured, and banded with black lettering. Hearne had his own sack, identical in colour, which he pinned beneath one foot. A passage led through the snow to where he stood, marking where he had slid down.

"What're you up to?" Then, without waiting for a reply: "It's fearsome cold today."

Saying this, Eamon unfolded the sack, laid it on the ground, and slipped his body inside. Then he pushed free. The snow cracked and soughed, and he was sliding down the hill, a whip of crystals around him catching the sun. He stopped to the left of Hearne, and a little further below. He had rolled onto his stomach to prevent him from descending any further.

"My, that was grand." He pointed to Hearne's sister, at the foot of the brae. "Though we've a fair bit to catch up with her yet. Fearless, your sister is."

"Aye, she's lacking a bit of sense when it comes to danger."

Eamon waved to the girl, shouted "Hellooooo!" and she waved in return. She wore red woollen mittens and a matching scarf.

"Helloooooo to you too!" she shouted back, her voice all wan and echoey, reverberating across the hill's still glare.

"Do you fancy her?" Hearne asked.

"Don't be daft. We're friends, is all." Though he said this in an over-emphatic fashion.

"I bet you do. I'll tell her. "Here, Catie," shouting mock theatrically, "Eamon's got something to tell you. He -"

Grabbing hold of him, Eamon pushed him so they both slipped in the snow, and together they began to slide downwards. Hearne dug his hand into the hard crust in order to stop their fall.

Eamon looked to the steep drop below. To avoid it, it was necessary to swerve abruptly on descent, and follow a milder gradient to the wire fencing that edged the roadside.

Hearne shoved him face down into the snow. "Fuckface," he said.

Catie had begun the steep climb back up the hillside. She too carried one of the plastic sacks. The climb to the top was the most difficult part, feet catching in the imploding crust, or slipping if it did not break. Still, she did not fall, although at moments she came close.

"Are you lads having fun there?" She was level with them, and then was above them. Her face was red with exertion and the cold.

Still laid flat in the snow, Eamon and Hearne were playfighting.

"Boys. I swear."

Hearne reached into the impacted snow and formed a hard, deadly snowball, which he threw at her. It fell short though, and landed by her feet.

"Boys," she repeated.

They lay and watched her reach the top, then rose and began to follow. Others would arrive soon and this was the best time, when the snow was still mostly untouched.

It was hard walking uphill. The air was so sharp it ripped at their lungs and they could not speak. Catie sat looking at them, her legs already slipped into the sack, and as they neared her, launched herself directly towards them, so they had to leap aside to avoid a collision. She slid down and down, practiced at avoiding the lurks in the land, picking up speed then swerving, as they knew she would, to settle safely at the bottom. There she let out a celebratory whoop and waved to them.

"She has a cruel streak, your sister." Eamon hunkered, breathing heavily. He wore a felted tartan jacket too big for him, once his older brother's, a hand-me-down. Hearne sat beside him and hoisted one arm around his friend's shoulder.

"You should see her sometimes, she's nothing but pure wicked. I really hate her when she's like that."

"Girls are all the same. I'm glad I've no sisters to fall out with."

From where they sat, they could see across to the far end of the village where a few browned cottages stood amongst the fields and, further back, a larger house, far from the others.

"That's a grand place you have. You can see it wherever you go. No chance of getting lost, eh?" said Eamon.

"Ach, I don't like it. It's too big and it's miles from anywhere, so you don't see anyone. If it's wet I get soaked when I head on out. That happens all the time."

451

"We can maybe go back and look at your comics? Is there anyone in?"

"My granny, probably. She'll not let us have peace. And if we go, Catie'll come too."

"She's not so bad. For a girl."

"There are worse."

They watched Catie climb back up again. She was getting tired and her feet slipped frequently, forcing her to catch and steady herself with her hands. The sun had risen full behind them and reflected off the snow so brightly they had to shield their eyes.

"Here here, what's this? A pair of poofs is what I think, lads."

The voice came from behind them, in advance of heavy, crunching footfalls.

"Ah shite, it's Jamie. Don't move your arm or he'll only mention it more."

They listened to his approach until he was immediately behind them, but did not turn, and then Hearne did only when Eamon was pushed hard in the back, causing him to fall face first in the snow.

"Pretending you're not hearing, huh? Poofs."

Hearne stood up. He was small for his age, and did not even come up to Jamie's shoulders.

"There was no need for that. We didn't do anything to you."

There were two other boys with Jamie, of similar age, but Hearne did not recognise them. They looked as menacing and bullying as Jamie did, but lacked his expression of sharp intelligence.

"You watch out for him now," his granny had said. "There's nothing more dangerous than a bright bully."

Eamon still lay on the ground, winded.

"You were practically sucking each other's cocks. It's fucking obscene."

"We're mates, is all."

"Aye, that'll be right."

He looked at the crushed track down the brae. "Here, is it proper slippy?" He walked to the start of the slide and tested it with his foot. "That'll send you flying right onto the burn, that will."

At the foot of the descent was a wire fence, then the road, and beyond that another brae led down to the burn, distant but clearly frozen over.

"See if I was to give you a good push? That's where'd you'd end up."

"That'd be fucking right." Catie's voice. While they had been talking, she had reached the top. She had been hurrying and her face was red, her voice rasping. "Always picking on lads half your age, you are." She stood alongside her bother protectively, her expression confrontational.

"It's just a bit of fun, that's all." Jamie would not meet her eyes as he said this.

"Aye, that'd be right. I've seen your sort of fun before and it's shameful the way you behave. It's bullying, that's what it is. Are you not ashamed of yourself?"

"Och."

"And those two." She pointed at the two strangers who stood behind, looking intimidated. "Do you have to take reinforcements along, just to pick on lads half your size?"

"They're my cousins, that's all. I was just going to show them the sights, maybe have a slide if we could borrow someone's sack. We could maybe have a shot of yours?" He looked at her, hopefully.

"You've a fucking cheek, you have."

He smiled at her: "Go on."

"Aye, here, have a shot, and I'll laugh if you break your fucking neck."

"And the lads' too, maybe...?"

"Now you're taking the piss. You'll share mine and be glad of it."

She handed Jamie the sack and he sat down to slip into it. His body was so broad it barely fitted. The two cousins stood to one side, watching. They had not yet spoken. When he pushed free and began to slip down, they craned forward as one, watching his descent. He slid smoothly, evidently practiced, avoiding the slope's treacherous lurks, and swerving, just as Catie had, to settle safely at the bottom.

"I was hoping he would crash." Hearne was hunkered beside Catie, who in turn stood beside Eamon.

"He's not so bad, really. He's not had a good life, you've got to make allowances."

"Just because you fancy him," Eamon said.

She looked at him, surprised, and reddened.

"Aye, I can tell, so don't deny it. And see, he fancies you too."

"Just don't you repeat it."

Now it was Hearne who turned to her, surprised.

Jamie was at the bottom the hill looking up at Catie.

"See, it's you he's watching, not us."

"If he gives you any more trouble, either of you, let me know. I'll get dad to tell the manager at the Co-op, and then he'll be in trouble. That wee Saturday job he has'll not last a bang. And you two -" pointing at the cousins - "if you say anything to him about this, it's me you'll be dealing with."

The cousins did not say anything.

"Are you fucking deaf?"

One of them pointed to his mouth and then to his ear, then pointed at his brother.

"Ah Jesus, ah fuck," she said, "I'm sorry."

The cousin nodded.

"Here," she said to the boys, "give them a shot of your sacks."

They looked at her.

"Just do it!"

That left the three of them standing at the top of the brae, watching the three lads slide downwards. Others had arrived, so the snow had grown hard and uneven, and the still had turned to noise.

"It'll be too dangerous to go soon," Catie said. "See the tumble that girl took?"

Eamon ran to help the girl. She had gashed her cheek, and there was a lash of blood over the snow.

"It's no fun when it gets too busy anyway."

"You're not a sociable animal are you, Catie?"

Jamie had come to sit beside her and had lit a cigarette. The smoke curled straight and blue in the cold sunlight.

"Here, give us a shot." Catie took the cigarette from him, took a drag, blew the smoke out again without inhaling, then passed it back. "I can be when I want to." She took the cigarette from him again. "It's just not very often I want to."

"Here, I'll give you a fag. I'm not that tight."

"Ach, a couple of pulls does me fine. Anyway, we should be getting off." To Hearne and Eamon: "You two coming home? Gran said she was going out and dad'll be at work now, so we'll have the place to ourselves."

Hearne looked at Eamon, nodded.

"We'd best set off then. You coming as well, Jamie?"

"Ach, I'd better not. I've that pair to look after."

"Bring them as well. The more the merrier, eh?"

They set off down the brae and met the cousins, who were trudging up.

"We're off to my house," Catie said. "You coming with us?" She pointed at the building in the distance.

The cousins nodded in unison.

Together they walked to the bottom of the slope and onto the road. From there they crossed to a dirt track that descended on the other side, leading to a small bridge that crossed the burn. They all slid and fell on the track. Catie and Jamie walked ahead, then the boys, and finally the cousins.

"They're a fair item, aren't they?"

Eamon nodded at Catie and Jamie. Jamie slipped his arm around her waist and attempted to kiss her, though she turned away, laughing.

"Ach, it's all the hard man talk. Girls always fall for that. And girls always pretend they don't like you when they secretly fancy you. Are you still seeing Rosie?"

Eamon shook his head. "Nah, she wasn't my type really. No, not my type at all."

Hearne looked back at the cousins who followed, in silence. "Do you think they understand what we're saying?"

"Not if you don't turn back and let them lip read, you daft gowk."

They crossed the bridge and looked down to the shallow, frozen water.

"Here, you see that?" Hearne pointed to where the burn twisted back into the hillside. A fox stood silent there, watching them.

"My dad'd have it shot the moment he saw it. One got in and killed all our chickens last year." Eamon stood alongside and they watched the fox, watching them. The sun caught at the animal's eyes and made them flare green. "But they're bonny beasts all the same. He's bold, that one."

A stone flew over their heads and landed near the animal, which took fright and hurtled around the bend, out of sight. It had been thrown by one of the cousins, both of them appearing on the bridge now, standing beside the boys.

"Here, what did you do that for? He wasn't doing you any harm. And you nearly hit us with that."

The cousins just stood and grinned.

"Ach, come on." Hearne pulled Eamon's hand. "Let's catch up with the others. Those two are just soft in the head."

A further track led up the brae, and from there they had to cross two long fields before they came to the house. When they arrived, Jamie was with Catie, standing in the driveway and looking inside the car parked there.

"Did your old man not take the car to work this morning? It's a fair machine."

"Nah. He was on the drink last night and Larson came and gave him a lift to work."

"See my old man, if he had money? He wouldn't bother even getting out of bed, much less going to work."

"It's not my dad's money. It's my gran's." Catie pursed her lips as she said this.

"Same as. Who's it going to go to when she dies?"

"She says she'll outlast us all and I wouldn't put it past her. Here, let's go in now, I'm cold and could do with a cuppa."

The door was unlocked.

"Hello?" Catie shouted, "We're home!"

There was no reply.

"We've the house to ourselves, then. Here, let's make a brew."

She led them into the kitchen. To the left, as they entered the door, a Raeburn stood, and in the centre a large, unvarnished oak worktop, which also served as a makeshift table.

"Christ, Catie, it's as big as my whole house," Jamie said.

"Takes a bit of getting used to. Here, Hearne, make us a pot of tea, will you?"

"I'll help him," said Eamon. He filled the kettle and put it on the Raeburn to boil, while Hearne hunted out the teapot and scooped tea into it.

"A nice wee domestic, isn't it?" Jamie had his cigarettes out again and lit one, which he passed to Catie. He lit another for himself.

"Less of your cheek. They're good friends, is all. Here, you two, sit." She gestured at the cousins, who sat obediently on the chairs at the far end of the table.

"Where're they from?"

"My uncle's here from Fort William just now, so they've come up for a few days."

"Poor bastards."

"What, Fort William or them?"

"Both, really."

They laughed, and Jamie pulled her to him and this time she did not resist.

The kettle whistled and Hearne lifted it off the heat then poured the water into the teapot. Eamon found mugs in one of the cupboards and counted out six.

"Milk? Sugar?"

"Just milk for me. Jamie?"

"Milk and two sugars, ta."

"What about those two?"

"They'll just get milk and be glad of it." He smirked at them.

Hearne poured the tea and handed the mugs over to Catie and Jamie, then the cousins.

"Ah, that's grand." Jamie wrapped his hands around the mug. "My fingers are fair stinging with the cold."

"We're heading up to my room. We're going to look at my comic collection," Hearne said.

"Aye, you do that," said Catie. "We're not going anywhere. Mind you don't spill the tea on the carpet going upstairs, or gran'll have your guts for garters."

"Aye, and you two behave up there," Jamie shouted at they left the kitchen.

The stairwell was steep and narrow and led up to a long corridor with rooms on either side. The doors to the rooms were closed, so the corridor seemed dark and claustrophobic. It turned a corner and then there were more rooms still.

"I always think this house will never end. It's a proper mansion, it is."

"Half the rooms are empty, though. Catie's moved her bedroom twice in the last year. That's hers there."

Eamon peeked through a half-open doorway. The room was papered with flocked green wallpaper, and on the walls were pictures of punk singers, all of them heavily made up with eyeliner and foundation.

"Man, that place'd give you a headache."

"I've moved too. It's bigger than the one I had." He indicated the doorway at the far end of the corridor.

Unlike his sister's room, which had clothes strewn around the bed and floor, his looked barely lived in. The sole evidence of his occupancy was a large poster of Captain Marvel, in red and blue costume, a yellow star on his chest. He was drawn in such a way that his muscles and sinews were clearly defined.

"That's what I want," Hearne said, "A body like that."

"In your dreams you will. We'll both end like our dads, bald heads and beer bellies you see before the rest of them arrives."

"You, maybe. I'm never letting myself get like that. Here, come see out my window."

Opening the window as wide as it would go, the two of them half-hung out the aperture, looking into the garden. A tall tree had grown in proximity, but did not obstruct the view down the close-cut lawn and its frame of trees that followed the surrounding walls. Beyond the walls were fields, and beyond the fields the distant village, barely defined by its clutter of rooftops and grey stone buildings.

"I'll bet no-one else around here can see this far. I'm fucking jealous, man."

"It's great at night. All you can see is black, and then a bit of light from the houses, but not much, not really. When the wind gets up you can hear the wheat in the fields rustling, and I swear it sounds like someone whispering."

"Do you not get frightened? I sometimes have to go into the barn at night to fetch stuff for my dad, and it freaks me out, I feel like someone's watching all the time."

"Sometimes. Sometimes I feel afraid." Hearne lowered himself back to the floor. "I wish we were still in our old house, the sort normal people live in."

"Here. I could stay some night. We can have a sleepover and I'll keep you company."

"That'd be great. I'll ask, but wait until my dad's had a few. He'll agree to anything then." He paused, uncertain. "Come look at my comics. I've got some new ones."

Alongside Hearne's bed was a built-in cupboard which, when opened, revealed stacks of neatly arranged American comics. He lifted a selection off the closest stack then sat on the floor, spreading them out before him. They had been sorted into alphabetical order. Eamon settled alongside and together they began to look through the titles: SON OF SATAN, MORBIUS

THE LIVING VAMPIRE, DEATHLOK THE DEMOLISHER.

"They're so cool. No-one else at school has anything like these."

"I've a friend sends them up. He lives in Glasgow and gets them all there."

"I wish I knew someone like that." Eamon was examining a comic in which Dr Strange was in the process of being pulled into an oversized crystal ball. "Jamie's cousins. They're a bit weird, aren't they? They just sort of lurch around after you and smile in that odd way at each other."

"The whole family's odd, if you ask me. I just wish the three of them weren't here and they'd leave us alone. You were right about Catie and Jamie though. I hadn't noticed that before."

"It's not so bad. He'll maybe be less the bully if he's going out with her. To us, I mean."

"There is that. Here, have you seen this one?" He handed Eamon a copy of WEREWOLF BY NIGHT. "It's good! It's all told by this person who becomes a werewolf, and in this issue his sister becomes a werewolf too."

"Don't let Catie see that, it'll give her ideas. She'll be out howling at the moon the first chance she gets."

"Bounding home with a rabbit in her mouth. My nan'll have it gutted and served for tea." Hearne giggled and his giggles spread to Eamon, until the two of them shook and they had to lean into each other to stop the laughter turning to hysteria.

"Oh, it's a good thing she can't see us." Hearne mopped the tears from his eyes with the hem of his pullover.

"Yes. Yes it is."

Eamon drew Hearne towards him and kissed him lightly on the mouth. Hearne pulled away, embarrassed.

"Don't."

"It's only a kiss."

Hearne stood. "We'd better go back down. The others will be wondering what's happened to us." Without waiting for a reply, he opened the bedroom door and hurried along the corridor.

"Here! Wait!"

Downstairs there were male voices loud and laughing.

"Who's that? Has someone else arrived?"

Hearne ignored the question and rushed down the stairs, Eamon following. At the bottom, he turned and looked up. He looked as though he would cry and he was trembling.

"Come in, you two," Catie called from the kitchen.

When they entered the air was fugged, all four talking and smoking. Jamie had opened a can of Tennants which was placed between himself and Catie.

"Don't look so dumfounded. Isn't it a great trick? They were having us on, the lads were. They're no more deaf than you or me."

The cousins laughed and one of them pointed at Hearne.

"Fuckface," he said.

The other pointed at Eamon.

"Fuckface."

And the two boys stood there, beetroot, glad of the cousins' deception to cover their embarrassment.

TWENTY THREE

"Is it my imagination, or is there a gap there, just a small one?"

"I can't see anything."

"There is. I'm sure there is."

"You're tired. Nothing's changed."

"We'll see."

"There it is again. You must see it now."

A smudge. An erasing. Mist perhaps.

"It's the way the light is here, it's always changing. You've been in the city too long."

"Why do you always contradict me? I know what I'm seeing."

"Don't get upset, it's not good for you. For me, for that matter. It's not very likely, is it?" A pause. "Is it?"

"You're right. I'm being silly and emotional and seeing things that aren't there."

"Getting snappy with it as well. It's been a long day for you."

When she was asleep, Hew traced a finger gently down one side of his sister's face. She was the colour of dust.

"Hew?"

"Ssh. I didn't mean to wake you."

"I was having the most terrible dream. I was so afraid. Then I dreamt I woke up and you weren't there. I didn't know where you'd gone."

"I was paying for the rooms. I'm not going to abandon you, you know that." He sat on the bed alongside her, kissed her on the forehead. "It was just a dream. Get some rest and you'll feel better tomorrow. Sleep, and dream some nicer dreams this time."

"You've always been there for me, Hew."

"Of course I'm there for you." A pause. Then: "Mind how you looked after me when we were young?"

But she did not answer: she was already asleep.

———————

Rain shattered on the car windshield. Wipers pushed the wash aside, along with a debris of pine needles and crushed insects.

"You'd hardly know it was daytime, would you?" Casey rested her head against the side window, buffered by a cushion.

"It'll be brighter when we get out of this. The trees are so thick there's no room for light."

The car jolted along a road barely dirt. Shadowed pines defined either side.

"And it's early yet," he continued. "We'll leave this behind and the sun'll come out, and everything'll look different. You'll see."

"You always were the optimist."

"One of us has to be."

"I've no optimism left, Hew, I really don't."

"There's always hope, I've always believed that."

———————

"Would you open the window a bit? It's so humid it's difficult to breathe."

Hew lowered the windows. Their familiar whine. A spray of rain entered. He pressed the controls again and, rising, the windows halted a fraction short of sealing the world outside once more. There was the scent of pine and damp, of rotting vegetation.

"You hear that?" Casey gestured vaguely at the surrounding trees. "Animals out there somewhere, moving."

"Sheltering, if they've any sense. Deer maybe. Or wildcats. There are wildcats here, did I already tell you that?"

"You did. And I already told you I knew that. Though it's odd to think there are still places in this country where animals like that can live. It's almost prehistoric, this part of the world."

"That's its beauty. You leave the concrete and noise and chaos behind, and you come here where everything's different."

"It just feels a bit claustrophobic. And a bit lonely. I'd forgotten how quiet it is. I'll put on the radio. That'll cheer us up a bit." She switched the radio on. It broadcast only noise. No ghost even of stray stations, their snatched voices and unfamiliar music. "Atmospherics. All that low cloud." She switched it off again.

"It can't be long before we're clear of this. The road's rising, so we'll be above the tree line soon." He turned the car abruptly, the bend ahead hidden by the trees' overhang. It wavered a little on the mudded ground, steadied itself.

A dead stag lay directly ahead, blocking their path.

"Hew!"

"It's all right. I see it. I've got it." He braked to avoid hitting the animal. "Christ. We can't just run over that.

469

I'll need to get out and move it. See that dip at the side if the road? We couldn't drive around it, even if there was room."

"I'll help. I can do that."

"No you can't, you're not fit. Stay here where it's warm and it's dry. I'll manage."

"We could wait for the weather to clear."

"It's only a bit of rain, it won't kill me." Reaching into the back seat, he pulled out a waterproof jacket.

Casey leaned forward to look at the crippled bulk blocking the road. "Poor animal," she said, "what did it ever do to anyone?"

———————

He wore soaked-through tennis shoes, shorts, and Casey's cagoule, which was too short for him. His feet skidded in the impermanent mud. There was a gash below his knee, gained when he had slipped moments before. The rain made it impossible to see clearly, or to gain a handhold easily. The stag remained an immovable object. Hew looked towards Casey, the blur of her image through the windshield, and gestured helplessly.

It was a young stag, but still its bulk was beyond him. The slick of its body – rain or blood, impossible to tell which – had an awful, clinging odour. It was the stench of death. When he wrapped his arms around its neck, it only twisted alarmingly and the nubs of its horns rasped against his skin. Its crushed skull was made stark in the car's headlights. Inches; it would only move inches at a time.

Somewhere, far off in the trees' depths, there was cacophony, the combined rush of wind and rain, but other sounds too, animal noises. The sounds of creatures blundering fearfully and stupidly through the forest.

"Move". He spoke to himself. "You Stupid - Bloody-Useless- Animal." He managed to gain a little leverage somewhere in the ground's quagmire and pushed back against the body. "Move. Move. MOVE!"

The carcass slid down the incline at the road's edge, and he nearly followed, caught in its gravity, its unexpected movement, but he steadied himself, wavering, arms on either side like a tightrope walker. Then there was only the roar in his ears, both the forces elemental around him and his own fear, his heart's insistent impact, the blood rush, and his breath which came too quickly, too frequently, and which struggled to remain within him.

"Your knee's bleeding."

Hew almost fell into the car. He pulled the rain in with him.

"I'm through. That used up every little bit of energy I had." A pause. "I can hardly even speak."

Casey reached over and held him. His body was shaking with exhaustion.

"Don't. You'll get wet."

"I don't care. I want to." She looked past him, at the landscape which was dark, its order unravelling. "I can drive a little while. You get your strength back. We'll

471

find someplace to stay, and you can wash and get your knee seen to. And nothing more today, we rest. You're not as fit as you used to be either." The wind rose, rocked the car. "I swear, you'd think something was conspiring against us."

"No. I'll drive. I just want to get out of here now." He bent down, levered off his shoes, ungummed his socks from his feet. "Driving barefoot. It's the best I can do for just now."

"Be careful then. Do that for me, at least."

The car moved forward, haltingly at first, lurching. Gradually the track it followed began to widen.

"Finally." Hew wiped forming condensation away from the windscreen. "We're getting away at last. Remind me never to take the scenic route again. Never, never, never."

"You'll change your mind tomorrow. It's me that's the pessimistic one. It would have been lovely, if hadn't been for the weather. And that poor animal."

"That poor animal's taken ten years off me, I swear. And I'm not sure I have ten years left."

He turned the car around a bend. The trees thinned, then were gone altogether. Ahead was the thin-soiled, rocky flank of hillside. Above, the sky was sulphurous.

"I think it might turn into a proper storm, you know that? We'll get off this road as soon as we can. Do you know where the map is?" He opened the glove compartment, looked inside.

"Hew," Casey said.

"I think it might be on the back seat, that's where I saw it last."

"Hew! Stop."

He halted, turned, concerned, to look at her. "You're not feeling sick again, are you? I can open the window a bit. It's the air –"

"Not that. Don't you see it? There." She pointed skyward.

What she pointed at: a strip of white, precisely cut, on the horizon. There was a thick mass of cloud, the rain's decent, and then blankness, an absence. It looked as though the edge of the scene had been guillotined.

"I told you, Hew. I told you I wasn't imagining it."

"It must be some sort of optical illusion. Or the ozone layer. Is that what they mean by the hole in the ozone layer? In the satellite photographs there's always a huge space where the hole is."

"Wouldn't that be on the news though? And there was nothing on the news last night, Hew. It was murders and wars and politicians cheating on their wives, as usual."

"Well, that settles it then. An optical illusion." He studied the strip of white, which seemed to be slowly expanding. "It's an odd one though. What on earth could be causing it?"

The rain slowed to something chronal, a grey drift of drear pushing from one side of the landscape to the next. Where it should have touched land there was instead a lack, a blankness, exactly defined.

Casey reached into the glove compartment for her mobile phone. "I'll call....who DO you call for something like this? The weather office? The police?"

"That's being overdramatic. Is there a signal?"

"Hard to tell." Casey held the phone's face away from what little light there was. "There seems to be."

"Phone the guest house we stayed at last night, they must be able to see it as well. They'll know what it is. You still have the number?"

"It's the last one we called." She dialled the number, shook her head. "It's like the radio, just noise." She leaned back. "I feel tired all of a sudden."

"You sleep for a while, and I'll drive on. It can't be long now before we arrive at something that resembles civilisation."

"I keep on thinking I'll miss something." She looked down the road scored in either direction, its scrubbed emptiness, entirely barren, dun, pocked, rutted. "Though it does seem unlikely."

"It's how it is here, Casey. You see a few sheep, a few buildings on the hills, that's all."

"I'd forgotten, it's been so long."

He indicated what may have been lights in the far, far distance. They may only have been splashes of water on the windscreen. "We're still in civilisation, it's just over there. We'll get away from this and it'll feel better."

"It feels lonely, that what it feels like. And THAT." She pointed at the sky. "That feels worrying."

He reached over to hold her hand. "Nothing to get upset about yet. It's an oddity, that's what it is. We're exhausted, and it's been a long horrible morning. It's strange, yes -" his eyes wandered to the band of white - "but everything's strange when it's unfamiliar."

"Let's go then. We both need to rest and clean up. And I want to sleep too, only not here."

"I agree. We go, as quickly as possible."

"You're afraid, aren't you?"

"A little."

They travelled all day. Hew periodically checked the phone and radio for reception, but there was only the dead squeal of interference. The rain had stopped, but grim, oiled clouds remained.

"There's nothing." Casey studied the map. "It definitely shows a village here. There's a little H for hotel. Or hostel. Or whatever it stands for. I just want to see someone now, and find a place to sleep. A bath too. I'd kill for a bath."

The car drove slowly through the raw landscape. The ground was flat and pocked, a combination of peat and heather and strange, isolated mountains. The ground steamed. Hew studied the roadside carefully, as though it might contain something hidden.

"It's an old map. Maybe it's out of date, or maybe it's down a turnoff somewhere."

"You see everything, in every direction. There's nothing here, Hew. Wherever we are, it's not on the map. And we haven't seen a single person all day – don't you think that's strange? I know it's remote, but surely there's some sign of life in this place?"

"A wrong turning then."

"I don't think so. That line on the horizon, whatever it is, has been alongside us all day. And it's a straight road." She sighed. "A never-ending road."

"Scotland's bigger than you think, especially this part. People come here to -" He stopped the car abruptly.

"You're right. We need to find someplace. It's getting dark and we're exhausted. That place down there? We could stay for the night. I'll find some wood and make a fire, and we've got our sleeping bags and food in the boot. It'll be an adventure. The alternative," he gestured at the long loop of empty road "is to keep on driving."

"Is it all right? To stay there?"

"It's a bothie, I think. Besides, if it's not, do you see anyone around who's likely to object?"

A footpath led down to the building. It was a bare, stone construction. A wasteland of used toilet paper met them by the door.

"Well, there's been people here before us, at least," Hew said.

Inside, neatly mounded, were crushed lager tins and emptied baked bean cans. There was the grave of a wood fire.

"It feels damp."

"I'll get that fire going again. That'll warm us up. Watch your feet." He pointed to a scattering of sheep turds on the floor. "We may have company during the night. Have I told you what they call sheep around here?"

"Yes, Hew. 'The local leisure centre.' Frankly, at this point, I'll be glad to see anything that's alive."

Hew returned to the car and fetched their sleeping bags, along with an armful of mismatched foodstuffs.

"The remnants of our shopping expedition. We have spaghetti hoops, carnation milk, two packets of cheese biscuits, an apple, and a tin of frankfurters. Oh, and two bottles of water." He placed them down before her, as

476

though they were offerings. "Also, essential, a tin opener. We won't starve."

"You're trying too hard to be optimistic. I know you."

"I try. Sit down and snuggle up in that sleeping bag. I'm off to find something to put on the fire."

An hour later, there was a smoulder of roots and branches, in the middle of which opened cans of spaghetti hoops and frankfurters sat unpromisingly. Both Casey and Hew had unzipped their sleeping bags and draped them over their shoulders.

They sat, silent. The daylight had almost gone, and there were stars amber in blue.

"It's dimmed, but it hasn't gone away." Casey indicated the strip in the distance. "If anything, it's getting bigger."

"It's thrown me a bit, I'll admit. It's the not knowing, that's the thing. That and the worry about why everyone has gone."

"Earlier on…you were going to say that a lot of people come here to die, weren't you?"

"I can't hide anything, can I? This is where the suicidal people come. They're not found for years sometimes. If they're found at all."

"Ssh."

"It's a long way off, Casey. Maybe it'll never happen."

"Not that, silly. Don't you hear it?"

Movement outside. Something walking warily on wet ground.

Casey pulled the sleeping bag tighter around her shoulders. In the doorway, a shadow. Then, uncertain, a young stag appeared. It started at them, its eyes catching the light from the fire, standing as still as they were. Then, snorting, it turned and bolted into the night.

They woke to find the landscape hidden by mist. It lifted to show part of the view obliterated. Mountains were sheared mid-way. The sky's inflexible blue was matched with white. It was as if the scene before them was paper, and someone had torn a precise, even strip from the bottom.

"It's odd. It doesn't seem to faze them." Casey indicated sheep determinedly grazing and birds webbed between the few bent, undernourished trees. She leant back against the bothy's stone wall, shielding her eyes against the sun. "It's so peaceful. It's strange, but I don't feel any sense of danger, not the way I did yesterday. It's a bit hypnotic, in fact."

"Rabbits and headlights come to mind. Though I agree: the world's disappearing bit by bit and we're sitting here as though nothing's wrong. Maybe it's a form of shock."

"Or because it's so unreal. I hope we meet someone today. To find out what's going on, if nothing else."

"We'll get by. We always have done, whatever happened to us." He stood, stretched. "It's time we moved, before we both fall into a daze." He fetched the two plastic bottles, now empty, and filled them from a nearby burn. The water was brackish, but they drank it eagerly.

"This is going to sound silly, I know it is." They were in the car again, preparing to leave. "But I was thinking last night, what if I've died? Is this some sort of afterlife I've wandered into?" She pressed Hew's hands. "But you feel real enough when I touch you."

"It's the drugs. They're making you think strange things." He pulled the car sideways, so the road stretched in both directions, on either side. "What direction – back the way we came or do we carry on? You choose."

"Away from that." She pointed at the absence in the sky. "If there's anyone else around, that must be the way they've gone. Away from that, as far as we possibly can."

They drove down the single track road, to an uncertain destination.

There was a village ahead. Eight stone bungalows sat on either side of the road; dun, cramped dwellings designed less for living than for protection against the weather. All the houses were unoccupied.

"We might have known." Casey stood on her tiptoes to peer into a bedroom window. "That's the pessimist coming out in me."

"Definitely an evacuation." Hew stood behind her, facing in the opposite direction. "Is it my imagination, or is that getting closer?"

Behind them, in front of them, around them, the landscape shrank before the void's advance.

"If the radio worked, or the phone, then we'd know more. I think we ought to break into the house to see if there are any clues," he said.

"We can't do that!"

"Clues and food, Casey. That's two days now, and there's been no-one. Who knows how much longer it'll be?"

The decision made, he lifted a stone and struck it against the back door window. It cracked. A further blow and it shattered. He pushed the shards of glass inwards then reached inside to open the door.

"It's an old person's home. Smell that? Lavender and stale tobacco."

"What it smells is homely." Casey followed him into the house. "Hello?"

No reply.

"I hadn't expected any." This to herself.

The living room was cluttered, a mishmash of furniture, any available free space taken up by photographs and kitsch, inexpensive ornaments. In the centre of the room sat a table with an ashtray. In it, a whole cigarette had turned to ash, burnt down to the filter.

"That's disturbing." Hew pointed to it. "Like finding a half-eaten meal."

Casey examined a framed photograph on the wall. "That must be who lived here. Who live here, rather."

A couple in their twenties, a formal monochrome portrait. From the style it appeared to have been taken in the nineteen sixties. On the opposite wall, a contemporary photo of the same couple, lined and heavier now. They looked as though they had been carved out of worn, weathered wood.

"I feel like a burglar, but I'm stealing people's memories. There's nothing here."

"Let's try the kitchen," he said.

On the kitchen table lay a newspaper, three days old.

"That dates it at least." Hew lifted and examined the newspaper as though it might contain a clue. "Odd we didn't see anything though. Or hear anything, come to that. Though I suppose we were stuck in that forest for quite a long time."

"We can't have been the only ones."

"If there are others, we'll find them. Priorities though. We need food."

He raided the cupboard, emerging with cans of food. He emptied out bottles of diluting juice and filled them with water.

"We really should leave a note."

"There's more to worry about than that." He hoisted the bags onto the table. "We take everything we can find. Anything that could be useful."

"You're panicking now."

"I think 'being sensible' is the term you're after. Though it has spooked me, this place. I feel defeated, all of a sudden."

Casey put her arms around him. "Don't give in like that, it's not like you."

"You've given in as well, I hear it in your voice."

"I've not given in, I'm just not sure it's as bad as you think. Either that, or it's worse. I can't decide. Though like you said, it's something to do with the weather. Probably something to do with the weather."

"I don't know any more. I just want to leave."

"Do you think we should try more of the houses, to see what's in them?"

"What we have here will last us a while. The road we're following can't go on forever."

They carried the supplies to the car. White had consumed more of the landscape.

"Miles. It's pushed in miles, I'm sure it has." Casey tuned to look at it. Where the absence advanced, the ground appeared to corrode. "We were in there what – an hour?"

"Too long. We're leaving now. Hurry up."

"I'm sore, I can't move quickly, Hew."

"I know you are. But we have to go, we have to."

They drove, panicked, away from the source of their fear.

They had been driving for hours. The road – single track, winding, stretched before them. The void, its cruel incision, lay behind them. No matter how quickly they drove, it kept pace. Not only kept pace: gained ground.

"I'm so sore, Hew. We can't just keep on driving."

They halted, temporarily, to avoid colliding with sheep gathered to lie in the road. Startled by the car horn's insistence, the sheep looked up, then slowly rose, unconcernedly, to reposition themselves by the roadside.

"We can. We will."

"I don't have the strength any more. I'm exhausted and I want to sleep. I'm beyond caring."

"You sleep. I'll carry on driving."

"Have you ever thought what might happen if we just stopped? Maybe it's harmless. Maybe it's like a dividing line and everything's behind it, just the same as it ever was. That's where everyone is now, maybe. There. Not here."

"I don't believe that. You don't believe that."

"I think it's natural to be afraid of something you don't understand. Maybe though, maybe it's not justified."

"Or maybe it is, Casey."

"We've stopped anyway. Let's walk nearer to it, we can manage that. See what it's like."

"And then what - we run away again?"

"If we have to. What difference does it make anyway? We're not escaping it, however quickly we travel."

They walked midway through the adjoining field, closer to the white than they had ever been. It's seemed to press in ever more quickly, as though aware they were approaching.

"It's cold. Can you feel that? It's like standing in front of an open fridge. We should go." Hew's breath had turned visible.

"A bit longer. Just a little bit."

"I think you want it to reach you. That's what it sounds like to me."

A sheep, startled by their approach, ran into the void. It vanished as quickly and completely and if it had fallen into an abyss.

"That stone by your feet? Throw it into that and see what happens."

Hew hurled the stone. It blinked and wavered a little in the instant of its crossing, and was gone. There was no sound of it falling.

"How still it is. It's even eaten the sound."

"It's dead, Casey, that's what it is." He held her hand and led her back to the car. "You've had your look and it's not good, even you have to admit that. There's nothing there."

"It's beautiful in a way. It's like a wall of ice, advancing."

"Ice has substance, and texture. This has nothing. It's like someone's ripped away a bit of our reality. We're leaving."

They returned to the car and drove away, more quickly than ever.

Casey turned back at the white, the inevitability of it. Her face wore an ambiguous expression.

———————

"Running on empty. I'd give it minutes, Casey."

Only meters behind them, there was nothing. Ahead, the same stretching, unending road. No people, only sparse, abandoned buildings. A flock of starlings spiralled and vanished into the emptiness.

"It's the end, isn't it? I'm not sure I mind."

"It's never the end Casey, I do believe that."

The car juddered, whirred, continued against expectations.

"There's a bend down there. And there's a house. That's the first one we've seen since the village." He pointed towards it, a large building, once grand.

"I can barely even make it out. I can hardly see, I'm so exhausted. It's a like a dream now, everything's so unreal."

"We'll make for the building. It's hope, isn't it? Never give up hope."

The car slowed and stalled. It died.

"That's it then." Casey turned to face the bleached approach.

"We can walk. We can hobble. We can run. Down there, down to the farmhouse."

They abandoned their vehicle. The void was only a little over a meter away. It moved glacially and quickly at the same time. Casey stood, then buckled.

"I'm not sure I can walk, Hew. I feel so weak."

"I'll carry you, if I have to. A ten minute journey, that's all. We can manage that. It'll be some protection against…whatever that is."

"I'll try. For you."

They walked, eyes fixed on the house. The white expanded behind them. There was no sound. Even the animals were still.

"Nearly there now." Hew turned, saw Casey lagging behind. The blankness was almost upon her. He ran back, pulled her hand. "You've got to hurry. I know it's hard. But you've got to."

She hurried, stumbled, rose again. Hew half-supported, half-carried her. Behind them, they could feel the chill getting closer. They dared not turn.

"I feel so cold, it's all through my bones."

"Keep going, Casey. We're almost there."

The white was by their feet, as they lost ground, gained again.

"Nearly there now." Hew lifted her, pulled her, cajoled her. Their breath was made evident in the air's chill.

"Run."

"I can't."

"Run."
"I'm trying."
"RUN – "

Also by Peter Campbell

Approaching Our Destination

London's miraculous underbelly. A family mysteriously disappears on the moorlands, never to be seen again. A vicious vendetta between two gunslingers escalates into a conclusion both unexpected and inevitable. A group of anarchic orphans transform Paris into a fabulist jungle. A future in which urban legend is thought reality and in which an angel is the obsessive centre of attraction at a party.

This collection of sharp, haunting short stories depict a world in which another reality hovers just below the surface of what we see, and nothing is quite as it first seems.

Due for reissue 2015

Blowing Hot and Cold

It's a time of mysteries. Why does the bible salesman arrive to the accompaniment of thunderstorms? Who are the secretive figures seen in the ruins on the outskirts of the city? What is the meaning of the prophecy given by the woman in the lunatic asylum?

Maybe Martin knows the answers. He's grown up in the midst of a war that never seems to end. Or perhaps one of the people in his life do: his father, once poor, now wealthy, though no-one seems to know exactly how he inherited his money. His mother, determined to follow desires that lead her inevitably to madness. Or one of Martin's many broken lovers, broken once he leaves them, if not before.

Updating the form of the gothic novel, Blowing Hot and Cold is as memorable and puzzling as a dream. Told from the viewpoint of five different characters, Martin's life and world are gradually pieced together, culminating in a surprising, haunting conclusion.

Due for reissue 2015

Strange Attractor

The 1990s. It's a time of ecstasy-fuelled raves, end-of the-world fatalism, the supernatural, wilfully extreme behaviour and freakish coincidences *(or are they...?)*

Against this backdrop, John hitches a ride with a travelling carnival. It's the start of a series of outlandish events that force him to leave behind the existence he's taken for granted.

Among those he encounters are an amnesiac midget; an angel or devil with very earthly desires and a cryptic mission; a drug-addled serial killer with whom he'll develop an unhealthy relationship; a fortune-teller whose dreams may or may not portend a coming apocalypse; and a pregnant bird-woman whose uncle's tastes veer towards the distinctly perverse.

Gradually this intricate, mystifying world unravels into chaos, throwing John's life and the lives of those around him into danger.

Due for reissue 2016

Printed in Great Britain
by Amazon.co.uk, Ltd.,
Marston Gate.